A KISS AT HOME

Tanner stood inside her front door, looking uncertain. "I thought you might need cheering up," he said. "I would have been here earlier, but Wing and I were at a dog show in Marion."

Sally managed a wan smile. "That was very kind of you."

"Not kind at all. More like self-serving." He held out an Abernathy's bag. "I brought some ice cream in hopes there was another of those cherry pies in your freezer."

"You're in luck." She led the way through the living room, dining room, and into the kitchen. Sure enough, in the freezer was a homemade, ready-to-bake cherry pie. Sally turned the oven on to preheat. "Better put that ice cream in the freezer so it doesn't melt. It'll take about an hour and a half to bake the pie, then it has to cool."

"I thought about you often today. I hope you don't mind me showing up like this."

Sally shook her head. "Not at all. Truth is, I'm glad you're here. I'm probably not the best company right now, but I didn't want to be alone."

"He'll come home again."

"I hope so."

Tanner reached out with his forefinger and tipped her chin up. "I know so." Then, oh so softly, he lowered his lips to hers in a gentle kiss. He drew her to him, wrapped his arms around her and held her close, her cheek pressed against his chest. . . .

HOME AGAIN

Annie Smith

ZEBRA BOOKS
Kensington Publishing Corp.
http://www.kensingtonbooks.com

ZEBRA BOOKS are published by

Kensington Publishing Corp.
850 Third Avenue
New York, NY 10022

All Kensington titles, imprints, and distributed lines are
available at special quantity discounts for bulk purchases for
sales promotion, premiums, fund-raising, educational or in-
stitutional use.

Special book excerpts or customized printings can also be
created to fit specific needs. For details, write or phone the
office of the Kensington Special Sales Manager: Kensington
Publishing Corp., 850 Third Avenue, New York, NY 10022.
Attn. Special Sales Department. Phone: 1-800-221-2647.

Zebra and the Z logo Reg. U.S. Pat. & TM Off.

First Printing: October 2002
10 9 8 7 6 5 4 3 2 1

Printed in the United States of America

My many, many thanks to:

Judy Meyers and Christina Canter of Canine Companions for Independence;

Diana Helt, Mellisa Jacobs, and Matt Gamret along with the other members of the Erie Mighty Otters and the Pittsburgh Mighty Penguins;

Josh Wirt and Kip St. Germaine of the 2002 U.S. Paralympic Sledge Hockey Team. To learn more about sled hockey visit www.sledhockey.org;

Ch Nab's Kelda Wallis CD HIC and Spered Dove Across the Water, as well as Nancy and Bill Buckland, who, fifteen years ago, introduced me to Cardigan Welsh Corgis;

Laurie Miller, Lori Baker, and Heather Embry for background information;

Pam Baker and Karen Beck for being there;

Mark who always looks on the bright side of life;

Meg Ruley, who really does walk on water;

John Scognamiglio who was patient through a dark night of my soul.

One

"Tanner could teach you how to train your gold-fish," Jessie said as she pulled into Sally's driveway. "Swim through hoops, do loopdy loops. *You* might even learn some new teaching technique or something you could use on your kindergartners. Like using food for motivation."

Sally Foster glared at her friend. "Number one, I'm a terrific teacher already. Number two, I don't believe in motivating children with food. Number three, I like my goldfish the way they are. Anyway, it's decidedly untactful of you to bring up trained goldfish." She opened the car door and got out.

"He could teach you to train your cats to keep off the kitchen counter."

Sally stuck her head back in the car. She pretended to be fierce. "Forget it. I'm not interested in some guy. I'm especially not interested in some dog person. And leave my cats out of this." Then she grinned. "I'm changing the subject. I think it was one of the best plays they've done. Sylvie was wonderful—couldn't tell she's pregnant—and that Connie Hewitt really does have an amazing voice.

See ya later." She shoved Jessie's car door shut and, humming "I Am Sixteen," waltzed up the walk to her front door, turning to wave as her friend drove off down the street.

"Hi, honeys, I'm home!" Sally closed her front door behind her and groped for the light switch. Predictably, there was no answer from the cats; they were always blasé about her comings and goings. The sinuous white feline who was stretched out languorously across one of the built-in wall perches did, however, deign to toss Sally a glance. "Raindrops on roses and whiskers on kittens," Sally sang as she dropped her coat and purse on the couch and scooped the cat up into her arms. She danced around the room with her cat in her arms. "But I don't care what anyone says, cats are better than babies 'cause I don't have to get a sitter for you guys if I want to go out."

Tess was not impressed.

Sally set the cat back on her perch and sighed. Tess shot her a most witheringly regal glare and proceeded to lick her rumpled coat back into place.

"You're such a prissy thing," Sally said with a chuckle. "You're the most gorgeous thing on the face of the earth. But you're still a priss." The cat patently ignored her.

Sally leaned down to say hello to the fish. "Hi, there, fishies." The two goldfish swarmed to the front of the aquarium. They both wore their best hopeful expression on their faces. Goldfish were always hungry, always optimistic about the possibility of food. "You already had your dinner. But you guys're sure cute. Even if you can't swim through hoops, or hit Ping-Pong balls with your nose."

She headed into the kitchen. "Hey, boy cats, didja miss me?" It was a purely rhetorical question. Jude was probably hiding out somewhere. Her third cat, Troy, crouched on top of the refrigerator, pretending to be a soldier on the ridge of a hill, scouting for the enemy troops below. He batted at her head as she reached automatically toward the cupboard and her stash of Leety's chocolates. "Hey there, Sergeant Troy." She grabbed a handful of chocolate with one hand and scratched his head with her other. "You'd've liked the show. It was about climbing mountains, and it had a military hero." Troy blinked at her. She popped a Leety's fine chocolate into her mouth. Chocolate was most definitely the food of the gods.

Sally leaned against the counter. Tomorrow was Friday. After school, she was going to come home, put on her bathrobe, and spend the whole weekend watching Mel Gibson movies and eating Thin Mints. It was well known among Hartley's Girl Scout troops that Miss Foster would order a box of Thin Mints from any scout who knocked on her door. Now it was the middle of March. All those Girl Scouts had been delivering all those boxes of Thin Mints since Monday. So far, she had thirty-seven boxes on her dining room table—the thirty-eighth had been her reward for finishing grade cards. Everyone said Girl Scout cookies were supposed to freeze well. Sally took this on faith; her cookies never lasted long enough to make it to her freezer. And now all those boxes stared at her, called to her, wooing her seductively. But no. She'd wait until tomorrow. Mel Gibson and Thin Mints. It didn't get much better than this.

This year, during spring break, she really would walk three miles every day. She still had those brand new walking shoes in her closet, the shoes she got last summer when she was going to start walking with Liz and Kathryn but didn't because too many things got in the way. If she started walking over spring break, after she finished all the Thin Mints so she didn't keep eating them, and if she ate salads for lunch every day, and kept it up until summer, she might be able to lose enough weight so she wasn't embarrassed to be seen in shorts. Maybe.

Then she noticed the blinking red light on her answering machine. One of her kindergartners had probably come down with chicken pox, or strep, or pinkeye, or lice. Sally fortified herself with another half-dozen of Leety's dark chocolate nonpareils and pressed the button. *"This is Joann Hedges of the Brattleboro Memorial Hospital calling for Sally Foster. Please call me as soon as you can at this number. It's a matter of great urgency."* Brattleboro. Vermont. An icy chill slithered up her spine. That was where Deborah and Kevin lived. The machine continued with a second message. *"Sally, this is Ethel Fennessy. Oh, dear. Please call me immediately. As soon as you get home, no matter what time it is. There's been a horrible accident and . . ."* Her voice broke. There was a pause before she continued in a shaky voice with a phone number. Sally knew that number. It was

the number for Deb's cell phone. Ethel Fennessy
was Deb's mother-in-law.

Leety's fine chocolate suddenly tasted like school
paste in Sally's mouth.

Heart pounding, Sally punched in the number,
but in her haste her finger slipped so she had to
hang up and start again.

Fourteen years ago, on the day Micah was born,
Deborah had said to her, "If anything should ever
happen to us, we want you to take Micah. We want
you to be the one to take care of him for us. Raise
him for us. Would you?"

"Of course I would," Sally had said. "You're my
best friends. I'd be honored." And with her entire
being she'd meant it. But they both knew that that
kind of "anything" never happened.

Until now.

Ethel, Kevin's mother, was the one who told her.

Sally wanted to throw up. Instead, she fumbled
open the phone book and called the airlines. The
first available flight to Boston was early in the
morning, out of Columbus. She booked the flight
and made arrangements for a rental car. She called
Jessie to tell her what had happened and to ask
her to come over and take care of the cats and fish
while she was gone.

Then, even though it was late, Sally called her
principal. "They were coming home from Micah's
hockey game," she told him. "They were hit by a

drunk driver. Kevin died while they were cutting him out of the car. Deborah's in critical condition, and they don't think she'll make it. Kevin's mother said they're not sure of the extent of Micah's injuries. I'm his guardian, so I have to be there to do all the paper stuff. Besides, it's Deb . . . I don't know how long I'll be gone. It depends . . ."

"Take whatever time you need," Peter told her. "Tell them we're thinking of them."

That was when she started to cry. "Thanks, Peter," she managed. "They asked me when he was born . . . to be his guardian . . . but I . . . they . . . none of us ever imagined, not in a million years. In a billion years . . . I'll call you when I know more."

It was eleven o'clock. She had to leave for the airport in four hours. No point in even trying to sleep, not that she'd be able to. What did she have to do before she left? Sally went over a mental list, trying to think of something, anything, other than Deb and Kevin and Micah. Concentrate on the mundane, she told herself. Pack clean underwear. Clean the cat box. Change fish water. Run the dishwasher. Purge the refrigerator of any stray leftovers. She had enough cat food to last for a while, and fish food, so she didn't have to run to the store. Jessie had a key, of course, so that wasn't a problem. What else did she have to do? She glanced around her living room at all the scattered cat toys. She tried to think where she should begin, how to organize it all, tried to fight off thoughts of Deb and Kevin and Micah. But she couldn't do it. No matter how she tried, they pushed their way into her thoughts. She gave up. She sank down into her comfort chair and gave herself up to tears.

A solid-black cat suddenly appeared by her feet, staring up at her, unblinking. "Hey, Jude," she whispered. "Don't be afraid."

The cat leaped, and landed lightly in her lap where he settled himself into a curl. Sally felt the rumble of his silent purr. Of her three cats, Jude was the one who knew her the best, was in tune with her emotions. Tess was acutely aware of her own beauty, Troy was always imagining some military maneuver or guarding his fish, but Jude was her empathetic cat.

Sally bent down and rubbed her wet cheeks on Jude's black head. Jude never seemed to mind her tears. Never seemed to mind sitting with her, as long as she needed him. She'd never needed him as much or for as long as she did now. But finally, when her tears were slowing, Jude rolled over on his side and reached out a paw to feather-touch her chin. His eyes were luminous and compassionate.

Sally's eyes felt like sandpaper. Her nose felt as big as a house and stuffed like a Thanksgiving turkey. It was time to get things done.

At quarter till three in the morning, Sally's doorbell rang.

Jessie greeted her with a huge and noisy yawn. "I'm driving you to the airport," she announced. "Karen and Sylvie and M'liss all agreed, so don't bother arguing with me. You won't win." She shoved her way past Sally, into the house. "Karen made me promise not to talk so you could pretend I was a cab driver or something, unless you really wanted to. Now, stop crying. I'm going to sit here and read and pretend to be a cabbie until you're ready to go, so just ignore me." She held up a thick paperback. "It's by one of the guys who stayed behind at the hut while Scott set off to be the first to reach the South Pole. Really cool book."

"Thanks." Sally wiped her eyes on the sleeve of her shirt and smiled at Jessie's pun.

"This is what we best friends are for." Her friend grabbed a tissue from the box by the couch and shoved it at Sally. "You'd do the same for any of us and we know it."

Deb always said that even though Brattleboro was nestled into the arms of short, cozy mountains, and Hartley held on by its fingernails to the flat land of northern Ohio, the two towns felt alike. They were both established, unshakable, and had well-developed grapevines. Sally reached Brattleboro early in the afternoon, a half-eaten fast-food burger on the seat next to her. It had tasted like recycled cafeteria leftovers, but at least the coffee had been hot and full of caffeine.

She followed the blue signs to the hospital where she asked the pink lady for the critical-care ward. There, she asked at the nurse's station for Deborah Fennessy's room.

The nurse consulted a clipboard. "I'm sorry, ma'am, but only immediate family is allowed."

"She's family."

Sally turned to see Ethel Fennessy leaning on her cane. She had aged greatly since Sally had seen her last, but maybe she'd only aged since yesterday. Sally went to her and wrapped her arms around her, hugging her tight. "Thanks," she whispered. "Oh God, Ethel, I'm so, so sorry about Kevin."

In her arms, the woman trembled. "Thank you for coming so quickly."

"I had to be here, you know. Kevin and Deborah are . . . family."

Sally's arm still around her shoulders, Ethel moved down the hall, motioning to a closed door as they passed. "Mary is with her now." Mary was Kevin's older sister—the one Deb always said was overbearing. Deb, who never said anything negative about anyone.

"Frank, Mary's husband, is with Micah," Ethel continued. "We've been taking turns sitting with them." She led Sally into an alcove where a small, institutional-type couch and a few chairs hunkered around a table. The chairs were draped with coats, the table crowded with baskets of fruit and cheese and crackers. "Friends," Ethel tossed a wave towards the food, "they've been bringing all sorts of things. I don't know what we'll do with it all." She sank down on the couch, suddenly appearing lost and frail.

Sally sat down next to her and hugged her close. "We'll all work together to figure it out."

Ethel relaxed for a moment, then took a deep breath. "Thank you, dear. You can leave your coat here, it'll be fine. Now. I know you want to see Deborah."

"How is she?" Sally asked.

"Not well. Her parents will be here first thing tomorrow. I couldn't reach them until this morning."

Sally nodded. "If there's anything you need me to do, anyone you need me to call, anyone at all . . . I'm here to help."

"Deborah always said you were pure gold," Ethel's said. "Let's get you in to see her now."

Sally nodded again. "But what about Micah?"

Ethel seemed to crumple. "They're keeping him sedated so he doesn't move around. They're giving him medicine to try to keep the swelling in his spine down. But they still don't know how bad it is."

"How bad what is?" Sally asked carefully.

"He has a spinal cord injury." Ethel's voice wavered. "It's low in his spine. When they brought him in he was able to move his arms, but they don't know if he'll be able to walk again."

Deborah's room looked like the set for *ER*. Machines and pumps were connected to Deborah by myriad wires attached to every conceivable body part. There was a tube in her throat, and one in her nose. One IV dripped blood into Deb's arm, another dripped a clear liquid. Dozens of thick bandages were stuck on her, even on her eyes, and where there weren't bandages there were bruises.

Sally remembered hearing somewhere that people who were unconscious could sometimes hear you when you talked to them, but she didn't know what to say. Didn't know if she *could* say anything; her throat was clogged and felt as big as all outdoors. She sat down next to the bed and, careful not to dislodge any of the wires, wrapped her hands around Deborah's. She held Deb's hand, petting it gently. "Hey there, it's Sally," she whispered at last. "Don't you think this is a little extreme for playing hooky?"

The only sound was the monitor beeping, the ventilator whooshing, and a rhythmic click from the IV pump. Deborah did not move. "Don't try to talk," Sally told her. "Just concentrate on getting better. You know how hospital food sucks."

A nurse whisked in, clipboard in hand. She checked monitors, changed a hanging bag, did nurse-type things.

"Why are those bandages taped on her eyes?" Sally asked, struggling to keep her voice even.

"To keep them closed, so her corneas don't dry out." The nurse's voice was calm and professionally reassuring, but also compassionate in a detached sort of way.

Sally nodded, as if the answer made sense of all the chaos. But it didn't. Nothing did. There was no sense at all in this, she thought as the nurse whisked out again. Sally groped in her pocket for a tissue, one-handed, because she didn't want to break her contact with Deborah. She swiped at her eyes. Nope. No sense in this at all. Not even a little bit.

There was not a time when Deborah hadn't been

a part of her life. Their mothers, both pregnant at the time, had met in the grocery store and become friends. Sally and Deborah were both born at Hartley Community Hospital, one week apart. For a brief instant, she and Deborah were kids again, squabbling over whatever it was that they used to squabble over, but always ending up very bestest friends forever and ever. Then that instant was over; there was no more forever. Now, in this hospital room, the forever was here. Now was all they had.

Suddenly Sally knew that Deb was going to die, probably very soon. These were the last minutes she'd ever have with Deborah. Deborah, who had never told anyone when Sally was so afraid on the first day of kindergarten that she wet her pants. In second grade for several months they dressed as alike as possible, and pretended to be twins. When they were eleven, they went to Flicker's Pharmacy together, to give each other courage, and bought their first boxes of Kotex. And in ninth grade, when Sally got all her hopes up because someone heard it from someone that Don Anderson was going to ask her to the freshman dance, and then he asked Trip Ackerman, Deborah came over with a video and a whole pound box of Leety's Fine Chocolates. Their senior year in high school they both sent applications to Ohio State. They were both accepted and they shared first a dorm room, and then an apartment. Sally met Kevin in a required psych class. She knew he was perfect for Deborah and at their wedding, Sally was Deborah's maid of honor. Deborah became pregnant and the three of them went to Lamaze classes together.

When Deborah went into labor, Sally was there, with Kevin, in the birthing room, encouraging her to breathe. "Breathe, Deborah, breathe . . . in and out . . . breathe." The three of them breathed together to help bring Micah into the world.

Now, because of some drunk driver, Kevin was dead, and Deborah, who was as much a part of Sally's life as air, was dying also. Micah would live with her. She would raise him. She would be the one to see him go on his first date, get his first after-school job, send him off to college. She would be the one to see him become a man. She sat with Deb, stroked her hand, breathed with her.

Finally, the nurse came in and said Sally had to leave while they did some nursing care.

Suddenly, there was so very much Sally wanted to say and no time to say it. "Thank you for being such a terrific best friend. God, I'm gonna miss you!" It was so inadequate. There were no words for how much she would miss Deb. "I'll take care of Micah for you. I'll make you proud of him. I promise. Cross my heart." She gently held Deborah's hand up and pressed their palms together, their childhood ritual. "Blood sisters to the last." And Sally knew that this was the last. "They're kicking me out now, Deb, so I gotta go. But I'll be right outside with Ethel." She bent down and kissed Deborah's cheek. "See ya later, alligator," she whispered, and because she listened so hard, she could almost hear Deborah calling back, as she had across hundreds of childhood nights, *In a while, crocodile.*

TWO

"Tanner," Corinne's voice sounded tinny over the intercom. "Lucy and Maxie are here."

"Be right there." Tanner closed the file of puppy testing scores and shoved his chair back. He took his time on the way down the hallway to the lobby. He knew Lucy would need these last few moments with Maxie. Sure enough, as he reached the end of the hall he heard her take a deep, quavery breath. Then he saw them.

Lucy, with the golden retriever sitting patiently at her side, stood motionless, staring intently at a photo on the wall. Tanner guessed it was the photo of Juniper and her handler. It was one of many photos that covered the walls of the training school. Each photograph represented a victory—and Lucy, like everyone who volunteered by raising a puppy for a year, was part of making those victories happen.

Right now, though, gripping Maxie's leash, white-knuckled, as if holding on for dear life, she looked anything but victorious. She had looked the same way a year ago as she'd held onto Juniper's leash. And Hal's leash the year before that. And Frieda's, and Delta's, and the others. Their pictures, too, were on this wall. Lucy turned her back on the wall of victories—*Le Wall de Triomphe,* she'd once called it—and gave him a wan smile.

"So you decided to show up after all," he teased. It was a joke between them that went back ten years, to when she was twelve and they were both new at this. He'd repeated the same words every year since then.

"I almost didn't," she answered, as she always did. He knew she always dreaded this day, knew she always struggled to keep her emotions in check. She looked miserable.

To give her time to gather her composure, he directed his attention to the dog, still sitting calmly at her side. "Hello, Maxie," he said to the dog. "I'm glad to see you again. We're going to have a lot of fun together."

But the dog leaned against Lucy's knee and looked up at her, a question in her soft brown eyes.

Lucy cleared her throat. "Corinne has all the paperwork. It's all signed and everything." Then her face crumpled. "Oh, damn!" she muttered, swiping futilely at the tears coursing down her cheeks. "I always promise myself I won't break down like this. And I always do." She crouched down and wrapped her arms around the dog. "You be a good girl, now, Max." Her voice was clogged with tears. "You have a very important job to do. You're going to make a big difference in someone's life. You make me proud, you hear?"

The dog scrubbed her cheeks with her long, pink tongue.

"I love you, Maxie," she whispered into the dog's fur. "I'm going to miss you so much. It's just so hard." This last was directed towards Tanner. "No matter how much I mentally and emotionally prepare myself for this, it's always harder than I remembered."

"If it weren't difficult it would mean you hadn't done your job," Tanner told her as he'd told her before, as someone had told him, many years earlier. Even though he knew the words were true, he also knew they didn't help.

"Then I guess I always do a terrific job, because it always hurts like hell. Take her quick." Her face set, determined, resigned, Lucy stood up and held the leash out to Tanner. "Before I change my mind."

Tanner knew she wouldn't change her mind. He knew that no matter how much she hurt right now, she knew that what she did would make a huge difference in someone's life. Lucy knew she helped make miracles.

The instant the leash was in Tanner's hand, Lucy pushed past him and was out the door and gone. Maxie, confused, tried to follow her.

"No, Maxie," Tanner told the dog. "You need to be here now. With me."

The dog whined in distress. Tanner reached down to stroke her lovely golden head. But Maxie, who had formed a strong bond with Lucy, all but ignored him. Tanner knew that would change.

Corinne called from out of the office. "Lucy's

already requested another puppy, you know." Corinne knew Lucy, too.

Tanner nodded and rumpled the dog's velvet ears. "She always does. She's one of the best." When he turned in his puppy he would have requested another puppy, if he'd been able, if things had been different. But things were what they were, his friend Karen often said, and it was up to us to decide what to do with them.

"Maxie, let's go." He made his voice cheerful. "Time to meet the vet, and settle you in your new home. Tomorrow we'll begin turning you into a service dog." After a slight hesitation and a look towards the door, the dog followed him.

"You'll be fine," he told her. "I promise. Lucy will be fine, too."

The afternoon was set aside for retesting a litter of nearly identical, seven-week-old, fat and cuddly golden retriever puppies. Each puppy sported a drop of a different color of food coloring so they could be told apart. Jake had tested the puppies last week; it was Tanner's turn today, and Patti would test them again in a couple of days. While one trainer did the testing, the other two, clipboards in hand, observed from behind a one-way mirror. When they were finished, the three trainers would discuss the puppies, and decide. With luck, one of them would go home with Lucy next week. Tanner hoped so.

"First up," Tanner said, "Blue Boy." He scooped up the puppy with the spot of blue on the back of its neck. "Let's go, buddy. Let's see what you can do." The puppy licked him on the nose. Tanner took the puppy into the testing room and set him on the floor.

Blue Boy had an abundance of self-confidence. Tanner liked him. Of course, Tanner had never met a puppy he didn't like. Still, he had to be objective about testing. No matter how appealing a particular puppy was, if it didn't have the right stuff it would be placed in a pet home. Even though these puppies were from the school's special breeding program, only puppies who showed great promise were placed with volunteer puppy raisers, like Lucy. Then, after a year, the dogs were returned to the school to finish their training. If they passed their training, the dogs graduated and became service dogs. They would be matched with someone who needed them. Their picture would be added to the *Le Wall de Triomphe,* and they would change the lives of their new owners.

Blue Boy did well—though he showed a little hesitancy at walking on the screen. Orange Girl had no hesitancy at walking on the screen, but she didn't show much confidence when faced with the wind-up duck. Green Foot Girl showed desired responses for all the tests they gave her. She was suitably curious when the umbrella popped open six inches in front of her nose. When the wind-up duck quacked at her, she startled, but quickly recovered her composure. All in all, Tanner felt that today six of the puppies appeared to be good candidates.

* * *

"Message for you, Tanner," Corinne called to him when he came out of the puppy testing. He caught her looking at him oddly as he reached for the green While You Were Out slip.

"What?" he asked.

"The woman said she was your mother."

Tanner felt his gut clench. He shut it off and forced his face into a neutral expression. "So?" Without looking at the piece of paper he shoved it deep into the back pocket of his worn jeans.

Corinne shrugged. "I never thought of you having a mother before. I've known you for ten years and I've never heard you talk about your family."

He tossed her a cocky grin. "You thought I was born in a whelping box?"

"Well, yeah."

"I was." In an odd way, it wasn't even a lie.

Tanner whistled for Wing, the sharp sound piercing the cold of the evening. The Border collie came streaking towards him, the white on her neck and tip of her tail acting as a beacon in the dark. She was a lovely bitch, Tanner thought. Swift and fleet. Intense and driven. He'd trained dozens of dogs in his career, but never a dog as easy as Wing. And the most joyful thing was that she was his. The two of them were a team. When she reached him, he bent down to rub her ears while she tried to glue herself to his legs. He should've named her Elmer. Her breath, coming in pants, sent clouds flying up into the night.

Together they moseyed down the long gravel

drive towards the road to pick up the mail Tanner had forgotten to stop for earlier. At the end of the drive he flipped down the door to the mailbox and glanced in to see a clump of white envelopes. He drew them out, snapped the door shut, and whistled again for Wing.

Together they moseyed back towards home again, Wing ranging from side to side. Home, Tanner thought. Home was a small, utilitarian apartment built into one end of a pole barn. The rest of the barn made up his dog obedience school, where he held classes two nights a week. He was well known among dog people, and his classes were always full.

Back on the porch again, Tanner opened the door for Wing and she whisked inside. He was about to follow her when he caught a glimpse of a small something slipping through the shadows of the peach tree. That cat was back, watching him. Tanner stepped into the kitchen where he pulled an extra dog bowl from the cupboard, and filled it with cat food. Back outside, moving slowly and quietly, so he wouldn't startle the cat, he set the bowl of food on the edge of the porch. The first time he'd seen the cat up close it looked like it needed some serious food, so he put cat food on his grocery list. He hoped it would have the courage to come up on the porch to eat. He hoped it had a warm place to sleep.

In the kitchen once more, Tanner shrugged out of his down jacket. He glanced at Wing. She sat patiently by her water bowl. It was empty. He took the hint and poured fresh water. The dog lapped noisily. She was thirsty after her run.

Only then did he remember the stack of mail he'd brought back. He flipped through the colorful advertisements to find a few bills. And tucked slyly between them was an envelope of thick, creamy paper. He should've expected it. She always sent a letter on his birthday. But this year she'd called, too. She'd never called before. Tanner picked out the bills and tossed them on the long table that served as his desk. The advertisements went in the trash. The letter he shoved aside.

Wing sat, panting, on her haunches, watching him intently, trying to figure out what he wanted her to do.

"Go lie down," he told her.

She trotted over to her folded blanket and curled up, her head on her paws, her eyes still trained on him. Ever watching. Ever ready.

He picked up one of the bills. The spring obedience trials in Columbus were three weeks away. He and Wing were entered in the highest level of obedience where there would likely be some serious competition. That woman with the Papillon had beaten them earlier in the year. Granted, Wing had been feeling flirty that day, and the Papillon was a terrific worker, and had only beaten them by half a point in the runoff, but half a point was all it took. Tanner dropped the bill onto the table.

"Wing," he said softly. "Shall we work?"

Wing bounded up and over to the door that led to the big, open classroom. Wing loved to work. Wing lived to work.

Tanner set up the white baby gates to imitate a competition ring. He gathered his scent articles, using tongs to pick them up, careful not to touch them; he didn't want his scent on them yet. He set the articles along with the three white gloves on the table. Then he led Wing inside the ring, to a spot marked on the floor with masking tape. Wing followed him and positioned herself in a perfect sit, watching him, waiting for the command. Tanner smiled at her briefly. "Good girl," he murmured. Then he gave the command as he stepped off on his left foot. "Wing, heel."

Wing joyfully heeled.

Three

Sally wanted to spend the night in Micah's room, while he slept, so he wouldn't have to be alone. But Mary and Frank said they'd take turns. Mary took Sally aside and suggested she take Ethel home—that would be the most help, Mary said. Mary was obviously used to managing things. Ordinarily, Sally would have spoken up—after all, she had an obligation to be with Micah—but she caught a glimpse of Ethel, who looked like a wreck. So she acquiesced. She kept her voice friendly as she told Mary that she'd be back first thing in the morning.

After she dropped Ethel off, Sally drove across town to Deborah's house. She knew the way. Even in the dark.

The house was set back from the street, with winter-bare trees tall around it, silhouetted against the glooming sky. Sally pulled the rental car into the driveway and turned off the engine. Ethel had insisted that Deb and Kevin would have wanted Sally to stay at their house rather than at a motel; Deborah's house was Sally's other home, as Sally's house was Deb's. Even Mary and Frank had agreed. Still, somehow it didn't seem right to rummage through Deborah's purse for the keys, even though she knew Deborah wouldn't mind. They'd never had any secrets from each other.

Ten years earlier, after Kevin's father died, Deborah and Kevin had moved to Brattleboro to be near Ethel. While hunting houses, Deborah had seen this one and had fallen in love with it instantly. She said she felt like she already lived in this house, as if she were coming home. Suddenly, Sally realized, there were lights on in the house. Without thinking, she said to herself, Oh good, they're home. Then she remembered. They'd never be home again.

A figure came running across the lawn from the house next door. Sally recognized Sheryl Benson, one of Deb's many Vermont friends. Sally opened the car door and got out. "Sheryl? It's Sally from Ohio."

"Sally? Oh, I'm glad you're here!" Sheryl came to a stop about two feet from Sally.

"I just came from the hospital."

"Deborah?"

Sally shook her head. She couldn't find the words to say out loud that Deb had died.

"Oh no," Sheryl breathed.

Together they trudged up the walk where they sank down on the steps side by side.

"Ethel wanted to be alone to call people," Sally

said. "Deb's parents are getting here in the morning, and everyone else should arrive tomorrow or the next day."

"What about Micah?"

"They're keeping him sedated. There's swelling in his spinal cord and they don't want him to move around and possibly cause more damage. They say they'll know more when the swelling goes down, which should be in a couple of days. They're giving him medication to help with the swelling. I sat with him for a while this afternoon, then again for about an hour this evening. That's all I could do, just sit and sing to him. I don't know if he heard me." She had to struggle to keep her voice even. "Mary and Frank are with him now."

Sheryl shivered. "It was on the news last night. They were on their way home from Micah's hockey game and they were hit by a drunk driver going way over the speed limit. Their car rolled several times. Oh, God!"

"One of the doctors I talked to said Micah was wearing his hockey gear when they brought him in. They had to cut it off him. The doctor said all that padding probably had something to do with saving Micah's life."

"Today on the news they said the drunk driver was a woman who'd had an argument with her husband and went out and got drunk."

Sally closed her eyes. She didn't have enough energy to express the rage she felt. "She ought to be locked up for the rest of her life."

"As soon as I heard, I came over to get Sophie.

She couldn't stay here alone. Today I brought in the mail and turned on the lights."

Sally's thoughts snagged. Sophie. Who was Sophie? Did Deborah get a new cat and forget to tell her? Sally couldn't remember Deborah ever telling her there was a Sophie. "This is going to sound really stupid, but who is Sophie?"

"Micah's puppy." Sheryl didn't sound as though it was a stupid question. "He practically worships her. After Smoke died they were going to get another cat, but Micah told them he wanted a dog." Sheryl's voice broke and she began to weep silent tears.

"We need some tea," Sally said. "C'mon." She stood up and fitted Deborah's key into the lock. They opened the door and went into Deborah's home.

Deborah's house. It was warm and unassuming, welcoming. Just like Deborah and Kevin were. Sally slid her coat off and hung it on the coat tree by the door.

Standing in the center of the living room, she turned all around, slowly, seeing Deborah and Kevin everywhere. Slung over the back of a rocking chair was the afghan Deborah had knitted their first year in college. Now, Sally picked it up and wrapped it around her shoulders. God, this was more difficult than she thought it would be. She wandered down the hallway to the bathroom and grabbed a box of tissues. Thank goodness it was almost full.

In the kitchen the teakettle was on the stove and Sheryl was taking dishes out of the dishwasher.

"When we heard the news on the television," she said, her voice sounding lost, "and I came over to get Sophie, I ran the dishwasher. You know how dishes are harder to clean when they've been sitting around for a while. Deborah wouldn't want that." She turned to Sally, her eyes wide and luminous with unshed tears. "What will happen to the house? And all of their things?" She closed the dishwasher and sank down on a kitchen chair.

Sally opened a cupboard and pulled out two earthenware mugs. She set them on the table next to the other tea things and sank down in the chair across from Sheryl. "I don't know," she said heavily. "I just don't know."

They sat in silence until the teakettle whistled. Then Sally heaved out of the chair and over to the stove. She brought the teakettle to the table and poured the hot water. In her chair again, she wrapped her cold hands around her mug to warm them. It didn't work. "From the time Deb and I were born until she married Kevin, we were practically inseparable. Our mothers used to call us The Bobbsey Twins."

Sheryl said, "Every fall Deborah and I went to an orchard near here and picked apples. Then we'd spend the weekend peeling apples and making pies together. We always made a couple dozen pies. Two for right away, and the rest to freeze and bake later. Kevin and Bob always tried to steal the baked ones as soon as they were out of the oven." Her face seemed to smooth out around the edges. "Then Deb and I figured out that if we made pies on a day when there was a big football game on television, they wouldn't bother us." She smiled through her tears at the memory. "Deb taught me how to make the best apple pie."

They sipped their tea and shared all the good things Deb and Kevin and Micah had brought to their lives. The tea in their mugs grew cold, the clock on the mantel struck twelve, but they had more stories to share. Some of their stories made them laugh, some of them brought sighs and nods, some brought tears. In Deborah's kitchen, with her presence all around them, comforting as a hug, they talked for hours.

The next two days Sally was so busy she didn't have time to think. As Micah's guardian, Sally was now the responsible adult. She discovered the hospital's small library and read everything she could find about spinal cord injuries. She learned how the spinal cord worked, how it could be injured. She learned the difference between complete and incomplete injuries, and the levels of injuries, and nerve functions. She talked to the neurologist, the orthopedist, Micah's GP, even a psychologist who talked to her about the grief process. Then she interpreted it all for Ethel and Micah's Aunt Mary and Mary's husband Frank.

Other relatives arrived at the hospital. Relatives who needed to be brought up to date on Micah's condition, and comforted and consoled. Relatives who took turns sitting with Micah so he wouldn't be alone, even though he was still asleep. Sally knew some of them, of course—Deb's parents and much-older sister, and she spent time hugging and crying with them. Others of them, from Kevin's family, she had never met. She hugged and cried with them, too.

The small alcove became filled with family and friends and, in the afternoons after school, Deborah's fellow teachers and Micah's hockey players and their parents. All were there to give support, to show their love. Even though there was nothing they could do, they freely offered to do it.

Sheryl Benson proved herself to be a gem. She coordinated a casserole drive, and arranged for Deb and Kevin's Vermont friends to shuttle relatives from the airport to the hospital, then to Deb's house for quick meals, and back to the hospital again. She took care of the kitchen chores and took out the garbage. She fielded phone calls. And she kept Sophie. Until things settle down, she said. But Sally didn't want to think about the dog yet. Sally didn't want to have to think about the dog at all.

The day of the funeral was sunny and bright and cold. The small cemetery was bursting with relatives and friends, all bundled-up and gathered together to say goodbye to Deborah and Kevin Fennessy. Sally stood in the front, between Deborah's mother and sister. Ethel Fennessy, surrounded by a very solicitous Mary and Frank, and Martin, her youngest son, who looked so much like Kevin that Sally's breath caught, looked frail and tiny. Other cousins and aunts and uncles and in-laws were thick around the two flower-heaped caskets. Sheryl Benson and her husband and son were there, as were all the casserole and carpool friends. Kevin's architecture firm had

closed their office for the day, so all Kevin's co-work-
ers could attend. Micah's whole hockey team showed
up, the not-quite young men visibly trying desperately not to cry, some more successfully than others,
their mothers' and fathers' arms around them. The
hockey parents had been the last people to see Deb
and Kevin alive—at the game where Micah had
scored three goals—a hat trick. Also in attendance
were parents and players from the opposing team—
including the goalie—and the referees, and the
coaches. Teachers from Deborah's school were scattered among a whole cluster of her students, crying
openly, unashamedly.

Only Micah was missing. His absence was a big
hole in Sally's heart. She took in everything deliberately, carefully, the sound of the voices in song,
the sight of the great group of mourners, the bite
of the cold air sharp against her cheek. In her
mind she wrapped the images as one painstakingly
wraps fine crystal, to preserve them. She wanted to
keep them intact, unbroken, so she could share
them with Micah later, when he was ready. In some
small way it might comfort him to know how much
his parents were loved and respected by the people
of the town.

When it was time to go, Sally turned for one
long, last look at the two caskets, side by side. "See
ya later, alligator," she whispered.

In a while, crocodile.

After the funeral, Sally hurried back to the hospital and Micah's room, where she met the neu-

rologist. The swelling appeared to be going down, the doctor told her, so they'd started easing up on the medication. As soon as Micah was fully awake, he'd begin physical therapy, and they would be able to do more complete tests.

"How does he look?" Sally asked. She knew the answer, but had to ask anyway.

"There's no way of knowing right now, without more conclusive tests," the doctor answered.

"Will he walk again?" Sally decided to be blunt.

"I don't have an exact answer for you. It depends on a number of things. Where the injury occurred and whether it's a complete or an incomplete injury. Which nerves are involved. We'll know some of these things when we've done more conclusive tests. Sometimes, muscle function returns over a period of months. It can't be reliably predicted."

"In other words, you don't know."

"In other words," the doctor said simply, "I don't know."

Sally put her hands over her face. "I'm sorry," she said at last. "I apologize for my rudeness. Over the last few days I've read enough to understand that you really don't know. I guess I hoped for a miracle. It's just that he's so young, and he's lost so much . . ."

"Yes, he has. You're going to have to help him learn not to wallow in self-pity."

Sally frowned. "He has to grieve."

"Of course. I'm not talking about grief. I'm talking about the self-pity that comes later, that will keep him sitting and staring out the window. That will kill him inside. But you'll learn about that later.

There will be some education classes for you, as his caregiver. There are things you need to know— how to help him, how to let him help himself, what his limitations are, how to make appropriate adaptations to everyday life."

Sally was silent for a moment, staring at Micah, so uncharacteristically still in the hospital bed. "How soon can I start?"

"He should wake up this evening, but he'll be very tired. He should feel better tomorrow morning. Then the physical therapist will begin his therapy. Try to be here, too. The therapist will show you what to do."

After the doctor left, Sally sat and watched Micah sleep. He looked so very much like both of his parents. He'd always had Deborah's smile and Kevin's eyes. Deb always said Micah had inherited the very best parts of them. She thought about Micah waking up and learning his parents were both dead, learning he might not walk again. How would he bear it? How could she help him bear it? The family had decided, and Sally had agreed, that Ethel should be the one to be there when Micah woke up. Ethel should be the one to tell him.

After college, Sally had moved back to Hartley to teach. Deb and Kevin stayed in Columbus, where Kevin had been hired by a top architecture firm. After Micah was born, Sally had driven down almost every weekend. She held baby Micah close and danced around, softly singing simple songs to him, all the songs she sang with her kindergartners. Now she took his hand, as earlier she'd taken his mother's, careful of all the attached tubes and wires. "Catch a falling star," she sang to him, as she had when he was a baby, "and put it in your pocket."

Late that evening, Sally stood staring blindly out Deborah's kitchen window into the backyard. She wanted her cats. She wanted to hug them and bury her face in their fur and hear their comforting purrs, feel the rumble. She wanted to call Jessie, find out how the cats were, even though she knew they were fine. She had complete faith in Jessie. But, she admitted to herself, most of all she wanted the connection with someone from home so she could pretend, if only for a few moments, that the accident had never happened.

As she reached for the phone, she caught, in the corner of her eye, movement in the Bensons' backyard. The dog, Micah's puppy, was running in a large circle. Sally's hand dropped from the phone. A dog. Why did there have to be a dog? Actually, the dog was just one of the things Sally wanted to forget. She wanted to forget that it had taken rescue crews two hours to cut Deborah and Kevin out of their car, and that Kevin had died while they were trying to get him out. That it had taken another thirty minutes to free Micah. She wanted to forget how beat-up Deborah had looked. She wanted to remember Deborah and Kevin as they had always been—vibrant, full of energy and life. These were the things she wanted Micah to remember about his parents.

Four

The physical therapist, Heather Snow, was terrific. She explained why Micah had to do his exercises. "So if muscle function returns he'll have normal range of motion instead of contractures." Sally must've looked confused because the physical therapist added, "So his joints won't be stiff." The lady never lost her cool, never raised her voice, never showed the least impatience no matter how uncooperative Micah was. Micah was mostly uncooperative. Heather told Sally this was not uncommon; everyone had a different way of dealing with life altering events. The lady would've been a helluva kindergarten teacher. Now Heather gently but firmly showed Micah, yet again, how to sit up on his own.

Micah wasn't interested in sitting up, on his own or otherwise. He wasn't interested in anything. He seldom spoke, and when he did it was in a voice without emotion, and his eyes were wooden.

Sally's heart ached for him.

"So Micah," the therapist said, "I need you to sit up, like I showed you, so I can check your blood pressure."

Micah went through the motions until, with her support, he was sitting up.

"Great." She nodded her approval. "And look, your BP is within the normal range."

After about ten minutes, Heather allowed him to lie back down. The therapist was sympathetic, but also matter-of-fact about it all. Sally knew from her years of teaching that kids picked up on the emotional state of adults. If adults were overly concerned or worried or tense, kids would begin to think there really was something to worry about. Obviously the physical therapist understood this, too. Maybe she'd been a kindergarten teacher in a former life.

"Let's work on your leg muscles now," she said briskly. She moved to the foot of the bed and then stopped, to eye both Micah and Sally speculatively. "Micah," she said at last, "it's time for Sally to learn to do this." Her eyes fixed Sally and she crooked her finger. "Come here."

She guided Sally's hands to the correct position on Micah's right foot. "That's right, his heel in your left palm. Start with his toes. Gently and smoothly, first up and down, then side to side. That's right."

Memories of playing This Little Piggie with Micah when he was a giggly-wiggly one-year-old swarmed to the surface of Sally's mind. She shoved them back down. This was no time to turn sentimental and mushy. Besides, the blank look on Micah's face told her he wasn't interested in hearing any baby stories.

"Now the top of his foot, that's right."

Sally followed the therapist's instructions, at first feeling clumsy, then, through foot, ankle, knee, and hip, becoming more comfortable. Finally she had a chance to do something for Micah other than sitting passively at his side, singing silly songs while he slept. This was active, definite, something that would help him recover, even if he wasn't interested.

He wasn't interested in the CD player Sally brought to the hospital, along with a stack of CD's she found on his desk. He didn't want to watch any videos, even though the hospital had a video player. Books were refused as well.

However, that afternoon, Micah did seem to cheer up a little when, after school, a couple of guys from his hockey team shuffled in on feet they hadn't grown into yet. One of them even swung an air stick at an imaginary puck, scoring an imaginary goal. Then he looked embarrassed, as if he'd just remembered Micah might never play hockey again. They tried to joke with Micah for a bit, chatting about school, but after a few more awkward moments, none of them seemed to know what to say. Thinking they might be more comfortable without a strange adult present, Sally slipped out into the hall.

What did she know about teenagers? she thought. Nothing. Now, five-year-olds, Sally knew them inside and out—but teenagers were a whole different species. How was she ever going to do this? Sure, she'd promised Deb and Kevin—but that was when Micah was a baby. What did one do with a teenager? How did one bond to a teenager? And what made her think this teenager was at all interested in bonding with her? Hey, Deb, Kev, you have to help me out here. She wandered down the hall, but stopped when she heard her name. They were talking about her in the alcove.

"Sally take him?" Mary's voice was clear. "That's preposterous. She's a nice person and all, but Micah should be with Family." She actually said it with a capital F.

"As far as Deborah was concerned," came the mild voice of Deborah's sister, "Sally is—was—family. In every way that counts. In every way but blood."

Kevin's sister snorted in derision. "It's not the same."

Then Martin, the brother who looked so much like Kevin, who was a lawyer, spoke up. "But it *is* what both Kevin and Deb wanted, Mary. You know it is. I drew up the papers myself. Taking this to court, trying to overturn their wishes, is not the best thing for Micah, and it will also upset Mother. It'll cost you a lot of money, and you *will* lose. I suggest you not attempt anything of the kind."

"Isn't Micah old enough to decide where he wants to live?" Mary kept on.

"Leave it alone, Mary." The brother's voice was firm.

From where she stood, in the shadows of the hallway, Sally felt as if she'd been punched in the gut. What if Kevin's sister was right? Maybe Micah did belong here, in Vermont, with his aunts and uncles and grandmother, where he had his school and his friends. Who was she to yank Micah out of his world and stick him in hers? Just because something was legally decreed, didn't mean it was right.

Sally rushed down the hall, back the way she came. She had no idea where she was going—only that she had to be away from Mary right now.

"Oh, hello." Heather Snow's voice broke into Sally's roiling thoughts. "Listen, do you have a moment? I'd like to talk to you about Micah."

"Sure." Sally was glad to have something to take her mind off Mary's words. Sally followed the therapist down a short hall and around a corner to a small conference room.

"Micah," Heather said, "has just gone through what is probably one of the worst things that could ever happen to anyone." Her eyes were full of empathy.

Sally felt her gut clench with tears. Tears would not help anyone right now. Right now she needed to listen and learn how to help Micah. So, not trusting her voice, she nodded.

"Micah has a very long way to go. Right now, as you can probably tell, he's not the least bit interested in his recovery. He needs to be part of it. He needs to fight for it. At times it will be difficult and he'll feel like he's not making any progress. He'll need courage to continue. I know he's a hockey player, so I'm sure," she added with a swift grin, "he has a fighting instinct. Can you think of something that will help him come out from behind his wall?" She leaned forward. "I'm not talking about grief. Grief is necessary and natural. I'm not trying to minimize that in the least. But in order to do the best for him, I need to be able to communicate with him, I need him to be willing to talk to me as we work."

"I know," Sally admitted. "I've worried about that, too." She frowned in thought. "Okay," she said after a moment, raising her eyes to meet the therapist's gaze. "I'm not sure what it'll be right now, but I will," she vowed, "come up with something."

But what, she asked herself that evening, standing in the middle of Micah's bedroom. What could that be? What would help him find his way through the darkness without denying that it existed? She studied his room. The walls were covered with posters of hockey players. Gordie Howe, Mark Messier, Jaromir Jagr, as well as others she didn't recognize. A computer sat on his desk, along with the normal desk clutter. Next to his desk, a bundle of battered hockey sticks leaned casually against the wall. Micah's top dresser drawer was halfway pulled out, with a T-shirt draped over the side. The bed had almost been made, as if Micah had been in a hurry that morning. On his bedside table a cluster of hockey pucks shoved against a book called *Endurance*. She scanned the crowded bookshelves. Tolkien, the Harry Potters, Terry Pratchett, and several books about exploration of Antarctica and the South Pole. All were well-thumbed. Micah was a great fan of fantasy, and shared Jessie's obsession with the Pole. Last summer, when Deb and Micah were in Hartley, Jessie drove Micah down to Columbus to see the Shackleton exhibition, and they spent the rest of the week planning an imaginary trip to The Ice.

Hockey, other worlds, and Antarctica. How could these things help him now? Sally sank down in a beat-up easy chair that huddled in the corner of the room. She stuck her foot on top of a red rubber ball and absently rolled it back and forth while she thought. And thought. And thought. And thought some more.

Early the next morning, impatient for her toast to pop up, Sally leaned against the kitchen sink, a cup of tea in her hands. She still hadn't come up with something for Micah. Next door, in the Bensons' backyard, the dog was again running stupidly in a big circle. The dog, she thought with a heavy sigh. She was now responsible for a dog, too. Micah's dog.

Micah's dog.

The realization smacked her in the face. Micah's dog. How could she have been so stupid? Micah's dog was the answer! She dumped her tea in the sink and whirled around to shove the jam and butter back in the refrigerator. Again she stopped. The refrigerator was plastered with a plethora of cheerful magnets holding up the usual flotsam and jetsam, including a photograph of Micah holding a puppy. His puppy. Why hadn't she seen it before now? She probably had, but hadn't paid attention. She slid the photo from under the dog-bone magnet and held it close to study it. In the photo, the

puppy struggled to lick Micah's nose. The look on
Micah's face was one of sheer delight. She turned
the picture over. On the back, written in Deborah's
careful hand—Sally would recognize Deborah's
writing anywhere—were the words *Micah and his
new best friend. Valentine's Day.*

Best friend. This concept, best friend, had far-
reaching ramifications. You did things for your best
friends. You did things without expecting anything
in return. Whatever it took, for your best friends
you did, even if it was difficult. Sally knew this. Deb
knew it, too. This best friends thing was why Jessie
had driven her to Columbus in the middle of the
night. You bore a responsibility to your best friend,
a responsibility that was not a burden, but a privilege. "Okay, Deb," she whispered, sliding the
photo back under its magnet, "this best friend will
take that best friend to your son."

Sally rummaged around in her purse until she
finally came up with the card that had the hospital
phone number on it. "May I please speak to
Heather Snow?" she asked the switchboard, keeping her fingers crossed that the physical therapist
was available. Luck was with her. "Heather, this is
Sally Foster. I know what will help Micah. Can we
bend the hospital rules?"

Sally was not used to puppies, especially puppies
with industrial strength enthusiasm. The whole way
to the hospital she drove with one hand on the steer-
ing wheel and the other on the creature's collar, to
keep it from jumping up and licking her face.

When they reached the hospital, Sally snapped the leash on the dog's collar before she got out of the car. She was glad she had. As soon as she set the thing down on the sidewalk, the miniature hellhound scampered around joyously until it hit the end of the leash, whereupon it bounced back to Sally's side only to begin again. At least, Sally thought as she picked the monstrous thing up, it was small enough to be carried. Sheryl said Sophie would fill out, but wouldn't get much bigger. Thank goodness, Sally told herself. A big dog with this much energy would be impossible to keep in the house, and the cats would become psychotic. A small dog was bad enough.

All the other dogs Sally knew—Melissa's dogs, Karen's dogs, Sylvie's dog—walked politely on leashes. *That's because,* she could almost hear Jessie's smug voice telling her, *they've gone to Tanner Dodge's dog classes.* "You," Sally muttered to the furry fiend in her arms, "would most definitely flunk." The little creature wildly wagged its tail in complete agreement.

Sally followed the sidewalk around to the side of the hospital, as Heather had told her to do. Suddenly she had a horrible thought. She took the dog over to the grass and set it down. Sure enough, the puppy wandered, sniffing, in a tiny circle and then squatted. It was the first time Sally had seen it hold still. Sally breathed a sigh of relief and picked the puppy up again before it could start surging against the leash. The critter actually seemed to settle down in her arms.

Heather met her at the side door, as they'd arranged. "What a sweetie," Heather exclaimed as she reached out to pet the puppy in Sally's arms. "And oh my, what big ears you have." The puppy slung her tongue around Heather's fingers.

Heather led the way through the maze of back halls and stairways until they came out in a hall Sally recognized. Micah's room was the third on the left. "Go ahead," the therapist told her quietly. "I'm off to work with another patient, but I'll be in to see Micah in a bit."

As the therapist turned to leave, Sally put a hand on her arm. "Thanks for arranging this."

Heather grinned. She understood.

Outside Micah's door, Sally took a deep breath. She hoped this was the right thing to do. "This is it," she told the dog. "It's time for best friends to do their stuff." She shoved open the door with her hip. "Morning, Micah, I brought a visitor."

Micah slowly turned his head to look at her with his usual blank look. Then he saw his dog. For a brief second he stayed still as stone, then, with a cry, "Sophie!" he struggled to sit up and reached for her.

The puppy frantically flung itself out of Sally's arms to get to Micah. Micah held onto his wiggling, whining puppy as if he were holding onto his life. "Sophie, oh Sophie," Micah murmured. He bent over the little dog in his arms and buried his face in his best friend's fur. And over the soft, joyful noises of the puppy, Sally could hear the small gasps as Micah began to cry.

Five

Two weeks after the accident, the doctors pronounced Micah stable and ready for a rehabilitation center. Mary said he should stay in New England, to be near his "real family." Dartmouth, she said, which was not far from Brattleboro, had an excellent rehabilitation center. But Sally, armed with information from Heather, told the family Micah would go to the center in Cleveland, which was one of the best in the country.

"Besides," she added, "it's about an hour from Hartley, so I can drive up two nights a week and on weekends."

Mary opened her mouth to protest, but Martin, the lawyer brother, shot her a quelling glare, and she snapped her mouth shut. But her face said it all. She did not approve of Sally's plan. Martin's face showed no emotion; Sally had no idea what he really thought—as a person, not a lawyer. Ethel looked drawn.

Sally took a deep, steadying breath. She reminded herself to keep her voice even. These people all loved Micah, and she had to do all she could to keep communication as smooth as possible. If communication between Micah and his family broke down, it would not be because of Sally. "The staff here talked to the people in Cleveland, and helped me make our travel arrangements. Micah will be in a wheelchair. Ambulance to the airport, plane to Cleveland, then another ambulance to the rehab center. In addition to rehab, they have a tutor on staff, so Micah will be able to finish the school year. I've written down the address, phone number, and web address so you'll be able to keep in contact with Micah. And Ethel, I gave them your address and asked them to send you their brochure."

Ethel gave her a weak smile. "What about Sophie?"

"The Bensons have offered to keep her until Micah is out of rehab." She caught the expression on Mary's face. "Sophie will be happier here, with the Bensons, than at my house where she'd be alone all day, and evenings and weekends when I'm with Micah."

So the next day, Sally and Micah flew to Cleveland. It was a long and tiring trip for Micah. By the time they finally arrived at the rehab center, he wasn't the least bit interested in looking around.

Sally signed an amazing number of papers while a nurse wheeled Micah off to his room. When Sally saw him again, he was in another hospital bed, propped up with a pillow. He looked pale. He looked lost and alone. He *was* lost and alone. How could she possibly leave him to the care of strangers?

"He'll be fine," a nurse promised her.

"He'll be busy," the social worker said. "Physical therapy, occupational therapy. recreational therapy, counseling, support group—and schoolwork. He'll be a busy guy."

She gave Sally a packet of papers—information about rehab, spinal cord injuries, bunches of names, and phone numbers. "And a reading list," she said, "to help you understand what is going on in Micah's mind, and what you can do to help him. And this," she handed Sally a business card. "This is the contact person for a support group for families of people who have spinal cord injuries. Don't hesitate to call them. Better than anyone, they understand what you're going through."

"What I'm going through?" Sally asked.

The social worker gazed at her appraisingly. "Yes. You. Your life is focused on Micah right now, and you're probably a little frightened. You know your life is going to change in ways you can't predict, and that may make you apprehensive. The only thing you know for sure is that it won't always be easy. You're right. It won't. Make sure you remember to take care of yourself, pay attention to your own feelings and emotions, or you'll burn out. If that happens, you can't help him."

* * *

Jessie drove from Hartley to pick Sally up. She brought Micah a T-shirt. "It's from all of us," she said. "All your new aunties."

Micah held it up. *"Fortitudine Vincimus.* By endurance we conquer." He looked at her. "Shackleton's motto."

Jessie grinned. "Yup. Hey, this morning it was minus fifty-eight degrees at the Pole."

A shadow of a smile flitted across Micah's face. "It's only autumn. It's gonna get a lot colder."

"Nah. Remember what that one guy at the Pole said? There's no such thing as cold weather, there's only inadequate clothing. Hey, Sally and I gotta get going. I'll see you later. Okay?"

"Sure."

Sally bent down to give Micah a brief hug. It felt awkward. It took her a second to realize that Micah hadn't hugged her back.

"I'll be up Tuesday after school," Sally told him. "You know my phone number, and you have that prepaid phone card I gave you. When the money's gone I'll get you another one. Call anyone you want."

Micah nodded.

"Well." Sally hesitated at the door. "See you later, alligator."

"See ya."

Once outside the rehab center, Sally swiped her eyes with the heel of her hand. She blinked hard. "Bright sun," she said.

Jessie nodded. "Yeah." She didn't point out that today there was a heavy cloud cover.

Sally stared out the window of Jessie's car. She didn't think she was ready to talk yet.

Jessie paid unusually close attention to Cleveland's traffic. She didn't initiate conversation.

A good thing about friends, Sally thought, a lump in her throat: they knew when to be quiet. When she was ready to talk, she knew her friends would be ready to listen. Right now, she didn't know what to say, so she didn't say it, all the way back.

"Welcome to Hartley, Ohio," she read the Chamber of Commerce sign. Hartley looked the same. Grape Street looked the same. Sally's house looked the same. The cats and the fish looked the same. But Sally knew it would never be the same again.

Sally returned to her kindergarten classes. This was a world she knew, where she felt comfortable, in control. She went to school to find order in the chaos of her life. She went home to play with her cats, and to read the books on the rehab reading list. When she ran out of her dark chocolate nonpareils, she drove to Leety's for more.

Twice a week, after school, she drove up to Cleveland to be with Micah at the rehabilitation center. After a day of work, both physical and mental, Micah and his fellow rehabees usually spent the evening watching videos and eating popcorn. After her first couple of visits, Sally took movie requests. She became well known at the local video place, and well appreciated at the center.

Saturdays at rehab were set aside for field trips. Sally went along—like a room mother, she thought. They visited fast-food places and Sea World and the NASA Research Center, and the Rock and Roll Hall of Fame. One Saturday, they went to the Metroparks Rainforest, where they saw the colonies of bats, and the zoo where they looked for the pack of wolves. Sally understood the rehab people made sure the rehabees experiences out in "the world" were successful and interesting, so they'd be willing to make future forays. The teacher in her approved.

One Tuesday evening, Sally brought a box of Thin Mints for Micah. He shared well with others; the cookies were such a hit that on Thursday, Sally brought a dozen boxes. She would have brought Micah the world if it would help him.

Back in Hartley, after every visit, she called Ethel in Vermont and Deb's parents out west. She encouraged them to call Micah on the evenings she didn't go up to visit. She wanted to make sure Micah felt he was still part of their lives.

Rehab was slow going for a kid who until now had never known what *slow* meant. Some days he was higher than a kite, promising everyone he'd be back on the ice by fall. After all, he said, look at Gordie Howe. He was injured and had brain surgery and everyone thought he'd never walk again, and he went on to play a bunch more years in the NHL, until he was really, really old—over *fifty*. Other days, Micah was depressed, glowering at his surroundings, muttering that all these stupid exercises were no use, he'd never be able to walk again. The therapists at the center assured Sally this was another variation of normal.

Gradually, in spite of his mood swings, Micah regained muscle control and some use of his legs. He was fitted with braces. He could wear them under his blue jeans. One evening Sally went up to Cleveland to see him take his first steps. He needed his braces, and his feet swung slightly sideways when he moved them forward—the therapist said this might become less pronounced over time—but he walked.

That evening, back in Hartley, Sally pulled out her photo albums and opened them to the pictures of baby Micah taking his first steps. Today she'd seen the same intense concentration on his face, but this time there was no great drooly grin of triumph. This time, there was no grin at all.

In all her albums, she found a group of drawings Micah had done in art class and sent to her. Micah had inherited his father's ability to draw. The next day, after school, she took three of them to the craft store, to have them matted and framed.

One late afternoon in early May, when Sally arrived at the rehab center, the receptionist beckoned her over to meet a red-haired girl in a wheelchair. "Sally, this is Terry Muldoon. She's a hockey player. She wanted to meet you."

Sally automatically held out her hand. "Hi,

Terry." Then she did a mental double take and her eyes widened. Hockey player?

"Do you have a minute?" Terry asked.

"I guess so."

"Let's go outside to sit on the porch," Terry suggested.

Sally followed her out. "You're a *hockey* player?"

Terry grinned widely. "Yup. I play sled hockey. The Cleveland Thunder. That's our team. That's why I came out here after school today. I heard about Micah, and I wanted to meet him, to tell him about us, and to invite him to check us out. We'd love to have him play. We have such a cool team!" Terry was one of those people who used her hands when she talked. Her face shone and her words fairly tripped over themselves in enthusiasm. "It's co-ed. We come from all over the area, so we only get together to practice one afternoon a week, and our games are on weekends. There are only a couple other sled hockey teams anywhere near here. Pittsburgh, Erie, and a new team in Detroit. So we travel for most of our games. All of us on all of the teams are really good friends. We e-mail each other every day." She grinned. "One time, my mom yelled at me, *If you're doing E-mail again instead of your homework, I'm gonna smash that computer!*" Terry laughed. "But I know she doesn't mean it. She's really glad I have my team."

Terry's enthusiasm was contagious. What a wonderful thing for Micah this could be, Sally thought. He'd love it. "Did you talk to Micah?"

Terry's expression fell and she shrugged. "Yeah.

He said he wasn't interested. He said he didn't want to play any *adaptive sports.*" She wrinkled her nose as she said the last two words.

Sally was at a loss for words.

After a moment, Terry turned earnest blue eyes to Sally. "I think he'd love it. Sled hockey isn't wussy and it isn't watered-down stand-up hockey. It's *real* hockey. If he could come to one of our games, he'd see. It's fast and it's competitive and it's not for wimps. People all over the world play. And last year, in the Paralympics, Team USA brought home the gold. The final game, against Norway, ended in a tie, so there was a five round, one-on-one shoot-out and Team USA won. Some of us from our team were watching it together on TV, and we were yelling and screaming, it was so intense." Her hands dropped into her lap and she shrugged again. "Anyway, after I talked to Micah, one of the therapists said you'd be up this afternoon. So I waited. I wanted to meet you, to explain it to you." She pulled a pamphlet out of the backpack hanging on her wheelchair. "This'll explain a little about sled hockey. Here, on the back, is my phone number and my e-mail address. Micah might not be interested right now, but someday he might be."

As Terry wheeled her chair down the sidewalk, towards the parking lot, Sally read the words splashed in red on her black backpack. *Give Blood. Play Hockey.* Micah had those same words on a T-shirt.

Sally looked at the pamphlet in her hand. She'd

have to put this somewhere where it'd be safe. She might need it someday.

It was in the end of May, at Katie Matheson's high school graduation, that Sally started to shake inside. Katie was Karen's daughter and they—Sally and Jessie and Melissa and Sylvie—had all helped raise her, in an auntie sort of way, so of course they all had to go to her graduation. They all sat in a cluster of seats in the middle of the auditorium with Karen's family. Karen's face was drawn and pale. Ordinarily, Sally would have put the squeeze on her until she 'fessed up about what was bothering her, but Sally was so busy being bothered by her own life that for once she didn't have time to put the squeeze on her friend. So now, crammed into the auditorium with hundreds of other families and friends of the graduating class, Sally scanned the long row of graduating seniors. They stood quiet for once, proud in their scarlet-and-gold polyester robes with those funny tasseled hats, waiting their turn to walk across the stage, grab their diplomas, and flip their tassels.

In four years Micah would graduate from this same high school. Four years. How am I going to do this? she asked herself. The enormity of it almost made her gasp. She knew the answer—*because Deb and Kevin trusted you*—but it didn't make her feel any better.

As the school band belted out the beginning notes of yet another play-through of *Pomp and Cir-*

cumstance, Jessie leaned over and whispered, "So Micah is coming home next weekend?"

Sally nodded. "I'm going up to Cleveland to the rehab center to pick him up Saturday morning."

"Why are your teeth chattering? It *is* sorta cold in here. You wanna borrow my sweater?"

"I'm fine," she lied.

Jessie gave her one more look before she settled back in her seat.

Sally listened to the band with all of their enthusiastic gusto butcher *Pomp and Circumstance* once more. Students came and students went, but the band still massacred Elgar every year. It had been that way as long as anyone now alive could remember. Playing P&C, as it was affectionately dubbed, at graduation was a *school* tradition. Playing it *badly* was a band tradition.

Jessie leaned over again. "Sagan, my puppy, is coming soon after that, and Sylvie's baby is due in two more weeks. So we'll all be gaining kids together, we'll all be turning into moms together. In a manner of speaking."

"If you can equate newborns, teenagers, and puppies."

"Sure can," Jessie chirped cheerfully. " 'Course, teenagers are sort of a different species. But still, they count."

"Shhhh!" Sylvie hissed at Jessie.

"Colleen Marie Martini," the principal announced. Colleen Martini trotted up the steps and across the stage. Colleen had been in Sally's first kindergarten class. Since then, Sally had taught four other Martinis, Jeremy, Lilian, Kathleen, and Joshua. Jeremy and Micah were the same age.

Sally was terrified. What if Micah hated her? What if he still wanted to go back to Vermont to live with his Aunt Mary? What if he stayed with her but she messed him up so completely that he turned into a lawyer or something? She'd promised Deb she would make them proud of Micah. It was easy to make a promise you never thought you'd ever have to keep. She didn't resent Micah; he was the next thing to having her own kid, but she was terrified. She wrapped her arms around herself and stared straight ahead.

"Katie's next!" Sylvie whispered, practically bouncing up and down.

"Katherine Eleanor Matheson," the assistant principal announced, and a grown-up Katie, who used to be little Katie, walked across the stage to accept her diploma. Where did she get all her poise, Sally wondered. Melissa shoved a tissue into Karen's hands, and Jessie clicked away with her camera.

"Soon," Sylvie whispered to Sally, "we'll be sitting here again watching Micah graduate."

Sally nodded. They were all excited for her that Micah was coming home. Home to her house. Home to her. She hadn't told them about Sophie. She hadn't told anyone about Sophie. Not even the cats, who were not going to be pleased, or the goldfish, who, as long as they were fed twice a day, wouldn't care.

In six days, on Saturday, she would go up to Cleveland to bring Micah home. But the day before

that, she would drive down to the Columbus airport to pick up Sophie.

"Are you all right?" Jessie asked. "You look sick."

"Sophie is arriving Friday," Sally said without
thinking.

Jessie frowned. "Who's Sophie?"

"Micah's dog."

"Dog?" Jessie shrieked into the auditorium.

Everyone turned around to shush her.

Sunday evening, after Tanner took Wing out for
her evening run, his phone rang. It was Jessie.

"Hey, Tanner. I have a sort of personal question
for you, and I didn't want to ask you yesterday, at
Katie's graduation party. Um. Are you involved with
anyone right now?"

"What?"

"I mean, um, are you seeing anyone right now?
As in a girlfriend or something."

Tanner thought. "What are you trying to ask
me?"

"Well, I have a friend and I think the two of you
would hit it off. If you're not seeing someone already."

"Are you telling me you want to introduce me
to one of your friends?"

"Well, yeah. She's not just *my* friend. Melissa and
Karen and Sylvie know her too. Anyway, I think the
world of both of you. I think it would be nice for
you two to . . . you know . . . meet."

Tanner scratched his head. "Gee, Jess. I don't

know what to say." That was an understatement, he thought.

"You don't have to make up your mind right now. Think about it for a while."

"Uh. I don't think so, Jess, I'm pretty busy. But thanks for thinking of me."

After he hung up the phone, Tanner turned to look at Wing. "Where did that one come from?"

Wing wagged her tail.

"I don't know, either."

Six

Monday morning, Tanner checked his E-mail, then went to the dog runs to collect his group of canine students. After a run and romp in the large backyard, he brought them all in, tails wagging, tongues hanging, eyes bright. They all headed for the water bowls and the room was filled with the sound of five dogs slurping. Then he herded the wiggling dogs into their classroom. He worked with them one at a time, while the others played. It was an excellent way to teach them to ignore distractions.

Tanner pointed to the cloth rope tied around the drawer pull. "Maxie, take it." Without hesitation, the dog took the rope in her mouth.

"Good girl," Tanner told her. "Pull."

Maxie backed up, giving the rope a little tug, and pulled the drawer open.

"What a good girl you are!" Tanner told her. Maxie wiggled under his praise. She loved praise. So far, Maxie was everything they'd hoped she'd be. She was bright and steady, showed great empathy, and learned quickly and well. Boredom was not an issue with Maxie. She was content to do the same thing over and over and over again, a trait that would make her an excellent service dog.

"The next thing we are going to teach you," Tanner told her, "is to grab a pair of socks out of the drawer and bring them to me. You think you can learn to do that?"

Maxie smiled her doggy smile and swished her tail agreeably. She was a pleasure to work with, to teach. Lucy had done an excellent job raising her and was doing an equally excellent job with Oliver, who'd been placed with her two months ago.

Later that afternoon, Tanner shoved back from his desk and stretched. He'd worked his way through half of the stack of new volunteer applications. Thank goodness they did not have a dearth of volunteers willing to raise puppies. They could not survive without their puppy raisers. Many raisers were repeaters who, like Lucy, were committed to the school and its mission. For them, raising puppies was part of their lives.

He looked out the window into the neighboring soybean fields. It was turning into a hot day for the end of May.

He needed something cold to drink. In the break room he opened the refrigerator, the door festooned with another cloth pull. Most of the doors and drawers in the building had pulls on them; the trainers never missed an opportunity to teach a dog, or remind a dog, or encourage a dog to practice. For the same reason, there were light switches three inches up from the floor as well as at the conventional heights. Inside the refrigerator, among bottles of salad dressing, oddly shaped hunks of wrapped cheese, and the other brown bag detritus, stood two plastic pitchers. He reached for the closest one and looked inside. Jake and Patti, the other two trainers, had made their infamous version of grape Kool-Aid. They made it so strong, they joked, it could almost stand up by itself. Tanner shoved the pitcher back in the refrigerator. How could anyone drink that sludge on purpose? He looked in the other plastic pitcher. Corinne had made lemonade again. He poured himself a generous glass.

"You're not drinking that grape stuff?" came a teasing voice. Corinne rolled into the break room with Aspen, her service dog. She maneuvered her chair around the table. Aspen was careful to stay out of the way of the wheels until Corinne came to a stop, then he settled down next to her.

"You could use it for mortar." Tanner reached into the cupboard and handed Corinne a glass.

"We could use it for sealing the driveway."

Suggesting new uses for Jake and Patti's grape Kool-Aid was a constant source of amusement for the staff.

Tanner poured lemonade in Corinne's glass. "It'd be great for cleaning whitewalls. We could probably market it as an all-purpose engine cleaner."

Corinne rolled her eyes. "It should be illegal in the first place."

"It should be a federal offense," Tanner added conversationally. "Cruel and unusual use of Kool-

Aid in a manner other than that intended by the manufacturer."

Corinne chuckled. "There's another can of lemonade concentrate in the freezer. Bring it out for the puppy raisers' class tonight."

"Jake is teaching the summer classes," Tanner reminded her.

"Oh." Corinne shrugged in feigned innocence. "I thought you were. Lucy called a bit ago and asked, and I told her I thought you were teaching the class."

"Nope. It's all Jake tonight." Tanner narrowed his eyes at her. She full well knew who was teaching tonight because she was the one who made up the schedules.

Corinne ignored the look he shot at her. "She said she is moving into a new apartment next week. I put her new address in the files—she'll call when she gets her phone hooked up. She asked me if we wanted to do a home visit, like we did when she applied for her first puppy. I told her I'd have you call her if we did. I figure, by now she's such a habitual puppy raiser she'd never move into a place that was inappropriate. Anyway, she went on and on about that Oliver puppy. She says he's a little cutie pie and a monster." She chuckled.

"I bet she's a little in love with him already."

"She's a little in love with you," Corinne said.

Tanner almost dropped his glass. "What?"

"Don't try and act surprised, Mr. Dodge. Most of our female puppy raisers are a little bit in love with you." She set her empty glass in the sink.

"But—they can't be." He wasn't the type of man women fell in love with, a little bit, or otherwise.

Corinne looked smug. "Don't take it personally. You're exactly the kind of man women fall in love with."

Before he could think of what to say, she'd wheeled out of the room and, followed by Aspen, was gone.

Monday after school, Sally found Jessie leaning against the door of her car. "Don't you dare try to shut me up," Jessie announced by way of greeting. "Yesterday you rushed away after Katie's graduation without telling anyone where you were going. You drop this bomb on us and then disappear. That's not fair, you know. So I asked Melissa if I could take a couple hours off to track you down. Don't try to run away again. I will find you."

"You do a crappy Daniel Day-Lewis."

"So tell me about this Sophie."

"It's Micah's dog. Puppy."

Jessie looked at her and gestured wildly. "Puppy. There are billions and billions of kinds of puppies. What kind? How old? Tell me."

"It's a corgi."

"Cardigan or Pembroke?" Jessie shot back.

"Huh?"

"Which kind of corgi is she?"

"I dunno. It has short legs and big ears." She didn't add she thought the dog was funny-looking.

Jessie sighed in dramatic exasperation. "Does she have a tail?"

Sally nodded. "Only it's hard to see because it's a blur. It never stops."

"She's a Cardigan, then. What color?"

Sally thought. How to describe it. "Mackerel. Mostly mackerel stripes, with a white tummy. And white neck. Blaze up her nose."

Jessie nodded wisely. "In cats it's mackerel. In dogs it's called brindle. Okay. So you're making me pull teeth here. I can live with that. How old is she?"

Sally shook her head. "I'm not sure. About eight months old. Look." She pulled out her wallet and opened it. "Here's a picture of the two of them." It was the photo from Deb's refrigerator.

Jessie studied it, wide-eyed. "Yup. She's a brindle Cardigan. What a cutie. So where's she been all this time?" She handed the photo back.

"The Bensons in Vermont, Deb's neighbors." Sally still felt odd saying Deb's name, afraid she might cry, but it felt good to say her name, too. "Deb's neighbors. They offered to take care of Sophie while Micah was in rehab because I had so much to do with the end of the school year, and going up to see Micah, and getting ready for Micah to come live with me. They offered to take care of the dog," she repeated.

"Sure you didn't bribe them?" Jessie slanted her a sly grin. "Thinking they'd fall so much in love with her that they'd want to keep her forever and ever."

"Jessica Albright!" Sally was shocked. "I'm not a totally horrible person. Besides, Micah loves that dog. Even though it is a monster." She told her friend about bringing Sophie to the hospital, and the difference it made in Micah's recovery. "So you see, after that, there is absolutely no way I would ever *not* have the dog for Micah. He loves the wretched creature," she repeated faintly. She stubbed at a small rock in the parking lot.

"This really puts you in a quandary, doesn't it?" Jessie's tone of voice lost its tease. "You and Deb were practically indistinguishable from each other when you were growing up. After Micah was born, Deb became your ideal of how a mother should be. So now you think *you* have to be the perfect mother to Deb's kid, whatever it takes—even if it takes Sophie. Thing is, you don't want Sophie. You say your cats don't like dogs—but because they're *your* cats they've never had the opportunity to decide the dog question for themselves, because *you* don't like dogs—though in all other respects you're really quite a wonderful person. I simply don't understand this little idiocy of yours—and Micah, who has known you practically since before he was born, *he* knows you don't like dogs because you've never made the least attempt to hide this fact." She paused to take a breath. "And now you're stuck with a dog, and not just any old dog, but Deb's dog. And, of course, Deb was probably the perfect dog owner, except she neglected to tell you she had a dog probably because she knew exactly how you felt about *canis familiaris* and she didn't want you to think she was a turncoat. So what do you do? You have to be graceful about it all. You're pretty good at graceful, but you don't want to have to be because this is not a mere weekend visit—this is the forever kind of thing. You refer to Sophie as an *it* rather than a *she* because that's a way you can make your true feelings known without being explicit. By the way, you might want to rethink the *it-she* thing through. Micah won't be fooled." She looked at Sally. "How am I doing so far?"

"You pinned the tail right smack-dab on the donkey." Sally heaved a great big sigh.

Jessie shrugged. "Actually, Karen smacked the donkey. She and M'liss and I had a long conversation about all this. She's very insightful, for a psychologist."

"Well, no matter who came up with it, it's all true." Sally scooped up a handful of gravel and tossed it, piece by piece, back on the ground. "The worst part is that I have no clue what to do."

Jessie grinned widely. "Tanner Dodge has puppy kindergarten classes. You should be able to relate to the kindergarten part." She said it simply. As if that solved all Sally's problems. "We'll take you to Tanner. He loves herding breeds."

Sally groaned. "Not the sainted Tanner Dodge."

"Puppy classes will teach you to communicate with Sophie," her friend enthused. "You'll develop a much stronger bond with her."

"No."

"Ah, c'mon, Sally. You'll love Tanner."

"No."

"He's great."

"No."

"And he knows more about dogs than just about anyone who's ever lived."

Sally shot Jessie a withering glance. "You are prone to hyperbole."

Jessie did not wither. "It's not an exaggeration. You'll see."

"No. I won't."

"Don't be dumb. You're gonna have your hands full with Micah, let alone adding a puppy. Look. I'll call Tanner tonight and ask—"

"No."

"Yes."

"No."

"Spoilsport."

"Pushy."

"Stubborn."

"Bossy Bess."

Jessie hooted with laughter. "You've been around kindergartners too long. They've pickled your brain."

"You don't relish kids?"

"Yeah. I can muster up a liking for kids. Especially when they belong to someone else. You now, you've always wanted hordes of babies. Which is probably why you teach kindergarten, because they're as close to babies as you can get in the public school system. Me, though, I'd rather have dogs—which is why I'm getting a puppy and you're getting a teenager which is about as far from babies as you can get—but you're also getting a puppy which makes the deal about perfect. Puppies are precious and miraculous." She shook her head in wonder. "Teenagers can talk and are able to reason, though it's not always obvious, and best of all, they're already housebroken." She looked quite pleased with her bit of logic.

Sally, however, was not amused. She'd known Jessie too long to be pleasant and cheerful under these circumstances. "I'm getting a headache. I want to go home now. I need to eat chocolate and hug my cats."

That evening, Tanner opened a can of soup and dumped it in the pan. He turned on the stove burner and reached for a spoon to stir. Then the phone rang.

"Hi, Tanner," came a cheerful voice.

"Hi, Jess. I heard your puppy was arriving soon."

"Sooner every day. Sagan has to be at least eight weeks old before she can fly."

"Let me guess. You're excited."

"Absolutely. People should be excited about getting puppies, don't you think? But look. That's not why I called. I want to talk about PK classes. I'm calling for a friend who's just inherited an eight-month-old Cardigan puppy."

"Great dogs, Cardigans. But don't you mean beginning obedience?"

"I know eight months is a little older than usual for PK classes, but in her situation, I think it would be the best thing. She knows nothing about dogs and inherited this one. She doesn't like dogs. At least, not as a generic. I can't imagine not liking dogs."

"Do you know why she doesn't like dogs?"

"Why? I never thought about the why. Hmmm.

I always assumed she hadn't inherited the dog-o-phile gene. I'll have to think about this one. Anyway, can we sign her up for PK?"

"Yeah. Sure, Jess."

"I'll make sure she has all the shot records and stuff. Oh. Hey, Tanner, I had an idea the other day. I was in the library and there was this alleged training video by that media vet. The blurb claimed even people like J. Q. Public could easily and quickly teach their dogs basic manners." She snorted in disgust. "As if teaching dogs is some deep, dark, secretive, difficult thing to do, where you need the secret handshake or something. Anyway, I checked it out and watched it, but it was mostly a long commercial for some of the stuff he peddles. Real waste of time. You know so much more than he ever will. So I was thinking. Why don't *you* make a training video? We could get several dogs in various stages of trained-ness—like Wing could portray perfection, Sagan could represent PK classes, and we could get one of Karen's dogs to be slow but steady, and we could borrow Jean-Luc to play the spacey but loveable poo-dle. I think it would be great."

Tanner bit his lip to keep from laughing. Jessie and her grand schemes. "Thanks for the compliment, Jessie," he told her. "But right now I'm pretty busy training for all the summer shows."

"You and Wing entered in Lima?"

"And Dayton the next day."

"Well, what about in the fall? Making a video."

"No, Jessie. I don't think so."

"But it'd be a best-seller. I know it would. You could do autographing at all the dog shows."

"Thanks for thinking of me, but I really don't have time to do a video right now. Not in the fall. Not anytime soon."

"That's your final answer?" She sounded disappointed.

"Yeah."

Seven

Tuesday was the last day of school for the kids. Little Carrie, in the morning class, brought Sally a bouquet of spring flowers. In the afternoon, James's mom arrived with a huge platter of baked-from-scratch chocolate chip cookies. Sally shared the cookies with her students before she set the platter on her desk, piled high with notes and small gifts from her students. She felt a little tug at her heart as she looked at her class. She would miss them. She always did. Last September, they had arrived in her class, brand new. Many of them nervous, or frightened, expressed in different ways. Now, they were ready for first grade. "I am proud of you. You are, each one of you, terrific and special. I expect great things from you. Have a wonderful summer, and remember, in the fall you'll be first-graders."

When the bell rang for the last time, her students erupted out of the classroom to join the flood of kids swarming down the halls and out the doors into the summer sun.

School might be over for the kids, but the teachers had two more days to finish paperwork and to pack their classrooms into boxes. The school was scheduled to be painted over the summer, which meant all classrooms had to be empty down to the bare walls before the teachers were free.

Two days later, Sally blew a strand of hair out of her face as she lugged her last box into the hallway for the janitor to move to storage. Her boxes made up a veritable mountain. No one appreciated the multitude of art supplies and counting beads and packages of construction paper and kid-friendly scissors and pencils and little plastic sorting bears and dress-up clothes and all the other just plain *stuff* that was necessary to teach kindergarten. She'd been in the same room for eight years. Teachers could collect an amazing amount of stuff in eight years. Now it was all packed up in neatly labeled boxes. Her classroom was as bare as Mother Hubbard's cupboard.

Sally was hot and tired and felt grimy and gross. She checked her desk one last time, hoping to find some stray piece of chocolate lurking in the back recesses of a drawer. No luck. She slung her purse over her shoulder and dragged down the echoing hallway to the heavy doors. She blinked at the sudden onslaught of sunlight and shielded her eyes with her hand. Surely there was symbolism here, moving from the darkness into the light, but at the moment, it was beyond her to figure out what it might be. On the way home, she stopped at Leety's Fine Chocolates. She needed some of that fine. She deserved it.

When Sally arrived home from school, chocolate

in hand, she found the UPS man had struck again. A box was on her porch.

After the accident, Ethel had moved into Deb and Kevin's house temporarily until they decided what would be done with all their things. Sally and Ethel talked on the phone often, discussing the things from the house Micah might want. For the past month, every couple of days, when Sally arrived home from school, she found one or two big boxes from Vermont. One box was full of videos and CD's. In another box, Deb's photograph album was wrapped up in the sweater she'd knitted for Kevin, which he had worn constantly. In another was Kevin's OSU sweatshirt and the quilt from Micah's bed.

Now, Deb's rocking chair, with one of Deb's quilts folded over the back, had become Troy's new territory—to defend from any enemy. One of Kevin's framed architectural prints—"some medieval church-type place"—Sally had described it to Jessie, hung in her living room. Sally took her battered old end table, the one under her Rockwell print, out to the garage, and in its place she put Deb's many-pigeonholed desk. Deb's small collection of Toby jugs was in the dining room in the open cupboard Kevin had built for them, and next to the Toby jugs Sally put the ceramic candle holder Micah had made in first grade.

After a quick shower, with the evening news as background noise, Sally sank down on the couch to open the box. The cats, having learned that interesting things came out of boxes, watched intently. Sally cut the packing tape and looked inside.

Whatever it was, was wrapped in cheerful wrapping paper. Sally reached in to pull out the envelope addressed to Sally. She read the note inside. *Dear Sally, I know Deb would want you to have this. Love, Ethel.*

"Oh, my," Sally murmured. It was one of Deb's shawls. Deb loved to sew, loved to work with fabric, yarn, needles of all kinds. She sewed and quilted and knitted. She loved to make cuddle things— sweaters and quilts and afghans, things to keep her loved ones warm. That was her way of taking care of the people she loved. Sally wrapped the shawl around herself. It was like a hug from heaven. Minutes later, Jude pushed his way onto her lap and curled up. Sally could feel the vibrations of his silent purr.

The doorbell rang. Sally swiped her eyes and went to answer the door.

"Hi, Miss Foster." It was little Joshua Martini. "Can I come in and visit your fishies?"

"Of course. They'll be happy to see you."

"Hey, Miss Foster. What did the hat say to the scarf?"

"I don't know."

"You hang around while I go on ahead." He laughed uproariously at his joke. "Hi, little fishies," he crooned to the goldfish. "Are you glad school is out? I am."

Sally left Joshua with the fish and wandered down the short hall to open the door to Micah's room. All of her things were now upstairs in the guestroom, and in their place were a dozen boxes from Vermont, all labeled, in Ethel's hand, *Micah's Room.*

"Hey, Miss Foster." Joshua Martini was looking around her into the room. "Why don't you open all those boxes?"

"They're Micah's things. His grandmother sent them here for him. I thought he might like to arrange his room himself. It might feel more like his own room that way." Karen had suggested it.

"You're giving him a *pink room?*"

Sally chuckled. "You sound appalled. Don't worry. It won't stay pink. As soon as Micah decides what color he wants, we're going to paint it." Even, Karen had said, if Micah wants dark blue paint, or black.

"Oh. I guess it's okay, then. When's he gonna get here? I have lotsa new jokes for him!"

"I'm going to pick him up Saturday morning."

Joshua pointed to the framed photograph on the bedside table. "That's his mom and dad, right? The ones who died?"

Sally swallowed. She had taken the photograph when they were all in college. Deb and Kevin were in the early throes of being in love and Sally had managed to capture it on film. "That's right. You remember Deb from when she came to visit every summer. I don't think you ever met Kevin, but you would've liked him. He knew lots of jokes, too."

"Hey, I'm real sorry they died." Joshua's shoulders slumped. "Not just because of the jokes. When your mom dies, it really sucks. I know."

Sally was touched. This was a subject Joshua Martini did not discuss. "Thanks, Joshua." She bent down so she was on his level and could look into his eyes. "It means a lot to me for you to say that. I'm real sorry your mom died, too."

"Well, I better go home now. My stepmom said I can't be late for supper."

Sally got out her list of things to do before Micah got home. She called the Bensons to make sure Sophie was ready to fly to Ohio in the morning. She gathered together all the documents she needed to take to the license bureau tomorrow morning to pick up handicapped license plates. She took the pink sheets off the bed in Micah's room and made it up with brand new plain blue sheets, topping them off with the quilt from Micah's bed in Vermont. She took the photograph of Sophie and Micah out of her purse and put it in one of those clear, magnetized refrigerator frames. She stuck it on her refrigerator right next to the cat picture four-year-old Cammie Maxwell from down the street drew for her. Finally, there was nothing left to do but wait.

She wandered into the living room. She sat in Deb's rocking chair and pulled Tess onto her lap. The night before Sylvie and Ray's wedding, Sally and her friends had taken Sylvie out for a feast of Mel films and pizza—that expensive pizza they only had on special occasions. They'd done the same thing for Melissa the night before she married Peter.

"We need a celebration," she told Tess. She reached for the telephone and ordered the expen-

sive pizza. When it arrived, she opened a can of
sardines for the cats, and chopped up a tiny bit of
frozen scallops for the fish. The cats wound around
her legs and reached for the sardines. Marina and
Gwendal shot up to the corner of the aquarium
where she always fed them. "Treats for everyone!"

Then it was her turn. She slid the first *Lethal
Weapon* into the machine and settled down with
her pizza and a tall glass of iced tea. But the pizza
didn't taste quite as good as she remembered, and
she had a difficult time keeping her attention on
the movie. She kept thinking about Micah. Kept
thinking about all the major changes that were just
over the horizon.

C'mon, Sally, she told herself, it's not as if he's
a stranger. You've known him since before he was
even thought of.

For the first time ever, she gave up on Mel. She
turned off the video and wrapped up the leftover
pizza to stick in the refrigerator.

Then she noticed the red light on her answering
machine.

It was Jessie. "Puppy Kindergarten classes—you
should like that—begin in mid-June." Jessie went
on to give the registration information. Sally de-
leted it. She was not going to take Micah and Sophie to the sainted Tanner Dodge, she thought
perversely.

"Are you really gonna get a dog, Miss Foster?"
a little voice asked her.

Sally looked up from the brand-new handicapped license plate she was screwing on to the back of her car. A cluster of the younger neighborhood children stared at her, all their eyes wide and solemn. "Yes, Jasmine, I am." She gave the screw another turn. "There." She set the screwdriver down and gave the kids her full attention. "Remember, I told you Micah has a puppy. Her name is Sophie and in about half an hour, I'm driving down to the airport in Columbus to pick her up."

"Can we come over and see her?" Jasmine was going into first grade, so, being the oldest of the group, as well as having a natural tendency to take the lead, she'd obviously appointed herself spokesperson. Sally figured Jasmine would grow up to be either a politician or a union boss.

"Well, sure. Sophie likes kids."

Four-year-old Erin, who lived next door, gazed at Sally with great solemnity, the middle three fingers of her left hand in her mouth. Some kids sucked their thumbs—Erin sucked her fingers. She took them out of her mouth long enough to ask, in her slightly lisping voice, "Does Sophie like cats?"

From the mouths of babes, Sally thought. "I don't know," she answered. "I guess we'll find out. But you know, I have some friends who know a lot about dogs, and they say Sophie isn't full-grown yet so her opinions about things like cats probably aren't set."

The children nodded wisely, as if they understood.

"Can we come visit Micah?" asked Jasmine, who did not seem pleased to have the attention go to some other, younger, child.

"Of course. Micah is going to live here. In fact, most of you have met him before, even though you might not remember."

Kelly, who would be in kindergarten in the fall, said, "Micah's a teenager."

Sally nodded. "He's fourteen."

"Teenagers," said Jasmine in the tone of one who really knows. "They wear ugly clothes and listen to weird music."

An excruciating squeal of brakes shattered the quiet of the neighborhood. A decrepit car pulled up to the curb.

"Hi, guys!" Jessie hopped out of the car, clutching a bulging, brown paper bag splashed with Abernathy's logo.

"What's in that bag?" Jasmine asked.

"Oh, all sorts of very important stuff. It's a puppy pick-up kit. I'm going with Sally to pick up her puppy."

"You are?" Sally asked.

"Yup. I invited myself. Acquiring a puppy is one of those momentous life events that you have to share with your friends. Besides, if I didn't go with you, what would I do with all this loot? Take a look, you guys." Jessie held the bag low so the kids could look in. "I've got paper towels and a bottle of spray cleaner. Little zippy plastic bags to clean up unmentionable things, and a dog bowl and some bottled water."

"What's that?" Erin took her fingers out of her mouth and pointed.

"It's a small bag of liver-flavored puppy treats. Would you like one?"

Erin popped her fingers back into her mouth and shook her head.

"Gross!" Jasmine wrinkled her nose.

"And," Jessie added, "a leash." She looked at Sally. "Unless you already have one?"

Sally slumped. "No."

"Then it's a good thing I came prepared," her friend said cheerfully. "I get by with a little help from my friends." She sang the Beatles song.

They left Hartley, driving west to pick up the highway going south to Columbus. Jessie said, "I assume you watched *Braveheart* last night, so you have plenty of courage."

Sally shook her head. "Wrong. *Lethal Weapon.* Why? You think I need courage?"

Jessie nodded emphatically. "Yeah. Besides, I've decided that Mel is definitely a dog person. Look how many of his movies have dogs in them. He interacts with them like someone who is totally used to them being in his life. Like in *The Patriot.* Those two Great Danes? And in *The Man Without a Face,* remember when he tosses that piece of meat to the dog? He's had real-life practice tossing meat to dogs."

Sally slanted a look at her friend. "You're trying to irritate me?"

"No. It's just what I think. Mel Gibson is a dog person." She leaned back in the passenger seat. "Imagine what it would be like to be the person from the Humane Society who's on the set to make sure no animals were harmed in the making of this movie. Have there been any dogs in Russell Crowe's movies? Hmmm. I don't think so. I'm sure I would've noticed them . . . There was that dog in the beginning of *Gladiator*—for about three seconds." She sighed. "Well, that scratches Russell from my list."

Sally groaned.

Jessie rummaged around in the paper bag. "I didn't tell your neighborhood kids, but there's something in here for you, too. I thought you'd need it." She pulled out one of the distinctively long and thin boxes of Leety's dark chocolate nonpareils.

The young, gum-chomping clerk at the freight office told them the plane was fifteen minutes out. After it landed it'd take about half an hour for the guys to bring the freight over.

Sally dropped into an ugly plastic chair and flipped through the stack of seriously out-of-date magazines. She chose the least unlikely looking of them and opened it to an article describing "Great New Ways to Cook Your Thanksgiving Turkey Your Family Will Love." She wanted to throw up. Instead she groped for her purse and the box of nonpareils. Jessie wandered around the waiting room and read the yellowed notices on the bulletin board. Sally nervously tapped her toe. Jessie, whistling softly, did a few steps of soft-shoe.

Finally, the gum guy appeared, carrying a plastic airline pet crate and a small shipping box marked *Sophie Supplies* in great big red letters.

"I'll take her," Jessie said and reached in front of Sally. "You take the box. I'll open the crate and get her out. Why, what an absolute sweetie pie!" Jessie cooed as she lifted Sophie out of the crate. "What a precious little girl." She cuddled the dog in her arms. "Sal, she's gorgeous!" Sophie, obviously thrilled to be out of the small airline crate, threw herself into the cuddling with all her might.

"Let's go," Sally said. She grabbed the shipping box and headed for the door.

"Sally, she's marvelous!" Jessie exclaimed, the dog still in one arm, the crate in the other.

"And you're not the least bit partial, are you?"

"No sarcasm, now."

"I'm not being sarcastic."

"She's terrific."

"She's Micah's."

"She's going to live with you. Oh, you sweetie!" This last as Sophie managed to slurp Jessie's face for the umpteenth time.

Sally opened the backseat of her car and shoved in the shipping box.

"We should find her a spot to pee before we leave." Jessie shoved the crate in next to the box.

Sally looked around. Outside the freight office there was a large expanse of pockmarked blacktop, but little actual grass.

"Over there," Jessie said, pointing to a splash of weeds next to a chain-link fence. She pulled the leash out of her puppy pick-up kit and snapped it onto Sophie's collar. "I'll bet you're glad to stretch your short little legs, aren't you?" She set the puppy down. "Here you go, Sal."

Sally took the leash. "Hi, Sophie," she said. Sophie didn't seem to notice her lack of enthusiasm. Sophie had enough enthusiasm for both of them. Sally led the puppy over to the growth of weeds. The little dog gave a couple of sniffs and then squatted.

"Good girl!" Jessie gushed.

Sally looked away. "Let's get her home."

She put Sophie in the crate in the backseat of her car. She glared at Jess, daring her to contradict her decision.

Jessie gazed at her speculatively. "I'm glad to see you're referring to her as a 'she' rather than an 'it'. I've been wondering. Why don't you like dogs?"

"I just don't."

"But there has to be a reason."

"Don't push it, Jessie."

"You're afraid she's going to chase the cats."

"She's a dog. Of course she's going to chase the cats. That's what dogs do."

"You're prejudiced. Not all dogs chase cats, you know. Besides, it'll do your kitties good to have a different species in the house. It'll be a good multicultural experience for them. Aren't teachers big on being multicultural?"

"We have a different species in the house. The fish."

Before she let Sophie in the house, Sally took a quick look around to make sure the cats were up on the catwalks. She felt like a traitor. Sophie zoomed into the house, running around in circles

until she caught sight of Tess and Troy. She jerked
to a halt to stare at the two cats who crouched
safely out of reach. Sophie stood up on her short,
fat little legs. Her tail was a blur. She looked eager.
The cats were not impressed. The cats were angry.
Their tails whipped back and forth. Sophie did not
understand the language of the cats' tails. She sat
her little bottom down and stared up at the cats.

"Don't worry," Sally told Tess. "I'll keep you
safe. I haven't really switched sides." She reached
up for her cat. Tess didn't want to leave the catwalk.
Her claws dug into the carpeting. Sally untangled
her claws. She needed to hug her cat. She needed
to feel a purr. Tess was not inclined to purr.

"I still love you the best," Sally said, rubbing her
cheek against the silky fur. "I'll always love you the
best."

Tess ignored her.

Sally set Tess back on the perch and reached up
to pet Troy. Ever the soldier, he glared at the puppy
on the floor and growled. Troy flipped his tail and
stared down at Sophie with narrowed eyes.

Sophie did not understand the threat. She
grinned her puppy grin, her tongue hanging out,
and wagged her tail.

After a supper of Thin Mints, Sally let the puppy
explore the house. Sophie found the cat box. Sally
moved it. Sophie pulled a sock out of Sally's closet.
Sally pried open the little canine mouth to rescue
the sock. Sophie discovered the fish food on the
shelf under the aquarium, and before Sally stopped
her, gobbled it all up.

Sally stood over the puppy and scowled her fiercest kindergarten teacher scowl.

"Do not hurt my cats. Do not hurt my fish. Or you are one dead puppy."

Sophie wiggled in delight.

Eight

Tanner brought his group of dogs into the middle of the training room. "Down," he said. The dogs downed. They wagged their tails. They knew they'd done the right thing. "Stay," Tanner told them. The dogs had learned to do a down stay when they were with their puppy raisers. However, doing a down stay in the middle of a living room, or in the middle of a backyard, was quite different from doing a down stay in the middle of a restaurant or a playground. When they graduated, these dogs would go everywhere with their owners—restaurants, airplanes, movie theaters. They had to be reliable in public, had to ignore any and all distractions, no matter what it was.

Today the distraction was Penny, the school bunny.

Jake, helping him with the lesson, brought in the bunny and set her down in front of the line of the dogs. Penny casually hopped around the room. She had been raised with dogs and ignored them. Murphy raised his head and his ears went forward. "Murphy, leave it," Tanner said quietly. Murphy put his head back on his paws.

"Good dogs," Tanner said at last.

After the bunny had gone back to her hutch, Tanner took a basket of toys from a shelf. Squeaky toys were squeaked. Tennis balls were bounced, some barely two inches from the dogs' noses. Jake and Tanner tossed a Frisbee back and forth, low down, where the dogs could easily see it. They invited the dogs one at a time, to get up and play with the Frisbee, while the other dogs remained in place. A hot dog was waved in front of their noses. The dogs stayed down. The dogs ignored what was going on in front of them. Maxie rolled over on her side, closed her eyes, and pretended to go to sleep. Even Murphy, after his one bit of interest in the bunny, ignored the rest of the act.

"Good dogs," Tanner told them as he put away the last of the distractions. "Good dogs." They had done well this morning. Now it was their playtime. "Okay." He released them from their down stays. "Outside recess today, guys." The dogs swarmed up and around his legs as he led them through the door to the backyard.

That evening, Sally's friends arrived bearing gifts of tennis balls, chew toys, and a stuffed plush bone. Karen brought a book called *The Newfoundland Puppy.* "But it's the best book about puppies I've ever read," she said. "Tells you everything you need to know." Sally was doubtful about this last statement.

Melissa handed her a jar of extra-super-chunk peanut butter. "Give Sophie a tiny spoonful of it a couple of times a week. She'll grow up assuming great food always has little *things* in it. So if you ever have to give her pills, put 'em in peanut butter and she won't have a problem with it."

Sally looked at the jar.

Her friends looked at the puppy. They unanimously pronounced the puppy wonderful, charming, and adorable. For her part, Sophie thought these four new people, who were all equally willing to gush over her, were great, too. She raced around the living room in a circle and barked in excitement. Tess and Troy crouched on the highest catwalk and glared down at the irritating and rambunctious invader. They were not amused. Jude, of course, was nowhere to be seen.

"He's being obscure," Jessie said.

Melissa pulled three little fur mice from her pocket. "I didn't want the cats to feel dispossessed," she said.

Late that night, Sally woke up to an unfamiliar noise. Sophie, shut in her crate in Micah's room, was crying. It was a pitiful, mournful sound. Sally pulled a pillow over her head. She pulled the sheet over the pillow over her head. She scrunched her eyes closed and sang nursery rhymes to herself.

Finally, she got up and went to Sophie. She opened the crate door and peered in. Sophie was huddled against the back of the crate. The puppy looked up at her with mournful eyes, looking for all the world like a lost kindergartner on the first day of school. Sally felt something inside start to melt. "Poor thing," she murmured. With a sigh, she pulled the puppy out. "You're just a baby."

She sat down on the floor and hugged the puppy close. She leaned back against the bed. "You've lost everything you've ever known. And now you're stuck with someone who doesn't like dogs. All because of some dumb drunk driver." She felt the warm tears slide down her cheeks. "I'm sorry I don't like dogs. I know it isn't your fault. But you're stuck with me and I'm stuck with you. You'd have had a terrific life with Deb and Kevin. Kevin grew up with dogs. He knew what to do with them." There was a great lump in her throat; she snuffled her nose and wiped her eyes on the sleeve of her nightshirt. The puppy snuggled in her arms and gave a deep sigh. "When I was little my dad had a horrible dog." Deb was the only one who knew what had happened that night when they were nine. It was Deb who'd found a shoebox and dug the hole, and had stood with her, cried with her. "That's probably why she didn't tell me about you." Sally leaned her head back against the wall and cried into the night. Cried for Deb, for Kevin, for Micah, and Sophie, and her own nine-year-old self.

The next day, Sophie wiggled all over Micah's lap all the way home from the rehab center in Cleveland. He alternately hugged her and stared out the window. He wore the T-shirt from Jessie.

Maybe he thought his life was something to be endured.

Sally saw the tension in his shoulders, in his face. He's nervous, she thought. This was the first time he had been in a car since the accident. "Is Ohio still as flat as you remembered?" Sally asked him, trying to make conversation. For the last five years, Micah had spent two weeks each summer at hockey camp at Bowling Green State University, about an hour west of Hartley. During those two weeks, Deb stayed with Sally.

"Yeah."

"I have a ton of cherries this year. They'll be pickable soon."

Still no response.

"Remember the year you sent me those mountain seeds? You warned me mountains took a long time to grow. I planted them in my back yard under my cherry trees."

Micah stared out the window.

"I think Sophie has grown, don't you?"

"Yeah." He pressed his face against his dog's fur.

Sally sighed silently, feeling like she was in position to fail here. "The rehab staff all seemed quite pleased with your progress." Micah's crutches were in the back seat next to the wheelchair.

"Your things arrived a couple of weeks ago and they're in your room. Alex—I don't know if you ever met him, he's a bus driver for the school—said he'd build bookshelves for you. Just say the word. Whatever you want." Sally felt she was babbling but she went on. "Right now the walls are pink, but we can paint them any color you want. Even black.

Same with curtains. You remember the roses on the curtains. I didn't want to get new ones until you . . . until you came . . . home. Of course we'll buy new ones. You might even rather have shades, or blinds." She was coming close to tears, trying to express to him that she cared, that she wanted him to be happy. If he didn't start talking to her, it would be a long trip back to Hartley.

It was a long trip.

Finally, though, they pulled into the driveway. "Home again, home again," she said lightly, falling back on one of the silly rituals she had built up with him over the years. But their rituals were from another time, another life, before the accident. Now there was no *jiggity jig* from Micah in reply.

Sally hurried around to the passenger-side of the car. She clipped on Sophie's leash and set the wiggly thing down in the driveway. Sophie immediately dashed off, only to jerk to a stop at the end of her leash. Sally turned to Micah and held out her hand.

Micah waved her away. "I can do it," he said. He climbed clumsily out of the car and reached for Sophie's leash. She bounded towards the house and nearly pulled him over.

Sally captured the leash and pretended to give Sophie all of her attention so Micah had the opportunity to steady himself without an audience. "She's full of energy," she said cheerfully, to lighten the situation.

Micah sort of grunted.

Well, Sally said to herself, this is certainly a most

inauspicious beginning. "Leave your bags. I'll get them later."

"Hi, Miss Foster!" called a delegation of the neighborhood kids. They clustered next door in Erin's mother's petunia patch. Sally waved to them. Micah didn't turn around.

"You remember the cats," she said as she held the door open for him. She quickly glanced inside around the living room, to make sure the cats were out of harm's way before Sophie charged into the house. "There's Troy, up over the window. He's the one who likes the highest catwalks. He always likes to look down on things."

"He's the one with only three legs." It was the first complete sentence Micah had uttered practically since they had left Cleveland.

"That's right. He was hurt somehow, and someone dumped him off at Melissa's clinic." Sally didn't remind him that they thought Troy had been hit by a car. "I told Melissa if she'd fix him I'd take him. He ended up with three legs and I ended up with three cats." Somehow she felt it was the wrong thing to say.

Sophie ran around the room, sniffing excitedly. She found Tess, up in the windowseat. The dog sat flat on her rump, her tail wagging, and barked at the cat. Tess, who the previous evening had discovered how far the puppy could reach, was not impressed. She swished her tail and patently ignored the puppy.

Sally spoke over Sophie's bark. "That's Tess, and Jude is hiding."

"He always hides."

Sally grinned at him. "Yup. He doesn't like commotion. He'll come out to see you when it's quieted down." Though when, with Sophie here, that would ever be, she didn't know. "Marina and Gwendal outgrew their aquarium, so they're in a bigger one, fifty-five gallons now. Over here on the same table." She gestured to the aquarium. "I remember how tickled you were, oh, about five years ago, when you learned that the cats had their own pets."

The fish had been the cause of a great deal of teasing between them. Sally had named them after her favorite ice dancers. Micah, hockey player to the core, insisted firmly that all figure skaters were wusses. To call a hockey player a figure skater was the biggest insult of all. But now, he said nothing. He bent down a little and put his finger to the glass. The fish swam over to see him. After a moment greeting the fish, he moved over to the window and reached out to rub Tess under her chin. Tess allowed it.

"I've given you the room you—" she'd caught herself. "You've stayed in before. You'll remember where it is."

"I think Sophie needs to go out."

Sally hustled the puppy through the dining room to the sliding doors that led to the backyard. "Go potty." Jessie told her that if she always told the puppy to go potty while she was going potty, then she learned that was what it meant and she'd do it on command which could be quite handy. Jessie also said to praise her when she did it, to tell Sophie what a good girl she was when she peed. Sally didn't think so. That's where she drew the line. She left Sophie in the backyard to return to Micah. But Micah wasn't in the living room.

She heard him moving around in his room. Help me take care of your son, she said silently, hoping somewhere Deb was listening. Help me help your son.

"Where's Sophie?"

Sally whirled around. She'd been so lost in thoughts about Deb that she hadn't heard Micah. "She's in the backyard. Don't worry," she added, as Micah started for the sliding door, "it's fenced. Jessie came over last night and went over it inch by inch. Sophie can't get out and get lost." Sally really didn't want the little monster to get lost. Not really. "She's fine out there."

But Micah hovered by the sliding door. "Is she allowed to come in?" he asked. He sounded worried.

Sally frowned. "Of course." She steeled herself. "This is her home now." No matter how Sally personally felt. "Of course she can come in."

Micah looked uncertain.

"Just make sure, when you let her in and out, you latch the screen door. Tess knows how to open it." Sally grinned. "Sometimes she actually does come down from the catwalks and then watch out. Behind that beautiful head of fur, she has the mind of a master thief. Actually, with all the catwalks, if they want to, the cats can go all over the house without touching the floor." With Sophie here they might do that, Sally thought.

Micah looked around the dining room and into

the living room at all the catwalks and perches connected to the walls by stairs and ramps. Cat toys, with and without tiny bells, dangled from all sorts of places.

"Mom used to say your house was like Disneyland for cats."

Sally swallowed. This was the first time Micah had talked about his mother, at least to her. "Yup. She said my house was a cathouse."

"She said you always told people that cats were the ultimate race on earth."

"Yup. They are."

Micah nodded, more to himself than to her. "I thought so." He moved to the sliding door. "Sophie," he called.

Out in the yard, under the nearest cherry tree, Sophie glanced up at him, then ran the other way.

"Sophie, come here, girl!" Micah called.

Sophie stopped running, looked over her shoulder at him, and turned to run in a totally different direction. She was plainly inviting Micah to a game of chase.

"Sophie!" Micah called once more. This time, Sally noticed a note of despair in his voice. Maybe Sophie noticed it, too, for the little dog ran in a large circle and headed back to the door, to her boy. Micah leaned over, nearly falling in the process, to catch her. But he had hold of his puppy. He held onto the dining room table to help himself upright again. Still he held his dog tightly in his arms. "You have to come when you're called," he told her.

Sophie thumped her tail against his chest. At

least, Sally thought, she was an agreeable little wretch.

"Micah," Sally said, "I wasn't sure what you like to eat these days, so I decided to wait until you got here before I did a big grocery shop. You've always liked macaroni and cheese, so that's what we're having for supper tonight. All I have to do is stick it in the oven for forty-five minutes," she said as she opened the refrigerator. "Oh my," she exclaimed faintly. "It looks like elves have been here." For a moment she thought she'd start to cry at the generosity of her friends. Next to her humble pan of macaroni and cheese was a huge fruit salad, a pitcher of lemonade—Sally would bet anything it was freshly squeezed—with violets floating on top, green beans, and a decadent-looking chocolate cake. There was also a note to look in the freezer. Sally looked. She found three kinds of ice cream. She shut the freezer and shook her head in wonder. "I hope you're hungry."

"What should I do until supper is ready?"

"Whatever you'd like to do. Little Joshua Martini was here the other evening. He said he has lots of new jokes to tell you. Jeremy is looking forward to seeing you again. You could call them. You could put on your bare feet and do those exercises—write the alphabet in the air with your toes. Or you could unpack all those boxes of your stuff, but that might seem too much like work."

Micah wanted to play in the backyard with Sophie. So Sally dug around in the box of Sophie

Supplies until she found a tennis ball. As soon as Sophie saw the ball she turned into a maniac. Micah couldn't hold on to her and he half-dropped her onto the floor.

Watching them out the window as she set plates and silverware on the table, Sally noticed that Sophie didn't obey Micah any better than she did anyone else. Jessie's voice floated up from nowhere to repeat over and over, *Tanner Dodge teaches puppy kindergarten classes. You should take Micah. You should take Micah. You should take Micah.* Micah needed a puppy who obeyed him, rather than one who was out of control and pulled him off balance. She'd promised Deborah she'd do whatever it took. Maybe this was what it would take. Maybe she would have to call the sainted Tanner Dodge.

Sally reached for half a dozen nonpareils and let the dark chocolate melt in her mouth. Maybe Sophie simply needed a little more time to adjust to living in Ohio. Yeah, and maybe pigs could fly.

After dinner they took their ice cream out to the patio. Sophie begged and begged until Micah gave her his bowl to lick out. Then he glanced guiltily at Sally, who smiled back, glad he couldn't know what she was thinking. After all, that's what dishwashers were for.

"It's probably time for her supper," Sally said. She poured fresh water into Sophie's water dish and showed Micah where she'd put the dog food. Finally, Sophie was fed, the dishes were in the dishwasher, and Micah was in the backyard with Sophie.

The cats still had not touched the floor. Sally felt them glare at her, accusation in their eyes.

As if on cue, the phone rang. "Hello, Sally, this is Micah's Aunt Mary. I would like to speak to him."

Sally was determined to be friendly. She took a deep breath and quickly counted to ten. Pleasant voice, she told herself, pleasant voice. "Hello, Mary. I hope you are all well. Micah's outside. Just a minute, I'll find him for you."

Sally found him in one of the lawn chairs on the patio. Sophie looked up and wagged her tail at Sally's approach, but Micah didn't turn around. "It's your Aunt Mary," Sally told him, holding out the phone.

To give him privacy, she headed back inside to the kitchen to reach for a handful of Leety's. The world may be arrayed against her, but Leety's would make it right. Or at least help.

Sally had intended to suggest to Micah they take Sophie for a short walk. But after his phone call, Micah took Sophie to his room and shut the door. Shut me out, Sally thought.

She needed more comfort than Leety's could give. She found Troy in the living room, keeping a careful eye on the fish in case they rose up in revolt. Sally gathered him in her arms, but he wiggled out. He wanted to get back to his fish. So Sally tracked down Jude to cuddle, and reached for the phone to call Jessie. She wasn't home. Neither was Melissa. She didn't want to bother Sylvie, whose baby was due any day. She called Karen. Karen was home.

"Am I bothering you?" Sally asked. "You sound stressed."

"No. You're not bothering me. How's he doing?" Karen asked.

"Not sure. He hasn't said much about his parents, or the accident. Or any of the things that are from his house in Vermont, like Deb's rocking chair in the living room. And I don't want to pressure him. He's practically not talked to me at all, let alone about what he's feeling. He's polite and all, but he's treating me as if I'm a stranger. I think we need help."

"What kind of help?"

Sally took a breath. "Remember last week, you told me he would probably need counseling. At the rehab center today, when we were having the going-home interview, they said he should continue counseling for a while. He wasn't too keen on the idea, but I think he's going to need some help coming to grips with everything that's happened. I think one of the problems is, he wasn't going home. He was coming here instead. He doesn't think of my house as home. I don't expect him to—not yet, at any rate. But he's been here for at least a week every summer, so it's not as if *everything* is strange. Anyway, I think he'll need someone to talk to. You said you wouldn't be the best person for him because you're my friend. The rehab people agreed—Micah might see it as a conflict of interest. The social worker gave me a list of people in this area. I wondered if you'd look at it and tell me who you'd suggest."

"Absolutely."

"Also," Sally paused and gathered up her thoughts. "Jessie said Tanner Dodge teaches puppy kindergarten. Sophie won't come when Micah calls her. She doesn't know how to walk on a leash and I'm afraid she'll pull him over. He can walk, but his gait isn't right yet. His therapist says that'll take time, and he's always had a terrific sense of balance, but today, Sophie almost pulled him over. I'd hate to see that happen."

"You're afraid he'd be hurt."

"If nothing else, his pride would be hurt."

"So do you want Tanner's phone number?"

"Do I want? No. But do I think I need? Yes."

"Okay," Karen said with a smile in her voice. "I caught that tone of uncertainty. Look. Tanner's PK classes are a great experience for everyone with a new puppy, but a class situation might not be the best thing for Micah. He might feel self-conscious in a group of people. Sophie would pick up on it—dogs are quite perceptive, you know. Let me talk to Tanner and get back to you. Other than that, how're things going?"

"Okay, I guess. The dinner was great. You guys are terrific." Sally stopped to work the great lump out of her throat.

"Yeah. We *are* pretty fine, aren't we? But you're pretty fine, too."

Nine

Tanner tossed a dumbbell over the high jump. "Take it," he said.

Wing ran, jumped, snatched up, turned, jumped, ran, and stopped in front of Tanner in a perfect sit. She held the dumbbell in her mouth, her eyes on his face.

Tanner reached for the dumbbell. "Out," he said and Wing gave him the dumbbell.

"You are terrific," he said.

She did not move. She waited. For Wing, waiting was an action.

"Okay," he said. She leaped into the air.

Tanner heard a car pull up. He wasn't expecting anyone.

It was Karen and her newest foster dog, Dinnie Burns.

"How'd you like to play obedience judge?" he asked her.

"Sure." She put her Newf on a down stay and took her place in the middle of the classroom ring. "You want a straight heeling pattern? Or is there something specific you want to work on?"

"Straight heeling pattern."

"Ready?" It was the question every obedience judge asked at the beginning of every competitor's turn in the ring.

"Ready." His reply was a signal to Wing that they were about to start. Wing's impeccable attention was focused on his face.

"Forward," Karen called.

"Wing, heel." And they were off. Karen had earned obedience titles with several of her Newfoundlands and was familiar with several different heeling patterns commonly called by judges. Wing heeled perfectly. Then they brought out two stantions to work on figure eights. Wing lagged a little on the outside turns, just enough to sneak a peek at Dinnie, who snored loudly. Karen chuckled.

"Wing, watch me," Tanner softly reminded her. Wing snapped her attention back on Tanner and hurried to catch up. This was the kind of mistake that could cost them the competition.

"Newfoundlands snore," Karen said apologetically when the exercise was finished. "It's practically in the breed standard."

"Wing still knows better than that," Tanner said. He rubbed Wing's ears. "You needed to be reminded, though, didn't you?"

Wing wagged her tail and jumped up to put her paws on Tanner's chest.

They took Wing through the drop on recall, the directed jump, the scent articles, and then another series of figure-eights. This time she ignored the still-snoring Newfoundland.

"Exercise complete," Karen said at the end of the pattern.

Tanner released Wing, who pranced around looking quite proud of herself. He ducked behind the counter and returned with two cans of cold root beer. He handed one to Karen. "So, I take it you didn't come all the way out here to help me with Wing. What's up?"

"Favor time."

"I owe you several."

"I know." She grinned at him. "But this may cancel them all out."

"Sounds important. What do you need?"

"It's not for me. It's for one of my best friends." Karen told him about Sally, and Sophie, and Micah. "He's lost everything," Karen said. "This dog is all he has and she's a firecracker."

Tanner thought. "Cardigan?"

"How'd you know?"

"Jessie called to tell me about a friend of hers who'd just inherited a firecracker of a Cardigan puppy. Same dog?"

Karen chuckled. "I should've known Jessie'd get to you first."

"She asked me to sign Sophie up."

Karen shook her head. "I think Micah needs one-on-one. Not just for the dog stuff, but because of his situation. He has always been a physically active kid—now he can't walk without braces. It has to be a blow to his self-esteem, and he's dealing with a great deal of grief. I'm asking you to work with him individually."

Tanner took a deep swig of root beer. The summer session of his obedience classes was about to begin. Even though he'd been teaching for several years, his classes took time, and filled two nights a week. He planned to spend the other three nights working with Wing. If he took on a private student, he would have even less time to devote to his own dog.

"I know you are very busy right now, preparing Wing for competition," Karen interrupted his thoughts. "I know this isn't the best timing, but I think you could help Micah. He's been displaced. He's lost his parents, and hockey, which was his great consuming passion. It's possible he'll never walk without his braces. He's a teenager, which is difficult enough without the rest of it. He's moved across the country, leaving his life and everyone he's ever known behind. Except Sally, of course. And he's met all of us when he's been here to hockey camp every summer. But I imagine he still feels completely on his own. His dog is the only thing he has left. He needs to have a good relationship with her, and she needs to learn to be a civilized dog. I think you are uniquely qualified to help him."

Tanner had known Karen for a long time—since his first year in college, when he was required to go to counseling. Karen, doing her doctoral studies, had been assigned as his counselor. She'd worked with him throughout the year, and afterwards they'd remained good friends, bound together by their love of dogs. It was Karen who had suggested he come to Hartley to train service dogs.

He owed her big time. "You're using privileged information to turn those screws."

She grinned briefly. "Yes, I am. But only because it's so important. Sally has no clue about dogs—she's a cat person through and through. Micah and Sophie need a teacher who knows how to teach people who have mobility challenges. A teacher who understands what it means to go through a life-altering experience. You're it." She reached down to stroke the head of her sleeping foster Newf. "Sally said while he was in rehab all his friends from Vermont quit calling him. Evidently, they didn't know what to say to him, didn't know how to react. You and I both know how isolated he must feel. He needs this dog, and I know Sally. She would never, ever do anything at all to hurt the puppy, won't ever show anything but acceptance towards the puppy, but inside she'll be tense. She'll try to keep her tension from Micah, but he'll pick it up and get defensive and then Sophie will pick up on all the body language, and it'll be an all-around mess."

Tanner shoved his hands in his pockets. He looked over at the corner where the bookshelves were crowded with books on training methods, and dog breeds, and dog magazines. The corner was made cozier by an old carpet and a pair of easy chairs from the Goodwill store. Karen was right, he did know what isolation felt like. He knew about losing parents—though his parents weren't dead. He knew about losing friends who didn't know what to say so they stopped trying to say anything. He knew what a dog could mean to a young boy in that situation. He remembered what a dog had meant to him. Many people had helped him when he was young. Now, he supposed it was his turn to help—even if the timing was inconvenient. Finally he nodded. "I'll talk to the boy. Meet the dog. See what I can do."

"Thanks, Tanner. This means a lot to me." Karen reached out and gave him a great big hug.

"You knew I'd say yes."

She nodded. "I know you well enough to know you'd never turn Micah down."

Tanner knew Karen well enough to know there was something else worrying her, and if she needed his help with it, she'd ask. And he'd say yes.

Tanner usually asked prospective students to come to the barn to be evaluated for lessons. But Karen had made him curious about Micah's surroundings. He thought he could gain a better understanding of Micah and Sophie if he saw them in their home. He followed Karen's directions to an established neighborhood where all the streets were named after trees, except this one. This was Grape Street. Grape Street, running between Fir and Hawthorne, was made up of what real-estate people called "starter" homes. The front yards were dotted with bikes, wagons, toy trucks, and an occasional wading pool; 198 Grape Street was a small, two-story house, devoid of any front yard kid litter.

As soon as she came to answer the door he recognized her. He'd seen her before at Melissa's vet clinic—she'd had her coat over one arm and a cat carrier in the other. He'd liked her eyes and her smile. He saw her again, across the crowded room, at Katie Matheson's graduation party, but she'd disappeared before he'd found out her name. Now he found himself standing at her front door.

"Karen said you were willing to come over to meet Micah and Sophie. I can't begin to tell you how much I appreciate it." She gave him a smile, opened her door wide, and invited him into her home.

Tanner nodded. Her smile started in her eyes, just like he'd remembered. "I'll see if I can help." He looked briefly around the living room. Then he took another look, a longer look. He'd never seen anything like this. Bookshelves, full of seemingly well-loved books, started and stopped all over the walls, interspersed with what looked like empty shelves—some carpeted, others painted in bright colors. Some of the empty shelves were arranged in a stair pattern, leading up the wall to a long shelf that ran the length of the room, then turned the corner and continued. Under the stair shelves, on a paint-splattered strong man of a table, bubbled a big aquarium with two huge fish. Crouching next to the aquarium, on another shelf, was a black-and-white cat. Then he understood. She had made her entire living room into a cat habitat.

He looked at her. "Does your cat like strangers?"

She grinned again. "I have three. Tess, up there over the door," she pointed up in back of him to a white cat, who stared down, "doesn't appreciate her fur ruffled by the hands of mere mortals. Troy, the one by the fish, has a soldier complex, and Jude, my other cat, is hiding."

Tess stared at him with one of those unblinking, inscrutable cat looks. Tanner decided she wasn't the best cat to make friends with first, so he crossed the room and held out his hand to the black-and-white cat. "Hello, Troy," he said, as if speaking to an equal. The cat stopped watching the fish and blinked at Tanner, then gave his hand the slightest of sniffs. Evidently the cat decided he was acceptable, for he allowed Tanner to pet him. But only once. The cat returned his attention to the fish.

Tanner had never seen fish this big outside of a pet shop. "Those are huge fish. What kind are they?"

As if recognizing his interest in them, the fish swam up to the glass, their tails fanning gracefully into huge butterfly shapes.

"They masquerade as fancy goldfish, but in reality they are stomachs with fins. Gwendal is the gray one, only in fish it's called blue. Marina is the one with the bright red cap. They're orandas. They don't do tricks, but I do hand-feed them."

He caught the slight edge of defiance to her words, then ignored it. It probably had nothing to do with him. He bent down to look more closely at the fish. He would have sworn they were looking back. "I've never seen goldfish this big."

She bent down next to him to look at the fish. "That's because most people get them from the pet store and within a couple of days, or sometimes weeks, unintentionally kill them. I got these guys when they were about an inch long. That was six years ago."

He was curious. "If most people kill them, how did you keep them alive?"

He caught her wonderful smile, reflected in the glass of the aquarium. He knew he'd willingly do anything for the reward of that smile.

"All through high school, I worked at Friendly's Fish Farm. You know, that place out on Wendell Road. I learned how to take care of goldfish. Change some of the water every week and don't feed them too much or they'll eat themselves to death. And give them enough space to grow."

Pretending to watch the fish, he watched her eyes, reflected in the glass. He could watch her eyes forever.

"I expect you want to meet Micah and Sophie." Her words splashed him like cold water, reminding him why he was here. She stood up. "They're in the backyard."

Tanner stood up, too, "Does he know why I'm here?"

She looked surprised. He hoped she never played poker—she'd never win. "Of course. I don't believe in springing things on people, especially people I care about. That's like handing someone a toad."

She led him through the dining room—equally decked out in cat places, he noted—and slid open the screen door. "Micah," she said, "Mr. Dodge is here."

Forget about her, he told himself. You've seen beautiful women before. Think of her as a very big distraction. Focus on what you're supposed to be doing. Tanner gave himself the mental correction, and followed her out onto the back patio.

"Hello, Micah." He held out his hand to the boy in the lawn chair.

After a slight hesitation, the boy shook it briefly.

Tanner looked into Micah's eyes and saw an inexpertly built wall, to keep the world out. Tanner was looking at a reflection of himself when he was a teenager. Not exactly, of course, but close enough. From behind the wall, he sensed Micah was teeming with pain, anger, resentment, fear, defiance, hopelessness. Tanner understood at once why Karen had come to him. "My name is Tanner," he said, careful to appear neutral. "I work with people and their dogs."

"Hello." It was the minimum required of civility. Micah wore blue jeans and a T-shirt with the words *Give Blood, Play Hockey* splashed over the front. It was an in-your-face shirt, seemingly at odds with a spinal cord injury. Then again, maybe it wasn't.

A brindle blur came streaking towards them, past the row of trees that ran the length of the deep backyard. This must be the firecracker. "May I pet your dog?" he asked Micah.

Micah looked surprised. "Sure."

Tanner knelt down and the puppy hurtled herself at him and erupted into wildly enthusiastic jumping and whining. "Hello, there. I take it you're Sophie." The puppy gave a last jump up on Tanner before she bounded across to Micah.

Tanner nodded to himself. This puppy needed to focus her energy. Micah would have to teach

her some control. She was almost full-grown, but hadn't started to fill out yet. When she did, she'd be strong enough to really knock him down.

Tanner watched carefully as Micah picked up his dog and settled her on his lap and let her lick his face. At some point in his life, Micah learned how to pick up a puppy correctly. It was obvious to Tanner that Micah loved his dog, and equally obvious that she adored him. Yes, he thought, if Micah was willing, he could work with them. Tanner settled into a lawn chair next to Micah's.

"My friend Karen Matheson said Sophie was a firecracker."

"She's a little crazy sometimes."

"When I talked to Sally, she said Sophie doesn't always come when she's called."

"Yeah." Micah seemed hesitant to say anything negative about his dog.

"You know," Tanner deliberately leaned back in his chair, to make himself appear relaxed and non-judgmental, "Cardigans are a very old breed. They were bred for thousands of years to herd cattle in the mountains of Wales. They're agile little guys, with lots of energy. And they're tough—any dog who herds cattle has to be a little tough. They're also highly responsive, which is part of their charm. They were bred to work very closely with their people." As he spoke, he continued to watch Micah closely. On the surface, Micah kept his gaze on Sophie, who was scrubbing his hand with her tongue, but Tanner knew the boy was listening. "I think their energy, their responsiveness, their willingness to do whatever they're asked . . . These things make them such terrific dogs."

"You think they're terrific?" Micah asked.

Tanner knew it was not an idle question. "Yes. I think for the right people, they're terrific dogs. But, you know, they're so bright you need to make sure they have something to do, or they'll be bored. Not many cows for her to herd here in Hartley. She needs something else." He nodded to the bright orange tennis ball on the patio. "Something like playing ball. I bet she loves to play ball."

Micah nodded. "She's manic. My—it's the thing she loves best."

Tanner wondered what he'd started to say. "Herding dogs usually have strong retrieving instincts. You mind if I throw the ball for her?"

Micah shook his head and set Sophie down on the patio. Tanner tossed the ball in the air a couple of times, catching it in his hand, to judge Sophie's interest. Her attention was glued to that ball. She seemed to have plenty of intensity and drive. He threw the ball out into the yard. He watched her fly out to it, grab it out of the air, wheel around, and hurtle herself back to him where she dropped it at his feet, willing him, with her eyes, to throw it again.

He threw the ball a couple more times, studying Sophie as she ran after it, keeping half an eye on Micah, observing his reaction. "Watch her," he told Micah. "She runs out, in front of the ball, watching the ball over her shoulder as she runs, judging where it will fall so she can be there before it lands, so she can catch it."

"Yeah," Micah breathed, watching his dog in wonder. "How does she know how to do that?"

"I'm not sure," he said honestly. "It's one of those things some dogs seem to know instinctively. It probably has its roots in prehistoric hunting behavior of wolves. Herding cattle or sheep or ducks, in terms of behaviors, is very close to hunting them."

Micah looked surprised. "I didn't know that."

"You ever seen a herding trial? You might find them interesting."

"Do you have a dog?"

Tanner nodded. "Wing. She's a Border collie."

"Does she herd?"

"She has the instinct for it, but she doesn't have a flock of ducks to herd. I compete with her in obedience."

Micah nodded, but Tanner could see he didn't know what obedience was. It was difficult for boys to admit they didn't know something. "There are three levels of obedience competition. You have to successfully pass the first level before you can go to second, pass the second before you can move up to the third level. To pass, you and your dog perform the exercises in front of a dog obedience judge. That's what Wing and I do. She and I are partners." He threw the ball again, and again, Sophie went after it.

"Which level are you on?"

"When you complete all three levels, if your dog is good enough, and if you have the determination, you can earn an obedience trial championship, but it takes a long time. That's what Wing and I are doing."

"Is it hard? Getting your dog to do what you say?"

"Well, now." Tanner picked up the ball, tossing it in the air and catching it. "That's not an easy question to answer. It depends on a lot of things." He handed the ball to Micah. "You and Sophie, I bet if you worked with her you could do very well."

Micah looked surprised and slightly pleased. Part of that wall was crumbling. He threw the ball for Sophie.

Tanner kept his voice casual as he continued. "You seem to love her, and she adores you. She's smart, corgis love to learn things, she looks like she enjoys life. I think the two of you would make a great team." He let this sink in for a moment. "What have you taught her so far?"

Micah looked down. "Um. Nothing."

"Who taught her to play ball?"

"I did."

"Well, that's something you taught her. You taught her to bring the ball to you and drop it."

Micah grinned. "At first she didn't know how to drop it."

Tanner grinned back. "You taught her to drop it. Didn't you?"

Micah nodded. "We bribed her with food."

"See? You taught her something. She learned. She loves it. Part of the reason she loves it is because she's working with you. And you learned she's motivated by food. Not all dogs are, you know. It's important to know what motivates your dog.

The way she goes after that tennis ball tells me you could probably also use that ball as motivation."

"Do you think I could teach her to come when she's called?"

"Yes, I think you could. Do you want to?" This was the crucial question. Unless Micah was interested, and committed, there was nothing Tanner could do.

"Yeah."

"What else do you want her to learn?"

Micah looked confused.

"I'll tell you what. Let's make a deal. I'll work with you and Sophie one night a week. We'll begin with basic obedience training, walking on a leash, not jumping up, coming when she's called, sitting, lying down, staying. That sort of thing. You, on the other hand, will work with her every day. *Every* day. No slacking off on weekends. In a couple of weeks we'll see where she is, where you are, and we'll figure out where you want to go from there. Is that a deal?"

"Sure!" Micah's face was a study in conflicting emotions. Relief warred with anger, despair with hope. "When can we start?" Micah could see the possibilities of a new beginning.

Inside the dining room, where she pretended not to overhear what Micah and Tanner were saying, Sally listened carefully. Micah's voice began to lose its edge. Glancing quickly out of the window, she saw his shoulders begin to relax. Tanner appeared to be relaxed and casual. Sally sneaked another peek.

Tanner was showing Micah how to teach Sophie to sit—a beginning lesson so they had something to work on before their first real lesson. That was thoughtful of him, Sally thought. Maybe it was more than that, though. Maybe Micah was being tested. She crossed her fingers.

Ten

Late that night, Tanner took Wing out to the backyard to run off some steam. Away from the city lights, the sky was bright with stars. The silence of the night was dotted by the cries of bats. Suddenly he heard a different sound, so tiny he wondered if he'd imagined it. He listened. There it was again. It was the desperate mewing of a young kitten in trouble. Tanner moved towards the sound, straining to see in the dark, careful not to step on the little thing, wherever it might be. The mew came again, and again, the demanding cry turned frantic. Tanner moved more quickly.

Finally, he saw it. A kitten fumbled around in a patch of bare ground, searching for its mother. Tanner picked it up. It was very young, maybe two weeks old. Its eyes weren't opened yet, and it didn't even fill the palm of his hand It was trembling. He held it close to shield it from the cool night air.

So that was why the stray cat had been growing fatter and fatter. But where was she? Tanner hadn't seen her for at least a week. Quickly he scanned the surrounding area, looking for any place a

mother cat might hide a nest of kittens. The
ground was bare all around—hardened dirt with a
few weeds. This was overflow parking for his obedience classes.

"Well, little one," he said to the kitten, "it looks
like you're going to have to stay with Wing and me
for a while."

He whistled sharply for Wing, then headed back
home, the kitten cradled in his hands. What does
one do with an orphaned kitten, he wondered. He
had a fleeting thought of the climbing habitat at
Sally Foster's house. She would know what to do
with an orphaned kitten. He thought of calling her.
He decided it was too late.

It was also too late to call Melissa, his vet. "Let's
take a good look at you," he told the kitten. "Look,
Wing, we have a baby, a black-and-white baby, with
perfectly symmetrical markings. Are you a boy or
a girl?" He lifted the kitten's tail, knowing that the
kitten might be too young to determine gender.

Wing nosed the kitten gently, sniffing it, then
licking it. Wing knew what to do with babies. The
kitten, obviously sensing something that resembled
its mother, squirmed towards Wing, yelling and
screeching. "Listen to you, demanding respect.
With that set of lungs, we're going to have to call
you Aretha."

He set the kitten down on the rag rug for Wing
to supervise. Then he dug out the smallest dog
crate he had, one Wing had used when she was a
puppy. He outfitted it with towels and set Aretha
in. Wing sat close, to watch over the kitten. Then
Tanner searched his drawers until he found an eye-

dropper. He didn't have any kitten formula, but he still had some powdered puppy formula in the freezer. Probably, if it wasn't too old, it would do in a pinch.

He made up a tablespoon of warm formula, then picked up Aretha. The kitten protested at the unfamiliar eyedropper.

Wing hovered close, worry on her face.

"Don't worry, Wing. Tomorrow we'll call Melissa for a real bottle and some kitten formula. This is the best we can do right now."

Wing was not convinced.

After flailing her head from side to side a few times, the kitten figured out what was in the eyedropper. Then she sucked mightily, kneading her tiny front feet on Tanner's thumb.

Wing watched intently, to make sure Tanner fed the kitten correctly.

When the kitten was finished, Wing licked the kitten's bottom until she got the necessary result. She curled up on the carpet with the kitten, now fed and warm, pressed up snuggly against her belly. Only then did she relax. Wing was an experienced nanny. She clearly decided Aretha was her responsibility.

Tanner set his alarm clock for two o'clock in the morning—the kitten was small enough to need a night feeding. Tomorrow he'd take the kitten to work with him—she was too small to go all day without food.

Wing gave the kitten a swift lick. The kitten stretched and settled back down to sleep. Two orphans, Tanner thought, Micah and now little Aretha. Like Wing, he took his responsibilities seriously.

The next Wednesday, after dinner, Sally drove Micah and Sophie out to Tanner's pole barn for their first lesson. She'd never been down this road before, corn on one side, beans on the other. She figured halfway through the summer, she'd have all the bumps and ruts of the old road memorized.

Micah had kept his promise to Tanner, at least so far. For the last week, several times a day, he'd taken Sophie into the backyard. Holding a nickel-thick slice of all-beef weenie—Jessie said we did *not* call them hot dogs—right in front of her nose he said, "Sophie, sit." Then he slowly moved the weenie back up over her head until, her nose following the bribe, she naturally plopped her little bottom down. Micah immediately told her "Good sit," and gave her the bite.

When he was working and playing with Sophie, Micah seemed to come out from behind his wall. He spoke to Sally in single words, and single sentences. Nothing even remotely resembling a conversation between them. He was polite. Nothing more.

"Hey, Micah!" she sometimes wanted to yell. "I'm not a stranger. I've known you since before you were born! When you were a baby I changed your dirty diapers!" Instead, she gritted her teeth and practiced the virtue of patience.

Sophie was wildly enthusiastic about her new obedience lessons. She was wildly enthusiastic about anything that involved food. She was as bad as the fish. Sally decided Sophie was a stomach with legs.

"That must be it," Sally said, pointing to a gray pole barn set back from the road. She pulled into the long driveway. In front of the plain structure was a gravel parking lot. Built onto one side of the barn was a small porch that held two Adirondack chairs.

Tanner came out to meet them, a black-and-white dog trotting by his side. This must be Wing, Sally thought. Tanner's dog seemed friendly enough. Sophie was delighted to meet a new canine.

Tanner greeted Sally briefly, then turned to Micah and Sophie. Sally didn't try to follow their conversation as she followed them into the building. If someone had told her, four months ago, that she would be going to one of Tanner Dodge's dog classes, she would have laughed. It was as likely as walking to the Pacific Ocean barefooted. It would have meant she had a dog. Three months ago the chance of Sally ever having a dog was so remote as to be a mathematical impossibility.

Yet, she thought as she stepped into the barn, here she was, with a dog, at dog school. The fact that Sophie belonged to Micah and he was the one with the lesson was immaterial.

Inside, the barn was one big room with a cement floor painted blue. In one corner, two shabby easy chairs crouched under tall, hulking bookshelves crammed with books and magazines. A four-foot counter surrounded what appeared to be some sort of office—Sally could see two file cabinets and a well-used bulletin board, and an old-style refrigerator. Between the easy chairs and the office were three steps leading up to a closed door. Built-in benches rimmed the rest of the room. In the middle of the room were two large squares, their areas defined by what looked like extra-long baby gates.

Tanner pointed to a small carpet at the foot of the stairs and Wing trotted over to it to settle down, head on paws. Then he led Micah and Sophie into one of the squares.

Oh, Sally realized. It's like one big, open classroom. She wandered over to the bookshelves to scan the titles. They were all about dogs. Nothing interesting. But on the wall, in a plain frame, was—Sally leaned closer to read it. Tanner Dodge was a certified pet dog trainer. Sally never knew dog trainers were certified. She settled into one of the easy chairs, ignoring the coating of dog hair. She had the foresight to bring her own book to read, the latest *Cat Who* by Lilian Jackson Braun. She pulled it out of her purse but it was difficult to concentrate on her cat mystery with all those dog books looming up behind her, practically breathing down her neck.

She found herself listening to Tanner as he instructed Micah. She liked the way he explained things in positive terms rather than negative ones. Instead of criticizing the way Micah held the leash, Tanner suggested Micah try it this way, not because it might be easier, but because Micah might find it more comfortable and he'd probably have more control of Sophie. He spoke to Micah as a peer, rather than from the distance of an instructor. As soon as Micah did something well, Tanner told him so. Her friends were right, Sally realized. Tanner was a good teacher.

She also noticed the way Micah listened carefully to Tanner and how he answered questions. With Tanner, his reserve was down. Micah was almost like his old self. What was it about Tanner? Sally wondered, idly watching him.

By Madison Avenue standards he wasn't conventionally handsome. He was medium height, medium build, medium brown hair that was straight and needed a trim—not much, just as if he hadn't gotten around to it recently. There was nothing outstanding about any one of his features—she couldn't remember what color his eyes were—and if she'd seen him on the street she wouldn't have looked twice.

"Let me show you," Tanner said to Micah. "Wing," he called his dog. "Come."

Sally saw a flash of black and white, then the dog was sitting next to Tanner, her head bent to one side as she watched him intently.

"Wing, heel."

Suddenly Sally saw what her friends saw. Suddenly she realized Tanner, like Micah, lived behind a wall. Now, with Wing, the wall was gone. For the first time, she saw Tanner Dodge. He was breathtaking.

Sally sat stunned.

"You look like you just won a life's supply of Leety's Fine Chocolates." Jessie's voice broke into Sally's thoughts.

"What're you doing here?"

"Came to see how things are coming along." Jessie peered into her face. "You sure you're all right? You look shaken up."

"You have an overactive imagination."

"No, I don't." Jessie pretended to be offended. "My imagination is totally grounded in reality."

Sally snorted. "Yeah, right."

"Hey, you two," Tanner called across the barn. "Hi, Jess—please keep your voices down. Sophie isn't ready for distractions yet." But he grinned at them.

Jessie plopped down in the other easy chair and leaned back. "Tanner's amazing, isn't he?" she whispered.

Sally was very glad Jessie couldn't read her mind. "He's doing a great job with them."

"The monster puppy seems to be doing well," her friend continued in a whisper, so she wouldn't be overheard. Jessie watched Sophie and Micah carefully for a moment. "She has forging issues, though."

"Micah," they heard Tanner say from across the ring, "she's forging."

"Told ya," Jessie whispered smugly to Sally.

"At least she's not tangling him up in her leash like she was before."

"She's turning into a civilized beast?"

Sally shrugged. "The cats don't think so."

"They're hardly an impartial jury."

Sally glared at her friend.

"Look, I like your cats, but they live dull lives. You don't even let them get up close and personal with their pet fish. I bet Sophie gives them something to think about all day. Keeps them on their toes. Troy finally has a real enemy to keep lookout for. I bet he's thrilled."

Sally glared again. "The cats like calm. Sophie is chaos."

"What a great opportunity for them to learn tolerance." Jessie paused meaningfully, but she kept her eyes on Micah. "You, too."

"I'm tolerant."

"You're *selectively* tolerant. You're tolerant of kids and cats. Not dogs."

Sally sighed. There really was no way she could argue. It was true. Having Sophie *was* a great opportunity for her to learn tolerance. "The problem with best friends is they know how to annoy you." But she said it without anger.

"The problem with best friends is they are willing to tell you the truth," Jessie said.

Jessie stayed through the lesson, whispering a running commentary about how Micah was doing.

Sally made listening noises, but in reality, she ignored her friend. She wanted to figure out why all of a sudden she couldn't keep her eyes off of Tanner Dodge. Tanner Dodge, of all people. Tanner Dodge, who was the dog person of all dog people. The God of All Things Dog, as Jessie often said.

All too soon, the lesson was over. Micah and Tanner were coming towards them. Sally quickly dropped her eyes. She'd figured out that Tanner was fairly perceptive. She didn't want him to see her looking at him this way. She jerked her attention to Micah. "Looks like you're doing a great job," she told him.

"Sophie is, too," Micah said. "Tanner says so."

Without thinking, Sally glanced at Tanner.

He caught her gaze. He held it.

Sally yanked her attention away from the man. Trying to act normally, she looked around the room for Sophie. Sally told herself she was behaving abominably. She was being perfectly absurd. She didn't have time to fall in lust with anyone right now—and lust was, in all likelihood, what this was all about. Or some raging hormonal thing. Right now, when Micah had just come to live with her, every little speck of her time and energy had to go to him. Not to mooning over some dog trainer. She had absolutely no business thinking about something as shallow as her own romantic fantasies. How unutterably selfish! How would she ever be able to face Deb and Kevin again? Once Micah was all settled, and adjusted, with lots of friends, and doing well in school, maybe then—*maybe*—she would allow herself to indulge in some personal fantasies. Maybe she would even cast Tanner in a starring role. But that would be then. This was now.

Now Wing and Sophie tore around the room like banshees playing some variant of chase.

"That's one excited puppy you have there," Jessie said to Micah.

Micah gave only a brief nod in acknowledgement.

"So, Tanner," Jessie started right in, "Sally says Micah's been consistently working with Sophie. She says the furry fiend might be morphing into something that actually slightly resembles something that is almost like a reasonable creature."

I did not—Sally started to say. Then she stopped.

"Micah's doing very well." Tanner agreed. "He's doing a fine job with Sophie."

As if on cue, the two dogs threw themselves down on the floor, panting and swishing their tails. They looked pleased with themselves.

"So what are *you* doing on Saturday? Any shows this weekend?"

Sally watched Tanner grin at Jessie. He was comfortable around her. He never seemed completely comfortable around Sally. She felt an unfamiliar twinge. Could it possibly be jealousy? No. Could it? No. Absolutely not. How could she concentrate on helping Micah if half of her mind was wandering off in some fairyland where knights on white horses rescued distressed damsels who were always stunningly beautiful and size minus two. Get a grip! she told herself firmly. Anyone who's under a size ten is probably anorexic.

"Not this weekend." Tanner's voice jerked Sally back from her musings.

"Good. Then you can come to Sally's house for our annual pick-and-pit party."

Sally felt her mouth drop open.

Eleven

"Sally," Jessie continued blithely on, "has five highly prolific cherry trees in her backyard. Every year about this time, they burst forth with glorious and great quantities of fruit. So we all go over and pick billions and billions of 'em. You know, Melissa and Karen and Sylvie and me. Then we sit around in a circle and pit them. So why don't you come, too?"

"Can you?" Micah asked. "Can you really?"

Sally caught the questioning look Tanner shot her. Nothing else to do but nod gracefully and smile. "Sure. There really are plenty of cherries waiting to be picked. It's an annual event. I have lots of buckets and freezer bags. Any that you pick and pit you get to take home." She shrugged a whatever kind of shrug, as if there weren't a whirling feeling in her stomach.

"Bring Wing," Jessie stuck in. "Karen will bring a Newf or two, and M'liss'll bring a dog, and Sylvie'll bring Jean-Luc unless she has her baby. All the dogs'll have a party, too."

Sally looked at her friend in surprise. Where did

the dog part come from? Then she saw the look on Micah's face and all of her silent protests came to an abrupt stop.

"It'll be sort of a welcome to Hartley party for Sophie," Jessie explained.

"Please," Micah added.

This was the first time Sally had seen Micah show interest in something. He hadn't made any attempt to make friends, even when Jeremy Martini came by to visit, and Micah had known Jeremy for years. The two of them played together every summer when Micah and Deb visited Hartley. For the most part, Micah sat in his room with Sophie and read. Or surfed the net. Or sat outside in the back and threw Sophie's ball for her. He hadn't told her what color he wanted his room—so it was still pink, and the curtains still sported flowers. He hadn't made a serious attempt to unpack his things; most of them were still in boxes. Only half of his new bookshelves were filled. Sally wondered if he didn't want to unpack because he didn't want to be a part of Hartley. Didn't want to be part of her life. So now, if he wanted Tanner to come, for whatever reason, she wanted Tanner to come, too. She had to ignore her own convoluted emotions about the possibility of developing some unrealistic fantasy relationship with Tanner. Micah wanted Tanner to come to the pick-and-pit party. Therefore, Sally would do whatever it took to get him there.

"Please," she said to Tanner, smiling at him, telling her stomach to knock off the butterfly dance. "Please say you'll come. And Wing," she added quickly. Then she had an inspiration. "You and Micah can be the token guys."

"Ray will be there," Jessie pointed out. "Unless Sylvie has her baby. These days he doesn't let her out of his sight. Wait until that baby comes. Ray will be totally obnoxious about it."

Sally ignored Jessie. "Please."

"Please," Micah added.

Tanner stuck his hands in his pockets and looked down at Wing. Wing looked back. Once again, Sally could almost see some kind of communication thing pass between them.

Please, she said silently. This is the first thing other than obedience lessons that Micah has sounded even remotely enthusiastic about. Please.

"Sure." Tanner said at last. "We'll be there."

"What did you invite Tanner for?" Sally hissed at Jessie. Tanner and Micah were in the back of the barn playing a quick game of Frisbee with the dogs. Tanner said it was Sophie's reward for a good lesson.

Jessie glanced at her. Then did a double take. "Oh, ho." Her voice was knowing and sly.

Sally felt herself turn red. Blast! She should have left it alone.

"So," Jessie said smugly. "We are having *emotions* about this, are we?"

"Cut the royal *we* stuff."

"So *you* are having emotions about this are *you*?" Jessie teased.

"All those dogs. The cats will be very upset."

"They'll love it. It'll keep them going for weeks."

"Tess will get constipated from the stress."

"So, feed her some frozen peas. You always say it works for the goldfishies when they're constipated. Besides, the cats'll be hiding. We can shut them in your bedroom. They won't know the dogs are there. Besides, the dogs will be in your back yard. Besides, it'll be good for Sophie to see how civilized dogs act. Dogs are highly imitative, you know. Doggy see, doggy do."

"I will ignore that last bit of alleged humor." Sally slumped against the side of her car. "I feel like my home is being invaded by dogs," she told her friend. "Granted, these are all dogs I know. Except Wing. The logical part of my brain tells me there isn't anything to worry about with Wing. Wing seems so perfect she's almost a Stepford dog."

"It'll be fun," Jessie tried to jolly her up. "You'll see."

He shouldn't have done it, Tanner thought as he watched their cars disappear down his driveway and turn on to the road. He shouldn't have accepted the invitation to go to Sally's house on Saturday. He should have said he had too much to do. He wasn't sure it was a good thing for him to be around her more than he was already. Micah was a fine young man. Sophie was a little delight. A firecracker, as Karen and Jessie had said, but a delightful firecracker. Tanner had a soft spot for firecrackers. Once you leashed their energy and they were under control they were fun to train, fun to work with, fun to watch. Micah and Sophie were not the problem.

No, it was Sally he was concerned about. He liked Sally. The instinctive attraction he'd felt when he'd first seen her last winter had stuck. Now he'd met her, talked with her, seen her commitment to Micah, that attraction had grown stronger. This was not a good thing. When he worked with Micah, he found himself sneaking glances at her. When he explained Sophie's actions and behaviors to Micah, he found himself mentally explaining them to Sally as well. It had become important to him that she begin to understand how Sophie's mind worked. He wanted her to relax around the puppy and see what a great dog she could become. These things he wanted. These were all reasonable things to want.

He did not want to be attracted to her. He did not want to want what he knew he could not have. That one time, at her house, when he first met Micah, that was enough to tell him she was way out of his league. Her house was open and inviting and full of light. She even had a bowl of those dried flower petals that made everything smell all girly. The catwalks and perches were proof that she saw her cats as unique—was willing to change her way of life to accommodate another species. She had one of those bodies painted by that painter— what was his name? Ru . . . something—whoever he was, he painted female bodies that were like Sally's. Soft and rounded and unmistakably female. Her smile was genuine, and her eyes were open and wide. She was the kind of person who still clapped for Tinkerbell, and believed all the fairy tales were true. The kind of person who hadn't seen the underbelly of life. No. She was not for someone like him.

He whistled for Wing. Together, they headed back to the barn.

He lifted Aretha out of her nest of towels. In the past week, her eyes had opened. Now they fluttered open and she recognized him and Wing. She opened her tiny mouth to yell loudly and with great indignantion, but it ended in a yawn.

Wing stood up on her hind legs to try to reach the kitten. Tanner let her lick the kitten once or twice. "See, she's fine," he told his dog. "Hey there, little Aretha," he said to her softly. "I bet you're hungry." He set her down on the floor for Wing to take care of while he prepared her dinner. He measured the powdered kitten formula into the bottle, added warm water up to the red line, and shook it vigorously. He tested it on the inside of his wrist and declared it dinner.

"Here you go, Aretha," he told the kitten as he picked her up. He sat down at his kitchen table and held the kitten in his lap as he fed her. The kitten knew what the nipple meant, and she glommed onto it heartily, making little tiny squeaky noises while she ate. And ate. And ate. Little Aretha was growing.

"You and I, Wing, we're good surrogate moms."

Friday at work, Tanner took his group of dogs into the playroom. He worked with each of them individually, for about five or ten minutes at a time, while the rest of them romped and played. Today they were going to learn how to turn on the high light switches. They already knew how to work the low light switches which were about ten inches off the floor. When the dogs understood how to work the low switches, they moved to the higher ones. It took many repetitions, on different switches, in different rooms, for the dogs to be fully comfortable working the lights. Dogs had individual styles of working lights. Some dogs grabbed the switch between their teeth, some used only their top teeth.

Later that morning, he took Maxie to town. She wore her royal blue service-dog-in-training cape. They worked on doors—the automatic doors at Abernathy's grocery store, the revolving door at Tuckers Department Store. Tanner took Maxie into the mall through those heavy doors that made that swishing noise. At the sound, Maxie flattened her ears and leaned toward him slightly. "You don't like it?" he asked her. "It's a harmless noise. Let's do it again." He took her out the other side, then right back through the noisy door again. This time she didn't lean, but her ears were still showing her unease. So they did it again. The third time she walked calmly through the swishing door. Tanner reached down to rub her head. "Good girl."

As Tanner strolled through the mall with her, he periodically paused in front of store windows, as people did when they were window-shopping. For the most part, the storeowners and clerks welcomed his dogs. They understood why visits to the mall were an important part of their training. To-day, he took Maxie into a bookstore. He spent a minute pretending to browse through the books, then he chose one at random and held it out to Maxie. "Take it," he said.

Maxie carefully took the book in her mouth.

"Good girl." Tanner didn't gush, for he had expected no less of her. "Let's go," he told her and Maxie trotted next to him up to the front counter. "Put it up," Tanner said.

The clerk was suitably impressed as Maxie stood up against the counter and set the book down.

Tanner pulled out his billfold and accidentally-on-purpose dropped it. He pointed. "Take it."

Maxie reached down and picked up his billfold.

"Put it up."

Maxie stood on her hind legs to put it on the counter next to the book. She gave her head a little flip to tell the world she was one smart girl.

"Amazing," breathed the clerk. "No matter how many times you bring them in here, I'm always amazed. I wish my dog could do that."

"You can teach your dog to do that," Tanner told her. "It takes time and a great deal of patience." Two years ago she'd come to dog school with her dog, a cheerful little guy of unknown heritage who had obvious aspirations to the sedentary life of a couch potato.

"You don't know my dog," she said with a roll of her eyes. "I adore him, but he's dumb as a rock."

"Maybe he's bored." He grinned at the clerk. They'd been through this same conversation before. "Give him something to do. It's been a long time since he's been to dog school. Bring him back. It's not too late to sign up for the summer session."

"Maybe I will." But she said it in a vague sort of way, and Tanner knew she wouldn't. She was one of those well-meaning people who loved their dog, but didn't go out of their way to challenge their dog's mind. With a wistful smile, she handed the billfold back to Maxie who held it out to Tanner.

"See you later," the clerk said. "She's one beautiful dog."

After the bookstore, Tanner strolled towards the other end of the mall. For an instant he thought he saw Maxie limp on her rear right leg. He stopped and looked carefully at Maxie's rear. He ran his hand down her leg. He didn't feel anything unusual. He told her to walk a few steps. He watched carefully. It was crucial for his dogs to be physically sound as well as mentally stable. He didn't see anything unusual, but he made a mental note to have Melissa take a look. "Let's go," he told Maxie and together they continued down the mall.

Tanner knew Maxie loved to swim, so he slowed to a crawl as they passed the floor-to-ceiling fountain. A clutch of small children excitedly tossed pennies into the water, squealing with joy as they were splashed by drops of water. After a quick glance at the water, Maxie looked back at Tanner.

"Good girl," he told her with a quick rub of her ears. "Where there is no temptation, there can be no virtue. You have passed temptation and left it in the dust. You are smart *and* virtuous. Let's see what you do at the cookie store." He came to a halt in front of the gourmet cookie store. Yesterday, in this same spot, Tanner had to remind Murphy not to pay attention to the fresh cookie smell coming out of the bakery. Today, Maxie sat calmly at his side, making no moves towards the store. Tanner stood in front of the store display windows for an extra few minutes, just to make sure. Maxie waited.

"Hello!" Sally Foster came out of the cookie store, a bulging bakery bag in her hand. "I thought dogs weren't allowed in malls." Even though she said it with a smile, he could hear the question in her voice. Before he could answer, she said, "I'm sorry, that was rude of me."

"No problem. This is Maxie. She's one of my students."

"Hello, Maxie," Sally said in a friendly voice.

Maxie started at the voice. She didn't move, but her entire body leaned towards Sally. Maxie wagged her tail, obviously promoting herself some petting. The woman and the dog stared at each other for a moment. Sally looked puzzled, as if she knew Maxie from somewhere, but couldn't quite place her.

He didn't know what to say. He wasn't good at small talk.

"So, do you normally stand around outside cookie stores?" she asked. "Or are you merely enjoying the fragrance wafting through the door?" She wiggled her fingers in the air and her eyes did that twinkle thing.

Tanner swallowed. "Maxie is learning to ignore those . . . um . . . fragrances."

"How is she doing at ignoring them?"

He looked down at the dog by his side. The dog looked up at him. She held his gaze and grinned at him; she knew what he was trying to do. Then she wagged her tail, forgiving him for making her sit through the cookie smell. He looked at Sally. "She's doing very well. She's a star pupil. She has learned she can't give in to temptation, no matter how great it is." Looking at Sally and talking about temptation was not a smart thing to do.

"Do you think Sophie will ever learn that?"

He nodded. "Of course she can learn—she's smart. The question is, does Micah have the desire to teach her?" Oops! *Desire* was another word to avoid around Sally. "Does Micah have the motivation necessary to teach her?" *Motivation* was a safe word. He had motivation of his own.

Tanner pretended not to watch her chest as she sighed. Talk about temptation and desire, he thought. He made himself remember his own motivation.

"I'm worried about him," she said.

"Worried?" He found himself resorting to the trick Karen used on him many years ago, to elicit more information by repeating the word as a question. Now it helped him create distance from Sally. He must maintain distance.

For a moment he thought she was leaning towards him. He thought he might be leaning towards her. He forgot about distance and thought about close. Then she seemed to catch herself. Her face turned pink. It looked good.

"Oh," she said with a short laugh. "I guess we always worry about people we love. I tend to over-react. Anyway, I'd better go pick him up. He's at the physical therapy center next door. I ran in over here to pick up cookies for tomorrow. According to the weather forecast we'll have a glorious day for cherry-picking. Bye." She gave him a last smile and hurried off down the mall.

He watched her until she disappeared through the heavy doors that made that swishing noise. He was sorry to see her go. He was lucky she went. "Well, Maxie," he said, "let's get back to work."

Back at the school he put Maxie in her run and made a note on the dry-erase board to ask Melissa to check the dog's right hind leg. He whistled down the hall to the front office to pick up Aretha. Corinne had twisted his arm until he agreed to let her play babysitter. Playing babysitter for Aretha was easy. Two nights ago, Wing had unearthed an ancient stuffed plush fish from under Tanner's bed and Tanner had given it to the kitten, who decided it was perfect for practicing climbing skills. So Aretha's day was now full of napping and fish-climbing. She was growing by the proverbial leaps and bounds, but she still wasn't allowed to explore the world at large. That had to wait for a couple more weeks when she'd be old enough for her kitten shots. Tanner hoped she'd also be big enough for a feline leukemia test. Right now, Melissa had told him, Aretha's tiny kitty veins were too small to get blood out of.

"She's been a little darling," Corinne told him. The little darling wasn't in her crate. The little darling was curled up in Corinne's lap, sound asleep. Corinne gave him a look of unrepentant defiance. "She wanted to be held. I couldn't say no to her. Even Aspen agrees with me, don'tcha, boy?" Aspen, asleep at the side of Corinne's wheelchair, opened one eye at his name and gave his tail a single thwop on the floor. He snorted and closed his eyes again.

"Those two must've had a tough afternoon," Tanner said teasingly as he reached for the kitten. She squeezed her eyes and opened her tiny mouth in a tiny yawn, her tiny teeth like the tips of needles. She shook her head, and sleepily opened her baby eyes. Then she realized who held her and she yelled with great enthusiasm. He snuggled her to the front of his shirt with one hand while he reached for the crate with his other.

He saw speculation in Corinne's eyes.

"What?" he asked, over Aretha's squalling.

"Just thinking. I talked to my brother last night. He and his wife had a new baby, so I'm an aunt again. Are you an uncle? Do you have any brothers or sisters?"

He knew what she was doing. Ever since his mother had called, Corinne had become increasingly curious about his family. "Nope. I'm from a litter of one." He winked at her, to let her know he knew what she was up to. "Gotta feed the big mouth here." He nodded to the yelling mouth in his hand. "Thanks for babysitting her. See you later." He grabbed up Aretha's crate and ducked out of the office before she could ask him anything else.

He set Aretha's crate on the long, counter-type table he used as a desk, and carried her to the break room where he made up a bottle of formula. "Here you go, little one," he murmured softly as he fed her. "Get big and strong. You are destined for great things."

"She's awful small." Jake came in and looked at the kitten. "Maybe you don't feed her enough."

"She's perfect. She's gaining weight like a trooper. She's about twice as big as she was when I found her."

"That's impossible. If she were any smaller than she is now she'd be invisible." Jake opened the refrigerator. He pulled out the blue pitcher and peered at the contents. "Almost out of Kool-Aid," he said disapprovingly. He poured the dregs of the sludge into his glass. "Time to make more."

"You could use that stuff to clean whitewalls," Tanner said.

Jake sighed dramatically as he gazed at the purple stuff in his glass. "Pearls before swine," he said mournfully. "Pearls before swine."

Aretha chose that moment to lose the nipple. She shrieked her frustration.

"Maybe she wants Kool-Aid instead of that stuff," Jake said. "It'd help her grow. Put hair on her chest."

Tanner helped her find the nipple again. "I don't think so."

Jake dropped into the other wooden chair at the table. "She'll be a great distraction for the dogs," he said. "Especially if we can teach her to make that noise on command. Any dog with a high prey drive'll go crazy."

"You sound real cheerful at the possibility."

"Hey. We have to test their prey drives. It's our job to find distractions that the dogs find irresistible. They must resist, and we must weed out the ones who don't. You always say, where there is no temptation there can be no virtue." Jake had a decidedly casual approach to life.

"Do you take anything seriously?"

"Sure." Jake took a swig of his Kool-Aid and closed his eyes in television-commercial-style rapture. "I take lotsa things seriously. The question is, is there anything *you don't* take seriously? Think about it." He shoved to his feet and, after raising his glass to Tanner in salute, he headed down the hall. "Always look on the bright side of life," he sang, adding the whistle to the next part of the song.

It had been a full week, Tanner thought that evening. At work, he had a full group of dogs. Maxie, Mystery, Marshall, Marmalade, Marlow, and Murphy were all enthusiastic and energetic students. Teaching classes here at home two evenings and working with Micah one evening a week didn't leave much time for Wing—and now, it was Friday night, and he didn't have enough energy to do more than a cursory heeling pattern with her before he went into his apartment. He opened the refrigerator and peered hopefully inside. With a sigh, he reached for a can of soda. He sank into his one comfortable chair and toed his boots off.

He thought about Jake's words. There were lots of things he didn't take seriously. He might not be able to think of any right now, but there were lots of them. Tanner was sure of it. It only looked like he took everything seriously because most of his life—okay, he admitted, all of his life—was taken up by dogs. Tanner was not casual about dogs. You could be casual about trees, he thought, or food, or movies. Even books. You could be casual about cars, as long as they worked. But dogs, no. Dogs were serious stuff.

A lone thought trailed through his mind. Sally Foster believed the same thing about her cats—she took them seriously, and expected her friends to do the same.

"Are you serious stuff?" he asked Aretha.

Under Wing's ever-watchful eyes, the kitten made little forays out of the kitchen area. She explored the world under the kitchen table where she batted at a stray sock. She crept out from the table and scampered across the room towards Tanner's bed. Wing followed her; careful to make sure she didn't venture out of bounds, picking her up and carrying her back when she did. Aretha had become Wing's pet, just like Sally said the fish were her cats' pets.

Tanner wondered what she would think of Aretha.

No. He was not going to think of Sally Foster. He would not give in to temptation. Instead, he would be virtuous. He would read that new book on dog psychology. He reached for the thick book and turned to the bookmarked page.

Twelve

Friday evening, Sally turned on the evening news. She wanted to hear the latest weather forecast. "That hot, moist air will reach us quicker than we thought," the weather person said, waving vaguely at one of those maps behind her. She was not the regular weather person.

"More quickly than we thought," Sally muttered to herself. "No wonder kids don't know how to speak."

"After pleasant temperatures tonight," the new girl continued blithely, "tomorrow will be sunny and humid, with afternoon temperatures reaching the high eighties." She looked pleased at the prospect. "It'll be a great day for fun in the sun."

"Temperature, you dummy. It's singular." Sally snorted in disgust. "And it'll be a *good* day." She turned to Tess. "What is happening to our language? And why do people not care?"

Tess didn't care, either.

"Hot and humid. That means more ice," Sally told the cat. She wandered into the kitchen. She emptied the ice into a freezer bag and filled the trays with water.

Sophie erupted into the kitchen and threw herself at the counter.

"You want ice." It was a statement. Sophie loved ice. "You and Sylvie's poodle, Jean-Luc," Sally told her, "you both love to chew ice." She reached into the freezer bag and pulled one of the smaller cubes. "Here." She tossed.

Sophie caught. Sophie crunched blissfully. Sophie crunched loudly.

"Aren't you ever quiet?" Sally asked.

Sophie wagged her tail and looked hopeful.

"Another piece?" Sally reached for the ice cubes again. "Dumb question, Sally," she told herself.

After Sophie had her second piece of ice, Sally checked her list of things to do before tomorrow. The patio was swept. Stepladders. Sally had one stepladder—she'd borrowed a second one from next door, and Ray said he and Sylvie would bring theirs—unless the baby decided to arrive. Three should be enough. She had five big boxes of freezer bags, and one box of trash bags for the pits. Lawn chairs. She had root beer, lemon-lime, and orange sodas in the refrigerator, and Sylvie had promised to bring lemonade—the baby thing again. Would that be enough? Sally wondered. Her friends weren't picky—Micah liked root beer, but what about Tanner? Did he like soda? Or lemonade? Or would he prefer beer? And what kind?

She called Jessie.

"Beer?" Jessie said. "I don't think I've ever seen Tanner drink beer. Hmm. The refrigerator at dog school is always full of sodas and stuff. 'Course, you probably wouldn't have beer at a dog school because dogs can tell sometimes if people are beginning to get drunk, and lots of dogs don't like it."

"This isn't about dogs, Jess, it's a simple question. Do you know if Tanner likes beer, and if so, what kind?"

"That's two questions, Sally," her friend said. "And the whole *world* is about dogs. Haven't you learned that yet?"

Sally looked down. Sophie had one of her ham-flavored chew things. Sophie chewed it noisily. Sally groaned. "It's a good thing we're friends, or you would proverbially drive me up the proverbial wall. So what about the beer?"

"I'm thinking. Nope. I've never seen Tanner drink beer. Hey. Why all this sudden interest in beer?"

Sally shrugged. "You know. People say that on a hot day nothing tastes as good as a cold beer. It's supposed to be hot and humid tomorrow. I thought cold beer might be a good thing. The hostess thing."

"Well, in my opinion, don't bother. We'll all be happy with sodas and stuff. I know Ray likes beer sometimes, but since Sylvie got pregnant he hasn't touched it—it's supposed to be one of those supporting-your-pregnant-wife things. Sylvie is so lucky. Sometimes I wish . . ." Jessie sighed long and hard. "Do you think we'll ever find our Mr. Rights?" She sounded serious.

How odd, Sally thought. How out of character. "I . . . I don't . . ." she stammered. "I don't know. I certainly hope so."

"I would like to hope that somewhere, out in

the universe, there's some guy with my name on him. Or maybe he's holding a sign—like limo drivers at the airport—that says *Jessica Albright, Hartley, Ohio*. And somewhere there's some guy with your name on him, too, Sal. And some guy for Karen. All we have to do is find them. And then we have to make them see us. The problem is, it's a big world, after all."

An image of Tanner Dodge flashed across Sally's mind.

But her friend continued. "Do you ever feel like you're invisible?"

"No," Sally said. "Do you?"

"Yeah." Jessie's voice was so quiet Sally held her hand over her other ear to shut out the sound of Sophie's fervent chomping on her chewie.

"When do you feel invisible, Jess?"

"Oh, whenever I'm around some guy I think is attractive."

"Anyone in particular?"

"No. Not really. Well, actually there are lots of guys I think are attractive. But they don't seem to see me at all. I guess I'm not the kind of woman guys are attracted to."

"You sound depressed."

"You sound like you're doing that teacher thing, affirming the feelings of a troubled kid."

"It's called active listening. They teach it to us in teacher school. So, you sound depressed."

"Yeah." Jessie also sounded discouraged. "I guess I am."

"Do you want to come over and watch *Lost Horizon?* We can sing along with all the Burt

Bacharach songs. Or *Mystery Alaska?* That's a terrific cheer-up movie. And Russell Crowe's in it."

"Nah. Thanks, Sal, but I'm okay. I guess my life is sticking its tongue out at me and blowing raspberries. I'm going to put on my jammies and crawl in bed with a good book. Hey, don't worry about me. It's probably PMS or something. I'll see you tomorrow."

"Hey, Jess. Any guy who doesn't see you doesn't deserve you. And if anybody says anything different, let me know and I'll punch them in the face."

Saturday morning, as predicted, started out hot and humid. "Sing praises to the gods in charge of air conditioning," Sally told the cats.

After lunch, before everyone and their dogs arrived, Sally unwrapped six raw scallops. The cats heard the plastic wrap and appeared as if on cue. All three of them jumped onto the counter. Sally scooped them up and onto the kitchen catwalk. "Not when I have a sharp knife in my hand," she told them. She sliced the scallops into the three cat bowls, the ones she kept for festive occasions. She was careful to make the portions equal—she didn't want any accusations of feline favoritism. Then, carrying the bowls, she went into her bedroom. The cats followed her willingly. Well, they followed the scallops. Sally set the bowls down.

Troy gobbled his without chewing, while Tess used her best company manners.

"It's all your Auntie Jessie's fault," she told them.

"She was the one who invited all those dogs." And Tanner. The cats ignored her.

She left her bedroom, and after a guilty look over her shoulder at her cats, she closed the door. They wouldn't suffer any emotional trauma, she told herself. She had no reason to feel guilty.

On her way down the hall, she bent her head down and gathered her hair into a ponytail. As she fastened it with a colored elastic, she looked down at her chest. Her T-shirt was older than dirt and looked it. She should change. Maybe that new—no, she told herself firmly. Cherry-picking is sweaty, and cherry-pitting is sticky, and the juice stains. Picking and pitting was not a good time to wear new clothes. It was also not a good time to try to impress a man. Which was why it really was okay for Tanner to come, because no one in her right mind would invite a man she was trying to impress to pick and pit cherries, so no one would ever even suspect her stomach was doing the butterfly thing, which, by the way, was not at all appropriate and had to stop.

When Micah was okay, when he had made friends, was settled in school, when she was sure he was on that road to recovery that everyone talked about, then, maybe she . . . Then she would start walking—every day. And she'd ban Leety's Fine Chocolates from her house. Ban all chocolate. Chocolate syrup, chocolate ice cream, chocolate cake, cookies, and even that refrigerated cookie dough. The Girl Scouts would have to do without her support. She would buy a full-length mirror and put it up on her closet door and she'd make herself look at her reflection every single day. When she could get into a size twelve again, *then* she'd do the man thing. Until those things came to pass, she'd forget about the sainted Tanner Dodge. Until then, she had Mel. And chocolate.

Back in the kitchen, Sally reached for her stash of Leety's. The chocolate hit her tongue with a burst of bliss. She closed her eyes to concentrate on the taste. Nothing like chocolate to help her feel better.

Thunk!

Sally jerked her eyes open at the sound. Then she relaxed. She knew what it was; Micah was in the backyard throwing that old tennis ball for that dog. Sally left the cool of the house and went out into the heat.

Micah was probably nervous about seeing lots of people, she thought. "You know my friends," she told him. "Jessie. And Melissa, my vet."

Without looking at her, Micah nodded and threw the ball again. Sophie tore after it.

"Sylvie—she's the one who puts flowers in food, her husband Ray is a mailman. Karen is the one who rescues Newfoundlands."

Sophie dropped the ball at his feet and Micah bent down to pick it up.

Sally tried again. "Are you sure you don't want to call Jeremy Martini to come over and help pick? You two have done stuff together every summer . . ."

Micah shook his head. "No, thanks."

Sally bit her bottom lip and thought. Of course, Micah remembered her friends, and Jeremy Martini—he'd seen them every summer when he came for hockey camp. That was it, she realized. They were from his life before. When he had a mother and a father. When he was a hockey player. Now he was a kid who didn't have parents. Now he was a kid who couldn't walk without braces, who couldn't play hockey. Now he was a kid who didn't know who he was.

She was glad Tanner was coming.

Sylvie was first to arrive, looking as big as a house. In one hand she held Jean-Luc's leash, in the other was a big pink plastic pitcher. With a grin, she held out the pitcher. "Take it—it's heavy and it's sweating!"

"I'll put it in the fridge." Sally took the pitcher.

"Ray took the stepladder into the backyard," Sylvie said. "He said the gate was easier to manage with a ladder than your house. Why don't you get the other two pitchers out of my car," Sylvie said. "Let me go out and see Micah by myself. I want to have a minute with him before everyone else gets here." Sylvie's eyes were unusually bright.

"Sure." Sally nodded. "That'd be good." When Sylvie was a teenager, she'd lost her mother, too.

As Sally made room in the refrigerator for the lemonade, she heard Sylvie slide the dining room door open. "Hi, Micah," Sally heard Sylvie say.

Karen showed up with Brian, her most geezer Newf who, at age nine, moved slowly and slept a lot. Jessie brought a photograph of Sagan. "She'll fly in next week," Jessie said, practically jumping up and down.

"You look like one of my kindergartners when they have to go to the bathroom," Sally teased her. But she agreed that Sagan was gorgeous—though personally, she thought the puppy looked like it was all skinny legs and huge eyes.

Melissa and Angie, her eight-year-old stepdaughter, arrived with Lady, the Sheltie who was the little girl's faithful shadow. But no Tanner.

"I saw Katie the other morning," Sylvie told Karen, "running with Gracie." Gracie was a random-bred dog who belonged to Karen's brother and sister-in-law. "They looked good together, both sleek and blond, like a matched set. Actually, I've seen them often, running in the mornings. You'd think Katie would take the summer off and relax before she goes off to college. Has she *finally* decided where she's going to go?" Katie had been accepted at four colleges.

"Not yet," Karen answered, but Sally noticed Karen seemed a little tense. She wondered why. Karen also didn't seem to want to continue to talk about Katie. Curiouser and curiouser, thought Sally. She decided to test her theory.

"Is Katie coming?" she asked. "You did tell her she was invited, didn't you?"

"She said she had some meeting with someone about something," Karen said vaguely. "So where's my bucket? C'mon, Bri, old guy. You can sleep under a cherry tree. Let's pick us some cherries."

Hmmm, Sally thought. She took a quick peek

out the front door. She told herself she was merely
admiring the lovely day. But she didn't see Tanner's
truck coming down the street. She followed her
friends into the backyard.

"Angie," said Sally, "because this is your first
pick-and-pit party, you may use my special yellow
cherry pail." Angie beamed like the sun. The little
girl, reaching for cherries, her dog at her feet,
looked very Mary Englebreit. Sally watched Melissa
smile at her stepdaughter and Angie grin back.
They had a good relationship, Sally noted with a
pang.

"Doorbell," Jessie sang out. "I'll get it." She set
down her bowl and trotted off through the gate
towards the front of the house. She returned a moment later, Tanner and Wing in tow. "Tanner's
here, everyone," Jessie called out unnecessarily.
"You all know him, and the dogs all know each
other."

Sally's insides turned all gooey, like chocolate left
in the sun, soft and darkly sweet. She felt herself
flush, willing herself to go to Tanner and greet
him. She felt rooted. She couldn't move her feet.
Her hand automatically picked another cherry and
dropped it in her bucket.

Jessie took Tanner in hand, handed him a
bucket, and led him to the tree where Micah was
picking. "Look. The really opaque ones aren't
ready yet. When the cherries are ripe they get
sort of translucent and they almost fall into your
hand. Be careful not to pull on the tree when
you pick them."

"Yeah," Sylvie added. "The spirits of the cherry trees will leave."

Ray set a lawn chair down beside Sylvie. "Why don't *you* leave the trees," he told his wife, "and sit right here while I pick the cherries for you."

Sally kept an eye on everyone, then brought out more cherry pails. "Mega Lots had a sale on sand pails last fall," she explained. "I bought all I could find." She noticed Micah was careful to pick near Tanner, on a different family of branches, but at the same tree. Near enough for comfort, but not so close it didn't appear casual.

Sophie was in awe of all the big dogs. She imitated them, followed their lead. The puppy was in the obvious throes of hero worship. She wanted to be just like them when she grew up. Sally hoped she was. For dogs, her friends had some nice ones.

Jessie said, "So Micah, I bet you didn't realize that when you got Sally you also got all of us. We're a package deal."

"It wasn't a surprise package," Micah answered.

Jessie chuckled. "Good. You're quick, kid."

Today wore a T-shirt with another hockey slogan splashed across the front. This one read *Their Goalie is Stupid*. Sally's heart went out to him. She needed to find a way to help him make friends. Girls made friends so much easier than boys did—especially teenagers.

She noticed Karen also watched Micah carefully, with professional as well as personal concern. Sally should talk to Karen later. Karen would have some ideas about how to help Micah make friends, how to cheer him up, how to help him feel more at home.

Jessie, swinging her bucket in a jaunty sort of way, ambled over to Sally. "Tanner seems to be having a good time," she whispered.

Sally scowled at her.

Tanner and Micah were in the middle of a conversation about something or other, but Sally couldn't hear what they were saying. She caught a wistful expression on Micah's face. Sally moved one tree closer to them, so she could eavesdrop. Ah. Micah was telling Tanner about Antarctica. Tanner was listening intently. Tanner was a good listener, Sally thought. He had turned from the branch he was picking and given all his attention to Micah, who was trying to hold onto his cherry pail at the same time he was using his hands to demonstrate something.

When he and Deb were in Hartley last summer, all Micah talked to her about was Antarctica. He and Jessie spent hours together poring over maps, polar weather conditions, the cold, the science, the polar station, Shackleton. Last summer, Micah found a way to bring Antarctica into every conversation.

He didn't talk to Sally about Antarctica anymore. He talked to Jessie about Antarctica, and he talked to Tanner about Sophie. But he didn't talk to her. Sally wasn't doing a very good job with Micah. Suddenly the number of cherries in her pail seemed pitifully small.

The dogs—except for Brian, who lay snoring and snuffling next to Sylvie in the shade—came tearing through the trees. Jean-Luc, in the lead, threw himself down. The others followed suit. Their tongues lolled out as they panted

"Hey, Sal," Jessie said. "I'm gonna get them some water. Where do you keep your biggest bowl?"

"Give it up, Albright," Melissa teased. "You really want to snoop in Sally's cupboards to find her chocolate stash."

"Yup," came the unrepentant reply. "Anyone who lets their chocolate be found, deserves to have it eaten." Jessie trotted off into the house to carry out her mission of mercy. Soon she came out again, a big bowl balanced in her hands. The panting dogs, their tongues lolling, left the shade of the trees to swarm up onto the patio. Jean-Luc shoved his way to the front of the pack. The other dogs, for their part, looked properly respectful while the poodle claimed his first dibs on the water.

"Hey, everyone," Sylvie called. "Look. Jean-Luc is top dog. He's never been first at anything before!"

"I told you last year, you should've painted him for that Halloween dog walk," Jessie said. "He'd've won first place in the costume competition."

Sally closed her eyes and lifted her face to the sun. It was a beautiful day to pick cherries. She stretched her back. Yes, it was a beautiful day.

From inside the house the phone rang. "I'll get it," Jessie said. "The dogs need a refill anyway." A moment later, she stuck her head out of the door. "Micah," she called, "it's your Aunt Mary."

Karen casually wandered over to pick at Sally's

tree. "Trouble?" she asked in a quiet voice. "You had that miserable look on your face while you watched Micah go into the house."

Sally shook her head. "She calls at least three times a week. She says she wants to give him all the news about his family and friends in Vermont. I suppose I ought to be glad. His friends don't call. I can't read him," she confessed to her friend. "I can't tell if her calls upset him or not. I *think* that somewhere deep inside she truly cares about him. I *hope* she truly cares about him. But I'm not sure she's doing her best to try to help him settle in here. She wanted him to stay in Vermont, and she can be pretty manipulative."

"You think she's trying to undermine your relationship with Micah?"

Sally thought about it. "That would be a horrible thing to think. It would be horrible if it were true. I hope it isn't, but I wonder."

"You still have that list of therapists?"

"Yeah. But Micah says he doesn't feel like talking to a counselor right now. Karen, I'm not sure he's healing. Oh, he looks like he's healing on the outside, but I don't think he's healing on the inside."

"Like an emotional abscess," Karen suggested.

"Yeah. The wound heals over, but the infection inside continues to grow and grow and sometimes if it's not lanced and drained, it bursts." She shuddered. "I'm glad I'm not a vet."

"Yeah. M'liss says it's a gross thing to do." She shrugged. "Emotional abscesses—and that's not a clinical term—can be equally unpleasant. For everyone. Thing is, most people want to avoid the gross part, the painful part, so they leave it alone; they think it'll go away on its own. But it won't." The two friends were quiet for a moment, picking cherries and thinking about abscesses. Then Karen asked, "How is he doing with Tanner? They seem to get along well."

Sally grinned. "Tanner is great. Micah actually talks to him."

"Tanner is a good person for Micah to talk to," Karen told her. "Not only about dogs." She thought for a moment. "You might talk to Tanner about Micah. Talk to him about what's going on. Tanner works with physically challenged people all the time."

"I thought he trained dogs."

Karen, reaching for a cherry, stopped midpick and gazed at her thoughtfully. "You don't know what he does, do you." It was not a question. She plucked the cherry and dropped it in her bucket. "Ask him sometime. You'll be amazed."

"Oh." Sally stood on her toes to reach an upper branch. She gently drew it down so she could reach the cluster of cherries. They were translucent. They were ripe and succulent, ready to pick. Any longer on the tree and they'd spoil, spilling their sweetness onto the ground. "I guess you're right." She focused her attention on the clusters of cherries on the branch, to give herself time to think. When she first met Tanner she hoped he could help civilize Sophie. Then she was glad that Micah seemed to like him, and that Sophie seemed to be learning stuff. And the other night, when she really looked at him, for some reason he looked better to her than even Mel. Now she snuck a surreptitious peek at him. He still looked better than even Mel. But she had never thought about him as an individual person in his own right—she'd only thought of him in relation to her. How self-centered that was! Suddenly she wondered what his life was like. What he did for fun, what he read, what movies he watched, what he liked to eat, what music he liked. And if he liked cats. And kids.

Micah came out of the house and headed over to the tree. He glanced around. She caught his eye and gave him a small wave. He returned her slight wave, but he went back to pick up his bucket where he'd left it, next to Tanner. Sally hoped, with all her heart, Tanner liked kids.

Angie marched over next to Tanner. She beamed as she held her pail up for his inspection. Evidently he approved, for Angie set her attention on the lower branches. As Sally watched, Tanner picked a handful of cherries and dropped them into Angie's pail. Yes, she decided. Tanner likes kids.

"Anyone," Karen said quietly so only Sally could hear, "who likes kids and dogs can't be all bad."

After picking bucketsful and bucketsful of cherries, they dragged lawn chairs into a circle on the patio. They put the dogs on a down stay, all except Brian who was still snoring under a cherry tree. They drank icy cold soda and lemonade in great gulps—Sally noticed Tanner chose lemonade—and Sally passed the platter of those amazing chocolate cookies from the bakery at the mall. She distributed plastic pit pails and plastic freezer bags and when at last she turned to sit down, she realized her friends had finagled the seating arrangements so her chair sat next to Tanner's. Sylvie caught her eye and gave her a wink. Sally blushed. The sun was hot today.

"Everybody, let's pit!" Jessie yelled.

Sally showed Tanner how to use his thumbs to release the pits, which made little squopping sounds as they popped out and into the pails. The cherries were then plopped into freezer bags.

"Remember," Melissa reminded Angie, "cherry juice splashes and stains."

"That's why you made me wear grubbies!" Angie said gleefully. Her eight-year-old face was radiant as she hugged her full bowl to her chest. She was proud of her very own cherries. Sally guessed she was also thrilled to be included with the big people.

The cherries were sticky and smelled sweet. Sally's fingers dripped with juice as she popped a pitted cherry in her mouth. It was glorious. Rapturous. Then she saw Tanner watching her. She turned red. He grinned at her, a private grin, the grin of a shared secret. He popped a cherry in his own mouth, a drop of juice on his bottom lip. Sally's mouth went suddenly dry, and the butterflies did that dancing thing in the middle of her belly, and she realized she liked the look of his lip.

"Hey," Jessie said. "I saw that. If you get to sample the goods, then Jean-Luc does, too. Hey, Jean-Luc, look." From his spot on the ground next to Sylvie's chair, Jean-Luc's eyes followed Jessie's every move. "Sylvie, I'm going to spoil your dog's dinner. Jean-Luc, catch!" Without moving from his spot on the ground next to Sylvie's chair, the dog caught the cherry on the fly.

"No more than about a dozen of them," Sylvie cautioned, "or you have to clean up the results. One year," she continued for Tanner and Micah's benefit, "he ate so many cherries he had diarrhea for two days. Talk about gross." She did that pregnant woman's rub-in-a-circle thing on her belly.

"He only ate them because you put them on your kitchen counter and promptly forgot about them," Karen added.

"That wasn't nearly as gross," Jessie countered, "as the time that foster Newf of Karen's—what did you name her, Karen?"

"Golden."

"Yeah, Golden." Jessie frowned, "Dumb name for a black dog. Anyway, this dog was a food thief. She'd eat anything, whether it was edible or not. Crayons, candles, those fake logs for the fireplace. Nothing was safe from that dog. She was a blue-ribbon counter surfer."

"Which is why," Karen added, "her first family turned her over to Rescue. They didn't want to deal with her, didn't want to learn anything about dogs. They should've gotten a pet rock."

"Anyway," Jessie interrupted her, "one day when Karen was in the middle of bringing in the groceries, she found a box of raisin bran in the grocery bag. Golden stole the box and took it into her crate and ate the entire eighteen ounces. Of *raisin bran*. Now, *that* was gross. I remember you calling the clinic as soon as you found the empty box in her crate. I couldn't tell if you were laughing or crying. Hey, I'm gonna get more lemonade. Anyone else want more anything?"

Sally wanted to sink into her chair. Her friends were talking about diarrhea in front of Tanner! She was mortified. She glanced around, looking for something safe she could change the conversation to. Instead, she saw Sophie, silently sneaking up to Micah's chair. The little dog stared intently at the cherry in Micah's hand. He quietly held it out to her. One snap of her sharp teeth and that cherry was history. Sally had horribly vivid visions of the results of Sophie eating too many cherries.

"Remember," Melissa said, "the time that Yorkie ate his owner's estrogen pill?"

They played *Remember When,* trying to outdo each other by recalling the grossest things their dogs had eaten, until finally, thankfully, they ran out of gross things to remember. Then the conversation turned to more pleasant subjects until, at last, the buckets were empty and the pit pails were full. Freezer bags bulged with the results of their work. Sally looked around the circle of her friends, all of them still sticky with the juice of pitted fruit. She wanted to gather them all up and hold them close. She closed her eyes for a moment and took a deep breath, willing herself always to remember this afternoon, the true blue sky, the cherries sparkling like rubies, the voices of her friends and their laughter. This was a magical moment. And Tanner was part of it.

"And think," Sally told her friends as they gathered up their freezer bags to take their bounty home, "the cherries will be coming for the next week or so. Any time you want to pick more, you all have standing invitations."

Thirteen

Sophie parked herself at Sally's feet while Sally rolled out piecrust. She felt the brown eyes staring at her. "Forget it," she told the puppy. She sprinkled a batch of cherries with a mixture of sugar and flour. The puppy sat, still staring. "I'm still ignoring you," Sally told her as she put the pie in the oven. But ignoring those brown eyes, so full of hope and optimism, was not an easy thing to do. "Cats don't beg for food," she told the dog, deliberately not remembering Troy's habit of jumping on the counter every time she cut open a cantaloupe. Or Tess's insistent meow whenever Sally made tuna sandwiches. That wasn't begging, she told herself, it was the cats' way of reminding her not to forget them. She looked at the dog, glanced at the clock, then looked at the dog again. Sophie, seeing she had Sally's attention, wagged her tail. "Well," Sally told her, "I guess you can have a treat now." She spooned out a small clump of extra-super-chunk peanut butter.

Sophie loved extra-super-chunk peanut butter.

"Micah," Sally called.

There was no answer, so she went to knock on his door.

"Come in," came Micah's voice, not very loud.

She opened the door to see Micah, stretched out on his bed with Jude curled up next to him. Micah's hand was on the cat's black head.

Sally smiled to see them. "Is he purring?"

"I can feel it, but I can't hear it."

Sally nodded. "That's Jude. He has a silent purr." And he always knows when his comfort is needed, she added to herself. "The pie is in the oven. It'll take a while to bake, then it has to cool. All that sun this afternoon wore me out. I thought I'd order in a pizza and put on a movie. How does that sound?" She held her breath. Micah hadn't been very social since he'd been with her.

Without looking up from the purring cat, he asked, "What movie?"

"I hadn't made up my mind yet. I thought I'd wait to see what you were in the mood for."

"All right," Micah said at last. "But I'm not in the mood for anything with Mel Gibson in it."

She grinned. It was something his mother used to tell her, too. "Whatever you want to watch." She felt safe. "You pick something out while I call for pizza."

Micah chose *Armageddon*. Yeah, it fit, Sally thought. It was a survival movie—with heroism. And there were some funny parts. She brought a box of Thin Mints out from the freezer.

They watched the movie, ate Thin Mints and pizza. They fed pizza crust to Sophie, who, even after scarfing down her own dinner, sat at their feet staring intently at theirs. The cats arranged themselves on the pole perch next to the couch, close enough for handouts but far enough to feel safe from Sophie. The cats weren't taking any chances.

For the first time since Sophie had arrived, Sally found herself relaxing around the puppy. For the first time half her mind wasn't busy planning what to do when Sophie decided to chase her cats. Sophie hadn't made a move towards them, but regarded them with a kind of respect.

By the time Bruce Willis and his crew of oil drillers were on their way to the asteroid, the pizza was gone. Micah pressed the "Pause" button. Sally went into the kitchen to cut generous pieces of still-warm cherry pie.

"This is really good," Micah told her with his mouth full. But before she could respond he pushed the "Play" button. Micah wasn't ready to talk to her yet.

Patience, Sally, she told herself. Patience goes well with pie.

Tanner worked with Wing, fed Aretha, and made himself a grilled cheese sandwich. After tossing Wing the crusts, he settled into his chair with a book. Wing spread out on the rug in front of the sink. Aretha used her tiny little claws to climb up his pants to his lap. Maybe she was part mountain goat. The phone rang. At the sudden sound, Aretha leaped straight up in the air, like a cartoon character, then shot off his lap to race across the room. Tanner picked up the phone. It was Katie Matheson.

"Are you going to a show tomorrow morning?" she asked. "If you're not, can I go running with you?"

"No, I'm not, and yes, you may. Can you be here about six?"

"Sure. Do you mind if Gracie comes, too?"

"You're dogsitting again?" Across the room, Aretha stalked some imaginary menace. The menace won. Aretha hurtled her kitten self back to him and swarmed up his leg to his lap.

"Yeah. Uncle Roger and Aunt Camille are off somewhere, so we have Gracie and Bob. Bob is too lazy to take on a run, but Gracie is great. She'd make a good marathon dog."

Tanner heard tension in her voice. Then he remembered the night Karen came to ask him to work with Micah. There'd been tension in her voice then, too. "I saw your mother today at Sally's." He stroked Aretha's little head. She closed her eyes and purred.

"Yeah."

"She said you'd been invited, but you had other things to do." Tanner heard big-dog barking in the background. Maybe Aretha heard it, too, for she suddenly grabbed Tanner's finger between her needle teeth and kicked with her hind feet. Tanner gently picked her up and set her on the floor. She dashed off to bother Wing.

"Yeah. I did. Hey, Brian," Katie's voice was muffled. "I'm over here. Turn the other way, old man. That's it." Then her voice was clear again. "Sorry.

Brian's becoming senile in his dotage. He goes down the hall and gets lost. Then he stands looking at the wall and he barks until we come and find him."

"Doggy Alzheimer's. He slept under a cherry tree most of the afternoon."

"Yeah. Hey, Tanner, I need to do some out-loud thinking. Can I talk to you tomorrow? Like, can I talk to you and you not tell Mom what I say? It's not dangerous, or illegal or anything. I want your opinion about something."

Many years ago, when he was in college, after Karen had helped him over his crisis, they'd become friends. Karen claimed him as an honorary younger brother, so Katie, who was in elementary school, announced Tanner would be her honorary uncle. Even now, she sometimes referred to him as her Uncle Tanner.

"Sure. As long as it *isn't* dangerous or illegal."

"Okay. Gracie and I'll see you bright and early in the morning, then. Oh, and thanks. I love my mom, but sometimes she doesn't understand."

Tanner idly watched Aretha terrorize Wing while he thought about Katie's last words. *I love my mom, but sometimes she doesn't understand.* Karen was a great mother. Katie was lucky. She was also smart enough to realize how great her mother was, and to appreciate her. *I love my mom, but sometimes she doesn't understand.*

Tanner glanced briefly at the drawer where he kept the handful of still-unopened letters from his mother. Did he love his mother? He didn't know. He never thought about her. She was irrelevant to him. She was part of a life that was so distant it was more like a movie, or like a book, a life lived by someone else. He hadn't seen his mother since—

Aretha squealed. Wing had her pinned with one paw and was giving her a bath. Aretha flailed her arms and legs. Wing calmly washed the kitten, taking all the flails and squeals in stride. Wing didn't lose her temper, didn't hit, didn't yell. Wing screamed no obscenities, hurled no heavy objects. Wing was a good mother.

"Do you know anything about my father?" Katie asked. She sped up for a few steps, looking back to see if Tanner was coming with her.

He wasn't. He shook his head. "Nope."

"Would you tell me if you did?"

Tanner thought. "Maybe. I don't know." They ran farther. Katie sped up a few steps, looking back again. Tanner didn't speed up with her and she fell back again.

"Did my mother ever say anything at all about him?"

"Nope."

"Weren't you ever curious?"

Tanner grinned. "Nope."

"Must be a guy thing."

"Yup."

They ran farther. Tanner was glad she didn't ask him more questions so he didn't have to answer.

"Don't you think it's odd that no one knows anything about my father?"

"Nope."

Katie made a frustrated noise. She put on speed. Gracie kept up with her. Tanner and Wing didn't. This time she didn't slow down.

"Hey," he called. "Slow down."

"Getting too old?" she teased, her voice floating back to him.

"For this fast, yes." His words came out in little gasps. He didn't know if she heard him.

Katie slowed down. She'd heard him. She and Gracie slowed their pace until they were doing a slow jog.

Tanner grunted at her. He was still out of breath.

"You've been slacking," Katie said. "You used to run every morning."

He grunted again. He didn't have enough breath to keep up a conversation. He mentally shook his head at himself. Katie was right. He had been slacking. It took a while for him to get his breath back enough to say, "I usually don't go this far."

"You're getting old." But she grinned.

"I'm not old."

"You're about my mother's age."

"Your mother," he gasped, "is not old."

Katie looked over at him and shrugged. "She's old to me."

They were almost back to his driveway, Tanner saw gratefully. They turned off the road to walk the long driveway, to cool down.

"Wow!" Tanner said. "You're in terrific shape. When did this happen?"

"I started working out at Steve Songer's gym. You

know Steve. He has that really nice black Am Staff, Lennox."

"He teaches boxing," Tanner said. "Are you telling me you've taken up boxing?"

"Not really." She grinned. "I don't like being hit. But it's a great way to get into tip-top shape."

Katie had always been in good shape. Tanner wondered why she suddenly needed to be in "tip-top shape." He didn't ask. He knew she didn't like to feel pressured. She'd tell him in her own time.

"When did you stop running?" she asked. Back at his house, they sank into the Adirondack chairs on his small deck. Well, Katie sank. Tanner fell. The dogs flopped down beside them, panting. The dogs were worn out, but they were both smiling doggy smiles.

"Oh, I guess, I cut back to once a week last fall."

"What happened?"

"Nothing specific. I suppose I've been reevaluating my life."

She nodded. "Yeah. I know what you mean."

He kept his chuckle to himself. She was eighteen. How much of a life did she have to evaluate? "Is that why you're asking about your father?"

"Yeah." She stuck her feet up onto the railing, leaned back in the chair, and pulled her ball cap farther over her forehead. "Mom wants me to go to college."

She pretended to be casual. He knew her well enough to know she wasn't. "And . . ."

She sighed heavily. "I don't know what I want to do with my life. What's the point of spending four years and bunches of bucks on college if I don't know what I want to do?"

"If you don't go to college, what will you do?"

She shrugged. "Maybe join the Marines."

Oh. "This is why you want to be in tip-top shape?"

"Yeah."

He chewed on this for a while. "Have you told your mother you want to join the Marines?"

"Nope." Katie stretched her arms over her head. "I decided not to tell her until I've actually signed up. Other than my recruiter, you're the only one who knows."

Tanner gave a low whistle. "She won't be happy."

"No. She won't."

"This is what you don't want me to tell her?"

"Yeah."

Tanner chewed some more. "So, do your out-loud thinking. Why do you want to go into the military? And the Marines, at that."

Katie tapped her foot on the railing. Tanner noticed she was fidgety. Katie was never fidgety—unless she was nervous.

"I don't want to go into the *military*. It's not like I'm some warmonger, or anything like that." She tapped her foot some more. "I want to be a Marine."

He had a sudden thought. "Does this have anything to do with your father?"

She turned her head sharply to pin him with her gaze. "What do you know about my father?"

He shrugged. "I told you. Nothing. What do *you* know about your father?"

She relaxed back into the chair. "Nothing. Not really."

"C'mon, Katie. This is your honorary Uncle Tanner, here. I'm not a dentist pulling teeth."

She grinned briefly. "Sorry." She tapped her foot. "I love my mom. I really do. She works hard. She's honest. She's smart. She helps teenagers, and she's obsessive about rescuing Newfoundlands. She's a really good person. Even if she weren't my mom, I'd respect her. I can talk to her about anything." She said it as if it were a litany. "Anything in the whole wide world. Except my father. She won't tell me anything. She shuts me out. I don't know. Maybe there's some deep, dark secret. Like, maybe he's a convicted murderer or something." She looked at him from under her ball cap. "Do you think that's it?"

"No. I don't."

"I don't either. It's making me crazy." She stood up abruptly. "Mom said to bring you back for French toast. You wanna come?" Evidently, Katie was finished with her out-loud thinking.

"Sure. Give me about half an hour to feed Wing and Aretha and take a quick shower. You know I never turn down your mom's French toast."

"Okay. But take your time. I'll head on home and tell Mom you'll be over."

She whistled for Gracie and trotted down the steps and off to her car. She started the engine and gave a quick wave as she backed up and headed off for home.

Tanner watched after her. "What do you think

about that, Wing?" he asked. "Katie Matheson wants to be a Marine."

Wing looked up at him, a question on her face. "I agree. I don't get it, either."

"French toast?" Sally said. She cradled the phone between her ear and her shoulder as she opened a can of cat food. "I *adore* your French toast." Three cats wound around her ankles and craned their necks to see what she was doing.

"I made cherry syrup last night," Karen said.

"Food for the gods," Sally agreed. Troy leaped up onto the counter. She set his bowl under the cupboard, Tess's bowl next to the sink, and Jude's bowl on the counter beside the refrigerator. Now, AD, After Dog, the cats ate on the counter so Sophie couldn't bother them. She knew, from experience, Sophie was quite willing to steal the cats' food. Or even their empty bowls, which she then chewed into bits and dribbled all over the house. Bit-of-cat-bowl was wicked on a bare instep.

"Sophie is invited, too, of course. She'll have a great time playing with all the Newfs."

"I'll talk to Micah. If for some bizarre reason we can't make it, I'll let you know."

But they did make it. They made it to Karen's house—and Sally saw Tanner's truck in Karen's driveway. Micah saw it, too.

"Is Tanner here?" he asked.

"I don't know," Sally said. She hoped he was. Then she remembered she had on a pair of ancient jeans and a faded T-shirt. She hoped he wasn't.

Her hand automatically went to her hair, carelessly pulled back in a quick ponytail. He was. She could see him in Karen's backyard. Maybe she could pretend she'd forgotten something and sneak away.

"Hi, Tanner," Micah called as he opened the car door.

It was too late. She was stuck.

"Great cherry syrup," she told Karen. The five of them sat at Karen's picnic table, their plates heaped with Karen's infamous French toast. Karen's currently eight huge black Newfoundlands, Gracie and Bob who belonged to Karen's brother, and Wing and Sophie were all lying down in a long line along the back of the house. The dogs were on a down stay, which meant they were not allowed to get up. Sally thought most of the Newfs looked like they were asleep. She could hear at least one of them snore. Sophie, however, kept her little eyes firmly on the food, on the table and out of her reach.

"It's Grandma's recipe," Katie said.

"I've made cherry syrup before," Karen said mildly, as if Katie hadn't interrupted her. "Last summer, in fact."

"I think it's great, too," Micah said, reaching for seconds. "Maybe Sally can learn to make it."

Sally determined to do just that. If Micah wanted it, she'd make it.

Tanner nodded. "As Angie would say, it's truly scrumptious."

Talk about truly scrumptious, Sally thought. She

kept her gaze firmly in check, which meant away from Tanner Dodge, who sat next to her. Why did he look so good? He smelled good, too, she thought, like sunshine.

Then she realized Katie had said something about something that happened when she was in elementary school in Indiana and Tanner . . . what?

"Tanner and I first met in Indiana, when I was in grad school," Karen said to Micah.

"He's sort of like my uncle," Katie put in.

"Were you in grad school, too?" Micah asked Tanner.

He shook his head. "Nope. Ordinary college."

"Is that where you grew up?" Sally asked. "In Indiana?" What she really wanted to know was if he and Karen had been romantically involved. Somehow she didn't think so. People who'd been lovers usually didn't turn into good buddies. Then she remembered—earlier, she stirred the orange juice while Karen finished cooking breakfast. And Tanner had opened one of the kitchen drawers to count out silverware. He didn't ask which drawer, she realized. In fact, he hadn't behaved at all like a guest.

Tanner shook his head. "No. Only school."

"Mom helped him move here to Hartley," Katie said. "He even lived with us for a while at first."

Sally's gaze shot to her friend. Tanner lived with Karen? That explained the kitchen drawer thing, but it brought up a whole heap of new questions. Maybe they *were* more than mere friends. If so, Sally thought, she had a way big problem. How to stop thinking lustful thoughts about Tanner Dodge, which she had to do anyway.

She raised her last forkful of French toast to her mouth, but stopped. Yuck. She pulled a long, black dog hair from her fork.

Karen shrugged. "Sorry. It happens."

Sally knew, from eating at Karen's before, dog hair in the food was not unusual. Still, she doubted she'd ever get used to it. Only, now—she had a dog. She'd be picking dog hair out of her food for the next however many years. What a horrible thought. She looked over at the row of obedient dogs. All those Newfoundlands had long fur. Then she looked at Sophie with her short coat. Maybe corgis didn't shed. She didn't think she was that lucky.

Katie said, "You know what Mom's friend Laurie says—and she's been an emergency room nurse for almost thirty years so she should know—she says no one ever died from eating a dog hair. Think of it as extra protein."

"Good thing," Karen added with a tired sigh. "Because around here there's always at least one."

"The one who finds it has good luck," Tanner added with a grin.

Karen turned red. "That's enough, you guys. You're embarrassing me."

"What if there isn't a dog hair?" Micah asked. He wasn't grossed out, Sally noticed, more curious. "Does that mean no one gets good luck?"

"Just because no one finds it," Tanner answered, "doesn't mean there isn't one."

How could they all make jokes about finding dog hair in their food? Sally thought.

"Hair of the dog?" Micah quipped.

"Yeah," Tanner said. Sally noticed he sent some sort of look to Karen. What was that about, she wondered. It seemed they had some shared secrets. Her spirits sank lower. It was time to change the subject. She set her fork back on her plate and turned to Tanner. "So, where did you grow up?"

"It's a mystery," Katie said with a grin. "He won't tell you. I used to try to tickle him to make him tell me, but he never would."

Tanner smiled briefly. "Used to drive you nuts."

"Still does." But Katie said it with affection. "I guess we all have deep, dark secrets." She turned to her mother and the affection was replaced by a hint of accusation. "Why is that, Mom? Why do we keep secrets from the people we love the best?"

Karen gazed steadily at her daughter. "Perhaps out of habit. Perhaps to protect ourselves, or the ones we love."

"Maybe the ones we love don't need our protection," Katie said.

Sally looked from Karen to Katie. Mother and daughter had locked gazes and looked like mirror images of each other. Something was going on here, Sally thought, something private and hurtful.

"Micah," Tanner said, "Sophie is up." Even though his words were spoken in a quiet voice, it was enough to break the sudden tension.

"Sophie," Micah said to the dog who was now at his feet, "you're supposed to be on a down stay."

Sophie gave an optimistic wag of her tail.

He gently led her by her collar back to her spot at the end of the line. "Down." He pointed to the grass. With a decided lack of enthusiasm, Sophie sank down. Micah brought the palm of his hand down in front of her nose. "Stay." Sophie put her chin on her front paws and heaved a sigh of sufferance.

"Hey, Micah," Katie said, "tell her to watch Mom's Big Dogs. They'll show her what to do."

Karen chuckled. "Don't worry, Micah," she said. "She understands what you're telling her to do. Pretty soon she'll figure out she has to obey regardless of what she wants to do."

"He's doing very well with her," Tanner said to Karen. "He should be proud."

Karen smiled at Tanner. "Thanks."

But she said it so softly Sally wasn't sure she'd heard correctly. She was sure, however, her friend and Tanner shared something special.

Fourteen

Over the next couple of days, Sally and Micah picked, pitted, and froze more than two dozen pies' worth of cherries. Sometimes, in the evenings, they were joined by one of Sally's friends, or a neighbor or two; sometimes they picked and pitted alone. Every morning, Micah did his strengthening exercises. And every day, he worked with Sophie on her obedience lessons.

Tess and Troy soon discovered the range of Sophie's reach. They each used that knowledge in their individual ways. Pretending to ignore Sophie, Tess swished her tail exactly one inch in front of the puppy's nose, teasing her, taunting her. The more Sophie barked, the more satisfaction Sally could read in Tess's eyes.

As for Troy, as soon as he discovered Sophie could not reach the aquarium he gave up watching the puppy and returned to his fish. He liked his fish. Gwendal and Marina didn't bark. They didn't have shiny, snappy white teeth. They didn't steal his food. They didn't race around the house or chew up his fur mice. Oh, no they did not. Gwendal and Marina knew their place in the world. Troy gazed approvingly at his fish and saw they were good.

Jude emerged from wherever it was he hid. He walked across the floor to meet Sophie, nose to nose, on her own level. They sniffed each other. Sophie got down on her elbows and stuck her butt in the air—Jessie said it was a play bow. From this unlikely position Sophie wagged her tail. Even Sally could read the expression on the doggy face, inviting, then pleading, and finally begging, Jude to play. Jude was not inclined to play. However, the two of them worked out their relationship on their own. Sophie treated Jude as somewhat of a stick-in-the-mud kind of pal. Jude treated Sophie with amused tolerance. When Jude entered a room he gazed around, looking for Sophie, not, as Sally thought at first, from fear but as one friend looking for another. Sally was amazed the day she came into the living room to find the two of them napping together. Sophie's head rested on Jude's belly. Sally reached down to feel under her cat's chin. Jude purred.

She looked at her fish and wondered about Karen and Tanner. She looked at Sophie and wondered about Karen and Tanner. She looked at Micah and wondered about Karen and Tanner. Her wondering had to stop. She decided to ask Jessie. Then she decided, since Jessie wasn't the most discreet person in the world, maybe she wasn't a good person to ask after all. She would think of something else. Right now, she needed chocolate.

Well, shoot! she thought, Jessie *already* figured

out Sally was interested in him. Why, Jessie was the one who invited him to pick cherries. She wouldn't have done that if he'd been involved with Karen. Besides, Sally thought, she'd known Karen since elementary school. Karen was a couple of years older than she was, so even though she knew who she was, she didn't really *know* Karen. Sally moved back to Hartley after college and a couple of years after that was when the five of them had become good friends. Jessie said they'd been Siamese quintuplets in a former life.

No. Sally put her mental foot down. There was no way Karen could be involved with someone and the rest of them not know it.

Wheee! She grabbed a handful of Leety's and whirled around the kitchen. It was a beautiful day!

Sally showed Micah how to do a water change and clean the filter intake on the aquarium. She showed him how to hold fish food—under the water, keep your hand still, be patient. Gwendal and Marina saw the unfamiliar hand in their water. They observed it from different angles until they decided it was not a threat, and, best of all, this new hand held food. The goldfish knew what to do with food. "It tickles," Micah said.

In the evenings Sally and Micah sat in the living room and watched movies. They ate cherry pie. Cherry cobbler. Sally made cherry jam, which they ate on buttered toast. They gave the crusts to Sophie, who was not particular. They made a special piece, with lots of butter, for the cats, who were.

On Wednesday morning, she made an extra pie to take to Tanner that evening, when they went to

Micah's lesson. Then she thought she probably shouldn't take it to him. She didn't want him to think she was trying to impress him with her domesticity, even if she was. Then she told herself it was merely the friendly act of anyone who had an abundance of cherries. If she had anything, it was an abundance of cherries.

That night she brought a book, but again, she couldn't keep her eyes off him.

An insistent noise woke Sally on Thursday morning. The telephone. Sally wrenched her eyes open and looked at the clock. "Who could be calling at seven in the morning?" she muttered through a yawn as she reached for the phone. She accidentally dislodged Tess from her regular place on Sally's pillow. The cat glared at her, stretched, and closed her eyes. Whoever it was, the cat's demeanor said, was certainly rude.

It was Sylvie.

"Hey, Sal, you wanna come to the hospital and meet the little boogaloo?"

Suddenly Sally was wide awake. "You had the baby?" she screamed. "You had your baby?"

"He's three hours old and he's perfect."

Sally took a two-minute shower, pulled on clothes, and dragged a comb through her hair. She brushed her teeth. She scribbled a short note to Micah and stuck it on the refrigerator. "Sorry, kitties," she said to them as she grabbed her purse and fished out her keys. "You'll have to wait for breakfast till I get back. I gotta get to the hospital."

She blew three kisses to the cats, and two for the fish, as she practically floated out the door.

Thank goodness, Sally thought as she wound her way through the streets of Hartley, the maternity ward was enlightened enough to have relaxed visiting hours. The hospital parking lot left much to be desired, though. She drove past the rows and rows of empty spots reserved for physicians and was practically out of the city limits and into the county before she came to visitor parking. Evidently, the hospital believed visitors would enjoy a long walk on their way to the entrance. Sally took it at a near trot, and was out of breath by the time she found her way to the maternity ward and skidded to a stop in front of Sylvie's door. She looked in.

She saw her friend Sylvie. The same Sylvie who put flowers in food, and forgot about spaghetti sauce on the stove while she went to the store so the pot burned past redemption, who named her poodle after a bald guy and then clipped his coat to look like a topiary, Sylvie who met her husband when she fell off her roof and landed on top of him, Sylvie who was unfairly naturally slender, with her flowing red hair looked like she should have the starring role in *Riverdance.* Sylvie sat propped up in one of those hospital beds, wearing a lacy bed jacket. In her arms she held, as if holding the whole world, a wrapped bundle. She was looking down at it and singing softly. She looked like every picture of the Madonna Sally had ever seen. Then Sylvie stopped her song and looked up to see Sally and she smiled.

Sally was filled with a rush of tears. "Oh," was all she could say. "Oh, Sylvie."

Then she was at her friend's side, hugging her close, careful of the baby in Sylvie's arms.

"Can I hold him?" she breathed.

"Of course." And Sylvie held out her son.

Sally blinked away her tears and carefully took Sylvie's baby. He was tiny and miraculous. He had lots of black hair, his face was all scrunched and splotchy from being born, his eyes were closed tight. Sylvie was right. He was perfect. Sally fell instantly in love with him. Careful not to disturb him, she refolded the bit of blanket so it better haloed his head.

"He has all his fingers and toes," Sylvie said. "Ray counted them at least a dozen times to make sure."

"Where is Ray?"

"He was up all night with me, so I finally sent him home to take Jean-Luc out and to get some sleep."

"What is his name?" Sally asked, still gazing in wonder at the miracle in her arms.

"Don't know yet. I wanted to look at him for a while before we decided for sure. I was sure he was going to be a girl, so we were going to name her Avalon, after one of my favorite art teachers."

"I hope you don't name him Merlin or Lancelot or Gawaine. Not even as a middle name." She tossed Sylvie a half-teasing glare. But only half teasing. She didn't think Ray would do such a thing—he had more sense than Sylvie did sometimes—but Sylvie had strange ideas about names. After all, she named her poodle after a bald guy. Who knew what she'd come up with for a baby.

Sylvie smiled beatifically. "No promises."

Sally looked down once more at the sleeping baby in her arms. "Oh, Sylvie, he's gorgeous," she breathed. "He's absolutely gorgeous. Name him Mel."

Sally also sang songs to the sleeping baby. "Twinkle Twinkle Little Star," and "Be Kind to Your Web-footed Friends," the fast-food song, and "Oh Hey Oh Hi Hello," that song about Ohio by Jim Gill which was the first song she taught her kindergartners at the beginning of every school year. The baby slept through them all. "You have to let me come over and sing to him at least once a week, so he develops a well-rounded musical vocabulary," she said. "You can give him all the classical stuff— Mozart is supposed to be good brain food you know—but I can teach him the songs real kids sing."

"But not those ones about dirty underwear," Sylvie said. "They're gross."

Sally gave her a look of pretend indignation. "Those are both Boy Scout songs, I'll have you know, and not the least bit subversive. Unlike the one you were singing to him when I got here." Reluctantly, she gave the baby back to Sylvie.

Sylvie sent her a slightly smug, saintly smile. "My mother sang that to me every night when I went to bed. I turned out okay. Besides, it's some kind of a hymn, I think, with words by Blake, and it was written a long time ago. No one protests the industrialization of England anymore—it's a lost cause."

"Still, it's an odd choice for a bedtime song. Whatever happened to good night, sleep tight, don't let the bedbugs bite? Course, it does end with that violent part, but you could always leave that part off and he'd never know the difference." She pulled a chair up next to the bed and perched on the edge of the seat, leaning her elbows on the bed so she could see the baby as he slept. "He's so perfect and pure. I could watch him breathe forever."

Sylvie nodded. "I could, too." Then she looked at Sally. "Is this how you felt when Micah was born?"

Sally nodded. She couldn't speak for the sudden lump in her throat.

"I thought so," Sylvie said in a cloggy voice. "I wonder if this is how my mom felt when I was born."

"I'm sure it is." Sally reached for a tissue and wiped her eyes.

Sylvie nodded. Without a word, Sally handed her the box of tissues. Sylvie took one and set the box on the bed between them. "After Ray left, before you arrived, I was sitting here, looking at my baby. My baby. And he's so tiny and he can't do anything for himself yet." She blew her nose. "Suddenly, I was absolutely terrified because I thought what would happen to him if I died before he's grown? Then I wondered if my mom had that same thought when my brothers and I were born. And Ray's mom. And Deb. And then they all did die, and they had to leave us and I know they must have absolutely hated that. I know how they must have felt. And it terrified me."

"Because you'd miss him, wouldn't be able to watch him grow up?" Sally handed her another tissue.

Sylvie shook her head. "Damn," she muttered, "I wish I could cry gracefully." She blew her nose again. "Because I wouldn't be able to protect him. And I don't mean I don't think Ray would. Ray would die for him. But I'm his mother. His mother." One of her tears dropped on the baby's head and she gently thumbed it away. Or maybe she rubbed it in. She turned her watery gaze on Sally. "I'm so glad Micah has you."

Sally smeared away her own tears and her friend handed her a tissue and Sally made good use of it. "I'm glad I have Micah."

"Is there anything you need me to do?" she asked before she left. "Anyone you need me to call, whatever, just let me know. Oh. Sylvie, are you sure you turned off the stove before you left for the hospital?"

"We're fine," Sylvie said as she reached out to hug Sally. "And would you believe it, as soon as we pulled out of the driveway I started worrying about the stove, so Ray stopped the car and ran back in the house to check for me. It was off. But if we need anything, we'll call. I promise." And Sally knew she would.

On the way home, Sally pulled up to the curb

next to a small city park and turned off the engine. She thought about the day Micah was born. She thought about Deb becoming a mother. Most people became mothers by giving birth. Micah wasn't a baby anymore, and Sally hadn't paid her dues by going through a labor and delivery—at least, not directly—but as far as she was concerned, her responsibility for Micah was as permanent as stone, and would last as long as they both lived. Not out of duty, out of love.

By the time Sally walked through her front door, the tears on her cheeks had dried into streaks. She heard Micah and Sophie in the backyard. She called out, to let him know she was home. Tess, crouched on the catwalk over the door to the dining room, shot her a regal scowl.

"I'm sorry, Tessie, I know you had to wait for your breakfast. But look, I'm opening the can now." Tess ran lightly down the cat ramp to wind around Sally's legs. Troy stuck his head in the kitchen and joined Tess in the rub-around. Even Jude appeared, seemingly out of nowhere.

All three cats leaped onto the counter. Sally set their bowls in their places. Without a word of thanks—after all, gourmet cat food was merely their due—they ate.

She wandered into the living room. Marina and Gwendal rushed to the top corner of the aquarium where Sally always fed them. "Here you go, fishies," she told them. She held a pellet in the water. Gwendal took it from her fingers. Sally made sure Marina got the next one. She fed them five pieces each. That was all they were allowed to have for breakfast. They were still hungry. Goldfish were always hungry.

She stood by the aquarium for a few minutes, idly watching her fish without really seeing them. The fish watched her, as always on the lookout for something else to eat. This time they were out of luck. She had something important to do. She stuffed a stack of tissues into her pocket. Then she went into the backyard, into the heat of the morning.

Micah tossed a glance at her before throwing the ball again for Sophie.

Sally sat down on a lawn chair and patted the chair next to her. "Come. Sit. There are things I need to tell you, and I'm going to be . . . um . . . emotional. So I need your attention." Rats. She didn't mean to sound like a teacher.

Micah gave her a long look. Then he sat. Sophie came, too, bouncing up with her slobbery ball in her mouth, sure Sally would give her a warm welcome. Sally gave her a welcome, but it was short.

Sally looked into Micah's eyes, searching for the boy she knew. She wanted to hold his hands while she talked to him about this, but he was a boy, and boys didn't like to see great shows of emotion. Boys didn't like other people to know what they were feeling. Sally wondered briefly how boys ever survived emotionally. But it was time to begin.

"I was with your parents, in the birthing room, when you were born," Sally said. "I don't know if you knew that, or maybe you did, but you might have forgotten. You were born at four o'clock in the afternoon. As soon as you came out, they put you on your mom's belly while your dad cut the cord; then the nurses took you and weighed you, and sort of wiped you off. Put a bracelet on your arm. Made your footprints. Did those kinds of things. Right in the room. Then they gave you back to your mom. She looked at you, really looked at you, and she cried. Your dad cried. I cried." Sally felt her eyes overflow again and she pulled out a tissue to blow her nose.

Micah wouldn't meet her eyes. He wasn't even looking anywhere near her. His face was turned towards the backyard, towards Sophie, who was snuffling around under the cherry trees, looking for fallen fruit.

"Your eyes were open and you were looking around. The lights in the room were dim. Then you saw your mother. She started talking to you—I forget exactly what she said, but your eyes latched on to her face and both of your thumbs went right into your mouth. You sucked your thumbs and you stared and stared at her while she talked to you. Then, after a while, the nurses came back in to clean up your mom and move her to a regular room, so your dad and I took you to the nursery. We sat in these rocking chairs and took turns rocking you, singing to you. Your dad sang Pink Floyd. I sang nursery rhymes. Then you fell asleep and we held you while you slept, watching you breathe." With the palm of her hand she smeared the tears off her cheeks. Micah still hadn't met her gaze, and except for one small, secret swipe at his eyes, he hadn't moved. The lump in her throat was the size of the moon, but she had one more thing to tell him—the most important thing of all. "Your mom said the day you were born was the happiest day of her life."

With a strangled sound, Micah made an ungainly move out of the chair. He lost his balance, reached blindly for the table to steady himself, and pushed his way into the house, sliding the glass door firmly shut behind him. Sophie trotted over to the patio to stare after him. Sally picked up the abandoned tennis ball and threw it. Sophie tore off, grabbed it up, and rushed back with it so Sally would throw it again. Sally threw the ball over and over until Sophie was panting heavily. "That's enough. You're worn out and you won't admit it," she said as she put the ball on the table.

Sophie threw herself down on the patio and shoved her short little legs straight out behind her. "You're doing your frog imitation," Sally told her. The dog, still panting with her mouth drawn wide to take in more air, answered her with a couple of token tail wags.

Sally sat outside for a long time, going over, again and again, the day Micah was born. That was the day Deb asked her to be Micah's guardian and she had said yes.

Thursday, after a quick sandwich for lunch, Tanner dropped down into his desk chair. He absently tapped a pencil on his desk.

"What's got you?" Jake asked.

Tanner tossed the pencil onto his desk. "Maxie."

"Ah. The brilliant one."

"The brilliant one who is a little stiff in the rear."

"Oh."

"Yeah."

"Maybe it's nothing. What does Melissa say?"

"Hasn't seen her yet. On Friday I thought I saw Maxie hesitate on the steps at the mall, but I wasn't sure. I checked her out and couldn't find anything obvious. This morning, though, she seemed a little sore when she stood up." Tanner nodded. "Yup. It's very slight, but it's definitely there. I guess it's time to make a visit to Hartley's best vet." With a sigh, he reached for the telephone. Before he could pick it up, it rang.

"Tanner," Sally's voice lost none of its usual warmth over the phone. "I'm sorry to call you at work, but . . . would it be possible for me to come talk to you this evening about Micah?"

Tanner thought. "I teach classes until nine. Karen is my assistant instructor, but she can't be here tonight, so it might take me longer to finish up. If you don't mind waiting until after then . . ."

"That would be fine. Um . . . Karen said you'd be a good person to talk to."

"Oh. Then I'll see you this evening." He didn't want to say goodbye yet. "By the way, thanks again for that cherry pie. It was great."

"I'm glad you liked it." She sounded like she was smiling.

There was nothing more he could say. "Well, 'bye."

After he hung up the phone, he sat and stared

at it. He realized he was looking forward to seeing her.

"Thickening plot?" Jake asked.

"What? Oh." He'd forgotten Jake was there.

"Did I actually hear Tanner Dodge make a date?"

"No. Nothing like that."

"Then like what?"

"It's this woman. I'm helping this orphaned kid, teenager, who has a puppy who needs to learn manners. Anyway, this woman is the kid's guardian. She wants to talk to me about him."

Jake grinned. "Which explains why you sort of leaned into the phone while you were talking to her."

"No." Tanner gave him a disgusted look.

"Yes. Remember, I'm a master of reading body language."

Tanner looked at his friend. "Go torture some grape Kool-Aid or something."

But after Jake whistled his way down the hall, Tanner tipped back in his chair and thought about leaning into Sally's voice.

That evening, while he fed Aretha, he realized he'd forgotten to call the vet.

Fifteen

Sally came to the pole barn early. She wanted to see Tanner interact with a class. She told herself it was merely professional curiosity—one teacher observing the methods of another. She slipped in the door and sat down in one of the old easy chairs in the book corner.

In the middle of the room, twelve people, each with a dog, were arranged in a large circle, trying to teach their dogs to do a down. Some dogs caught on, some dogs didn't. Sally wondered if it was the other way around—maybe some of the *people* caught on, and other *people* didn't. She watched Tanner work with a middle-aged woman and her dog. The woman didn't have a clue, Sally realized, but the woman's dog had it already figured out. Tanner was calm, patient, showed the woman yet again what to do. This time she did it correctly. Tanner nodded. He was too far away for Sally to hear what he told the woman, but she beamed. Sally could almost see her grow two inches. Tanner was a fine teacher.

At five minutes till nine, Tanner excused the

class. People and dogs swarmed over to the benches to gather up their things, chattering all the while. Some, mostly female and young, stayed behind to talk to Tanner, including one very pretty young lady who couldn't take her eyes off him. Sally knew how she felt.

Tanner looked over to Sally and gave her a short wave. The cluster of students all looked, too. They wanted to see what their teacher found interesting. They all stared at her for a moment before they turned back to the object of their adoration. The very pretty one stared at Sally for a longer moment before she, too, decided Sally, who did not even have a dog, was not a threat and turned her attention back to Tanner.

"The god of all things dog," Sally murmured to herself.

When even the very pretty one had left, Tanner came over to Sally. "Sorry," he said with an apologetic grin. "Sometimes they have lots of questions . . ."

"No problem." She smiled back at him.

He shoved his hands in his jeans pockets. "It's hot in here—let's go out on the porch to talk."

She followed him out the door and up the steps to a porch where two Adirondack chairs sandwiched a small, round redwood table.

Well, Sally thought, here she was, ready to talk, and Tanner was ready to listen. The night was warm, the sky was clear. A bug zapper gave off a faint yellow glow against the dark.

"Where's Wing?" she asked, mostly because she didn't know how to start.

"Inside." Tanner leaned over to open a door wide enough for Wing to brush out. Wing greeted Tanner effusively. She even turned to Sally to give her a nod.

Sally nodded back to Wing, who wandered off down the steps out into the country night, as if giving them privacy, Sally thought.

"This might take a while, to tell it all," she said, giving him an out.

"I'll listen." He didn't take it.

"You might have heard some of this from Karen or Jessie."

"I can hear it again from you."

Sally started to speak. "I don't remember a time when Micah was not in motion. Kevin went to OSU on a hockey scholarship. He knew he wasn't good enough to play professionally, but he wanted the education. He earned his degree in architecture. And he married my very best friend. Anyway, for Micah's second birthday, they gave him a pair of skates. I never knew they even made skates that small! They looked like little toy doll skates. And a helmet. They put this miniature helmet and these itty bitty skates on this two-year-old kid—still in diapers—and he took off. He went zooming around the ice rink. I swear he knew how to skate before he was born. Maybe he learned by osmosis. I don't mean to sound overly dramatic, but from the first moment they put those skates on that kid, he didn't want to get off that ice. Ice was his own special biome. He'd rather be on the ice than anywhere else in the world. He was manic about it. And he never fell down. *Never.*

"When he was almost four, Deb and Kevin moved back to Vermont. Kevin found a men's hockey league—just for fun. Micah had to play, too, so they signed him up and he started playing hockey with a team of other preschoolers. They're called mites." She chuckled at the memory. "Micah was a mighty mite. I remember the first time I saw him play. I went up to Vermont for Thanksgiving that year, the week Micah turned four. He had a hockey game. These little kids on the ice—most of them were so small their moms tied their jerseys around their waists.

"You could tell, right away, Micah was different. He wasn't a skating helmet, like the others. He was a four-year-old kid playing real hockey. Every summer he and his mom came back to Hartley for two weeks. Well, he was here for a week; then we drove him over to Bowling Green for hockey camp. Later in the summer he went to another hockey camp up in Canada. Micah was going to play for the NHL someday. It wasn't opinion, or a topic for discussion, it was a cold hard fact. We knew it, and Micah knew it. He wasn't a snob about it. To him, hockey was like breathing. It was what he did. It was his life.

"Now it's gone. He won't talk about it, never brings it up. He hasn't even put up his hockey posters. He has about a dozen of them. They were all over the walls in his room in Vermont. Now, here, they're in a mailing tube in his closet. It's as if hockey gave him a definition—he was a hockey player. Now, because of his spinal cord injury, he doesn't have that anymore. On top of losing his parents, and moving here—but *he* didn't move here, someone else moved him here. It was done to him, he was the object, not the subject, of the sentence." She shot him a quick grin of apology. "Sorry. My kindergarten teacher persona is showing.

"Thing is, he wears T-shirts with hockey slogans and team logos on them. So I know he's thinking about it. But he also always wears blue jeans, no matter how hot it is, to cover up his braces. Up in Cleveland, when he was at the rehab center, one of the therapists talked to him about all kinds of adaptive sports, but he won't have anything to do with them." She remembered the girl in the wheelchair who played sled hockey. "Karen says he's processing."

"What would you like me to do?" Tanner asked.

Sally blinked in surprise. "I don't know if there's anything you can *do*. I guess, more than anything else, I needed to talk. And I thought it might be good for you to know this—you know, because you're working with Micah. Besides, Karen said you worked with people who had gone through life-altering experiences so you'd probably understand him."

She glanced at him. The expression in his eyes was soft as a caress. Their gazes held each other like lovers. In the faint yellow glow they were the sum of existence. The rest of the world, in the dark, did not even exist. She was aware that Tanner was so close she could almost feel him. No more was he merely the phantom, the insubstantial specter who tantalized her in her dreams at night. He was real. She knew his skin was warm and smooth. She could reach out and touch that skin if she wanted to. Explore the whole expanse of his warm skin if she wanted to. He would explore her, for she had become beautiful. In his eyes she read seduction. In her eyes she knew he read acceptance.

Wing hurtled herself up the stairs. The world in the faint yellow glow shattered. Tail wagging, Wing flopped down on the porch and panted.

Sally blinked. It was over. She wasn't beautiful after all. She was only herself. Dummy! she mentally chastised herself. What was she thinking? Her imagination was working overtime. She swung a mental hammer to pound those feelings down deep into the dirt. She had no right to think of herself right now. No right to do anything to complicate the relationship Micah had with Tanner. If Sally came on to Tanner, that would create a complication. Micah needed help. She had no right to think only of herself at a time like this. She had to stay focused on Micah, not follow her own animal instincts. Thank goodness Wing had interrupted them, or who knew what would have happened.

Sally needed that hammer back. Quickly. How embarrassing! She'd practically thrown herself at him just now, imagining she read seduction in his eyes.

Tanner cleared his throat. "You're saying Micah is searching for an identity?"

Thank goodness for the dark—he wouldn't see her blush. "Um . . . Yeah. On top of the normal teenage angst stuff. He doesn't seem to have any interest in meeting new kids his age—or even in spending time with the kids he used to. You know, when he was here in the summers. I'm afraid when school starts he's going to have a difficult time." Sally felt herself grow warm.

"It might be difficult to meet new kids if he feels like he doesn't have an identity." Tanner spoke quietly, without judgment, as he did so much of the time. That was one of the things Sally liked about him—his voice and the way he used it. "If he's self-conscious about his braces it'll be even more difficult."

"You think when he knows more about who he is that he'll find it easier to make friends?"

Tanner nodded. "It's a thing to hope for, at any rate."

"Then how do I help him find out who he is?"

"By giving him as many opportunities as possible to try new things. What did he do in the summers, other than hockey camp?"

"He's always been on the move. We used to joke that he was a perpetual-motion kid without an 'Off' button." She grinned at the memory. "Once school was out he practically lived at the ice rink. If he couldn't get there, he'd shoot baskets, ride his bike, or his roller blades. Now he and I watch videos at night. It's good for *our* bonding, I guess, and it keeps his mind occupied so he doesn't think about the accident, but I'm not so sure it's good for him. I never thought I'd say it, but I'm really glad he has Sophie. Doing things with her, the things you've taught him, gives him something constructive to do every day. Besides his physical therapy exercises."

Tanner was silent for a moment. "Would you say he has a competitive streak?"

She nodded. "Always has. He wants to be the best at everything he does, he has to be perfect—and he usually is. At least, he usually was. I'm afraid he thinks he doesn't have anything to be best at anymore."

Tanner leaned back in his chair, tented his fingers, and gazed at Wing, stretched out on the porch. "If Micah wanted to compete in obedience with Sophie," he said slowly, as if feeling his way, "his braces wouldn't be an issue."

Sally frowned. "They wouldn't?"

Tanner shook his head. "Obedience is not about how fast or how high. It's about how close you can come to perfection, which is described in a written set of rules. The highest marks will go to the one who is closest to the ideal. Some days everyone passes, other days everyone fails. Micah wouldn't have to be the fastest, or the strongest. He *could* be the closest to the ideal." He snapped his fingers. "Come to think of it, there's a woman up in Michigan who competes in a wheelchair, with a Cardigan Welsh corgi." Tanner looked at her at last. His eyes were shining in the dim light. "You say Micah always wants to be the best. This is an area where—if he worked at it—I think he could excel."

Sally sat in thought. "I wonder," she said. If Micah could get excited about this, if he could succeed—and Tanner seemed convinced he could—maybe he'd feel like he had his life back, or at least a life.

"It would take a lot of work," Tanner continued. He caught her gaze again, and held it. Now, even though the intensity was the same, the sensuality was absent. "It would take a lot of work and time on your part, too. You would have to take Micah and Sophie to matches and trials all over the state. You would have to spend many weekends at dog shows. That means you'd spend lots of time with Micah and Sophie, but you'd also be surrounded by lots of other dogs, and lots of other people who talk about nothing but dogs." He seemed to search her soul for the truth. "Are you willing to do that?"

Sally had to escape from his gaze. He saw too much of her. She was afraid he wouldn't like what he saw. She closed her eyes and leaned back in the chair. Even so, she wasn't free of him. If she opened her eyes she'd be caught again. Deep cleansing breath, she told herself, in and out. Now another, until she was calm. "You didn't ask me how I *felt* about it," she said without opening her eyes. "You asked me if I was willing."

"That's right. They're different things. My dog teacher persona is showing."

Sally smiled at his use of Jessie's joke. "If Micah wants to do this, I am willing." She opened her eyes to see the approval in his eyes.

"I knew you would," he said, almost as if to himself.

Oh my, Sally thought, they were going to have another one of those earth-stopping moments.

Just then, Wing sprang up to scratch insistently at the door to Tanner's apartment.

Sally heard a tiny sound—a sound she recognized. "Kitten?"

Tanner pulled away from her and held still for

a moment. Then he nodded. "Yes, kitten. I guess she's awake and hungry. You want to meet Aretha?" He opened the door and Sally followed him into his home.

She hadn't thought before about where he would live. But whatever she'd imagined would be nothing like this. The room ran the width of the pole barn, and was about twelve feet deep. On one wall was the kitchen area, with a door Sally guessed led to a bathroom. There was a sleeping area with a hanging rack for shirts and an unfinished dresser. Sally would not allow her gaze to linger on the neatly made bed. On the other side of the room was a table—made out of a door, Sally realized, a door on legs. There was a computer on the table and a neat pile of papers that looked like bills. An old office chair. On the fourth wall was a small television and shelves full of neatly stacked books and a few videotapes. The only thing that looked spontaneous was a jam jar crammed with ribbons—most of them green. Sally knew these were ribbons Tanner had won at dog shows. Finally, by that fourth wall was a small sofa, old and worn.

It was neat and utilitarian, nothing was out of place, nothing extraneous. Wing stood by a dog kennel, staring at the noise coming from inside.

Tanner opened the latch of the kennel and out shot a black-and-white ball of screaming fluff. Tanner picked it up and showed it to Wing. "She's fine," he told the dog. Then he nuzzled the little thing briefly. "I want you to meet Sally," he told her. "She loves kitties." Then he turned to Sally. "Sally, this is Aretha."

Instinctively, Sally reached out for the kitten. "She's so tiny!" she exclaimed, hugging the wee thing close. The wee thing had a loud purr.

"She was about ten days old when Wing and I found her. Her mother had abandoned her. Yeah, she's tiny now, but she's twice as big as she was and she's growing like a weed. Hold onto her while I fix her bottle."

"You hand-raised her? By yourself?"

"Wing does a lot of it. Melissa says she's in excellent health—but can't test her for leukemia until she's bigger and they can get blood out of her arm."

Sally petted the kitten on her tiny head. The kitten's purr was loud and emphatic. "Hey, little one, look. Your bottle is ready."

Tanner reached for her. As soon as the kitten saw the bottle coming, she lunged towards it, using both paws to clutch it tightly, eagerly sucking, all the while making little wild animal noises. Suddenly, she lost the nipple. She flailed around furiously. Tanner chuckled as he helped her find it. "She eats solid food now—she isn't sure she approves of it yet—but I still give her a bottle in the evening."

Sally watched in wonder. This man was full of surprises.

After Aretha was fed, Tanner cleaned her up—a process that left her wet from being held under the faucet while he rubbed her bottom with a warm washcloth. "We're still working on the litter box thing. Right now she doesn't approve of that, either." He set her down on the floor right in front of Wing.

Sally's gut clenched. Her heart pounded. "You're not nervous about your dog around the kitten?"

"No. Of course not. Wing is very protective of her."

It was all Sally could do not to cry out when Wing put her paw on the kitten, trapping her, holding her down. Sally had a sudden vision of another dog holding down another kitten. No! This was different. See, she told herself, the kitten is not afraid. Wing is washing the kitten.

Still, Sally held her breath, ready to snatch the kitten up at the least sign of trouble. There was no trouble. The kitten seemed to be used to the dog holding her down. Used to the dog's tongue. In fact the kitten took it all in stride. The kitten was not afraid of the dog.

Tanner gave her a slight frown. "Lighten up. Wing would never hurt her."

Sally nodded. Intellectually she knew he was speaking the truth. But her heart still pounded. Adrenaline still rushed through her. A vision of a kitten long ago insinuated itself into the front of her mind—no. She refused to think about that night, that kitten. Shove that memory back down where it belongs. Think about this kitten, here, now.

Only when Wing finished bathing the kitten, when the kitten clambered to her feet, shook her head, and scampered away to swarm up the bedspread, was Sally able to relax. She saw Tanner looking at her curiously, but this was something Sally was never going to talk about. She hadn't talked about it in almost twenty-five years and she wasn't going to talk about it now. Besides, she had to get home to Micah. If she stayed any later her car would turn into a pumpkin. So she said, "Will you talk to Micah about this obedience thing? If you think he can really do it."

"Sure. And yes, I think he really can do it. If he wants to." Tanner still had that speculative look on his face when she climbed into her car and waved good night.

As soon as she was home, Sophie leaped up and rushed over to see her. Micah, watching a video and sharing his popcorn with Sophie and the cats, gave her a brief hello. The cats acknowledged her presence from their royal perches. Sophie's tail was going full speed. Sally looked down at Sophie. She might have short little legs, and huge, funny-looking ears, but at least she was up-front and honest about her emotions. Sally tried to imagine a Sophie who was as obedient and well behaved as Wing. She discovered she actually liked Sophie whether she was well behaved or not.

"Hey, Micah," she said, "if we could find a way to hook a generator to that tail, this dog could probably produce enough electricity to provide power for a third-world nation."

Tanner sat on his porch, staring into the night. Sally's reaction to Aretha and Wing was way out of proportion. Her reaction was not that of someone

who was simply unfamiliar with dogs. She had re-
acted as someone who'd had a frightening experience with one. Tanner wondered what had
happened to frighten her. It wasn't idle curiosity.
He was in danger here. He was in serious danger
of falling in love with her. Even if she liked dogs
it would be a mistake to fall in love with her. Add
her obvious fear and he only asked for disaster.
Years ago, a dog had saved his life. Now his life
was committed to dogs.

A relationship with Sally Foster was out of the
question.

Sixteen

Friday morning Tanner called the vet clinic.

"I'm sorry, Tanner," Suzette said, "we don't have an opening until next week. We're closed on Monday and Tuesday, for Hartley Days. Melissa's going to do her Tuesday surgeries on Wednesday. How about Thursday afternoon at three o'clock?"

Tanner marked the master calendar. He was thoroughly disgusted with himself for allowing his personal life to interfere with his professional responsibility to a dog. No cookies for you, he told himself, and stop thinking of Sally. He tried, but it was like pink elephants. Hopeless as it was, he could think of nothing else. He gave up. He set the timer and let himself think of her for three minutes. That should help get all these thoughts and half-expressed wishes out of his system. When the timer dinged, it was time to go to the dogs.

He pulled the wheelchair out of the cupboard and unfolded it. He sat down in the wheelchair and rolled himself towards the kennels. Some dogs spooked the first time they saw people in wheelchairs. Maxie, of course, behaved as if she'd been born next to a wheelchair. Her kennel mate, Mystery, took it all in stride after a thorough sniffing of the chair. It took Melody a few minutes to figure out where he had to be in relationship to the chair so he wasn't accidentally run over, but was still close enough to do his job. Today it was Murphy's turn to meet the chair.

On his way down the hall, he met Corinne and Aspen coming towards him. Corinne's lap was piled high with a stack of dark blue T-shirts, all imprinted with the school logo in lime green. One of their big benefactors had donated the money for two hundred T-shirts to be worn by staff and volunteers for various publicity events. The benefactor had also decided upon the color scheme. Tanner did not think much of this decision. Neither did Corinne. Patti, however, used the word *luscious*. But then, as Corinne said, what could you expect of someone who turned innocent grape Kool-Aid into purple toxic muck?

"How are plans for The Parade?" he asked. One of Corinne's many hats was parade coordinator. She wore it well.

"It'll be great. Everyone I asked said yes. Now remember, we're meeting at the shopping center at ten o'clock. That'll give us time to water the dogs and give everyone a new T-shirt." She looked at one of the shirts in her lap and grimaced. "I keep telling myself, it was very generous of him to donate all these shirts. The new pamphlets arrived from the printer's, so we'll hand them out along the way. Several volunteers are stationed along the route to help out in case it gets too hot for some of the younger puppies. So, are you walking with Maxie in The Parade?" Corinne asked.

"No." He hadn't mentioned his concerns about Maxie to anyone but Jake. He hadn't thought about which dog he'd walk with in The Parade. He decided on the spot. "I think I'll take Murphy."

Corinne's eyes widened. "Not take Maxie, the Perfect Dog?"

He ignored her teasing tone. "That's exactly it. She's already perfect. Murphy isn't. He could use the experience."

Corinne continued down the hall, shaking her head and muttering about the mysterious ways of those who trained dogs.

Tanner watched Murphy carefully all morning. He wasn't a perfect dog like Maxie. She was intuitive; he was a bit dense. She was content to do the same task over and over again. Once Murphy had a task figured out, unless he was kept in check he liked to try his own variations. The trainers could pair Maxie with almost anyone. Murphy would probably do best paired with someone who had some experience with dogs, or someone who could quickly learn how to outthink this one.

Saturday morning, bright and early, Jessie called. "Sagan was set to fly into Columbus today," she said, "only, my car just fell apart last night with all sorts of steam and stuff pouring out, so I don't know how I'm going to get there."

"Of course I'll take you," Sally said. "How soon do you have to leave?"

Micah didn't want to go. Sally didn't want to leave him home alone for several hours while she drove halfway across the state.

Micah rolled his eyes and reminded her he was old enough to stay by himself. He promised her he'd be fine. The phone numbers of all her friends were on the speed dial. Anyway, he said, it's not as if he had anywhere to go. He'd stay home and surf the net, or read, or play ball with Sophie.

Sally narrowed her eyes and looked at him closely. She didn't tell him he'd have lots of places to go if he'd put forth the slightest effort to make some friends.

"I'll be fine. Honest," he said. "Sophie will protect me, won't you, Soph?"

She had to believe him. Still, she stooped down to lecture Sophie. She tried to scowl, and speak to Sophie in a stern voice, so she would understand this was important, but it was impossible to scowl in the face of Sophie's exuberance. She gave up and grinned at the puppy. "You take care of Micah, and the cats, and the goldies, or else. You hear?"

Sophie wagged her tail.

Jessie bubbled with excitement the whole way down to Columbus. She practically bounced up and down on the seat.

"Knock it off," Sally said at last. "You're acting like a kindergartner."

"Then you ought to be used to it," was the answer. But Jessie did settle down, limiting herself to tapping her foot. "Okay. I'll quit bouncing. Let's talk about something else. How're things going with Tanner?"

"Things?"

Jessie looked at her closely. "Don't be coy. I know you're aware of the famous Tanner Dodge spell. Every female who has anything to do with dogs is halfway in love with him. You ought to see them at dog shows while he's in the ring. It's almost obnoxious."

Sally didn't pretend she didn't know what Jessie meant. But she was puzzled about one thing. "Why do all these women go gaga over him? I don't get it. He's not all that good-looking."

"True." Jessie nodded. "But there's some mystery about his past—no one knows what it is. And then something happens when he's with Wing. I don't know what it is, but it's real." She looked closely at Sally again. "You can't tell me you haven't noticed it."

"Usually when Micah has his lesson I bring a book to read."

Jessie snorted.

"Okay," Sally confessed. "I've noticed it. I have no clue how to explain it either, though."

"There's something odd about Tanner with all these women hanging all over him all the time, though," Jessie said. "His Tanner fans. He never takes advantage of them. Not ever. And it's not because they don't try. It's as if he's not interested. And I know he's not gay."

"Then what is it?" Sally had to ask. "Maybe he's really a monk in disguise. Maybe he took a vow of celibacy."

Jessie shot her a withering look. "I really don't think so. Karen knows something, though—she's known him longer than anyone. But she won't talk about it. Believe me, I've tried to worm it out of her."

Sally chuckled. She knew Jessie's worming capabilities. "What does she say?"

"Nothing. She shuts up tighter than the jaws of a pit bull. She says Tanner is who he is and that's all there is to it. All there is to it. Yeah, right. And I'm the Queen of Sheba."

Sally was glad she was driving so she could pretend to watch carefully for the signs to Columbus while she casually asked, "Was there ever anything between Tanner and Karen?"

"What? You mean like a relationship?"

"Well, yeah."

Jessie was silent. Sally knew the thoughts were swirling around in her brain because whenever Jessie thought seriously about something, she made all sorts of interesting faces.

"I don't think so," she said at last. "But I wouldn't swear to it."

Sally nodded. "Yeah. Me, too."

"I know they're not involved *now*. Karen and I have both assisted with some of his classes. Believe me, if they were involved romantically, I'd know. I don't think they were involved way back when. I mean, if they'd been lovers or something a long time ago, it's not likely they'd be as comfortable around each other as they are."

Sally nodded. "Yeah."

"But at the same time, there's this communication thing they have with each other. You don't get that from being ordinary friends. Even extra ordinary friends." She thought some more. "I know Karen loves Tanner. And she's one of the people he trusts the most." She scrunched her eyes while she thought some more. "I think they have a kind of sibling-like relationship. Yeah. That's it. I think they sort of adopted each other as siblings when Karen was in grad school, because Katie used to call him her Honorary Uncle Tanner. So. It looks like you don't have to worry about the turf thing."

Good, Sally told herself.

Sally looked around the small airport freight office. It looked the same as it had when she picked up Sophie. Same magazines, even older now. Jessie, having forgotten about Tanner, drummed her fingers.

"Here." Sally shoved a tattered magazine at her. "Read about 101 ways to recycle your Christmas tree."

Jessie waved the magazine away. "Can't read. Too nervous."

Sally found she looked forward to meeting the puppy, too. Hmmm. It must be because baby anythings, even puppies, were cute.

They waited. Finally, the airplane was on the ground, unloaded, and they heard the *beep beep beep* of a truck backing up. The chewing gum guy disappeared into the back. He returned a moment later with a small dog kennel.

"Ooooh," Jessie breathed. She took the kennel

as if it were the greatest treasure in the world. She set it down in the middle of the floor and opened it up. "Hello, Sagan," she crooned. "Hi, sweetie." Jessie practically crawled into the tiny kennel. She backed out, pulling a trembling puppy, all long, skinny legs and huge wide eyes. The puppy looked terrified.

Sally mentally compared this puppy to Sophie's in-your-face-I'm-so-terrific arrival. No one had to peel Sophie off the back wall of her kennel.

Jessie held the puppy close to her chest. "Sagan, baby," she murmured. "It's all right. Nothing to be worried about. You're home now. Look, Sally. Isn't she the most amazingly gorgeous thing you've ever seen?"

You never, *ever* disagreed with a mother who thought her baby was beautiful. No matter what you thought, you kept it to yourself. Sally reached out to touch the trembling head. The fur was softer than it looked. She rubbed the tiny head. Peered into the two huge brown eyes. It was impossible to resist the frightened puppy. "Hi, there, Sagan. I'm your Auntie Sally. Poor thing. She looks anorexic." Oops! Wrong thing to say.

"She's a sight hound," Jessie said, without taking offense. "She's supposed to be skinny. No extra padding to slow her down."

All the way back to Hartley, Jessie cradled Sagan in her arms. Sagan trembled.

Halfway home they stopped at a rest area, where Jessie snapped a collar around the puppy's skinny neck and attached a soft nylon leash. She set the puppy down on the grass. The puppy stuck to Jessie's side like an extra appendage. Wouldn't even pee. After a few unproductive minutes they got back into the car and headed north again, for Hartley.

"You should name her Velcro," Sally said.

Jessie tossed her a disgusted look.

"Or, oh, I know! Burdock."

"I would never name a dog after a noxious weed."

"You'd rather name her after a dead astronomer?"

"He was a great man."

"Yeah. Okay. I'll give you that."

"Look, Sagan," Jessie pointed the puppy at the window. "This is Hartley. This is where you live now."

The puppy was not impressed. Not even when Sally pulled into the vet clinic. "To C'lumbus, to C'lumbus, to get Jessie's dog. Home again, home again, jiggity jog," she said. Then, "What?"

Jessie shrugged. "Your kindergarten teacher persona is showing."

"Deal with it," Sally said with a grin. "I'll carry the kennel and stuff. You get the puppy." She needn't worry. No way was Jessie going to set her puppy down. Not even while she dug one-handed in her purse for her keys.

Sally hauled the airline kennel and the puppy pick-up supplies in the back door of the clinic and up the stairs to Jessie's apartment. She dumped it all on the floor. The puppy startled at the noise. "I'm sorry, baby," she said. She reached for the puppy. To her surprise, Jessie let her take her. She held the puppy up to look her in the eye. "Welcome to Hartley, Sagan," she said. "When you get settled in, you have to come over to meet your new cousin, Sophie. You're the two new girls in town. Two new girl babes. You'll drive the guys crazy."

Jessie looked thoughtful. "You know, when you first told us about Sophie, we were sort of concerned."

"Why?"

"It's no secret that you don't like dogs. We weren't sure you'd be able to adapt to life with a canine. You seem to be doing quite well. Thanks in no small part to Micah and Tanner. And Sophie herself."

"Tell you the truth, I'm surprised myself." She tickled the puppy's soft little belly. "It's impossible not to like Sophie. The little wretch is actually delightful. Tanner says she has a high pack drive, which is one reason she's so responsive. Speaking of which," she handed Jessie her puppy, "I have to get home to said teenager and said hairy hound."

Jessie chuckled. "You're beginning to sound like a dog person."

"I am not a dog person," she called over her shoulder as she started down the stairs.

"You have a dog," Jessie called after her. "You're starting to talk to dogs as if they're cats. You're well on your way. Next thing, you'll start keeping a spare leash in your car and a dog comb in your purse."

"I am not going to be a dog person."

"Why ever not? We're great."

Sally stopped at the bottom of the stairs and

turned to glare up at her friend. "Dog people are enthralled by the effect of various foods on their dogs' stool. Then they sit around talking about the grossest things their dogs ever ate. Dog people are infinitely fascinated by what goes in and comes out of all their dogs' orifices. It's embarrassing. Besides, I have three cats and have had to move their litter boxes twice so Sophie can't get to some of those gross things that dogs eat. Yuck! I am, and intend to remain, a cat person. Good-bye." Sally closed the door behind her.

After she dropped Jessie off, Sally picked up some drive-through to take home for lunch. "It's such a lovely day," she told Micah, "let's eat out on the patio."

So they did.

"So, Sophie, you did a good job taking care of everyone, eh?"

Sophie ignored her and stared at the french fry in her hand.

"Okay," she said. Sophie liked french fries.

"I see you picked and pitted while I was gone."

"Yeah."

"Was this an unsubtle hint for me to make another pie?" she teased.

Micah shrugged. "I guess."

After lunch, Sally pulled out flour and shortening to start a piecrust when the phone rang. It was Aunt Mary. She wanted to speak to Micah.

Micah, as usual, took the phone in his room.

Sally smashed the shortening into the flour.

She measured sugar and flour into a pan on the stove, then added the cherries and all their juice. The mixture had to be stirred constantly until it thickened. While she stirred, Micah came back into the kitchen.

"She wants to talk to you."

Sally didn't want to talk to Aunt Mary. But Micah was there, holding out the phone, so she smiled and moved the pan off the burner. "Thanks," she told him. She took the phone.

"I'm concerned," Mary stated, "that he doesn't seem very cheerful. Not like his usual self at all. He says he doesn't have any friends there. Micah has always had friends."

Sally bristled. Why did the woman always rub her the wrong way? She glanced into the dining room to make sure Micah had closed the sliding glass door after he took Sophie outside. It was time to stand up to Aunt Mary. "Actually, he's beginning to come out of his depression." She hoped it was true. "So far he hasn't been interested in meeting any kids his own age."

"Why not?"

It had been easy to talk to Tanner about him, she thought, but she wasn't able to talk to Mary. Maybe because she always felt on the defensive when she talked to Mary. She always felt like she had to justify Micah being with her instead of back in Vermont. "I imagine he'll make friends when he's ready."

"What does his counselor say?"

"He's not going to counseling right now."

"Not going to counseling? What are you thinking of? You know the doctors here told you he needed counseling."

"He did go. He had a counselor at the rehab center, and when he got home I took him to a doctor here—but he wouldn't say anything, so finally the counselor said it would be best to wait until he is ready to talk. That hasn't happened yet."

"He needs to!"

"And he will. When he's ready. I have a good friend who's an adolescent psychologist and she said the same thing."

"I still say he should be here, in Vermont, where we can take care of him properly."

"I'm sorry you feel that way." Sally struggled to hold on to her temper. She thought back to the books on adolescent grief she'd read. "I think he's still finding ways to process everything that's happened to him. I don't think you can expect him to react the way you think he should."

"It's still not good for him to sit alone all day and wallow."

"First of all, he's not alone all day. I'm on summer break. I'm home most of the time. Secondly, he doesn't wallow. He does his physical therapy exercises. He works with his dog a lot. Tanner, who's teaching him to work with Sophie, says he's doing very well with her." She found herself getting upset. A black cat leaped up onto the counter next to her. It was Jude. She gathered him up, holding the phone under her chin. Jude's silent purr started its calming magic. "Look, I know you're concerned about Micah. I am, too. We both want what's best for him. Right now, I think he's doing what he feels he needs to do. When he's ready to do more, he will. Even if I have to move mountains for him."

When she hung up the phone, Sally pulled a chair over to the refrigerator to reach the cupboards on top. Leety's Fine Chocolates took care of everyday tension, but talking to Mary called for something stronger. She needed The Big Guns. Stretching, she reached behind her waffle iron and fondue warmer and carefully felt around for her most secret, hidden, hard-to-get-to, only-in-case-of-dire-emergency stash of Godivas.

When the mail was delivered, there was a letter for Micah. He looked at it with a stone face. He opened the envelope, pulled out the letter, read it, then tore it in two and tossed it in the wastebasket. Then he went into his room and shut the door.

Sally fished the letter out of the wastebasket. She put the pieces together and read.

Dear Micah,
    Our sled hockey team is having a games weekend in Cleveland in the end of July. The Mighty Penguins from Pittsburgh, and the Mighty Otters from Erie— the two teams I told you about—are driving over from Pennsylvania, and the Ice Bears are coming down from Detroit. Over the weekend, each team will play about a dozen games. We'd love to have you come and see us play. You could meet everyone— we're all good friends, even though we play on different teams. Maybe you could even play a game with

*us. I'm sure someone on one of the teams will loan
you a sled to try out. Trust me, we all love to see new
players. Think about it. Give me a call any time you
want to talk. Either about hockey or anything else.*

   Terry

Under her name, she'd written her phone number, her e-mail address, and the words "Hockey is life. Everything else is details."

Seventeen

Late Saturday afternoon, the doorbell rang. Sophie hurtled herself towards the door, barking and yelling up a storm.

Sally opened the door. It was Tanner, with Wing sitting politely at his side. "Is Micah here?" Tanner asked.

"Sure, come in." Sally held onto Sophie's collar as she opened the door. "Sophie, knock it off," she muttered. She glanced over her shoulder to see where the cats were. Tess sat in the middle of the living room. Troy was stretched lazily on the catwalk next to the aquarium, where he could easily keep a close eye on his fish. Jude was, of course, hiding.

Tess stood up and stalked regally over to Wing, then turned around and whipped her tail in the dog's face as she moved away.

Tanner chuckled. "I guess she told Wing what she thinks of her."

"I guess so."

"Sorry to drop by without calling first, but I was driving by . . ."

"Not a problem." She smiled. "I'm glad you came by. I think he's upset about something. He's been in his room most of the afternoon. I'll get him."

She knocked softly on his door. "Micah, Tanner's here to see you," she said.

A moment later, the door opened. Glancing over Micah's shoulder, Sally saw Jude on Micah's bed.

"If you don't have anything planned," Tanner told him, "I thought we might take the dogs for a walk."

"Okay," Micah said. He didn't show much enthusiasm. But he made his way into the dining room where Sophie's leash was on the counter. Sophie, seeing the leash in his hand, started bouncing up and down, whimpering excitedly. She had enough enthusiasm for both of them.

As they walked around a red bicycle dropped in the middle of the sidewalk on its side, Tanner observed Micah out of the corner of his eye. The boy's shoulders slumped. His awkward gait was more pronounced than it had been recently. That emotional wall was back up. Sally was right, Tanner thought. Micah was upset about something. He wondered what had happened. Tanner paused a moment, so Wing could sniff. "So how do you think you're doing with Sophie?" he asked.

"Okay, I guess." Sophie chose this moment to squat. "Good girl," Micah murmured.

"I think you're doing a great job. Look. She isn't hitting the end of the leash anymore."

"Yeah."

"She seems to be adjusting to life here in Ohio." Tanner waited to see if Micah felt like talking about his own adjustment. Evidently not. "Have you thought any more about what you want to do with her, as far as obedience goes?"

"Not really."

"Tomorrow there's a dog show over in Lima. Wing and I are entered in the obedience trial. It might be a good opportunity for you to see what it's all about. Then, if you think it's something you'd be interested in doing with Sophie—I'll help you do it. I think you could do well. If you'd like to go tomorrow, you can come with me."

Micah watched Sophie discover some intriguing smell in the grass. "Thanks. It'd be okay. If Sally will let me."

"I think she will. She seems like a reasonable person." Visions of Sally danced through his mind. "In fact, if she doesn't have other plans, maybe she'd like to come with us." This wasn't part of his original plan, but the more he thought about it, the more he liked the idea of spending the day at a dog show with Sally.

By the time they got back to Sally's house, Micah seemed to feel better. He stood up straighter, and he even chuckled when Sophie threw herself down on the grass and wriggled around to scratch her back. Then she stood up and a shake started at her head, moved down along her body, and ended up at her tail.

"We're having chili for supper," Sally said. "Would you like to stay?" Then she added the clincher. "I have a cherry pie fresh out of the oven." Like Karen's French toast, he couldn't say no to Sally's cherry pie.

So he stayed. After supper, he and Micah put the dishes in the dishwasher and wiped the counter. He looked at all the stuff on her refrigerator: a child's drawing of a colorful blob, a photo of Micah, and a younger Sophie. Then he noticed the little white words on the refrigerator. "What's this?" he asked. He read, "Who has seen the wind?"

"It's Sally's magnetic poetry. Yeah, I know. It's dumb."

"What's it for?"

Micah looked disgusted. "The other night we watched *Conspiracy Theory.* Mel Gibson had magnetic poetry on his refrigerator, and Sally decided she had to have some, too, so the next morning we drove all over until we found some. She likes to move the words around. There's a whole bunch of 'em in the drawer there. You wanna change it? You can. She won't mind. She'd prob'ly think it was cool." Micah opened the drawer. He pulled out a plastic box crammed with words, all on some magnetic stuff. "Here." He spilled some of the words on the counter. "Make something up."

"Okay, but don't tell her. Let her find it on her own." Tanner sorted through the words. *Round. Big. Hot. Red. Will. Good. Very.* Oh, he could make up something with these words, all right. He'd better not. Instead he pulled out a handful of different words to arrange on the refrigerator. There. He wondered what Sally would think of that.

He grinned a conspiratorial grin at Micah. Micah grinned back.

"This looks familiar." It was a pen-and-ink drawing of a woman leading a group of children of various ages over a mountain. The woman had a sense of urgency about her. The older children carried younger children on their backs, leading others by the hand. In the distance, following them, were shadowy figures that resembled dragons. The whole picture had an atmosphere of imminent danger.

Sally came to stand next to him. "Sylvie did it. She's really good, isn't she? She gave it to me for my birthday a couple of years ago." She pointed. "She even put in the cats. And the fish." Sure enough, among the children he saw a snooty white cat, a black-and-white cat with three legs, and a third cat—this one, solid black, must be Jude. And there, tucked under the arm of one of the older children were the two fish in a round glass bowl. It was an odd choice for a birthday present. Tanner looked closer. "That's you," he said. "The woman is you. But who are the children?"

Sally turned pink. It looked good on her. "For years, I've had this recurring dream where I have to save a group of children from some great evil. The details change, but the basic plot is the same. I told Sylvie about it one time. She said it was a highly symbolic dream."

Tanner thought about Sally in bed. He quickly turned to the next thing on the wall. "What's this?"

So Sally told him to sit on the couch next to
Micah and she would give him a tour of her living
room walls. Books, drawings, a weird statue of a
cow-thing painted to look like that starry night
painting. He didn't get it. Finally, she came to a
large technical drawing of some medieval church-
like building, drawn from several different angles.

"This belonged to Kevin, Micah's father. I don't
know anything about it. Micah, can you tell Tanner
what this is?"

"It's the Hagia Sophia. It's a mosque." Micah's
voice was low. "It was built in the sixth century in
Constantinople. It was my dad's favorite building.
We named Sophie after it. Her full name is
Spered's Hagia Sophia. It means Spirit's Holy Wis-
dom." He pulled his dog onto his lap and hugged
her. "Because Dad said she was awfully smart."

Early Sunday morning, Tanner fed Aretha,
cleaned her off, and set her in her crate. "Take
it easy," he told the kitten. "We're off to a show.
Wish us luck."

Wing gave him an impatient look. Wing didn't
need luck. Wing was ready.

Tanner grabbed the two canvas bags he'd packed
the night before. "Let's go," he said.

Wing bounded over to the door.

Sally would never in a million years have ever
imagined herself on a Sunday morning, earlier
than she ever got up on a non-school day, walking

with Tanner Dodge, his dog, and Micah through a massive and crammed parking lot, past lots of big vans with dog stickers on them, on their way to the entrance to a dog show. But then, lots of things had happened lately that she'd never have imagined in a million years. Just goes to prove, she told herself, your imagination needs some work.

"On the eighth day, God created Dachshunds," she read a bumper sticker. Then she saw another one. *"I heart my Beagle.* Oh, and there's a *I heart my French Bulldog.* I guess lots of dog people heart their dogs." When she didn't get a reaction, she said, "Lighten up, you guys. It's a beautiful day in the neighborhood." Then she recognized the look on Micah's face. Uh-oh. "I'm embarrassing you, aren't I?" she asked. "I'm sorry."

But it was Tanner who answered. "You don't sound sorry."

"You caught me." She swung her arms and grinned. "I'm not the least bit sorry. Micah, kiddo, you'll have to put up with it. However, I promise I won't be offended if you pretend you don't know me."

"Your kindergarten teacher persona is showing," Micah said in the exact tone Jessie had taught him three years ago.

Closer to the building, they passed lots of people and dogs connected to each other by leashes. Sally saw dogs sitting politely, dogs running alongside their people, dogs squatting or lifting their legs. Some dogs stood on little black, rubber-topped tables exuding great forbearance while people combed them. Sally touched Tanner on his arm to get his attention. "Is that a poodle?" she asked in a quiet voice so she wasn't overheard.

"No. It's a bichon frise."

"Oh," said Sally. She realized she knew as little as she'd known before.

They went through the doors after a short woman with at least a dozen leashes in her hand, each leash attached to a little dog. "Pugs," Tanner whispered to her.

Tanner paid for their tickets and bought them a catalog. The person taking the money stamped the backs of their hands. Sally held her hand in front of her face and squinted to try to see what it was, but the image was smeary.

Inside the building, Sally looked around at what appeared to be utter chaos. The building was teeming with people and dogs, standing, moving, brushing—the people, not the dogs. Oddly, all these dogs were not barking at each other. Still, the noise level was akin to that of a school lunchroom, but without the clanging of plates. Sally caught glimpses of various levels of triumph and tension in the expressions on faces. Groups of people and their dogs clumped and clustered together by kind, sometimes with an odd kind thrown in.

Tanner stopped to consult the catalog. "Ring eighteen," he said. He peered over heads looking for . . . "Over there." He pointed. He and Wing threaded them through the throng until, at last, they came to a stop. "Rings eighteen, nineteen, and twenty are the obedience rings," he told them. "I have to get my armbands. Wait here."

Sally looked around. Beside her, Micah looked

as confused as she felt. Then Tanner was with them again. "I have about an hour before I have to prepare for the ring," he said. "Let's walk around. I'll explain it to you."

This was Tanner's world. But for Sally, it was a foreign country where the inhabitants spoke dog. It sounded like English, but Sally overheard people using phrases such as "taking breed," and "winners bitch," and "fresh-chilled semen." In elementary schools people usually did not speak of semen, fresh-chilled or not. Sally wasn't sure what fresh-chilled semen was. She *was* sure she didn't want to know.

She learned collies came bearded, Border, rough, and smooth. There were Border terriers, and Welsh terriers, Irish terriers, and two kinds of fox terriers. Tanner pointed out three kinds of dachshunds and told them all three came in two sizes. Beagles came in two sizes, too. And that dog over there, the one she thought looked sort of like a German shepherd, was a Belgian Tervuren. They walked past tall, skinny dogs. "Those are Scottish deerhounds, and that one there, is an Irish wolfhound," Tanner told them. Sally's mouth dropped open. "Jessie's puppy is one of those? They're huge."

"Look over there, Micah." Tanner pointed.

"Cardis!" Micah said.

Sure enough. Sally counted twelve Cardigan Welsh corgis who were all as funny-looking as Sophie. "Different colors?" she asked.

"Yeah," Tanner said, his lips twitching in a barely

suppressed grin. "They come in different colors and everything. Imagine that."

Sally felt herself turning pink. "You're teasing me."

"Are they going to be judged?" Micah asked.

"Yes." Tanner glanced at his watch. "We have time. Do you want to watch?"

They claimed three of the folding chairs loosely arranged around the ring. Wing sat politely at Tanner's feet. The first four dogs went into the ring. Their owners knelt down in a line and had their dogs stand in front of them, their sides to the judge. Sally leaned towards Tanner. "They all look alike," she whispered. "Except for their color. How can a judge tell them apart?"

"They only *look* like they look alike." Tanner gave her a grin. "Micah, look at the last two. Do you see any differences?"

Micah wrinkled his forehead in concentration. Kevin had wrinkled his forehead exactly the same way, Sally thought with a pang.

"The black-and-white one has a straighter back than the brindle one."

"You're right. He does have a better topline," Tanner said. "He's also smaller, not filled out yet— he's probably a younger dog." He opened the catalog to the correct page and ran his finger down the listing. "Yes. Look. He is fourteen months old—the other dogs are older."

Micah looked at the catalog, but didn't seem to know what he was seeing.

Sally asked the question, so Micah wouldn't have

to. She pointed to the listing. "What does all that mean?"

Tanner met her gaze, and gave her a barely perceptible nod of approval. "The dog's number, worn on the armband, name, who the owner is, the sire and dam, and who bred the dog." He pointed to a listing farther down. "This puppy is nine months old—the same age as Sophie. Number fifteen." He glanced around the group of dogs gathered near the entrance of the ring. "There. The woman in the purple flowered skirt. Her dog."

"I see her," Micah said.

Sally leaned in front of Tanner for a better view. She found the woman—who had the slender blond kind of pretty that always made Sally feel big and clumsy—and followed her leash to the dog. "Sophie is prettier," she whispered. She noticed Tanner's lips twitch and she forgot about everything but his lips. How could she ever have thought him plain-looking? she wondered. She must've been blind.

The judge must've been blind, too, for he gave the puppy a blue ribbon. However, after some more shuffling of dogs in the ring, the judge redeemed himself when he gave the purple ribbon to a stout, middle-aged woman and her brindle dog. Sally clapped along with the rest of the observers. Jessie had drilled into her that the important ribbons were purple.

"That dog won, right?"

"Yes. That's the winners bitch."

On their way back to the obedience ring, Tanner guided them to the AKC table where he picked up a tall, thin booklet and handed it to Micah. "Obedience regulations."

As they moved through the crowds, Sally noticed several women waving to Tanner, calling a greeting to him. He waved back. Then the women looked curiously at Sally. As a matter of fact, now that she thought about it, ever since they arrived she'd noticed women watching Tanner, some more obviously than others.

Back at the obedience rings, they found three folding chairs. Tanner drew Micah's attention to the three rings, one for each obedience level. Micah promised he'd watch carefully. Then Tanner took Wing outside to warm up.

Sally was glad they could sit; she wasn't sure Micah was up to all the walking around. In the first ring, a miniature poodle heeled smartly next to a grizzled man who looked like he should have dried egg yolk on his tie. In the next ring a sleek gray dog—Micah whispered it was a weimaraner— nosed through a group of little metal dumbbells before he found one he liked and, with the dumbbell in his mouth, hustled back across the ring to sit at the feet of his owner. She turned to the third ring and found herself smiling at a bulldog, who wagged his whole stubby body so enthusiastically he heeled in a crooked line. "His sit is crooked," she heard someone behind her whisper. In the ring, the woman tossed a dumbbell over a white board, and after a pause, called out, "Bill, get it." Bill the bulldog trotted out to the white board and threw himself over—describing his movement as a jump would be generous—wiggling so much he almost knocked the board down. The person in back of Sally gave a slight gasp. Bill's owner took him to one end of the ring. "Bill, sit. Stay." She walked to the other end and turned around. Then she called him. He rushed to her in an ungainly gallop. "Bill, down!" the woman called. Bill slowed to a halt. For a second he stood doing his whole-body wag; then, looking desolate, as if being denied heaven, he lowered his heavy body down. "Bill, come!" He struggled to his feet and rushed to her, to sit wiggling crookedly at her feet, to stare up and worship. Applause broke out all around them as the woman and Bill emerged from the ring. Sally thought Bill was the most beautiful dog she'd ever seen, and for some inexplicable reason, tears welled up in her eyes. She understood, finally, what Tanner meant when he said Sophie was willing. He meant she was like Bill.

"So, what do you think?" she asked Micah. "About doing this with Sophie."

The rapt enthusiasm on his face instantly cooled. He was once more the teenager who lived with her. "It might be okay."

She grinned. She was not fooled by his off-handed manner. Maybe Micah could get excited about doing obedience with Sophie and that would give him something to look forward to, a goal to work for. She crossed her fingers.

She watched the dogs for a while longer but none of them held a candle to Bill, so she watched the people watching the dogs.

Then she heard a man call out, "Open B, number 312."

Tanner and Wing strode into the ring. Sally was aware the rest of the crowd had grown suddenly quiet. Then the rest of the world disappeared. There was only Tanner and Wing.

Wing had Bill's enthusiasm, but her movements were precise and graceful. Wing stayed by Tanner's side because it was her natural place in the universe. Not because he told her to, but because the two of them were invisibly connected. At times, Wing, balletlike, flowed away from his side, only to do her task and flow back to him again. Sally had no idea what the judge thought, but she thought Tanner and Wing were flawless. This is what a relationship with Tanner would be like, she realized, freedom of equals brought together and connected by love. He would accept nothing less. She wanted nothing more.

The rest of the world returned with a rush of applause. "Wow!" Micah breathed beside her. "That was really something."

Sally watched Tanner make his way through the smiling crowd that had gathered to watch him. Some reached out to shake his hand, others to pet Wing. Some looked at him with envy. Some, mostly women, looked at him with the same barely concealed adoration Bill had for his owner. They were restrained groupies, the Tanner fans. He showed courtesy to everyone, friendship to some. Jessie was right, Sally thought, he didn't take advantage of them.

Tanner dropped into the chair between them. Wing gave a contented sigh as she parked her nose on his knee.

"That was really good," Micah told him.

"Thank you." Tanner took him seriously. Tanner treated Micah as an equal.

"What happens now?" Sally asked. She could practically feel the evil stare of one of the groupies, a woman with a hard expression and a Doberman. Sally felt fat and frumpy. She felt like the typical tourist except without the madras shorts and camera.

"Now we wait for the rest of the group to finish; then we all go back in for the long sits and downs."

"Oh." Clear as mud.

Micah consulted the booklet. "It means all the handlers in this group put their dogs on sits and downs and leave the ring and go out of sight."

"Oh." It also meant she couldn't escape from the Tanner fan. But, then, it also meant she could sit next to Tanner, close enough that their knees brushed. She settled back in the uncomfortable chair and let the sounds of the dog show wash over her. She was content to be where she was, by his side, which was her natural place in the universe.

Later that afternoon, after they'd arrived back home and Micah was outside in back with Sophie, the phone rang. It was Cheryl Benson, Deb's neighbor in Vermont. "On Friday," Cheryl said, "two days ago, the woman who caused the accident was in court. The judge fined her two thousand dollars and sentenced her to two hundred hours of community service. He also suspended her license for ninety days. He went easy on her because this was her first drunk-driving charge. Scuttlebutt says the judge and the woman had some connection."

Sally felt sick. "That's why Micah was upset after Mary called yesterday. Mary told him. She ought to be strung up," Sally muttered.

"Shot," Cheryl said.

Sally didn't know if they were referring to the drunk driver or to Mary. She guessed it didn't matter.

Eighteen

The Fourth of July was a big deal in Hartley, Ohio. Yes, it was an important date in the history of the United States, but that was icing on the cake. As every child in town knew, the Fourth of July was important because it was on this day, almost one hundred and fifty years ago, that Benjamin Hartley founded his town.

Every year, on the evening of July 3, at the end of an all-day beauty pageant, the town crowned Miss Hartley, Junior Miss Hartley, Little Miss Hartley, and Baby Beautiful Hartley. The Fourth, itself, was a daylong event beginning with a pancake breakfast in the high school parking lot, followed by The Parade down the main street of town. All morning at Kedrick Park, small booths had been springing up like mushrooms. In the afternoon, the Hartlians wandered among them, counting out their money to buy homemade jams and jellies, pies, crafts, woodcarvings, quilted pillows and jackets, and scented soaps, to name only a few of the treasures. A local quintet wearing nineteenth-century garb strolled through the park to serenade anyone who cared to stop to listen. If no one listened, the quintet sang anyway. And when the sun went down, and the booths had been packed away for next year, the citizens of Hartley, full of barbecue and lemonade and cotton candy, gathered by the lake for the annual display of fireworks. The Fourth of July had always been celebrated in this way. The day's events were an institution.

This year, for Sally, the day began with an argument.

"No, thanks," Micah said. "You can leave me here. I don't mind."

Sally put her hands on her hips. "I will not leave you here. It's the Fourth of July."

"I don't want to go to the high school to eat pancakes."

"You've always loved pancakes. I happen to know that a couple of years ago at Brattleboro's Maple Syrup Festival you ate so many pancakes you made yourself sick. You particularly loved the chocolate coconut ones. Your mom sent me the recipe."

"Yeah, well," Micah muttered, "that was then, this is now."

"Yes. It *is* now. And now we're going to the pancake breakfast."

"I told you. I don't want to go."

"But why?"

"I just don't."

"That's not a reason."

Micah shrugged.

Sally flopped down in Deborah's rocking chair. She supposed she should be happy Micah was at least behaving like a normal teenager. She decided the normal teenager mode wasn't fun. She took a deep breath. "Okay. Let's start all over again. Micah," she said brightly. "Today is the Fourth of July. It's Hartley Day. In Hartley we always begin the day with a pancake breakfast in the high school parking lot. Your turn."

"I don't want to go."

"Wrong answer."

"True answer. You always say honesty is important."

"Then please be honest with me now and explain why you don't want to go." She made an unsuccessful attempt to capture his gaze. "Micah, I'm not an unreasonable person. I want to understand why you feel this way." When she didn't get a response she fished. "Is it because you don't want to see anyone?"

Shrug.

"Or because you don't want people to see you? Because if that's it we are going to have a big problem in six weeks when school starts."

Micah stood at the window with his jaw clenched and his shoulders tight. He stared out into the morning. Sally guessed his hands, shoved in his pockets, were fisted.

"I think the biggest issue here is that you don't trust me with your emotions. I know teenagers like their privacy, and I respect that. I have tried really hard not to push you, not to try to make you tell me what you're feeling. But I'm at a loss here."

Micah spun around to face her. "You really don't get it, do you?"

"Obviously not."

"This pancake breakfast thing. It's a family event. This whole stupid day is a family event. People go with their families."

"So?"

"You're not my family!"

Sally was stunned. She stared hopelessly at the angry teenager standing in front of her. She opened her mouth, but nothing came out. There was nothing to say.

"You treat me as if you think you're trying to be my mother or something. You and my mother were friends. So what. You're not my mother. I don't have a mother anymore. And I don't have a father. Some damn drunk driver saw to that!" His anger had turned to anguish.

Tears streamed down Sally's cheeks. Oh God, how she hurt for him! How she ached for him!

"I didn't even get to tell them good-bye!" His chin began to tremble. Immediately he strode from the room. Sally heard his door slam.

She leaned her head against the back of Deb's rocking chair, pulled Deb's quilt around her shoulders, and wept. Micah was right. She wasn't his family.

Out of the corner of her eye, she saw Sophie, crouched behind the sofa, trembling. Poor little thing, Sally thought. So she scooped up the puppy and settled back into Deb's chair. Sophie huddled under the quilt with her. "I bet you were scared, weren't you? You're not used to hearing Micah yell. I'm not, either."

Sophie heaved a tremulous sigh and relaxed into

Sally's lap. Sally rubbed Sophie's soft ears. It was oddly comforting.

Sally sat with Sophie on her lap, in Deb's chair, for what seemed like hours. She didn't know what to do. She wanted to go to Micah, hug him, hold him close, as she did when he was a baby. Once, when he was two years old, he tripped on her sidewalk and fell down. She scooped him up, kissed his boo-boo, and he wiggled out of her arms and was off and running again. That was fine then, but this was no child's boo-boo. Micah's pain couldn't be kissed away.

Finally, Micah opened his bedroom door. He came into the living room and sat down on the couch. His eyes were red and puffy. She knew hers were, too.

He said, "It's probably time to go, if we want to see The Parade." It was his way of apologizing.

"You're probably right." It was her way of accepting it. "It's Melissa's turn to stake out our spot and bring the lawn chairs. You and I are bringing cookies and popcorn. If you want to bring a book to read, or your Gameboy, or something, I have a tote bag. Or," she added hesitantly, not knowing how he'd react, "if you think it'd be better to use your wheelchair today, we can put all our stuff in the bag on the back."

Micah stared at the fish. The fish stared back. "I don't want to use the chair."

She wanted to tell him he'd be so tired, with all the walking, all the wandering around the booths in the park. He's not a baby, she told herself. He's been to Hartley Days before. He knows what's involved. Let him make his own decision. She wanted him to be a baby again, or a kindergartner, so she'd know what to do, how to protect him, what decisions to make for him. She took a deep breath. "Okay. We'll leave the chair at home."

"Can I bring Sophie?"

"Yes. She'll probably have a great time." She attempted a grin. It was shaky, but she thought it got the meaning across. "I have fifty dollars for you—you might see something at one of the booths—but you remember the rules. If you buy it, you have to carry it."

Early that morning, Hartley's finest closed the main street and put up signs directing drivers to the detour around the downtown. Parking was at a premium downtown, even more so on the Fourth of July when every side street and alley was lined with cars. It was only half a mile from Grape Street to Main, so Sally always walked—except when it was her turn to get there early and bring the lawn chairs. She knew this year, with the handicapped license plate, she'd be able to find a spot closer to Main. But Micah didn't want anything to do with it. "That's for crips and geezers," he said. So they walked. It was slow going. Micah couldn't walk quickly, and Sophie had to stop and smell all the smells along the way.

The Parade was a grand event. Wise Hartlians arrived early to stake out their seats along the side of the street. They brought folding chairs and blankets, jugs of ice water and packets of snacks—some people brought books to read, others spread out blankets and played cards. A good seat meant a long wait. By the time The Parade passed by, the sidewalks would be seven or eight people deep. Everyone not in The Parade watched The Parade, filmed The Parade, and applauded The Parade.

By the time Sally and Micah and Sophie walked all the way to Main Street, the sidewalks were already crowded with spectators. "Look for a red, helium-filled balloon," Sally told Micah, "tied to seven empty lawn chairs."

Mrs. Carruthers, who ran the diner, and Mrs. Wilde, who owned the yarn shop, had found a shady spot under a tall tree and sat knitting while they waited for the festivities. Sally and Micah stopped to say hello. "Remember, Sally," said Mrs. Wilde serenely, but with a twinkle in her eye, "any time you want your next knitting lesson give me a call."

Sally laughed. "Thanks, Mrs. Wilde. I will."

"Are you gonna learn to knit?" Micah asked when they were out of earshot.

Sally shook her head. "It's a very old joke. Mrs. Wilde lived down the street from us when we were growing up. When your mom and I were in fourth grade, she taught us how to knit. Well, she taught your mom. Your mom took to it like a duck, but I couldn't figure it out—no matter how loudly I yelled at the yarn. Finally, one day I told Mrs. Wilde I couldn't come for a knitting lesson because I had to do an errand for my mother. I told her I'd come back later." She grinned. "She never forgot it. She never let me forget it, either."

They found the red balloon tied to six chairs, only two of them empty. Besides Melissa, Jessie, and Karen and Karen's daughter, Katie, were already there.

"Minus forty-seven degrees down there," Jessie greeted Micah.

"Heat wave," Micah answered.

It took Sally a moment. "Oh. Antarctica."

"The Pole," corrected Jessie. "They're having a heat wave. Probably in honor of Hartley Day."

Sophie was excited to see Brian Boru, who was stretched out asleep at Karen's feet, and Gracie, who was not. "What, no puppy?" Sally asked Jessie.

"Sagan hasn't had all her shots yet. I don't want to expose her to all the nasty, evil germs floating around."

"Sylvie said to tell everyone hi," Melissa said. "I talked to her this morning. She's staying home with the baby, of course," she added. "She didn't want to bring him."

Jessie nodded in agreement. "Germs. The little boogaloo hasn't had his puppy shots yet, either."

"Ray'll be in The Parade, though," Karen said. She held up a camera. "I promised to document The Parade for Sylvie to put in the boogaloo's baby book. Baby's First Parade—and he wasn't even there."

The friends chatted together to pass the time. Micah, sitting at one end, kept his attention on his Gameboy. Katie, sitting at the other, kept her attention on a book. On the sidewalk in front of them, Sophie and Gracie chewed on each other. Brian Boru snored.

When Melissa mentioned that Tanner was going to be in The Parade, Sally instantly perked up her ears and Jessie shot her a knowing look.

"Micah," Karen said, "wait till you see Tanner and all the Helper Dogs. This great big whole group of dogs—the puppies are so cute I can't stand it."

Sally had a vision of Tanner walking with a canine herd, like sheep. She still didn't know what Tanner did for a living—she made a point to ask Jessie later.

"Hey, Miss Foster!" It was Joshua Martini from the other side of the street. She waved to him and he darted across to see her.

"Hey, Miss Foster, I got a good one for you. Why do gorillas have such big nostrils? Because they have such big fingers." He laughed uproariously and slapped his leg.

Sally chuckled more at him than at the joke; then she realized that Micah, beside her, was laughing.

"Joshua, you remember Micah. This is his dog, Sophie. And this is Katie's uncle's dog, Gracie."

Joshua sat down on the sidewalk to better gush over the two dogs. The two dogs were quite agreeable to this.

"Hey, Miss Foster! You have a dog now? I thought you didn't like dogs."

The silence was instant and strained. Beside her, Sally could feel Micah emotionally pulling away.

"Well, now, Joshua, I've always said that there are certain dogs that I like a lot. Like Hugo, Dr. Winthrop's dog. You remember when he visited our class? And I like Jean-Luc, you know him, and Gracie here, and Brian. But most of all, I like Sophie, because she lives with me." As if to prove her point, Sally reached out and fondled the puppy's ears. Sophie wagged her tail. Suddenly, Sally realized it was true. She did like this little dog. For a dog, she really wasn't bad at all.

Finally, the crowd stirred and the excitement began to ripple up and down the street. Books were closed, playing cards were put away. Cameras were focused, flashes tested. In the distance Sally heard the faint beating of a big bass drum. The Parade was about to begin.

Leading The Parade was the mayor of the town and a contingent of veterans carrying the American flag. As always, Sally felt a lump in her throat when the crowd stood up in respect as the flag went by.

Next was an antique fire engine, and then came the Hartley High School Marching Band playing the school song. Cheerleaders cheered, flag girls waved their flags, baton twirlers twirled, and gymnasts did cartwheels. Political candidates and their supporters tossed wrapped candy to the kids along the way. Melissa's husband, Peter, and Angie, along with a group of children from their neighborhood, rode bicycles decorated with crepe paper and streamers. Every Bible School had a float, as did the Boy Scouts, the Girl Scouts, the dance school, and the gourmet pizza place.

Local letter carriers handed out candy from their mailbags. A group of mostly young and very fit men came by wearing shorts and *Songer's Gym* on their

T-shirts. One of the men had a powerful-looking black dog on a leash. "That's Lennox," Jessie said. "The dog, I mean."

"Is he a pit bull?" Micah asked.

Sally's eyes widened and she looked more closely at the dog in question.

"He's an Am Staff," Jessie said. "American Staffordshire. He was in for shots the other day. Really nice dog."

"That doesn't mean anything, coming from you," Sally pointed out. "You think all dogs are nice."

"Shhh!" Jessie said. "Be respectful. Hartley's plethora of pulchritude passes the peasants." The winners of the beauty pageant, supervised by their mothers and wearing more frills than dress, did the pageant wave as they were carried along on the pageant float. All except Baby Beautiful Hartley, who'd fallen asleep in her mother's arms. The local square dance club danced their way by on a flatbed truck. The next flatbed carried a local jazz team.

"There's Tanner," Micah murmured. He pointed. Sally looked.

Down the street, after yet another group of little girls in tutus, came two teenagers in dark blue T-shirts carrying a banner for Helper Dogs. Tanner walked between a woman in a motorized wheelchair and a young woman carrying a tired puppy. There were several other people, all with matching dark blue T-shirts, each with a dog on a leash. Some tossed candy, some handed out pamphlets.

"Jake!" Karen called out. She waved. A man

called back. Gracie leaped to her four feet and stood staring at the man, her tail going full speed.

"Micah!" Tanner called, and waved.

Micah waved back.

Sally felt left out. Here was Tanner with a whole other life, and she didn't know anything about it. All these people, including the pretty young woman carrying the puppy, had a claim to him. Then he caught her eye and gave her a smile and she felt better.

"Hey, Sal," Jessie nudged her. "Look, there's the fish farm!" Indeed, coming down the street was a truck pulling a gargantuan papier-mâché smiling goldfish on wheels. The sign around its huge neck read *Friendly Fish Farm—for friendly fish.* Three high school students walked alongside the goldfish, handing out flyers. Sally remembered the summers, long ago, when she and Melissa and Jessie had walked in The Parade, handing out the instructions for taking care of goldfish. She automatically looked for the man driving the truck. It was Don Anderson, of course. Sally frowned. How, for so many years, could she have thought he was so gorgeous? She had lusted after Don Anderson for so long it had become habit. Now she wondered why. He didn't hold a candle to Tanner Dodge.

Karen said, "I heard Trip was coming home soon."

"Trip Ackerman?" Jessie said, as if there were another Trip. "Home from China?"

Karen nodded. "I heard it from Carol Sewel who heard it from Don Anderson's mother. She's coming home to take care of her uncle. We should go over and see her."

"It would be the neighborly thing to do," Sally agreed. The thought of Trip Ackerman coming home to Hartley didn't bother her at all. Not even a little bit.

Then Sally noticed Micah's attention was glued on a young girl in the group of cheerleaders from Garfield Middle School. Micah would be attending Garfield in the fall. Sally knew that girl. She was Lilian Martini, Joshua and Jeremy's sister, and as pretty and as nice a girl as they came. Micah and Jeremy had been friends for a long time, so, of course Micah knew Lilian, too. Sally looked at Micah looking at Lilian. Oh, ho, she thought.

Nineteen

After The Parade, they packed the lawn chairs and other paraphernalia into Melissa's car and all moseyed on over to the park.

"Thanks for going slow," Karen said. She nodded at her elderly dog. "These days Brian's old bones can't move very quickly."

Sally caught her gaze and gave her friend a little nod of thanks. Micah couldn't walk quickly either anymore.

Gracie strained at the end of her leash. Katie said, "I'm going to take her for a run. We'll find our own way home, Mom. See you later." And with a wave to the rest of them, Katie broke into a run, Gracie beside her.

Karen bit her lower lip as she watched her daughter run away. Micah, too, watched Katie run.

Then they were at the park. "Look how many booths!" Melissa said.

"You say that every year," Sally said.

"Every year there are so many booths," Melissa said. "Yell if you see that dollmaker's booth. You know, Paris McIntyre's dolls. Angie wants one of them in the worst way."

"Angie's into dolls?" Karen said.

"These aren't dolls to play with, like all her Barbies. These are different. You put them on a shelf and look at them. They're called art dolls."

They walked among the booths, slowly, "maintaining geezer speed," said Jessie, admiring the myriad pretty things to be had.

"Pretty useless," Micah said.

"Spoken like a true man," said Karen.

Micah looked embarrassed.

Lilian Martini and a bevy of her friends giggled together across the way. "Sophie needs a drink," Micah said. "We'll be over there." He pointed. The drinking fountain was nowhere near the giggling girls.

"When you're done with the water, I'll be up there, at the doll booth," Sally said.

"So how is life with a teenager?" Karen asked when Micah was safely away.

Sally shook her head. "Not anything like I ever imagined." The two of them slowed their steps to keep pace with Brian Boru.

"What did you imagine?"

"I imagined it would be the same as it's always been when he's come to visit. It's like he isn't the same person he's always been."

"He isn't."

"Oh." Sally stopped and blinked at her friend. "You're right. I guess . . . I guess I didn't see that."

The big, black dog lowered himself to the ground and put his head on his paws. Karen reached down to stroke the huge head. "He's had a life-altering experience. Most of the people he knows—his peers, I mean—probably none of them has had anything like this happen to them. Micah doesn't have an example to follow. He doesn't know how to do it. He is figuring it out on his own."

When Karen put it that way, it was obvious.

"Oh."

"How is he getting along with Tanner?"

"Fine."

"Good. Tanner is one of the best people Micah could ever have as a friend." Karen shaded her eyes from the sun as she smiled up at Sally meaningfully. "So, how are *you* getting along with Tanner?"

Sally blushed.

"He's a terrific guy," Karen went on. "I think the world of him."

Sally cleared her throat. "Um. Yeah. I mean, I think he's pretty terrific, too."

"And speaking of something terrific." Karen pointed back the way they'd come. "Here they are now."

Sally looked where Karen pointed to see Tanner and Micah, each with a huge smile and a dog, coming towards them. It was so good to see Micah smile again. Sally's heart wanted to burst with the joy of it. Instead, she did the next best thing. She smiled back.

"Who's this?" Karen held her hand out to Tanner's dog.

"This is Murphy."

"This isn't the dog I saw at the mall?" Sally asked. They looked the same to her.

"That was Maxie. She stayed at home today."

Karen, doing some heavy-duty dog chest rubbing, said to Tanner, "So, do you have plans for the rest of the day? Or can you hang out with us?"

"Can you come with us?" Micah asked.

"I guess so. Until it's time to take Murphy back."

Sally told herself she was glad for Micah's sake. She knew she was lying.

Melissa met up with her husband and stepdaughter. Angie proudly clutched a plastic bag to her chest. "I won a goldfish!" she exclaimed. "His name is Smokey."

Peter caught his wife's look and shrugged.

"Well, then," said Melissa, a smile twitching her lips, "we'll have to go buy an aquarium for Smokey. We can't keep him in that bag for long—he needs oxygen. I hope that superstore is open all day." She turned to the rest of them. "I guess that's it for us. We'll see you at the fireworks."

Sally and the other four continued around the park. Sally saw the school secretary, who said the painters were finished so Sally could unpack her classroom any time now. She gushed over Sophie. After a look from Sally she didn't say a word about the superiority of dogs over cats. But she looked quite smug.

They listened to the singers, drank lemonade, ate corn dogs and barbecued pork sandwiches, pickles, and huge slabs of homemade bread with

butter right out of the churn. They bought a slab
of bread to split between the dogs. Tanner said
Murphy wasn't allowed to have any, so Sally tore it
in two. Sophie snapped her piece up and it was
gone in two seconds. Brian Boru took his piece
gently and chewed. And chewed. And chewed.

"Brian believes in thorough mastication," said
Karen. "It drives Gracie insane."

Sophie scouted around on the ground, searching for any dropped tidbit. Murphy sat quietly and
politely at Tanner's side.

"Why doesn't he scrounge around for food?"
she asked.

"He's not allowed to," was the answer.

Sally blinked. "Lots of dogs aren't allowed to,
but they do anyway."

"I didn't train them."

"Brian doesn't look around for food," Micah
pointed out.

"He's too old," said Karen. She bent down to
hug her dog and to whisper in his ear. Brian leaned
against her and groaned in pleasure. He gave his
tail a lazy swish.

Finally, Tanner said it was time to take Murphy
home. Jessie said she had to go too, to take Sagan
out. "I'll take Brian and Sophie home for you guys
if you stake out a spot for the fireworks. Fireworks
aren't a good experience for dogs," she added to
Micah.

"So it's down to the three of us," Karen said.
"Without dogs."

* * *

They stopped at the glassblower's booth and watched a woman making glass beads. She held a long, thin rod of glass in a flame till it was all soft; then she wound the molten glass around a metal rod, adding colors from other glass rods, and like magic, there was a glass bead.

"Those are amazing," Sally said. She studied the glass beads for sale and selected several for herself. "Micah, help me pick out some beads to send to your grandmother."

She and Micah stood close together, poring over the beads. It was almost like old times, Sally thought. Then Karen joined them to choose another group of beads for Sylvie. The woman at the cash box strung them all together on a thick silk cord and Sally wore them as a necklace.

They sat on a bench and listened to the quintet, ate more barbecue, and drank more lemonade until the sun dropped low in the sky. Karen said, "I'll get the lawn chairs from my car, and you guys stake out a spot for fireworks. No, I don't need help. When Melissa dropped the chairs off at my van, after The Parade, she put the wagon in, too. I parked my van near that gas station—so I can get ice for the drinks in the cooler." She nodded. "We're clever women. We have this Fourth stuff down to a science."

Sally and Micah tossed their lemonade cups in a trash can and headed off slowly towards the lake. "Whew! It's been a long day. I'm bushed." Sally knew Micah must be exhausted. Even in the heat, he wore jeans, as he did every day, to conceal his braces. Sally knew the effort it still took for him to keep his legs from swinging out to the side as he walked. The therapist said Micah's gait would continue to grow smoother and easier, but like everything else, it would take time.

"Shall we go up close?" Sally asked. It was a rhetorical question.

"As close to the lake as we can get," Micah said.

They found a large spot almost at the water's edge and dropped down to the grass. Sitting down felt really good. "I don't think I can walk home," Sally said, closing her eyes. "Let's camp out here and go home in the morning."

Micah snorted. Then he said, "There's that kid you talked to today."

Sally opened her eyes and saw Joshua Martini jogging by with a Frisbee in his hand. "Hey, Joshua," she called to him. He swerved his jog and came over to them.

"Is your family here?" Sally asked.

"Yeah. Over there by that big tree." He shuffled his feet. "Everyone but my dad. He doesn't like fireworks so my stepmother brought us." He turned his attention on Micah. "Hey, you wanna play Frisbee?"

Micah looked around, looking for escape, Sally thought. He gestured to his legs. "I don't think I can." Sally's heart broke at the embarrassment she heard in his voice.

"Betcha can," Joshua said. "You just gotta throw it to me, and catch it when I throw it back to you.

You don't gotta run, or anything. I can't throw it very far anyway."

Micah looked at her, seeking permission, maybe.

She shrugged, as if it were no big deal. "Try it," she suggested. Then she grinned. "You might like it."

Micah struggled to his feet, his face slightly red.

"Hello, there!" It was Tanner, wending through the patches and groups of people, carrying all their firework-viewing paraphernalia. Sally's hope level shot sky-high. If there was anyone who could help Micah right now, it was Tanner Dodge. A knight on a white horse if ever there was one.

Her gaze met his and for an instant, the whole earth revolved around the two of them.

"I hoped I'd find you," he said. "Can I join you for the fireworks?"

"Yes." She answered his unspoken question as well. Then she blinked. What was she thinking? "Joshua has asked Micah to play Frisbee."

Tanner seemed to grasp the situation immediately. "Great," he said. "Mind if I join you guys?"

It would be all right now. Tanner would know how to help Micah save face in case he couldn't handle it. She settled back to watch. Surprisingly, Micah did quite well. Tanner spent time with Micah, suggesting ways he could catch the Frisbee more easily, and with Joshua, showing him how to throw it more accurately. What an amazing man, she thought. Able to help both boys in a way that neither of them felt embarrassed to accept his assistance. It was a gift, a rare gift he had.

He worked with the boys for a bit, then settled

down on the grass next to Sally. "What's going
on?" he asked.

"Going on?"

Tanner nodded. "All afternoon you've been
treating each other as if you're made of glass."

"That obvious?"

"To me."

He listened carefully, while Sally told him about
the argument that morning. Other than Kevin,
she'd never known a man as comfortable to be
around as Tanner Dodge. She'd never felt as free
to be herself as she felt with Tanner. Maybe that
was why she was able to be so honest with him. "I
feel like a complete failure. I should have seen it,
but I guess I wasn't paying close enough attention.
He's right. He didn't get a chance to say good-bye
to his parents. That's what funerals are for, aren't
they? To say good-bye. I keep hoping he'll get used
to life here, but he hasn't. Maybe I should send
him back to Vermont for a visit. But I'm afraid if
he goes, he won't ever want to come home again.
He's all I have left of Deb and Kevin."

"He's all his grandmother has of them, too."

That was another thing she hadn't thought of.
She wrapped her arms around her drawn-up knees.
"I was a horrible teenager. If I'd been my mother,
I'd probably have torn my hair out—but once my
mom told me mothers try, and sometimes they get
it wrong. But they try anyway, because they're our
moms and they love us enough to try, even though
they know they might fail, because sometimes it's
the only way they know how to show us how much
they love us." She looked up at the sky, her eyes

open wide so tears wouldn't fall down her cheeks. "I guess I have to let him go back, don't I? I have to hold him close to my heart with open hands."

"You don't have to. But it would probably be good for him."

They were silent, watching Micah and Joshua play Frisbee until Karen arrived with Angie's red wagon heaped high with blankets, chairs, mosquito repellent, and a cooler with cold drinks.

After a while, Sally noticed Lilian, Joshua's sister, make her way through the pattern of blankets towards them.

"Joshua," said Lilian, "Barbara says you need to come back now." Though she spoke to her brother, her eyes were on Micah.

Sally had to do something quickly. "Lilian," she called out. She got to her feet and, brushing grass off the seat of her jeans, went over to the girl. "This is Micah Fennessy. He lives with me now. He'll be going to Garfield Middle School in the fall. That's where you'll go, too, isn't it?" She turned to Micah and held out her hand to him. "Micah, you remember Joshua and Jeremy's sister, Lilian."

"Hi, Micah," Lilian said in a soft voice. Her eyes were curious. But she had more tact than her brother, and didn't ask.

Micah, after starting at her voice, turned bright red. He didn't know what to do with the Frisbee in his hands. Sally decided they'd have to figure it out for themselves. She returned to her spot on the grass and watched the two young people standing near each other, but not together. They each said something brief—Sally couldn't hear what it

was. She supposed what they said wasn't important—it was more important that they said anything
at all. Then, with a small wave to Micah, Lilian
called to her brother once more.

"See ya later, Micah. 'Bye Tanner." Joshua waved
at them as he trudged off after his sister.

Sally caught Tanner watching Micah. Then he
glanced at her, and she knew he had seen what
she had. Micah was interested in Joshua's sister.
Oh, no. She wasn't ready for this. How could she
ever hope to help Micah through girls? She didn't
know what to do with a boy. If Micah was a girl,
she would know exactly how he was feeling. After
all, she was well acquainted with the pangs of un-
requited love. She felt that way herself right now.
She felt that way about the man who was, right
now, settling down on the grass beside her.

"We'll have to see what we can do about that,"
he said softly to her as his breath tantalized her
neck and sent delicious shivers down her back.

She blushed, even though she knew he couldn't
possibly know what she'd been thinking. Thank
goodness!

"Micah! There you are!" It was Jessie, trotting
towards them, waving her arms. "I'm glad you were
standing—or I would have never found all you guys
and I'd have to watch the fireworks all by my lone-
some." She dropped to the blanket and patted the
spot beside her. "Sit." Micah sat beside her and
Jessie started in telling him about what she'd just
seen on the web about how the scientists at the
Pole celebrate the Fourth of July. "They have a pig
roast!"

They all chatted companionably, passing the mosquito repellent and sodas while the sky grew darker and darker until, finally, with a *bang!* the firefighters shot off the first of the fireworks.

All of Hartley oohed and aahed as the colored lights exploded overhead.

Jessie, her eyes on the sky, leaned over to whisper to Sally, "Aren't fireworks the perfect metaphor for an orgasm?"

Twenty

Wednesday morning, Tanner worked in the wheelchair with Murphy again. They went up and down the halls, around the auditorium, through the front door, into the side door until Murphy finally figured it all out. "Atta boy, Murph!"

Murphy did the great big body wag.

On the way back to the training room, Tanner took Murphy through as many doorways as he could, backtracking and going through several of them twice, until he wheeled into the front office. He took one look at the terrier-like glint in Corinne's eyes and stopped short. Murphy looked back over his shoulder and gave Tanner a look of reproach.

Corinne continued to pin Tanner with her stare. She held out a green While You Were Away note.

He took the note and gave it a quick glance. In Corinne's ultraneat handwriting were the words *Please call Sally. You should know her number.* He glanced back up at Corinne. "Thanks," he said.

He knew she wondered. He knew she pondered. He knew she bided her time. But for now, she let him go without a word, and he made his escape.

He called Sally on his lunch break.

"Micah and I thought," she said, "you might like to come over for supper tonight."

"I'd like that very much."

"Macaroni and cheese. It's not very fancy, but it's from scratch, and there's cherry crisp for dessert. We're still working on all those cherries."

"Macaroni and cheese sounds wonderful." He didn't think he'd ever had homemade macaroni and cheese before. He hadn't known much home-cooking at all, until he met Karen. She'd taken him under her wing and fed him well. She'd rescued him. Now she rescued dogs.

"Show up whenever you get off work. If Wing is with you, she's invited, too. If she likes macaroni and cheese. Well, I'll see you then."

"I'm off at five. I'll be there a little after." He wanted it to be five o'clock now. It was only one.

Tanner stared at his nameless, faceless sandwich. Sally Foster baked him cherry pie, she invited him to supper. Like their mutual friend, Karen, Sally also took in strays, human as well as feline. And, if you counted Sophie, canine. Even though she was afraid of dogs, he was certain she was, she opened her home to Micah's puppy, treating Sophie not as an outsider, an invader, a creature to be endured, but as family. Sally Foster was one special lady. Sally Foster deserved the best. He was not the best. He dumped his sandwich in the trash.

Corinne, in her wheelchair with Aspen at her side, blocked the doorway. He was trapped.

Corinne smiled at him. It was a terrier-like smile.

When terriers took hold of something, they did not let go. "Jake said you had a date last week."

"No. I didn't. I talked to a woman about . . ." It was all too complicated to explain. "No. Jake is wrong."

"Then during The Parade I see you wave to a woman. Then, after The Parade, I see you in the park with the same woman. And later I see you at the fireworks. With this same woman and you were leaning awfully close to her. Today you receive a message to call some woman named Sally, and you know her phone number. Now, I hear you tell someone you'll be there a little after five." Her eyes twinkled. "Sounds to me as if you're making another one of these dates."

"I'm helping a boy train his dog. We have a lesson tonight, so they asked me to supper."

"Someone asked you to supper?" Patti stood in back of Corinne's wheelchair.

Corinne wheeled aside so Patti could get into the lunchroom. "He has a date," she said.

Patti's face lit up. "Really?"

Tanner shook his head in disgust. "Women," he muttered.

"Very observant," Patti teased.

As soon as Sally hung up the phone, she knocked on the door of Micah's room. "I'm going to Sylvie's. I'm taking over a pan of macaroni and cheese. Tanner's coming for supper tonight. While I'm gone, would you please vacuum?"

"Yeah."

"I appreciate it. I won't be gone long. You know Sylvie's number."

"Okay."

Micah certainly was not a great communicator. Was it the teenage thing or the guy thing? Or was it all the emotional upheaval on top of being a teenage guy? Sally wrapped the pan in aluminum foil and headed out the door. She needed some girl talk.

She pulled in Sylvie's driveway, climbed the porch, and knocked.

"It's open! Come in!" came Sylvie's voice.

So Sally went in.

"Hi, Sal, I'm in the living room."

Sylvie sat in her rocking chair, holding her baby to her breast.

"I brought you some macaroni and cheese. Bake it for about forty-five minutes at three-fifty. I wrote it down and taped the note to the foil so you wouldn't lose it."

"Good thinking," Sylvie said. "Must be the teacher in you."

"I'll put it in the refrigerator."

When she returned to the living room, Sylvie looked up at her. "Do you and Micah want to come over for supper? Jean-Luc will undoubtedly be able to dredge up some energy to play with Sophie."

Sally shook her head. "No, thanks. Tanner's coming over."

Sylvie's eyes opened wide. "Now that's something new."

"I don't know if there's anything to get excited about, so don't make a big deal of this."

"But it *is* a big deal. Maybe not for you, but it is for him. He's always been a rather solitary creature."

"He's not antisocial."

"Of course not." Sylvie switched her baby to the other side. "I think the world of him. Everyone does. But to me, he's always seemed so alone. Like he doesn't have anyone."

"What about Karen?"

"There's having and then there's having. Karen is pretty much like a big sister to him. She tends to be like that, you know, always everyone's big sister. I think it's a way she can keep men at a distance. Tanner, now. I think he keeps people at a distance, too. Which is why I'm thrilled he's going to have supper with you. He won't be alone."

"Don't get your hopes up."

"My hopes are perpetually up. I have high hopes for all the people I love. Oh, speaking of the people I love. I love my rocking chair. It was the best baby present I could ever have. Thank you so much."

"It's from all of us."

"I know. I wanted to tell you how much I love it."

"Where's Ray?" Sally asked. Ray would be a good person to talk to Micah. Ray had lost his parents when he was young. Sylvie had lost her mother. Under normal circumstances, she'd have immediately asked them to talk to Micah. But not right now, after the birth of their baby. This was probably not the best time to ask them to talk to Micah about how it felt when a parent died.

"He took Jean-Luc next door, to Karen's to play

with the Newfies. He didn't want Jean-Luc to feel slighted by all the attention everyone has heaped on the baby."

"So how do you like motherhood so far?" Sally asked.

Sylvie looked up and smiled a Mona Lisa smile. "It's more wonderful than I ever thought it would be. I knew I'd love my baby. But no one told me I'd love him as much as I do."

"Maybe that's one of those things that no one can ever tell you."

Sylvie nodded. "Probably."

Sally looked around Sylvie's living room. She could see the floor. "Katie's still cleaning house for you this summer?"

Sylvie nodded. "I don't know what I'll do when she leaves for college."

"You'll be fine."

"Everyone keeps telling me that. You know, before the boogaloo was born, I was afraid I'd be a terrible mother. I was scared to death I wouldn't know what to do with the baby."

Sally was dumbfounded. "You were?"

Sylvie nodded. "People assume women automatically know what to do with a baby. Most women do. You do. You've always known what to do with kids. You didn't have to learn, you just knew. It was hardwired into your brain. But not me. I've never known. In some ways, the idea of having a baby scared me to death."

"Why didn't you tell me?"

"It's not the kind of thing you mention to people. It's something you keep hidden. Something

you're ashamed of. That you're afraid you'll fail
miserably at something so basic, so utterly com-
monplace. Something that everyone else seems to
be able to do without even thinking about it. Sort
of like cleaning house, only with major cosmic
ramifications."

"So how do you feel about it now?" Sally asked.
"Motherhood."

Sylvie smiled again. That same beatific smile was,
this time, aimed down at the baby at her breast. "I
don't know why I ever worried. Somehow the old
hormones kicked in and I seem to know what to
do. It amazes me how instinctual it is." She looked
up at Sally and grinned. "You must feel the same
way about Micah."

Sally gathered her thoughts into a coherent jumble. She wanted to pour her heart out to Sylvie.
She wanted to express all her frustration and anguish and her fear of failure. She was sure Sylvie
would understand. Then she noticed the dark circles under Sylvie's eyes. She saw how even through
the joy, Sylvie was tired. She knew she couldn't add
to her friend's full load. Friends didn't always share
with friends. So she swallowed back the rush of
words. She nodded. "It's a miracle, isn't it?"

Sylvie lifted the baby to her shoulder and patted
his tiny back. He let out a tiny belch. Then she
lifted her eyebrows. "Want to hold him?"

Sally reached for the baby. "Stupid question.
And here I always thought you were smart. I was
sure fooled." She held Sylvie's baby in her arms,
softly sang him silly nursery rhymes until his little

eyes closed. She looked back to Sylvie. Their eyes held. "I'm glad you're my friend."

Tanner enjoyed the macaroni and cheese. He had seconds. He even gave in to Sally and allowed her to put a small—very small, he insisted—amount on a plate for Wing. Wing thought it was excellent. As did Sophie, though Sophie inhaled her food so quickly it was difficult to tell if she actually tasted it.

Sally scooped another helping of macaroni and cheese into a plastic container, "For your lunch tomorrow," she said. She filled another with cherry crisp, and one with broccoli. He looked at the three containers she set down next to him on the table. He didn't know what to say. No one had ever done anything like this for him before.

Taking his plate into Sally's kitchen, Tanner glanced at the refrigerator. Then he stopped and read. Sally's original words, *Who has seen the wind?* were still there, along with the words he'd added, *no one.* Sally—he assumed it was Sally—had added the words *one who sees not the wind does not live.*

"What's wrong?" she asked.

He gestured at the words. "I don't get it."

She smiled tolerantly and patted his arm. "That's okay. Men often don't 'get' magnetic poetry."

He and Micah went into the backyard to have their lesson. Sally stayed in the cool house, behind the closed glass doors. He missed her. He wondered what she was doing.

He and Micah and Sophie worked on heeling,

and sits, downs, informal recalls. Sophie loved recalls. Tanner liked watching the expressions on Sophie's face while she waited at one end of the yard to be called. She leaned towards Micah, concentrating intently, listening for the command. When Micah called, "Sophie, come," she shot across the distance separating them and threw herself into his arms. This evening, Micah caught her up, lost his balance, and the two of them went over in a laughing, tail-wagging tangle. Tanner indulged himself with a quick thought of crossing the distance to Sally and tangling himself in her arms. And legs.

"Was that good, or what?" Micah called to him.

"Great. It was great." He shook the vision of tangling with Sally out of his mind. "I like her enthusiasm, her energy." He had to shake that vision out again. "Soon we'll begin working on formal recalls."

"What we'll do in a trial."

"Yes. What you'll do in a trial."

"How soon do you think we'll be ready?"

"If you continue as you've been doing, I'd say you'll probably be ready by spring."

Micah had that typical teenage expression that said he was pleased, but didn't want to appear geeky about it. For an instant, Tanner could see Micah as he must have been before the accident.

After Micah's lesson, she invited him to stay to eat popcorn and watch a movie. Micah wanted him to stay, too. They were all looking at him—Sally, Micah, Sophie, Wing. Even the cats looked at him—at least

Tess and Troy did. He'd never seen Sally's third cat. Then he noticed the fish. The fish watched him, too. They all watched and waited for his answer. He knew it would be dangerous to stay. It was dangerous for him to be here now. He knew over the last few weeks, he'd come awfully close to feeling things he shouldn't feel. But they watched and waited, wanting him to stay. He wanted what he had when he was with them. "What are we watching?"

"Anything that doesn't have Mel Gibson in it," said Micah. "Sally loves Mel Gibson."

"Why don't you pick?" Sally said.

"Me?" He didn't know anything about choosing movies, especially for other people. "Okay. If Micah helps."

So he and Micah looked through the movies on Sally's shelf and decided that even though she had a lot of chick flicks, there were enough real movies to choose from.

"T2," Micah announced.

Sally brought out three huge bowls of popcorn. They sat together on the couch, sharing their popcorn with the dogs, and Tess and Troy. Tanner finally met Jude, who promptly curled up on his lap. They had all seen the movie so many times they could recite half of the lines, which they did.

Tanner felt good. He felt warm and accepted. He hadn't felt like this in a long time, not since he first came to Hartley, when he stayed with Karen and Katie while he built his pole barn. He felt like he was part of a family. He felt like that now. He could become used to this. Even so, it was very dangerous.

Twenty-one

Thursday morning, after Micah finished his exercises, Sally said to him, "Would you like to go back to Vermont for a visit?"

Micah's head jerked up. For an instant he froze, then he said, "Yeah, it'd be okay."

"I talked to your grandmother earlier. I wanted to make sure she wasn't going to be out of town, or anything."

Micah didn't say anything. He didn't want her to know how important this was to him. She didn't want him to know how difficult this was for her. She had to open her hands, still holding him close to her heart. She had to let him make this decision based on its own merits, not because of how she felt about it.

"The Wylys are driving Shane down to Bowling Green this weekend for hockey camp." She held her breath. She didn't want to upset Micah by bringing up hockey camp. Micah didn't react, so she continued. "They said they'd be happy to give you a ride back to Vermont." That wasn't right, though, Sally thought. Micah shouldn't be going *back* to Vermont, he should be going *away* to Vermont, and then coming home again to Hartley. Thinking about grammar and word structure helped keep her emotions in check. "If you want to, they'll pick you up very early Sunday morning."

"Yeah," Micah said. "That'd be okay."

She wasn't sure yet how he'd get back to Hartley. She didn't want to say anything to him, didn't want to give him the chance to tell her he wanted to stay in Vermont.

His gaze suddenly shot to Sophie.

"Sophie can stay here with me, of course. That's not a problem at all." Then she hoped he didn't think she was holding Sophie hostage—to make him return. "Unless you want to take her. I don't know what the Wylys would say, but we could talk to them about it. She doesn't appear to have any car issues. But then, she hasn't gone on a twelve-hour, straight-through car trip before, has she?"

Micah shook his head. "No."

Sally bent down and held out her hand in an invitation to Sophie. Sophie heaved herself up and rushed over to Sally, her tail doing that electricity-generating thing again. Sally pulled the little dog onto her lap. I'd miss you, she said silently to the dog. I'd really miss you. Sophie sighed and snuggled into her arms.

"So, if you want to go, we need to make a list of all the things we have to do before you leave. Call your grandmother and the Wylys. Make sure all your clothes are clean. Is there anything you need? Shirts? Socks? Whatever. Anyone you want to call? A new book to read in the car, a new CD for your Walkman? Just name it. This evening, we can go to the mall, or if you'd rather go somewhere else . . . Or if you want to think about it tonight and go tomorrow . . . It's your show, here."

Now she had to not cry in front of him. She had to wait. She had to trust him. The next move was his.

"Will you practice with Sophie while I'm gone so she doesn't forget?" Micah asked. "Not heeling, or stuff like that. That's something she only has to do with me. I mean, stuff like using the right words, like, if she's on the couch you say *off* instead of *down*. Stuff like that."

Sally nodded. "Every day. I'll ask Tanner to make sure I'm doing things correctly so I don't confuse her."

"And when you want her to down, you say *down*, not *lie down*."

"Vocabulary words."

Micah blinked. "Yeah. Vocabulary words."

Sally grinned. "I'll be speaking fluent Sophie before you know it." The little dog in her lap heard her name and thwapped her tail.

That afternoon, Tanner loaded Maxie into the van and drove to Hartley Veterinary Clinic. He was early for his appointment, so he took Maxie for a short walk in the park next door before he took her in.

"Hi, Tanner," said Suzette.

"Hi, Tanner," said Jess. "Hello, Maxerooni.

What's happening with you?" She gave Maxie a head rub. Maxie loved head rubs.

Tanner followed her into the exam room. Melissa breezed in. "Maxie!" Melissa loved Maxie. Everyone loved Maxie—it was an involuntary reaction.

Tanner told her about Maxie's slight hesitation to do stairs, how she got up gingerly—it was very subtle, you had to look close for it—he looked at his dogs closely.

Melissa gave Maxie an overall look. Looked at her eyes, in her ears, checked her gums and teeth. Palpated her belly, listened to her chest. Tanner held her mouth closed so she didn't pant while Melissa listened to her heartbeat.

"Everything checks out up front," Melissa told the dog. "Let's look at your rear end, girlie."

Melissa ran her hand down each back leg, picked up each furry foot to wiggle toes, check pads, flex and rotate ankles, then knees. Maxie's left side was fine, but she winced when Melissa began to rotate her right hip. "I see why you brought her in," said Melissa. "Good girl, Maxie. I won't do that anymore."

Maxie wagged her tail and looked apologetic.

Melissa consulted the dog's records. "You're seventeen months old. You're a teenager, that's what you are."

Maxie shoved her nose in Melissa's pocket.

"That hip is bothering her. Do you want me to x-ray? She's not two years old, so they can't be sent in to OFA, but we can take a look if you want."

Tanner nodded. "If there is a problem, she can't continue with the program. We need to know."

Melissa led Maxie into the back area. "Why don't you wait here," she suggested.

Tanner shuffled his feet while he waited. He wandered back out into the waiting room and looked through the *AKC Gazettes*—but he'd read all of them already.

"So, Tanner," Suzette said, "isn't that Sophie puppy cute as a bug?"

Tanner had never thought of bugs as cute. "Yeah," he said. "She's a great little dog."

"Sally has been bringing her cats here forever," Suzette said, by way of explanation. "She brought Sophie in for a just-to-be-sure checkup. What a cutie!" Suzette sighed. "I want a dog in the worst way, but I can't have one until I move out of my parents' home, and I can't do that until I'm finished with school. And here Sally, who doesn't like dogs, of all people, ends up with one who is as adorable as Sophie. It's not fair."

"You'll have your dog someday, Suzette."

"When I finish school, and that won't be for another year." She sighed dramatically, presumably at the gross injustices of life.

"Say, Suzette, do you know why Sally Foster doesn't like dogs?" he asked.

Suzette shook her head. "Nope. I never even thought to ask her. It's one of those things. Some people are dog people and some are cat people. She's a cat person."

The phone rang, taking Suzette's attention.

"Tanner," Melissa beckoned from the doorway, "look at this picture."

Back in the exam room, Maxie greeted him with a great wagging of tail.

Melissa had two X rays snagged up on a light box on the wall.

"This is the left hip." She pointed. "And here is the right. Look at the shape of her right hip socket. It's not bad, but it's a little shallow. Right now it looks like she might be borderline dysplastic. I don't know what the OFA people would say about it. It's one of those judgment calls. It's certainly not serious—at least, not right now. There's no need to start saving pennies for a hip replacement just yet. If she were a family pet I'd tell you to keep an eye on her, and let her be a dog. If she seemed to be in pain we'd look into pain medication, and when she was two years old we'd take new X rays and send them in to OFA. But she's not supposed to be a family pet, is she?"

Tanner stuck his hands in his pockets as he looked carefully at the film. "No, she isn't. It looks like she will be, now."

"I'm sorry."

"Thanks. I'm really sorry, too. You don't know how sorry I am," he said.

Maxie sat at his side, where she belonged. She watched his face, looking for clues to his mood. Right now, her face wore a worried expression.

"Well, Maxie," he said. Then he didn't say anything else. There was nothing more to say.

Melissa bent down to pet Maxie. "You are a beautiful girl. If I didn't have two dogs right now I'd take you in a heartbeat."

Maxie spared a token tail wag, but her gaze on Tanner's face never wavered.

"Do you want me to send some pain meds with her?" Melissa asked. "Just in case."

Tanner drove back to the school with a bottle of pills in his pocket and Maxie at his side. At a stoplight, he looked over at her beautiful face. She had no idea she was going to be placed in a pet home.

Now here was an example of Suzette's idea of cosmic injustice. Mentally, temperamentally, Maxie was everything a successful service dog should be. She was that one dog in a million, like Wing. Training them was as easy and smooth as silk. Now he couldn't use her. He felt like he'd been punched in the gut. It did not feel good.

He drove back to the school in a blue funk.

Maxie put her chin on his knee and looked up at him with soft eyes.

It was impossible to resist her. "You are a good girl."

Maxie wagged her tail in agreement.

Back at the school, Corinne caught his gaze, dropped her eyes, and went back to her typing. She didn't ask.

Patti, the third trainer, was in the workroom at her computer. She swiveled around in her chair to gaze at Tanner for a minute. She did ask.

Tanner told her.

"Oh, I'm so very sorry," she said. "I know how you had such great hopes for her." She gave Tanner another long look and then patted her leg. "Come see me, Maxie."

After checking with Tanner to be sure it was all right, Maxie went to Patti for some attention. Patti fondled Maxie's ears. "It isn't your fault, sweetie," she said. "Let's blame it on that old Mendel and his dumb experiments with peas. It's *his* fault we have genetics. You are such a special dog! And you know, right now, somewhere in the world there is some unsuspecting person who needs you. Your job will be to help them. Not the way we thought you'd help—they may not even know they need you, but they do. And when you go live with them they will realize how incredibly lucky they are and they won't know how they ever lived without you. Tanner could've told you all this, but he's a guy, and guys don't like to talk about mushy stuff." Maxie heaved a great sigh.

Patti tossed Tanner an impish smile. "I made grape Kool-Aid. If you want some, it's in the refrigerator."

It was her way of giving him a hug. "Thanks, Patti."

He opened a computer file and found Lucy's phone number.

He sat and stared at the seven numbers. Then he looked at Maxie. He didn't want to have to scratch her from the program. But he had no choice. It would be unconscionable to place an even slightly dysplastic dog in a working situation. It was crucial for every Helper Dog to be perfectly trained *and* perfectly able. One out of two was not good enough. Maxie had to be dropped from the program and placed in a pet home. Lucy, as Maxie's puppy raiser, would have the first opportunity to adopt her.

He opened a file drawer, pulled out a form, filled in all the pertinent spaces. He reached for the stapler and attached the vet's report to the form. He realized he was only delaying the inevitable. He looked down at the dog lying at his feet, her head on her paws. Her eyes were trained on him. "You know something's going on, don't you?"

She gave her tail a twitch, but the expression of concern never left her face.

Lucy wasn't answering her phone right now; he knew what to do, so after the beep he left a message. "Hi, Lucy, it's Tanner. Please give me a call as soon as you can. Thanks."

Maxie stayed at his feet for the rest of the afternoon while he did paperwork, talked to puppy raisers, read their monthly reports. Now that his time with Maxie was over, he found he did not want to give her up. So she accompanied him to the break room, where she opened the refrigerator. She brilliantly ignored Patti's grape Kool-Aid and instead neatly pulled out a can of soda and, holding it carefully between her teeth, she went over to him. She sat in her perfect sit and waited for him to take the can out of her mouth. He knew if he asked, she would wait for him all day. "You truly are Miss Perfect."

* * *

He wandered up to the front office to give Corinne Maxie's release form and to check for messages. Corinne took the completed form without comment and put it in a folder on her desk. Only then did she look up at him. She held a letter in her hand.

"My twentieth high school reunion, this summer." She sighed. "Gee, the time has gone by quickly. Where's all that fun I was supposed to have?"

"We make our own fun," Tanner said. He knew she was trying to cheer him up.

Corinne looked surprised. "You mean I've waited all this time for nothing? Rats. I was looking forward to a great bunch of fun. All I get is an invite to go back and see the people I went to school with. Big deal. I don't know if I'll go or not," she said. She looked thoughtful. "They say you can't go home again. You can go to the place, but home is an entire gestalt of place and time and people. It's a long way to Iowa—in more ways than one. I never thought I'd ever want to leave that town—and here I am, all grown up, smack dab in the middle of Ohio. So, Tanner. Where did you go to high school?"

Her conversational tone did not escape him. "Further away than Iowa," he said. In more ways than one, he added to himself. He would never receive an invitation to a reunion. For him, going back was not an option.

Lucy hadn't returned his call by the time he left

for home. He took Maxie home with him. He told himself he wanted to give her an opportunity to become used to family life again, like a halfway house. He recognized the irony.

Wing was pleasantly pleased to meet Maxie. Both dogs had immaculate manners. They sniffed various portions of each other's anatomy and each accepted the other as equal in all things.

When Aretha saw Maxie, she leaped straight up in the air and scrabbled around to tear off in the opposite direction, only to whirl around and dash right up to Maxie, putting on her brakes at the last possible moment. She looked like a cartoon. Maxie, who had grown up with Lucy's parents' cats, gave her a friendly greeting. Aretha made an abysmal attempt to appear important and intimidating. But she soon gave up and decided Maxie was a great big new giant-sized, lifelike toy.

The kitten would soon be old enough to live at the school, where she would help teach the dogs to ignore cats. "You'll do an excellent job at it," Tanner told her. He picked her up so he could look her in the eye. "You'll be a working girl."

Aretha squealed and squirmed. Tanner put her down. She immediately decided to play Mountain Climber. She was The Climber; she would allow Maxie to be The Mountain. Maxie played her part like a trooper. Aretha climbed all over her. She made not the slightest move to stop her, not the slightest protest.

* * *

"Hi, Tanner, it's Lucy," she said. "Your message sounded urgent. I hope it's okay to call you at home."

"That's fine," he told her. "Thanks for calling back." There was no pretty way to bring this up. "I took Maxie in to see Dr. March. It looks like she's dysplastic. Her right hip. It's not bad, but . . ."

"It's enough," Lucy said.

"Yeah. It's enough. It's nothing we could have predicted—it's one of those genetic things. Both of her parents have great hips and elbows, and all the dogs for a couple of generations back. So, because she has good, clean genes behind her, it might not even ever bother her much."

"But it's too much for her to work with."

"Yes. It's too big a risk."

"So you'll be releasing her?"

"Yes. I completed the paperwork today, all but the director's signature." Then he waited. Lucy had been a puppy raiser for a very long time. She knew what this meant. She knew Maxie was now hers.

There was silence. Then Lucy moaned. "Oh, no! Oh, Tanner, I just moved! I signed a lease! I can't have pets! They said I could raise puppies because they're Helper Dogs, they're not pets, and all the ADA stuff. But I can't have pets! Maxie would be a pet!"

Tanner looked at Maxie. He felt real bad. He knew how much Lucy loved Maxie. "Do you want a couple of days to think it over?"

"No," she said. "A couple of days won't make

any difference. I can't leave here for another eleven months, and she needs a home now." Lucy began to cry. "It's just so unfair!"

"Yes. It is. I'm sorry." He was.

"Promise me you'll find her a terrific home. The best home. Promise me she'll live with someone who will adore her, who will think she's perfect, where she'll be family instead of dog."

"I promise."

"This sucks big time."

"Yes. It does."

He had enough time for a quick bowl of soup before his class arrived. He finished his soup and remembered he hadn't checked the mail. "Maxie," he said, "would you like to go for a walk?"

She most certainly would, so they walked the long driveway to his mailbox. He opened the door and pulled out half a dozen envelopes. Most of them were bills. But one of them was addressed in familiar handwriting. He didn't have to read the return address to know it was from his mother. She was like the terminator, he thought. She was dangerous. And, like the terminator, she would never, ever give up.

Twenty-two

Somehow, it was difficult to keep his mind on his class that night. Tanner was glad Karen was an experienced assistant. She was a pro. He should really turn one of the beginner's classes over to her completely. He would talk to her about it. Maybe in the fall, after she passed her certification test, she'd want to teach her own class instead of assisting him with his. That would give him more free time to . . . to do what? What did he do when he wasn't doing dog stuff? He didn't think he was ever not doing dog stuff. Except when he was with Sally.

The other night, before the fireworks started, when he sat with her while Micah played Frisbee, that was nice. He thought about Micah and Sally. Then he remembered what she said. Even though they know they might fail, mothers keep trying because sometimes it's the only way they know how to show their love. Maybe his mother kept sending him letters because—

He didn't want to think about his mother. "Good," he said to his class. "Now let's see how your sits are. Who wants to be first?" He chose a portly woman with a boxer puppy, leggy and energetic.

The woman led her dog to the middle of the ring. "Brownie, sit." The puppy, after thinking about it for a moment, sat. "Good dog," the woman said. The puppy was so excited he bounced up to lick her face. The whole class chuckled.

One by one, his students asked their dogs to sit. One by one, the dogs sat. Some more quickly than others, some sat and waited, some sat and bounced up.

"Good," he said. "Let's talk about the word *stay.*"

Class was over at nine o'clock. As usual, Karen stayed to help put things away after class and sweep the floor.

"Thanks," he said.

"No problem." She picked up a stray sweater left on a bench and hung it on the coatrack. "So," she said, dusting her hands on the seat of her jeans, "how're you doing in your life?"

"Okay." He thought. "Today I had to release a terrific dog from the program, but other than that, things are fine. How're you doing in your life?" he wondered if Katie had told her about the Marines thing.

"Pretty decent."

So Katie hadn't mentioned it yet, he thought.

Karen studied him, deciding whether or not he was telling her the truth. "You planning to enter the trials in August?"

"Yeah." He held the door open for her, and followed her out into the night.

"Soon Wing will have her OTCH. Then what will you do?"

"What do you mean?"

"When Wing finishes her OTCH, she'll be at the top of AKC obedience. She can't go any higher. She will be one of the best-trained dogs in the country. What will you do? With your life? Start a new puppy?" Her eyes twinkled. "Maybe an Airedale, or a saluki. Now *that* would be a challenge for you. I don't remember ever hearing of any OTCH salukis. Or Airedales. Maybe another Border collie. If you don't have Wing to train and trial, how will you spend your time?"

He shoved his hands in his pockets and leaned against the doorway. "I don't know." He remembered being with Sally and Micah, the family feeling. He thought of Sally's house. "Maybe I'll take up coin collecting."

Karen continued to gaze at him. It made him uncomfortable.

"What?" He tried to joke. "You don't approve of coins?"

She leaned against the side of the barn, next to him, and looked up at the night sky. "Look at all those stars. It amazes me that Jessie can tell them apart." Then she said, "You can trust Sally, you know. She's one of the people I'd trust with my life. With Katie's life. Even with my dogs if it came to that."

"How did Sally come into this?"

Karen ignored his question. "She's one of the

best people I know. The kind of teacher every thinking parent hopes their kid will have. She's good. She's honest and straightforward. She's fiercely loyal, as you've probably guessed. She doesn't live her life around the opinions of others. She does what she knows is right. She is worth more than gold and diamonds."

"Why are you telling me this?"

Only then did her gaze leave the sky to land on him once more. "I figured you knew it already— you can be pretty perceptive. But I wanted to tell you anyway. Sometimes hearing something verbalized makes it more real. Sally Foster is someone you, Tanner Dodge, can trust." She gave him a quick hug. "Call this a push in the right direction from your honorary big sister."

Later that night, he called her. "I know it's late."

"That's okay. What's up?"

"Were you asleep?"

"No. Reading in bed."

His mouth went dry. "I hope it's a good book."

"Another one from the rehab list. I hope they're helping me learn how to deal with Micah."

"You know how to deal with Micah."

"I don't know. Some days he seems to be doing better, seems more . . . I don't know . . . maybe content. Maybe it's resignation. Then all of a sudden, he doesn't want anything to do with me, or with Hartley. You're the only one he seems to be able to relate to. Other than Sophie and Jude."

"Have you thought any more about counseling?"

"I don't want to nag him."

"It isn't something you can make him do," Tanner agreed. "He has to be willing."

"The old horse and water thing. I know. Right now, he's not the least bit interested in that water." Sally sighed. "I'm afraid I'm failing him."

"No. You're not."

"What makes you so sure?" she asked.

"Because you care. Because you're willing to re-arrange your entire life to make him part of it, and because you *are* concerned that you might be failing him. If you were failing him, you wouldn't care whether you were or weren't. The possibility of failing him, and of what that might eventually mean to him, wouldn't even enter your mind."

"I guess it's like my mom said. Sometimes the only way mothers have of showing their love is by continuing to try. Like drops of water landing on a stone will eventually wear it away."

"I guess it's like that."

She gave a small, sad laugh. "Maybe in an eon or so, Micah will let me into his life."

He wondered what it would be like for Sally to be part of his life. He gazed around the room he called home. No, Sally did not belong here. Sally was from a different world, a world where the edges were round and smooth and soft, not harsh and angular. He wanted his world to be Sally's kind of round and soft. "Deep down Micah knows you love him. I think he'll be okay."

"You're going to tell me to be patient?"

"I don't have to. You are patient. I know you'll do the right thing."

"I'm glad you have confidence in me," she said.

"Yeah. I do. I also have confidence in Micah."

His eye caught the letter from his mother on the table, where he'd tossed it. Sally said mothers didn't give up because they loved their children. After a moment, Tanner reached in the drawer underneath his computer and pulled out a stack of unopened letters—all addressed in the same hand. His mother hadn't given up. He couldn't go so far as to say it was because she loved him, but he flipped through the envelopes and arranged them by their postmark date.

Aretha tore across the room to leap onto his lap. She didn't make it. She clung by her claws to the leg of his jeans. He unsnagged her and set her in his lap where she promptly curled herself into a fluffy ball and purred. Wing and Maxie took up positions on either side of him like bookends. They watched him. Maxie put her head down on his knee, her way of offering comfort.

He opened the first letter and began to read.

Friday morning, after Micah finished his physical therapy exercises, Sally drove him to the mall. There was no way she would let him go back to Vermont without at least a couple of new T-shirts. She didn't want to give Mary the least opportunity to complain about her ability to take care of Micah.

Waiting at a stoplight, she had an idea. She turned the corner and drove a few blocks and pulled up at the curb. She turned off the engine. "This," she pointed to the large brick building, "is Garfield Middle School, where you'll be going this fall. Hartley has three middle schools. There's Hoover, the first middle school. It's in the old part of town. Your mom and I went to Jackson, over on the east side, back in the days when there were only two middle schools. Garfield was built about seven or eight years ago. Do you want to go in? We can walk around the halls so you can get a feel for the school, and meet any teachers who happen to be here today. I know some of them, of course."

Micah had seemed to shrink back into the car seat. "No."

Sally sighed mentally. "Okay. No big deal. Maybe another time."

She turned the key, started the engine, and pulled away from the curb. She felt totally defeated. She was a failure as a new mom. It looked more and more as if Deb and Kevin's faith in her had been misplaced. They parked in a "Handicapped" parking space and went into the mall. Sally made a straight line for the cookie store and bought them each a huge chocolate-chocolate-chip cookie.

Micah picked out four nondescript T-shirts and three pairs of jeans. He showed a definite lack of enthusiasm about the entire business. Sally assumed it was typical shopping behavior of teenage boys when accompanied by a female adult. She wondered if Tanner would be willing to take him shopping for school clothes.

Hold it, she told herself. She had no right to assume Tanner was at her beck and call to pick up the pieces and take over whenever she felt unsure around Micah. It was time to stop telling herself she didn't know anything about teenagers. This wasn't a random teenager. This was Micah Fennessy, and more than once she'd changed his diapers when he was a baby. This was the kid she'd taken to the state fair one year; she let him eat as much cotton candy and hot dogs as he wanted and then he threw up on the Ferris wheel. This was the kid she sent dozens of books to every year. This was the kid who sometimes looked so much like his father that her breath caught. Kevin never paid attention to his clothes, either. Then it hit her. Micah's behavior wasn't teenage, it was genetic.

Suddenly, for some unknown reason, she was happy. "May I assume," she said to Micah, "you're not a clothes horse?"

"Huh?" He gave her a funny look.

"When you look confused like that, you look exactly like your dad. I seem to remember your father always wearing jeans. Except when he and your mom got married, of course. She wouldn't let him wear jeans."

Micah nodded slowly. "Sometimes," he said shyly, "he had to wear a suit to work. You know, when he was doing some presentation for some bigwigs or something. He only had one suit, and he hated it. He said suits made him feel boa constrictored. So one year, for his birthday, Mom bought a tie and she painted it to look like a great big snake."

"I'm being eaten by a boa constrictor." Sally sang the words softly so no one else in the mall could hear. She couldn't help it—her kindergarten teacher persona made her do it. She continued with the song until—

"And I don't like it very much!" Micah finished the last line with a flourish. He looked at her, she looked at him. For the first time since the accident, he grinned at her. And it was a great big, face-splitting grin.

They ate lunch—peanut butter and jelly sandwiches and iced tea, with the ubiquitous cherry cobbler—outside on the patio. In the warm summer sun, the tall glasses of tea got all wet and slippery with condensation. By the time they were finished, the sun was hot on top of Sally's head and bright in her eyes, but she didn't feel like expending the energy to get out the big shade umbrella. Instead, she shaded her eyes with her hand as she tried to capture the last bit of cherry goo on her fork. She gave up and put her plate on the ground for Sophie to lick.

Micah looked at her questioningly.

"What?"

"I thought," he said, "you didn't approve of dogs licking plates."

"Oh." Sally thought. "I guess I changed my mind." She shrugged. "Sophie made a convert out of me. Now we don't have to scrape the dishes— they can go straight into the dishwasher."

Micah looked at her for a moment, then put his

plate down for Sophie, too. Sophie immediately abandoned the tongue-scrubbed plate and headed for Micah's plate.

"Greener pastures," Sally said. She drained her glass of the last of her iced tea and leaned back in her chair. She decided this would be a good time to bring up a touchy topic. "The other day, I talked to that therapist up in Cleveland. He told me they had a peer group that meets once a week. He said you'd probably enjoy it."

Micah snorted. "I don't think so."

"You'd meet other kids your age who are going through the same kinds of things you're going through."

Micah looked at her as if she was crazy. "No one is going through what I'm going through. Besides, what makes you think I'd want to talk to anyone else about it anyway? You always want to talk about things. About *feelings*. As if you think it will help. Well, it won't. Talking won't help. Meeting other kids won't help. Nothing will help. Nothing."

He grabbed his plate and glass and stomped back into the house. Sally heard him open the dishwasher and thump it closed. A few moments later, she heard the door to his room slam. She looked at Sophie. Sophie looked at her.

Twenty-three

Late that afternoon, while Sally was peeling potatoes for supper, Micah's Aunt Mary called. The woman seemed to have a perverse sense of when would be the most disruptive time to call, Sally thought sourly as she knocked on Micah's closed door.

Without a word, Micah opened the door, took the phone, and shut the door again.

Sally sagged against the wall. Seemed like some days she couldn't do anything right. She felt like the ugly sister in the fairy tale. When the beautiful sister spoke, her words fell like roses and gold coins. But when the ugly sister spoke, her words fell like toads that sat on men's hearts. Yup. That's just how Sally felt.

When Micah finally came out of his room and put the phone back on its cradle, he didn't speak. Didn't even meet Sally's eyes. Instead, he went back into his room and Sally heard his computer booting up.

Supper was hamburgers and Sylvie's special potato salad, minus the nasturtium petals and water-

melon. Sally set everything on the table and stood
back to look at it. It looked pretty good. Since Micah arrived, she was eating better than she'd ever
eaten before. When she'd lived by herself, she'd
often have a bowl of Cheerios or ice cream for
supper. It seemed silly to waste time cooking just
for herself. She didn't like to cook for cooking's
sake, as her friend Liz did. But now, now when it
was important to be able to cook, she found she
could manage. She did more than manage. She
thought she was doing a fine job.

The meal properly admired, it was time to call
Micah.

"So how are your aunt and uncle?" she asked,
keeping her tone deliberately conversational. Start
with something innocuous and then gradually work
around to the real problem. It was a technique one
used with kindergartners. Sally was good at it. At
least when she was talking to kindergartners.

"Okay." Micah muttered.

"And your grandmother?"

"She's fine. I guess."

Hmmm. Kindergartners were usually more forth-
coming. Sally took a bite of potato salad. Maybe
she'd have to chuck the technique and take the
bull by the horns.

But then, Micah spoke. "Aunt Mary said if I want
to, I can stay with her instead of Grandma." It was
thrown out like a challenge.

Warning bells went off in Sally's mind. This is
not a drill. Her instinctive reaction was to scream
no, no, a thousand times no. Asking Mary to take
care of Micah was like asking the fox to guard the

henhouse. Mary would insinuate, and twist her words, and manipulate Micah into wanting to stay. But before she could manage to speak, she caught sight of Micah's face. The words died in her throat. She swallowed. "Do you want to stay with your aunt Mary?" She felt like she was asking more than the simple question.

Micah looked uneasy. "Not really. It's not my house."

"Well, then, that's settled."

"She said it would be hard for Grandma to take care of me."

Sally frowned. "Wait a minute. Is something going on with your grandma that I don't know about?"

Micah shrugged. "I don't think so."

"Then why would it be difficult for her?"

Micah seemed to shrink before her eyes. "Aunt Mary said Grandma was too frail to take care of a disabled teenager."

Ten, nine, eight—Sally counted furiously—seven, six, sheer force of will holding back the angry words, five, four—she hoped Mary would break her foot—three, two, deep breath, one. Another breath. There. "You are not disabled."

"Yes, I am."

"Well, okay. Technically, I guess you are. But there is nothing you can't do for yourself. You are not an invalid."

"I know," he muttered.

"Neither is your grandmother, no matter what—" She had to stop herself before she said something nasty about Mary and made him feel like he had to

defend that woman. She took another breath and
made a conscious decision to gentle her voice. "Your
grandmother is looking forward to your visit. She
told me she was going to go shopping today to buy
stuff to make Chicken Alfredo. Micah, she is so looking forward to having you stay with her."

Behind the wall in his eyes, he seemed to be
pleading for something. She took a stab.

"Do you want me to talk to Mary?"

Micah gave her an eloquent shrug. "I guess."

Sally kept her smile to herself. "I'll call her tomorrow." Maybe by tomorrow she could gather up
enough control to talk to Mary civilly. Then she
had a thought. "If there's anyone else you want to
call, back in Vermont, to tell that you're coming
back for a visit, you can call them, too, you know."
She knew Micah hadn't called any of his Vermont
friends since he'd arrived, but she wanted him to
know that he could.

Saturday, Micah seemed more down than usual.
Sophie picked up on his mood and didn't wag her
tail. She held her head low and looked up as if she
were guilty of whatever it was that was making Micah unhappy. She didn't even perk up when Tess
wandered across the room right in front of her
nose. She followed the cat with her eyes, but didn't
move. Jude spent the morning in Micah's room,
on Micah's lap as he surfed the net, then on the
bed supervising as Micah packed. Micah waved
away Sally's offer of a suitcase; instead, he brought
his hockey bag out of the closet.

Sally finally settled down on the couch with another one of those rehab list books. She didn't even want to look at it. She slipped it under the couch and reached up onto a bookshelf and pulled off *Madensky Square*. She would fall into turn-of-the-century Vienna and leave Hartley behind. Sophie jumped onto the couch and curled up next to her, as close as she could get her little body. She gave Sally a worried look. "It's okay," Sally told the little dog. "You can stay here." She petted Sophie's head. Sophie sighed and closed her eyes.

Well, this is something new, Sally thought. Micah with a cat, and me with a dog.

That afternoon, Tanner called and offered to pick up Micah and Sophie and work with them in a park nearby. He'd drop them off afterwards, if that was okay with Sally. It was.

"Would you like to stay for supper?" she asked.

"Of course."

After supper she packaged up leftovers for his lunch again. "I could get used to this," he told her.

She turned pink. "No problem."

"It might not be a problem for you, but it's certainly a boon for me."

"I'm glad you like leftovers."

"Anything is better than my bologna sandwiches." He kept his gaze on her face, to try to encourage her to look at him, but she kept her eyes to herself. He thought she was upset about something.

Tanner took Micah to the park, neutral ground. "Let's see how she's doing." He stuck his hands in his pockets. "Micah, get your dog ready."

"Sophie," Micah gave the leash a gentle tug. Sophie scampered over to him. "Sophie, sit." Sophie sat. Micah scooted her around until she was sitting next to him, instead of in front of him, ready to heel.

"Forward," Tanner said.

"Sophie, heel." Micah stepped off on his left foot, as Tanner had instructed him, holding the folded leash in his left hand. Sophie trotted off beside him, sitting when he stopped, as she was supposed to. It wasn't perfect, but it was quite an improvement. "Loosen the leash," he told Micah. "She needs to be on a loose lead."

Finally, Tanner called for Micah to go fast. This was always their Waterloo. It was difficult for Micah to break into a run with his braces; however, he did manage to make a definite increase in his speed, which was all that was necessary. Sophie, however, took off and bounced against the end of her leash.

"We have to work on that," Micah admitted.

Tanner smiled. "Yes. It does need some work. But then, anything that's worth anything at all, requires work."

"No free lunch?"

"Not even a free snack." He grinned briefly at the boy. "You're doing very well with her."

Micah ducked his head. "It's fun. I like working with her."

"She likes working with you."

"You think so?"

Tanner nodded. "Of course. She holds her head up, her tail wags, she has a bounce in her step. She has a great attitude. She's fun to watch. If we're going to get the two of you ready for the summer shows, we have lots of work. You might not have a lot of time left over for fun stuff once school starts, what with homework and lessons with Sophie."

Micah took a deep breath. "I'm used to that," he said quietly.

"Hockey?"

Micah nodded. Tanner pulled a tennis ball from his pocket and handed it to Micah. Micah threw it. Sophie was after it in a shot.

"Sally told me you were a terrific hockey player. She said you were going to make it to the NHL." Then he held his breath, wondering if he'd gone too far.

"It was just a stupid dream." Micah took the ball from Sophie and threw it for her again. Threw it hard.

Tanner waited until Sophie had the ball and was on her way back. "Doesn't sound like a stupid dream to me."

"Yeah, well, dreams ruin everything. What's the use of having dreams if some dumb drunk driver comes along and ruins your life?"

Tanner refused to take that personally. Instead, he thought about Micah's comment. What was Micah trying to say? He reached out into the dark. "Are you saying that if you hadn't been following your dreams, the accident wouldn't have happened?"

Micah threw the ball again and nodded.

"Do you think the accident was your fault?"

This time it was Micah who waited till Sophie returned with the ball and dropped it at his feet before answering. "Well, wasn't it?" His voice was harsh. He threw the ball again. "If it weren't for me, we wouldn't have been on that road at the exact time that stupid drunk driver came by."

"What do you mean, *if it weren't for you?*" Tanner kept his eyes on Sophie, to give Micah space.

"There was a Cannucks game on that night. They were my favorite team. I didn't want to miss it." Micah's voice was strained. "But we—my team—had a game that night too. I told my dad, if we left as soon as my game was over, if I didn't take time to take all my gear off, we could get home in time and I wouldn't miss the game." He stopped. Then he went on. "There was ice on the roads." He shrugged. "So now I can't play hockey anymore."

Then Tanner understood. Micah felt responsible for the deaths of his parents. There was so very much he wanted to say to the young boy. He wanted to say that accidents happened. That no one blamed him—though what did that matter when he blamed himself? He wanted to tell Micah that his spinal cord injury was not punishment for causing the accident. But he knew, from the rigid way Micah held his shoulders, that anything he said right now would be the wrong thing. So he said nothing. All the while knowing that nothing was the wrong thing, as well.

* * *

Sunday, the Wylies arrived at seven in the morning to pick up Micah. He told Sally good-bye, but he held his arms close to his side, telling her he didn't want anything remotely resembling a hug. When the Wylies' car was out of sight, Sally plopped herself down in Deborah's rocking chair, wrapped herself in Deborah's afghan in spite of the heat, and cried. Still wrapped in the afghan, she padded into the kitchen. She opened the freezer and brought out a box of Thin Mints. Then she went into the living room and stood in front of her shelf of videos, looking through them. First, she decided, she'd watch *The Patriot*. She spent the rest of the morning on the couch, wrapped in Deb's afghan and the cats, with Sophie pressed close to her. She watched Mel Gibson movies and ate Thin Mints. It didn't help. Not even a bit.

Mid-afternoon, her doorbell rang. She pressed the "Pause" button on the remote and padded to the door. It was Tanner, with Wing in her usual place at his side. Sally didn't even care that her hair was all tangled, her face stained with tears, and her nose was red. She didn't care that she had on one of her oldest, and most comfortable, T-shirts. She merely stood aside to let them come in.

Sophie, on the other hand, was thrilled to see Tanner and Wing. She leaped off the couch and rushed over to incite Wing to play. Sally told her to knock it off. Troy ran lightly over to his aquarium, to make sure his fish hadn't broken out of jail. Tess stretched languorously and gazed at Wing with a look of serious speculation. Even Jude wrapped around Sally's ankles and touched noses with Wing. The four-footed critters knew where they stood with each other.

Tanner stood inside her front door, looking uncertain. "I thought you might need cheering up," he said. "I'd have been here earlier, but Wing and I were at a dog show in Marion."

Sally managed a wan smile. "That was very kind of you."

"Not kind at all. More like self-serving." He held out an Abernathy's bag. "I brought some ice cream in hopes there was another of those cherry pies in your freezer."

"You're in luck." She led the way through the living room, dining room, and into the kitchen. Sure enough, in the freezer was a homemade, ready-to-bake cherry pie. Sally turned the oven on to preheat. "Better put that ice cream in the freezer so it doesn't melt. It'll take about an hour and a half to bake the pie—then it has to cool."

"I thought about you often today. I wondered if the people picked Micah up on time, and how you were doing. I hope you don't mind me showing up like this."

Sally shook her head. "Not at all. Truth is, I'm glad you're here. I'm probably not the best company right now, but I didn't want to be alone."

"Roads go ever on." Tanner read the words on her refrigerator.

"Tolkien," Sally said. *The Hobbit.* I decided it was appropriate for a day when Micah was leaving."

"He'll come home again."

Sally's eyes were filled with all the sand in the Sahara. She had no tears, only grit. "I hope so."

Tanner reached out with his forefinger and tipped her chin up. "I know so." Then, oh so softly, he lowered his lips to hers in a gentle kiss. He drew her to him, wrapped his arms around her and held her close, her cheek pressed against his chest. She closed her eyes and listened to his heart beat.

Twenty-four

They spent a quiet afternoon in the backyard
throwing the ball for Sophie and Wing until the
timer dinged and the pie came out. They decided
to eat dessert first, and then, holding hands, they
walked the half-dozen blocks to that new pizza
place. After finishing off an extra-large pizza, they
walked back to Sally's for more pie and ice cream,
out on her patio, under the night sky. The dogs
licked the dishes clean. For the first time in weeks,
Sally felt at peace, and content. She had held Micah close to her heart with open hands. It was the
right thing to do.

Sally felt better knowing that Tanner was there.
He was always calm and relaxed. He always made
her feel confident. She didn't want him to leave.

Tanner couldn't stay. "Much as I'd like to," he
said. "I have to get up early in the morning."

They stood together in the dark, arms around
each other, holding each other close. Then they
let go.

* * *

They had supper together on Monday, and took Sophie and Wing for a long walk in the park. Sally asked Tanner to tell her about Helper Dogs. He did. She was amazed. How could she have ever thought he was "just someone who taught dogs"? She was touched by his commitment to his work, to his dogs, to helping other people live a fuller life. He was such a mystery! His commitment to others juxtaposed on top of his solitary life—it didn't make a lot of sense. Unless he really was a monk.

Tuesday evening, Tanner taught classes at his barn; then he called her and they talked until late.

Wednesday, on his lunch break, he called her. She said she was on her way to school—to unpack her classroom. It was a multiday task, she said. Driving home from work, Tanner felt at loose ends. For the last several weeks, Wednesday evening was spent with Micah. Now, with Micah gone, he had the evening to himself. Somehow the prospect of being alone wasn't appealing. He wondered how Sally was doing with her classroom. She said she had a mountain of boxes to unpack, books to arrange, and something about centers, whatever they were. He made a turn at the next corner and found himself at Montrose Elementary School. Her car was in the parking lot.

He parked his truck in the spot next to hers. Pocketing his keys, he jauntily strode up the walk to the school. The doors were open. Peter Winthrop, looking not at all like a principal, wearing jeans and a T-shirt, stuck his head out of the office. "Hello, Tanner," he said.

"I came to help Sally unpack." Tanner knew he didn't really have to explain himself to Peter. "She said she had a lot of boxes."

Peter grinned. "She's not exaggerating. Kindergarten teachers have a lot of stuff. Her classroom is down that hall," he pointed. "Last door on the right."

Tanner nodded his thanks and headed off down the hallway.

He helped Sally unpack boxes and line up books on shelves and set up her computer. They loaded up the newly painted shelves with a wide variety of art materials. Tanner unpacked coffee cans full of little red-and-blue plastic bears, and clothespins, and big buttons. He found he enjoyed helping her. He liked seeing her in her own world where she knew exactly what she wanted, how she wanted her classroom to be. She knew her world well. She was confident here, sure of her abilities. He thought she was beautiful.

Finally, Sally threw up her hands. "I'm beat. Follow me home and give me enough time for a quick shower, and I'll feed you leftovers and the last of that cherry pie. If you want, you can bring Wing."

It was an offer he couldn't refuse, even though he knew he should, even though the warning bells were ringing, reminding him to take care.

He arrived at Sally's house with Wing and waved to the two children in the front yard next door. The older one waved back but the other stood silently, her fingers in her mouth, and gazed at him with a solemn expression on her face.

The evening was warm and pleasant, so he suggested they eat on Sally's patio. Supper was a simple meal made glorious by Sally's smile. She smelled like some fancy soap. He liked it. He wanted to keep her with him forever. But she looked beat. Her shoulders sagged. All that unpacking wore her out, he thought.

When she rose to take the dishes into the house, he took them from her and carried them into her kitchen. She opened the dishwasher and he put the dishes in.

"Thank you so much for all your time. For Micah. I don't know what I'd have done without you this summer."

"Hey," he tipped her chin up, but she closed her eyes. He shoved the dishwasher door closed and turned her towards him. "Hey, are you crying?" It was a purely rhetorical question. "Don't cry," he told her. Then, as if it were the most natural thing in the world, he gathered her into his arms, her head on his chest, his arms around her, his cheek pressed against her hair. He closed his eyes and breathed in the clean smell of her. He would hold her as long as she needed him. And then as long as she would let him.

"I seem to have spent a good deal of this summer in tears," she said at last, her words muffled against his shirt.

"It's been an emotional summer for you." His breath ruffled the tendrils of her hair.

But she made no attempt to move away from

him. He made no attempt to release her. He knew
it was dangerous, knew he was standing on the
edge, knew there was no future for them. But still,
he held her. He could not do otherwise.

Suddenly, he was aware his heart was pounding
and he could feel Sally's heart pounding. Holding
her was no longer an act of giving comfort. Holding her had become an act of barely restrained
passion. He raised his head to see into her eyes,
to see if—please God—she felt it, too. For a long
moment their eyes held. A moment when the air
around them became charged, when the earth
paused in its spinning, when all existence held its
breath, waiting. Waiting. Knowing that what happened in the next moment, were they brave
enough to seize it, would change their lives forever.

Even though he knew what he knew, that there
could be no place for them, he could not bear to
leave her, could not bear to be left. Quickly, before
he lost his courage, he seized the moment. He
kissed her. Not the brief kiss of friendship he'd
given her before. This was a kiss of passion, a kiss
of seduction, a kiss full of heady promise. Wonder
of wonders, she kissed him back.

He led her down the hallway to the door of her
room where he stopped and kissed her again, a
questioning kiss. Her answer was yes.

He undressed her tenderly, trailing kisses down
her neck, over her shoulder, down her breast. To
him she was fragile, infinitely precious. Above all
else, she was to be cared for. To give her pleasure
was what mattered to him. In the giving he re-
ceived.

* * *

They lay in her bed, entangled and drowsing. His thumb gently caressed her shoulder. She decided skin on skin was her favorite feeling, better than any chocolate, even Godiva. How had she survived without it?

"Sally," he said, his voice warm and full and rich.

"Mmm," she answered without opening her eyes.

"Why are you afraid of dogs?"

She was instantly alert. "What do you mean?" She lifted her head.

He gently pressed her head back down on his shoulder. "You're afraid of dogs. Why?"

"I've never liked dogs."

"But why are you afraid of them?"

"I never thought," she said slowly, "anyone knew that."

"The anyones of the world probably don't. I do."

"Oh. Well, I guess now, it's more of a habit. I've never told anyone about it. It was a long time ago. The only person who knew was Deb, because she was there. And after that night, we never talked about it." Then she reached back in her mind to pull out the memory and unfold it carefully so he would understand. "When I was little, more than anything in the world, I wanted a kitten." Her father didn't like cats, wouldn't have one in the house. But he had a dog. Buddy. He thought the sun rose and set in that dog. Nothing was too good for Buddy. The year she was nine, one day on the way home from school, Sally found a stray kitten, a little tiny thing, and brought it home. She snuck it upstairs and hid it in her room, keeping it a secret. Her parents would make her get rid of the kitten if they found it, but she wanted it beyond all reason. Deborah was the only one who knew about the kitten, and helped her sneak cans of cat food into her bedroom. The kitten slept on her pillow and purred her to sleep each night. She had the kitten for about a week.

Then, one morning she was late for school. She evidently didn't close her bedroom door tightly. The dog got in and killed the kitten. She came home from school and found the kitten in the middle of her bedroom carpet. It didn't move. It was twisted. She picked it up but it was limp. Half of the kitten's fur had been pulled off. Its neck had been broken.

She and Deborah tenderly wrapped the kitten in a pink blanket and put it in a shoebox. They took it outside to the woods in back of their yard. Deborah brought her dad's shovel and dug a hole under their favorite climbing tree. Sally didn't want to let go of the box, but Deborah made her. They put the box in the hole, covered it up. Deborah said the Lord's Prayer because it was the only prayer they knew, and they held hands and cried.

That night, she threw up and her mother kept her home from school the next day. She spent the whole day in bed, her covers over her head, crying. Partly it was grief, but now, after reading all those books from the rehab list, she realized part of it was her feelings of guilt because she hadn't protected the kitten better. Then, of course, she was a child, keeping all these intense emotions inside, having no way to process them. Maybe it would have been easier if she'd had someone to talk to about it, but she didn't. She couldn't tell her parents—after all, they had forbidden her to have a cat.

Buddy often tried to get into her room after that. She yelled at him when her parents weren't home. She couldn't ever look at that dog again without thinking of what he'd done, without remembering the poor, broken body of her tiny kitten. "Now, of course, after listening to Karen and Jessie and M'liss, and you, now I understand that he was a terrier, bred to go after vermin. He thought the kitten was vermin." Sally thought about the kitten. Somehow the memory didn't hurt as much as she thought it would. "The funny thing is, I actually like Sophie a lot. I know she likes me, too, but she knows she's Micah's dog. The other day, Micah told me he wants to compete with Sophie, so I guess, as you said, I'll be spending a lot of time at dog shows. You asked me if I was willing and I said I was. You never asked me how I felt. I feel fine about it. In fact, if someone came up to me and said, 'Sally, this dog is for you. This dog is perfect, and I guarantee, it will never, ever hurt your cats,' I'd seriously consider it. And you know what? That surprises the hell out of me."

Tanner nodded and held her close. "Doesn't surprise me at all."

"I suppose you're going to say something about how we grow and develop new interests."

"I wasn't going to. But now that you mention growing and developing . . ."

A glorious hour later, Sally pulled on her robe and wandered into the kitchen in search of two glasses and something cold to drink. As she opened the refrigerator, the telephone rang. She ignored it. "Let the machine get it," she said to herself as she filled tall glasses with ice. After the beep, she heard Cheryl Benson's voice. "Sally, this is Cheryl, in Vermont. You told me to let you know what happened with that drunk driver—"

Sally grabbed the phone. "I'm here, Cheryl. What happened?"

"Oh, good. I'm glad I got you. Everyone up here, including Micah, we're all sort of in shock. It was on the evening news. She did it again. That drunk driver. There was another accident. No one was killed this time, but there was a baby in the car that she hit. A ten-month-old baby girl. They think the baby'll be okay, but they're not promising."

Sally sank down into a chair. She wanted to throw up. "What," she asked harshly, "are they going to do now? Another slap on the wrist?" She felt her voice rise, but she let it fly, she set her anger free. "More community service? Fat lot of good *that* did! That drunk driver—no, Cheryl, *all* drunk drivers—every one of them should be strung up from the nearest tree and eviscerated. There's no excuse for drinking and driving. No one held a gun to that woman's head and forced her to drink, forced her to drive her car. Driving a car is not a Constitutional right, it's a privilege. As far as I'm concerned, drunk drivers have forfeited that privilege. What did the judge say this time?"

She heard Tanner come down the short hallway past the kitchen to stand in the dining room door. She glanced up and noticed him, in his T-shirt and jeans, his feet bare, but she kept her attention focused on Cheryl's words.

"Prison time?" she asked. "Good. At least the people of Vermont will be protected for a couple of years. Thing is, there's always another drunk driver waiting to get behind the wheel of a car."

Behind her, she heard her front door open. She turned in time to see Wing follow Tanner outside and her door close behind them. He probably took her out to go potty. He'd be back in a moment. Maybe he wanted to bring something in from his truck. Cheryl was talking about the crooked judge. Sally heard Tanner's truck door slam, the engine start. She wanted to run outside to stop him, to ask him where he was going, but she had to know about this drunk driver. For a brief moment, she was torn; then she decided Tanner wouldn't leave without saying good-bye, not after the amazing lovemaking they'd shared. She turned her attention back to Cheryl.

Twenty-five

Tanner pulled into the parking lot in front of his barn and turned off the engine. He sat and stared at the wall of the barn. Karen was wrong. No matter how much he wanted her to be right, she was wrong. He couldn't trust Sally.

He yanked the door open. He climbed out and held the door for Wing, who gave him a hesitant look before she hopped out. Then he slammed the door shut.

He wanted to pound something. He wanted to roar. He was flooded with rage. He didn't know what to do. But he remembered this feeling of betrayal. He'd felt like this once before, when he wasn't much older than Micah. His breathing was hard and ragged. Inside his apartment he grabbed up his phone. Today, now, he would say the things to his mother he couldn't say before. He punched in a number he thought he'd forgotten. He gathered the words he'd say first, ready to spit them out.

"Hello?" Her voice came to him from more than the other side of the country—it came to him from out of his past.

All the words he'd intended to say went silent. Instead he said the last thing in the world he expected to say to her. "Hi, Mom. It's me."

Sally sat on her couch, dumbfounded. Sophie took this as an invitation to cuddle, but Sally ignored her, so Sophie tried to promote a game with Tess. Tess batted at Sophie from the catwalk a few times, then leaped gracefully to the floor where Sophie pounced. Tess grabbed the puppy around the neck and kicked her with her hind feet, biting her on the muzzle. Sophie wagged her tail. Tess jumped up, ran a few steps, whirled around, and rushed back to Sophie.

Sally stared at the two of them without seeing them. She realized they were playing some feline-canine game. Deep down, Sally knew Tess was in no danger. She knew Sophie would never hurt her cats. She didn't know how she knew, but she did. She didn't have to worry about the cats, which was a good thing, because she also knew that Something Had Happened when Tanner left. She didn't know what.

Probably, a wicked voice told her, he was grossed out by how fat she was. She thought about that. No, she didn't think so. She wandered into the kitchen and reached for a handful of chocolate. She looked at the chocolate in her hand. Leety's dark chocolate nonpareils did not appeal to her. She put it back. She leaned her head against the cabinet. Earlier, before Cheryl's call, she felt miraculous and beautiful—now she felt totally defeated. Micah was gone. Tanner had said Micah would be back, but how could she trust Tanner, when he was gone, too? What more could she possibly screw up?

Thursday morning, Sally realized she was almost out of cat food. She left for Abernathy's early, before the sun had a chance to throw its vicious heat around. The store was cool, especially near the milk and ice cream. Her favorite black raspberry chip ice cream was on sale, so she grabbed two. She wandered over to the produce section. How could anyone eat all the vegetables recommended by the food pyramid pundits? She gazed around at the broccoli, and the onions, and the lettuces. This was what people ate to lose weight. She couldn't deal with all those veggies right now. Carrots were as healthy as she was willing to go, so she tossed a bag of mini-carrots in her cart. She snagged a bag of Oreos on her way to the poultry.

At the checkout stand she glanced at the magazines while she waited in line. "Lose Fifteen Pounds on Our Miracle Diet!" she read, and "Our Chocolate Cake Is Better Than Sex!" Both headlines shouted from the cover of the same magazine. It was positively schizophrenic, she thought.

She finished her shopping and lugged her bags out into the sponge that was Ohio in the summer. It was the kind of hot and humid day that made people want to stay inside. What did the pioneers do, Sally wondered, without air conditioning, and all those long skirts and petticoats and no deodorant. Her bare legs stuck to the hot car seat as she drove home. Yuck. Humidity made her grumpy. There should be a law against it.

She hauled the groceries into her house, put them away, and went back out into the heat and humidity to drive to school to work on her classroom. At least it was something constructive, and she didn't have to talk to anyone so she could be as grumpy as she wanted to and no one would see her. She planned to stay and finish, as long as it took. But at two o'clock, she remembered that Sophie, unlike the cats, needed to be let outside. Sophie was evidently a high-needs critter.

Sally drove home and took the puppy outside. She pulled the bag of mini-carrots out of the refrigerator. She looked at the carrots. They were orange. She hated orange. She could not be enthusiastic about eating mini-carrots for lunch. She made a peanut butter and jelly sandwich instead. Then she made another, and tore it into little pieces to share with the cats. Sophie had the carrots.

Sally told herself she would not look at her answering machine. But it wasn't blinking, anyway. Sally was willing to apologize—if she had any idea what she'd done. She picked up her keys and Sophie looked hopeful.

"C'mon, Soph," she called. "You can come to school."

Sophie did have an adventure, sticking her nose into every box and can and jar, knocking them over and pulling things out. Sally was busy rescuing kindergarten supplies from sharp little dog teeth.

"You aren't much in the way of help," Sally told her. "But you certainly are cute."

Sophie sat flat on her little rump and wagged her tail.

"Let's go home," she said at last. "It's too hot and humid to be here."

For supper, Sally ate a bowl of cold cereal while she watched *Castaway*. For dessert she ate ice cream with chocolate sauce.

The phone rang. But it was only Jessie, who said, "Let's take the two puppinos for a romp in the park."

Sally didn't feel like it. She didn't even ask Sophie's opinion. In the distance she heard the faint rumble of thunder.

Thursday, Tanner found his patience wearing thin. All dogs, but especially these dogs who had been trained to be aware of his every move, were aware of everything that went on with you emotionally, which is why one of the basic tenets of dog training said you never, ever train a dog when you're upset. Tanner was upset. He tried hard to tamp it down, shove it out of his mind, tried hard to use body language that would tell the dogs he was cheerful and in charge. It was a dismal failure. "You know I'm a fraud, don't you?" he asked them.

Yes, they knew. They knew him well enough to know he was faking his enthusiasm, and because he was upset, they were upset, too.

He decided teaching the dogs new skills might

be too stressful for them today, even though these dogs were experts at learning new skills. Instead, he decided to reinforce things they already knew, opening drawers and doors, turning lights on and off, dropping keys and blank credit cards so the dogs could pick them up, so when they did the task correctly—which they did because they were well trained—he could give them praise. They sensed his frame of mind and worked hard to please him. Still, they were subdued, even when he took them out into the sunny backyard for recess. This made Tanner feel worse. He felt he was even failing with the dogs.

Finally he sat down, leaning against the wall, and called them over to him. They came with their heads slightly down, their tails slightly tucked, using their body language to tell him they were submissive. Tanner sat in the shade, surrounded by the dogs, scratching their bellies, saying soothing things to them until their heads came up, their tails swished, and they felt secure and happy again. Then he pulled a ball out of his pocket to throw. They were fine dogs, he thought, watching them bound off. They were the best. Hand-picked, hand-raised, carefully trained, exceptionally sensitive to the emotions of others. These dogs were the elite. They would do anything he asked them to. But today, he was not worthy of them.

After lunch, he put the dogs in their kennels and brought out Maxie. He took her down to the front office where Corinne handed him a thick file.

"Find her a winner," she said. "Lots to choose from."

"Yeah," he muttered. Back in the workroom he dropped the file onto the table, and himself into his desk chair. Maxie sat down next to him and put her head on his knee. Her gaze turned to his face.

"Applications for released Helper Dogs?" Patti asked.

"Yeah," he muttered.

"I know how you feel," she said as she turned off her computer and slipped her shoes back on. "I hate that file, too." She grabbed up her purse. "Not because I hate the people—I'm sure they're all lovely people—but because it means I've failed. You, however, did not fail with Maxie. Remember that. You. Didn't. Fail. Mendel and his stupid genetics did. I'm off to interview a potential puppy-raiser. See you later." She gave Maxie a brief pat on the head and was gone.

No, he hadn't failed with Maxie, but he had to place her in a pet home anyway. The result was the same. He opened the folder. "Here we go, Maxie. Let's see if we can find a perfect home for a perfect dog."

The first application was from a first-time dog owner, a woman who worked a forty-hour week, sometimes longer, and therefore didn't have extra time to housebreak a puppy. Her sister told her she should have a dog for company, and she'd heard that Helper Dogs placed dogs that were already trained. The woman referred to dogs as *that*s not *whos*. Objects, not beings. The woman should have a pet rock. Tanner turned her application over. The next family lived in a large, three-story house. The people seemed to be lovely, but he didn't like the idea of Maxie living in a house with all those stairs. He glanced at the dog with her head on his knee. Her eyes were trained on his. He smiled at her. She wagged her tail, but her eyes didn't leave his face. He stroked her head. "You are a perfect dog," he told her. "You need the perfect home." He went back to the stack of applications. He found something wrong with every one of them.

He took the file back to the front office and dropped it on Corinne's desk.

She looked up at him. "You look terrible."

He managed a shadow of a grin. "Always nice to have your support."

"Friends tell friends when they look like hell. You look like hell."

He felt like hell, too. His eyes were gritty and thick-feeling from lack of sleep.

"You look," she continued, "like you've been drinking some of that grape Kool-Aid. It's lethal, you know. Those doctors from the Centers for Disease Control should be here any day to move it into one of their hot zones."

"I haven't been drinking grape Kool-Aid," he said. He wanted to thank her for trying to cheer him up, so he told his face to grin. The best his face could do was a grimace. He really wanted to go out and get screaming drunk. But that was not an option.

* * *

Home, after work, he didn't feel like eating. He sat out on his porch and drank a soda while he watched thick clouds roll in from the west. The thunder matched his mood.

When Karen arrived, before his first students, he asked her to teach the class by herself. He told himself it would be good practice for her. He told her he thought he was coming down with the flu. The truth was, he didn't have enough energy to give to his class. He didn't want his attitude to affect them. The people might not be aware of his turmoil, but the dogs would be.

Karen said she'd be glad to teach the class solo, she hoped he wasn't coming down with the flu, and he should drink hot tea with lemon and honey. She looked at him with that level gaze of hers, that gaze that told him she knew he was not telling her the truth. He had seen a lot of that gaze in the early days of their friendship. He wasn't used to people seeing through him, but Karen always had. She saw through him and still called him *friend*. Sometimes she pushed, to make him be honest with her, or with himself. But tonight she let it pass. "You don't look well," she agreed. "You should take it easy before the dog show this weekend."

He'd forgotten about the dog show this weekend.

Tanner slunk into his apartment and closed the door. He felt like he was running away. He knew he was. He stretched out on his bed with Wing and Aretha curled up next to him. Even the sound of the kitten's purring couldn't put him to sleep.

* * *

When Sally awoke Friday morning, rain came down in sheets. She felt like she was moving through a fog. The rain matched her mood. She took Sophie to school with her to work on her classroom. This time she was smart. She brought a brand new chew toy for Sophie to play with.

By noon, the rain still splattered against the windows, and her classroom was as set up as she could make it. The week before school started, when she had her class rosters, she'd make name tags for coat hooks and name tags for seats, for cubbies, and attendance charts. The week before school she would have dozens of last-minute things to do. But for now, she decided she was finished. Everything else could wait. If she spent any more time in this room she felt she'd go stark raving mad. Besides, Sophie's new toy was demolished. "Let's go home," she said.

Sophie was willing.

"You are an agreeable little wretch."

Sophie thought so, too.

The light on Sally's answering machine was blinking. The message was from Ethel: everyone was fine, Micah was okay. Sally called her back, but Ethel's machine answered, so Sally left a basic message.

Sally gazed around her living room. Troy crouched by the aquarium, keeping an eagle eye on his goldfish in case they made a break for the border. The goldies ignored the cat. The cat never brought them food, and so was of little interest to them. Tess gave Sophie a couple of half-hearted swats, but neither of them seemed interested in pursuing a chase game. Jude had appropriated Deb's rocking chair.

Her house felt empty. Her house was too quiet. She missed Micah, even Micah when his teenager persona was showing. Sally found herself at loose ends. That's what you get for being off all summer while your friends are all at work, she told herself. Besides, her friends all seemed to be involved in their own worlds right now. Jessie was totally wrapped up in Sagan, Sylvie was enthralled with her baby. Melissa seemed to be spending all her time working on the plans to enlarge her clinic. And Karen seemed preoccupied these days, listening with only half an ear—not a good thing for a psychologist.

So Sally cleaned house. She changed the water in the aquarium. She changed the litter in the cat boxes. She did laundry, she vacuumed the carpet, and then the catwalks. She scrubbed the top of the refrigerator, the bathtub, even the kitchen floor. She pawed through the magnetic words and made new sentences on the refrigerator. Then she decided they revealed too much of her emotional state, so she tossed them back into the box and shut the drawer. She leaned against the counter and stared out at the rain.

She called that expensive pizza place, but the delivery time was an hour and a half, so she drove out into the rain and picked it up. The warm box filled her car with pizza smells. But when she got it home, and inside, and opened on the kitchen counter, she didn't feel hungry anymore. She took one bite and shoved the rest away. Sophie and the cats had pizza for their bedtime snack.

All the four-footed ones ended up on her bed, but Tess insisted she was the only one allowed on Sally's pillow. Sally finished off her box of Leety's fine dark chocolate nonpareils and read *Madensky Square* until her eyes burned with fatigue. She turned out the light, and suddenly was wide awake. This was where she and Tanner—no. She listened to the rain on her roof and counted to one hundred over and over until she finally fell asleep.

Twenty-six

Saturday morning she followed Sophie into the backyard. After the rain, the whole world was bright and green. The air was fresh and the humidity was low. She threw all the windows and doors open wide to let the outside in. Then she challenged Sophie to a couple dozen throws of the ball. Sophie took her up on it.

Sophie won. Sally let her keep the tennis ball, spoils of the game. She stood in the middle of her backyard and held out her arms and twirled around and around and around until she was dizzy; then she dropped down flat on her back on the damp grass and watched the true-blue sky spin. Sophie thought this was a great new game and came over to investigate. "Deb and I used to do this," she said to the little dog. "And Micah, when he was little. My kindergartners do this. If you were a person instead of a dog, you could do this, too. Spin around till you're dizzy, and when you stop it looks like the world is spinning. But it really isn't. It's an optical illusion."

Sophie lost interest and wandered across the

yard to nose through the grass under the cherry trees.

"Spin around till you're dizzy," she repeated. That's what she'd been doing for the last two days, spinning around, losing her equilibrium so the whole world looked off-kilter.

She sat up. "Enough is enough. No more optical illusions. No more morose moods. No more metaphorical spinning. Sally Foster," she told herself, "you are a terrific person and you deserve the best. If that Tanner Dodge doesn't see it, then he's not the person you thought he was, and he isn't worthy of you."

Sophie appeared with the tennis ball and dropped it in Sally's lap. She looked willing.

"And you know what?" she asked the dog. "If Micah wants to stay in Vermont, we'll talk about it, and if I decide that's the best thing for him, well, I'll have to figure out how to do it somehow because I promised his mom and dad I'd take care of him, but I didn't promise where, and if it ends up I have to take care of him in Vermont, well, you do things for the people you love. I suppose they have kindergartens in Vermont, too. Because, remember on the Fourth of July when he was upset?"

Sophie was not interested in the Fourth of July. Sophie wanted to chase the ball, so she barked, and she shoved the ball with her nose so it rolled closer to Sally. But Sally wasn't finished thinking out loud yet.

"Micah said he didn't have a family. He was wrong. He and I are family. And that makes you my family, too. That makes you my dog. So whad-

dya think about that? I know, I know. Okay. Go get
it." She threw the ball for her dog. Her dog
brought it back.

After a while, they went inside and Sally went
into her bedroom and pulled on dry clothes. She
found her sneakers in the back of her closet. She
sat on her bed and pulled them on and called Jessie. She cradled the phone between her shoulder
and her chin while she tied her shoes. Finally her
friend answered. "Hey, Jess, you wanna take our
poocheroonies for a walk in the park?"

Tanner and Wing took first place in Utility, and
second place in Open B. After the judge handed
out the scores, he beckoned Tanner aside and told
him he'd seen Wing make a slight hesitation before
she dropped on her recall. He shook his head with
honest regret on his face. "I've seen her before.
She's a terrific dog."

"Thanks," Tanner told the judge. "She is terrific."

Tanner left the ring and looked over the crowd
to find Laura, the woman with the collie who'd
taken first place. Other competitors congratulated
him as he guided Wing through the mass of people
and dogs. Some wanted to talk to him, to ask him
if they could call with a question; he always said
yes, but he didn't stop to talk. He continued working through the crowd until he found Laura and
her dog. "Congratulations!" he said. "You finished?"

Her grin was as wide as the Grand Canyon.

"Thank you! Yes! He finished his UDX," she said in an excited rush. "We got Utility earlier this morning—of course you know that, you and Wing got first place—and his score was good, but not in the ribbons. All we needed from Open B was a qualifying score, and we took first! What a way to go out! I'm so happy I can't stand it!" She bent down to hug her dog. "What a good boy you are!"

Three years earlier, when Laura rescued the dog from a shelter, he was skinny and skittish. Now he was healthy and self-confident. "You've done an excellent job with him," Tanner said.

She gave her dog a final kiss on the head and stood up again to look Tanner squarely in the face. "I couldn't have done it without you."

Tanner was embarrassed. "Yeah, you could've. All I did was help you with a little fine-tuning. You did all the work."

"You never let me pay you for those *fine-tuning* lessons. Say. We're both done for the day," she checked her watch. "Let me buy you lunch. To tell you thank you."

Why not? he thought. After all, it was a three-hour drive home, and he didn't have any reason to rush. Besides, he liked Laura—not in a romantic way, but as someone he saw at dog shows, a fellow dog trainer. "Let me buy you lunch and we'll celebrate."

"We celebrate, but I get the check."

They put the dogs in their crates, and Tanner drove a couple of blocks to a Mexican restaurant where they ordered enchiladas and guacamole and talked about dogs and training methods and other dog shows.

Laura took a chip and scooped up the last bit of guacamole. "I feel like I'm a kid again. You know that feeling? You've spent all this time with school always in the back of your mind, what test is next week, what paper is due. And then one morning you wake up and it's the first day of summer vacation and you automatically think about tests and papers and stuff because you've developed that habit. Then you remember it's summer. And for an instant, you're lost, because you have to change mental gears. You know that feeling?"

Tanner leaned back in the booth. "Friend of mine said something similar to me the other day. What was I going to do when Wing finished her OTCH." He grinned briefly, then, to stop her question, he added in a teasing tone, "That may not be for a long time if people like you keep stealing first places." Truth was, he didn't know what he would do, what goals he would set for himself. He didn't know what he'd do about Micah and Sophie. He couldn't let the boy down, simply because he and Sally . . . he and Sally what? he wondered.

When they finished their meal, Tanner took the check.

"It looks like a minivan convention," Jessie said as they pulled into the parking lot of Kedrick Park. She pointed to an SUV. "There's a minivan on steroids. I wonder if they do random drug tests on SUVs."

"Very funny," Sally said.

"I thought so. I bet Sagan thought so, too. Didn't you, Sagan?"

Sagan kept her opinion to herself.

Sophie barked.

"Yeah, okay," Sally said. "Hold your horses. Let me get your door open."

"Don't let her bolt out," Jessie said. "Tell her to wait. Remember, Micah always tells her to wait before she's allowed to jump out of the car. It could save her life someday."

Sally opened the back door cautiously. "Wait," she told Sophie.

Sophie wagged her tail with great enthusiasm, but she waited. Sally clipped her leash on her collar. "Okay," she said.

Sophie leaped out of the car.

"That dog is fearless," Jessie said. "This dog is not. Here you go, Sagan. It's okay, this is the park; you've been to the park before."

"My dog is older than your dog," Sally pointed out. "Sophie's had more experience with strange places than Sagan has."

"Oh, ho!" Jessie said. "So Sophie is *your* dog now?"

Sally tried to look casual. "Of course. What did you expect?"

"You don't want me to answer that," her friend said with a grin. "Look, Sagan, this is the park. You remember the park."

They set off down the walk, the two puppies craning their necks to see everything at once.

"So, what happened between you and Tanner?" Jessie asked.

"You're not subtle."

"Nope. Life's too short to be subtle, especially with friends. I figure I've known you long enough and well enough to dispense with all the social formalities. What gives?"

"I don't know."

"Yeah," Jessie muttered sarcastically. "Sure."

"It's the truth. One minute he was there, and the next minute—while I was talking on the phone to Cheryl Benson, Deb's neighbor from Vermont, so I couldn't drop the phone and run after him— he was gone, in the proverbial cloud of smoke."

"He wouldn't disappear like that, without a word. I know him."

"He did."

"What were you doing before you talked to Cheryl?"

Sally felt herself turn red.

"Oh!" Jessie said, a great grin splitting her face. "Cool!"

"Yeah," Sally admitted. "It was amazingly cool. Past tense, because he left."

Two little girls, probably four years old, Sally thought, came running towards them across the green lawn of the park. "Can we pet your dogs?" they called out.

Sally and Jessie stopped. "Sure," Sally said. She stooped down so she was on eye level with the kids. Kids had enough adults looking down at them without one more. "You can pet my dog. Her name is Sophie, and she likes kids. In fact, in dog years, she's a kid, too. And this other puppy is Sagan. In dog years she's a toddler. Much younger than you are."

The children were impressed. Sophie was delighted. Sagan was quietly curious, but her tail twitched. The children plopped down on the sidewalk next to the puppies. The puppies climbed on top of them. The children giggled. The puppies' tails wagged.

How her life would've been different, Sally thought, if she'd met dogs like this when she was a child. But she hadn't. Her father's terrier nipped at children, nipped at her, and was not corrected for it. Her father had not been a responsible dog owner, she thought in surprise. He was her father, and she loved him, and she'd always thought he was perfect, even if he hadn't let her have a kitten, but he probably didn't let her have a kitten because he knew that dog would kill it. At least, she hoped that had been his reason. He'd never shared a reason with her, just said no.

"Mommy!" one of the children called. "Come see the dogs! They like us!"

The mother came and said the puppies were lovely, though it would be difficult to do anything but admire two puppies who were obviously enthusiastic about one's children.

"Can we have a puppy?" one of the children asked.

Let them have a puppy, Sally thought, as long as you take care of it.

"Puppies are a lot of work," the mother said. She caught Sally's eye and Sally nodded. "Almost as much work as you two. Not to mention your brother."

Jessie added, "Puppies are a great time commitment. Maybe when you're older your parents will let you have a puppy, and you can help take care of it."

"Maybe," the mother said. "You never know. Right now you need to say good-bye to the nice puppies."

" 'Bye, puppies," the children said, hanging back for one last puppy hug before they each took one of Mom's hands and allowed themselves to be led away. " 'Bye, puppies."

Jessie hugged Sagan and Sophie. "You guys are great ambassadors for the nation of dog."

"Nation of dog?" Sally asked as they continued along the sidewalk. "What happened to species?"

Jessie shrugged. "There's this old Indian saying that we and the dogs are brothers, but of different nations. I'll track it down and give it to you."

Sally wasn't ready to go that far yet. "Too bad," she said, "all kids can't meet such nice and friendly puppies."

"Too bad all puppies can't meet such nice and friendly kids."

"Too bad all puppies aren't this nice and friendly."

"Too bad all kids aren't that nice and friendly."

"Too bad," Sally went on, "all kids don't live with people as nice as their mother was, and as we are."

"Too bad all *puppies* don't live with people as nice as we are," Jessie said. "Because then, all puppies would be this nice and friendly." She held her hand up. "Enough of this. Let's get back to this cool time you were having with Tanner."

Sally sighed. "Let's not. It happened, it was cool, now it's over. No more cool."

"How do you know?"

"Cool means never leaving without a good-bye. Cool means you at least call. Cool means you drop by. Cool means you don't leave the other person to wonder."

"Oh." Then she added, "But something *must* have happened."

Sally shrugged. "I agree. Unless he was grossed out because I'm no sylph."

Jessie snorted. "He's not that superficial."

"I didn't think so."

"You think so now?"

Sally thought. "No. I don't. But if he is, then he doesn't deserve me, and I deserve better."

Jessie patted her on the back. "That's my girl! You're the best." Then she frowned. "I always thought he was the best, too."

"What made you think something had happened?" Sally asked, curious.

"Thursday night he asked Karen to teach class. He said he didn't feel well. He's never sick. Most disgustingly healthy person I've ever met. Karen said he didn't look sick, he looked depressed. And when I called you to ask if you wanted to take the doggy bambinos for a walk, when you said no, you sounded depressed, too. Karen said Tanner looked depressed. I thought you sounded depressed. It's not rocket science to figure out something happened."

"And it's your obligation to find out what?"

"That's what best friends are for."

Sally sighed a huge sigh and tried a smile on for size. "Thanks. I appreciate it. But I decided it doesn't matter. What does matter right now is Micah. I had no business getting sidetracked. I did, and the responsibility is mine. I only hope I didn't destroy any possibility of a friendship between Micah and Tanner. That would be the real tragedy. Tanner has been the best thing for Micah this summer." Then she remembered twirling in her backyard. "I'm the best thing for him, too, in a different way."

"Yes," Jessie said. "You are."

Twenty-seven

Sally pulled her car into her driveway and stopped. She looked at the house. "That's funny," she said to Sophie. "I thought I closed the front door when we left."

Visions of burglaries danced in her head. Until she put her mental foot down. This was Hartley.

That was Micah, standing in the doorway!

"Micah!" she called. She opened the door and Sophie scrambled out sans leash and dashed up to the front door, barking wildly. Micah scooped up his dog and managed to hold on to her in spite of her enthusiastic wiggling.

"When did you get home?" Sally asked. "Why didn't you let me know? I'd have been here."

"I only made up my mind last night. The Manlys were driving down to Bowling Green to pick up Bo from hockey camp, and they offered me a ride. I called you, but you weren't home, so I left a message on the machine. We had to leave really early this morning, so Grandma said she'd wait until a decent hour and she'd call to let you know."

"I didn't check my answering machine." Something was different about him, but she couldn't put her finger on it. She went into the kitchen. "Look," she said. She pointed to the counter where evidently she'd tossed a newspaper and it had landed on top of her answering machine. She moved it. Sure enough, the red light was blinking, and the readout said there were two messages.

"I'm so sorry. Your grandma must've called while I was outside with Sophie this morning. Jessie and I took the dogs for a walk in the park."

"That's okay. I had a key. I figured you and Sophie were somewhere because her leash was gone. So the cats and I sat on the couch and read."

The phone rang. Micah grabbed it off the hook. "Hello," he said. "Oh, hi, Jess. Yeah, she's here. Just a minute." He handed her the phone. "It's for you."

Sally took the phone. "Hi, Jess." She couldn't figure out what was different.

"Micah's back and you didn't mention it?"

"Yeah. Um. I forgot to check my machine last night. He got here while we were out with the dogs."

"I'm glad." Sally could almost hear her nod her head. "Hey, you left your purse here. Stay there, I'll be right over with it. Oh, I have something for Micah, too. I finally got a copy of that Shackleton movie. I told him I'd loan it to him."

"Okay."

As soon as she hung up the phone she realized what was different. Micah had answered the phone. Micah never answered the phone before. Oh, and Micah said he'd been reading in the living room on the couch, with the cats. Before, he'd always spent most of his time in his room, with the door shut. Now he was trailing a bright ribbon for Tess to chase. Tess wiggled her bottom and pounced on it.

"Jessie's coming over," Sally said. "She has something for you."

"Cool," Micah said. He flipped the ribbon from Tess and trailed it again. "I have something for her, too."

"You do?" she asked in surprise.

"Yeah. I have something for you, too. Wait a minute. I'll get it." He dropped the ribbon and disappeared down the hall. He returned with a brown packing box. "Grandma and I thought you should have this."

She fished a pair of scissors from a kitchen drawer and cut through the packing tape. She opened the box and looked in at a tangle of knotted cloth. Sally recognized it. "Your mom's knitting basket. When we were seniors in high school, she made me help her tear up bunches of cloth into millions of strips so she could crochet this." That lump was back in her throat, the lump she got when she talked about Deb.

Micah sat down on the couch next to her. "We had to squish it to get it in the box," he said apologetically.

"That's okay," Sally reassured him.

Sally reached in the box and pulled out Deb's handiwork. "There's something inside," she said. She looked at Micah.

He nodded. "Yeah," he said.

She reached inside the basket and pulled out a jumble of deep rose-colored wool and needles attached to a partially completed something. Then Sally noticed the paper in the basket. It was a pattern for a shawl.

"It was supposed to be your birthday present," Micah told her. "Grandma told me you always said you wanted to learn how to knit someday. I told her about that old lady we met at the parade. Grandma and I thought this would be a good kick in the seat. The pattern is in there, too. If you want to finish it."

Finish something Deborah had started? She didn't know if she could ever learn how to knit well enough. Still, the thought of a shawl Deborah had started . . . It would be like a hug. Sally smoothed the half-finished shawl on her lap. It had always amazed her how Deborah could casually take up two needles and a ball of yarn and turn it into something beautiful. "Are you sure you wouldn't mind? If I finished it?"

Micah shook his head. "Nah. Go ahead."

"All through high school, your mother worked at Mrs. Wilde's yarn shop. I'll take you there sometime, if you like."

Micah looked down at his feet. "Uh. Sure. Okay."

It was a great step forward for Micah, so Sally went on. "The summer we were sixteen, we read about how people could go to Ireland and rent a gypsy cart and travel around the countryside. We wanted to do that, but it was expensive. So we decided we would go out and get jobs, and we'd save every penny until we had enough. Deborah loved to knit. She could do anything with a ball of yarn, and Mrs. Wilde knew that, because she'd taught Deb to knit. It made sense for her to apply for a job at the yarn shop. There was no way I could work in a yarn shop—my experience with knitting lessons was *not* a success. I told Deb we could both work at the fish farm. She said thinking about all that water, the ponds and pools of fish, made her seasick." Sally chuckled. "I told her it was because she probably drowned in a former life." Then she realized that was a horribly tactless thing to say, but Micah nodded.

"I remember you used to tell her that," he said.

Sally went on. "So she worked at the yarn shop and I worked at the fish farm. It was the first time we'd ever done things separately." For a moment, Sally was sixteen again, feeling lost and alone without Deborah at her side. Deborah who always gave her courage, who always had more faith in her than she ever had in herself. Now, for a moment, Sally could almost hear Deborah say, as she'd said so often, *You can do it, Sal. I know you can.*

For the first time, she believed Deb. She *could* do it. Whatever life threw at her, she could do it. She could do *anything*. She reached out and gave Micah a hug. He didn't quite hug her back, but he didn't resist her, either. Yes, she thought, she could do anything.

"I guess I'll have to call Mrs. Wilde and tell her I'm ready for my next knitting lesson."

The front door opened. "Yoohoo!" Jessie stuck her head in and grinned at them. "Sagan and I arrive bearing gifts!" She held the door open for Sagan. "I decided we all needed to watch the Shackleton video, so I brought pizza."

Sally couldn't see the connection.

Micah did. "It's to bribe you, so we can all watch it together."

"Bright kid," Jessie said. "I also brought Sagan, so she and Sophie can wear each other out."

But it was Tess who greeted the new puppy first, running lightly towards her and offering her nose for a sniff. Sally blinked. Tess had decided she liked dogs? When had that happened? After a good sniff of the cat, Sagan caught sight of Sophie. She made a play bow. Sophie play bowed back. At the same instant, they leaped towards each other. "No roughhousing in the house," Sally told them. She called the puppies, encouraging them to follow her to the sliding door. "Go terrorize the squirrels," she told them.

Sagan followed Sophie into the backyard, so they could explore the great outdoors.

"Sophie isn't used to being number one," Sally said. "All her other canine buddies are older than she is."

"Let her enjoy it while she can," Jessie said as she put the video in the player. "Where did you hide the remote?"

"Should be in the magazine rack, by the couch," Sally called back. She found a tray and loaded it with paper plates, napkins, and cups of ice and carried it into the living room. "Sodas, lemonade, and iced tea are in the fridge. Micah?" she called.

Then she remembered. "We also have leftover cherry pie."

"Great!" Jessie said. "I'll take pie any day."

Micah came into the living room, holding out an envelope. He handed it to Jessie. "This is for you."

"Me?" her eyebrows lifted in surprise.

Micah shrugged. "You said when I got Sally, I got all of you."

"So, this is an I-Got-You-Babe present, eh?" She winked outrageously at him.

Micah colored. He stubbed his toe in the carpet. "Yeah. I guess."

"Cool," said Jess. Then she opened the envelope and peered in. "Really cool. No pun intended. Look, Sal, it's an Antarctic dollar bill." She grabbed Micah in a brief one-armed hug. "This is great. Thanks. I won't spend it all in one place. In fact, I won't spend it at all." She looked closely at the artwork. "Look at the color! Much prettier than our old paper money, which is pretty boring. This here is pretty enough to frame and hang on the wall. In fact, I think I'll do that. Micah, where'd you find it?"

"A few years ago, some company printed them to raise money for an Antarctic conservation project. My dad," Micah's voice trembled for a second. He cleared his throat. "My dad gave me a couple of them for Christmas last year."

Silence.

"Gee," Jessie said after a moment, "all those spices from this pizza are making my eyes water. Sally, you said something about drinks? Don't move, I'll get 'em. I know where your refrigerator is. Hey, Micah," she called from the kitchen, "it's minus 83 degrees at the Pole today, with a wind chill of minus 104."

"How do you know that?" Sally asked.

"Up-to-the-minute weather reports from the South Pole right on my desktop. Micah, I'll show you how to find it so you can put it on your computer." Jessie came into the living room and held out a pitcher. "I'll pour lemonade. Micah, you're closest to the remote. Grab some pizza and press 'Play.' Get comfortable, everyone. It's a long movie."

They ate pizza and finished off the cherry pie and watched Kenneth Branagh as Shackleton. They fed bits of crust to the cats. "Be glad you're not Mrs. Chippy," Jessie told Troy as she held out a bit of piecrust. "Mrs. Chippy, the cook's cat, was not a she but a he, and didn't make it."

Sally wrapped Deb's afghan around her shoulders and pulled Tess onto her lap. "Makes me cold just watching," she muttered. "And they said that year wasn't even a seriously cold winter for Antarctica."

Micah said, "They didn't reach Antarctica—haven't you been paying attention? Their ship was frozen into the ice before they ever reached shore. They were hundreds of miles from the Pole."

"Still too cold for me," Sally said.

As if on cue, Jessie and Micah recited together, "There's no such thing as cold weather. There's only inadequate clothing."

"I'll remind you of that in the middle of January," Sally threatened with a smile. She turned back to the video, pretending not to notice Jude curled up on Micah's lap. For the first time, she knew Micah would be in Hartley in January.

"Say, Micah," Jessie said after the movie, when the video was rewinding, "let's hie ourselves into the backyard so Sophie can instruct Sagan on the finer points of retrieving tennis balls. Sally, why don't you stay here and keep the cats company so they don't feel left out." She looked meaningfully at Sally.

Sally shrugged. "If anyone should feel left out, it's the goldies. The rest of us all had food." She bent down in front of the aquarium and watched Gwendal and Marina hustle over to the glass, wearing their hopeful look. "I bet you two'd like a slice of orange."

As she sliced the goldies' orange, she glanced out the kitchen window and watched Jessie and Micah with their heads together, in some sort of earnest conversation. Not a single tennis ball was in sight.

Monday morning Tanner stopped off at the vet clinic on his way to work. Aretha squalled through shots and a blood test. A little later, Melissa pronounced her in excellent health and ready to live at Helper Dogs. "You and Wing have been excellent foster moms," she said.

So Tanner took the kitten to work. "This is your new home," he told her. He carried her into the office.

Corinne looked up from the mass of papers on

her desk and grinned at the kitten. "So you've decided to join us?"

"Our newest staff member," Tanner said.

"Glad to have you aboard, Aretha." She turned
to the dog at her side. "Aspen, come see the new
baby."

The dog clambered to his feet and stuck his nose
on Corinne's desk. As soon as she caught sight of
the dog, Aretha arched her back, hissed, then sat
down to take a better look. Aspen gave a few snuf-
fles in her direction and wagged his tail. Aretha
danced over to him and batted at his nose.

"Her claws weren't out," Corinne said. "She
wants to play with him."

Aspen wagged his tail faster. He barked. Aretha
sat down to give him her haughty cat look. Then
she turned her back on the dog and stalked away
across the layout for the next newsletter.

"Typical female," Corinne said with a chuckle.
"Tease 'em and leave 'em."

"Yeah," Tanner muttered. "Tease 'em and leave
'em."

"You don't sound amused," Corinne said. "You
speak from experience?"

Tanner scooped up the kitten. He didn't answer
Corinne. "I'll take her in the back to meet everyone."

Sally was afraid Micah would ask about Tanner. She didn't know what she would say. But,
he didn't. Instead, the next morning, after
breakfast, he took Sophie out in the front yard

to work on her heeling. This, also, was new. He never took her out front, where people would see him. Sally went outside to sit on the front porch step and watch them.

Pretty soon, Micah had an audience. Three of the neighborhood kids gathered by the driveway to watch him.

"Whatcha doin'?" asked Jasmine when Micah and Sophie came towards them.

Micah stopped. Sophie stopped, too, and sat next to him. "We're practicing our heeling," Micah told her.

"Oh," said Jasmine. Then she turned to the other, younger, children. "He's practicing," she told them.

"Oh," they all chorused.

Little Erin from next door took her three fingers out of her mouth long enough to ask, "Why?"

Micah smiled down at her. "Because Sophie and I are going to do competition obedience next summer. It takes a lot of work."

"My daddy works," said the little girl. "Does your daddy work?"

Sally's breath caught.

"My daddy died," Micah told her. "But before he died he worked. He was an architect. Now Sophie and I are working. We're going to work a lot. You'll probably see us out here on the sidewalk. Sophie, heel."

Erin stuck the middle three fingers of her left hand back in her mouth.

"He's practicing," Jasmine said again, to reinforce her position among the younger kids.

* * *

After lunch, Micah asked Sally to drive him to the library. "Is this the same library that was here when you and my mom were kids?"

"It's a new building, but it's on the same spot." Then she had a thought. "On the way home, would you like to see the house where your mom grew up?"

After a brief silence, Micah nodded.

So after they checked out their books—Sally had a book with the auspicious title *Knitting for Dummies,* while Micah, after a conversation with the young-adult librarian, checked out *Rocket Boys* and all three volumes of *The Wind on Fire* trilogy—Sally drove across town to the neighborhood where she and Deb had spent their childhood. She hadn't been over here for a long time. She took a detour to pass Hartley Community Hospital. "That's where your mother and I were born," she said.

Then she drove Micah to the street where she and Deb had grown up. She stopped the car by the curb. "Your mom grew up in that house, there. Her bedroom was on the second floor, on the side of the house, there, above that lilac bush, but the lilac bush wasn't there then. My bedroom window was over there, on the second floor, next door. We could see into each other's bedrooms. When we were in college, your grandparents moved to New Mexico and my folks moved down to Florida."

She drove Micah to her old elementary school, then to the middle school and the high school. She took him to the park where, when they were seven,

Deborah had fallen off the swings and skinned her knees and Sally had helped her hobble home. She drove down to the corner bakery. "Every Sunday morning, your grandfather walked to this bakery and brought home fresh sweet rolls. Breakfast was sweet rolls and scrambled eggs. I haven't had those sweet rolls forever," Sally told Micah. So they went in and bought one dozen to have the next morning with scrambled eggs.

"Can we call Grandpa and Grandma in New Mexico and tell them we're continuing the tradition? Even if it isn't Sunday?"

"Sure."

They drove two more blocks down the street and Sally stopped again. "This is Wilde Woman's Wool, the yarn shop where your mom worked." Micah didn't want to go in, but Sally wanted him at least to see the shop. Not that he was interested in yarn, but it was a way to bring his mother closer, a way to share with him a part of her he could never otherwise know.

He asked lots of questions about their childhood, but he didn't ask about Tanner. Not once, Sally thought. She wondered why.

Micah helped her put lunch together, and they carried it out to the patio. In the middle of eating a deviled egg, he said, "I've been thinking. When I was in rehab, this girl came to talk to me about sled hockey."

"Terry something," Sally said.

Micah looked at her in surprise.

"I met her up there one afternoon," Sally explained. "She was leaving as I arrived."

"Yeah. Well, I thought I might give her a call. Talk to her about stuff."

Yes! Sally's heart leaped. She told herself to play it cool. "You have her number?"

"No. I thought I'd call the rehab center. They probably know. They'd probably tell me."

Sally grinned. "You're probably right."

"As opposed to left," Micah said with a straight face.

After lunch, he took the phone and disappeared into his room, closing the door behind him.

Sally wanted to dance. She wanted to sing. She wanted to fly. Micah, the Micah she knew, was almost home again at last. She didn't dance, or sing, or fly. She turned the oven on to preheat and pulled a cherry pie out of the freezer. She opened a can of kippers. "Kitties," she called. Instantly, the cats were at her feet, on the counter, rubbing, winding, playing at passion. They snatched the kippers out of her fingers.

"Rude things," she told them. They ignored her.

She sliced an orange, licking the juice off her fingers as she carried a slice into the living room. "Goldies," she called. She opened the top of the aquarium. "Gwendal, Marina." Calling her fish was unnecessary. They were at the surface as soon as they saw her coming. "Here's an orange." She floated the orange slice on top of the water. The goldies went to town.

Sophie was last. "What can I give you?" she asked the puppy. "I know. This is Jean-Luc's favorite treat." She opened the freezer for an ice cube. "Catch."

Sophie caught. Sophie crunched. Sophie loved ice cubes, too.

Micah finally emerged from his room and returned the phone to its cradle.

"Okay," he said, "here's the deal."

"I'm all ears."

"The Thunder, that's the Cleveland team, have a practice Saturday morning at a rec center on the east side of the city. Can you take me? We'll have to leave about eight-thirty."

"You bet."

"Great."

"You have directions?"

"Terry said she'd e-mail me a map."

That evening, after supper, instead of watching a movie, Micah suggested they take Sophie for a walk around the neighborhood. Jasmine was in her yard. She wanted to come with them, so they waited while she asked her mother, who said yes. Then they waited while Erin asked her mother, who also said yes. And Cammie Maxwell, whose mom said yes.

Twenty-eight

Tuesday afternoon Patti asked Tanner how the search for Maxie's new home was going.

Tanner said he was still working on it. He lied.

Tuesday evening, before the puppies for puppy class arrived, his phone rang. It was Micah. "Are we on for my lesson tomorrow night?" the boy asked.

"Absolutely," Tanner told him. "I'm glad you're back."

"I'm glad, too. See you tomorrow."

All through the puppy class, the back part of Tanner's mind was thinking about Sally, figuring out what he'd say to her when he saw her. He had not a clue.

"I'm glad you're here," Sally told Micah late that evening. Micah had taken Sophie out in the back-yard for her nightly constitutional before bed. Sally followed them into the dark. It was easier to share personal thoughts in the dark.

"I am, too," he said.

"I didn't know if you'd come back."

"I didn't know, either."

"You don't have to tell me, if you don't want, but . . . What made you come back?"

For a while he was silent and Sally didn't know if he would answer, but she knew she wouldn't press him if he didn't.

"Grandma showed me all Mom's scrapbooks. She said she'd pack them up in a box and send them." Then he was silent again. "You were in almost all of the pictures, you and my mom together, and sometimes my dad. I guess they wanted you to be my guardian, and they knew you better than anyone. Besides, I've known you all my life. I've known Aunt Mary almost that long, too." He made a slight grimace. "Grandma says she means well, but I'm not sure. Aunt Mary, she's bossy, and she treats me like I'm a baby, like I can't do anything for myself. I don't like that. You treat me like a person. And besides . . . I . . . um . . . I like you."

Sally put her arm around his shoulders. She ignored the tears on her cheeks. "I like you, too. In fact, you've always sort've been my kid, too, and I love you."

"Me, too."

He'd given her the sun and the stars and the moon. She raised her eyes up to the sky, to whisper a silent thanks to Deb in the night, and she saw a shooting star blaze across the sky. She pointed. "Catch a falling star," she sang, watching the spot where it had disappeared, "and put it in your pocket."

"Save it for a rainy day," Micah finished.

* * *

"I'm not going to stay," Sally told him. "I'm going to drop you off, and then I have some grocery shopping to do."

"Okay," he said.

Sally frowned to herself. Micah was not the slightest bit surprised. Maybe this complete lack of curiosity about people and relationships was some kind of a guy thing. Sally turned into the long driveway to Tanner's barn. Sophie, in the backseat, began bouncing up and down, whimpering and whining.

"You know where we are, don'tcha girl?" Micah said. "You like Tanner, don'tcha?"

Sally's heart pounded for a moment; then she realized Micah had been talking to Sophie, and Sophie adored Tanner. *I know what you mean,* Sally silently said to the dog.

Tanner was nowhere in sight, but the door to the pole barn was propped open. Sally dropped Micah off. "I'll be back in an hour," she said.

"Okay." Micah scrambled out of the car and took Sophie to potty in the field, a pre-lesson ritual. He tossed Sally a wave.

She drove back to town to Abernathy's, where she walked the aisles for almost an hour, pushing an empty grocery cart.

Tanner was tense. He had been tense before Micah arrived, not wanting to see Sally, yet wanting to see her desperately. Wanting to hold her, to taste her. Wanting to breathe in the smell of her. But he stayed in his apartment. He heard her car pull up on the gravel and stop, its engine idling. He stayed behind his closed door while he heard a car door slam. He didn't even look out the window as he heard her car drive off down the long driveway. He didn't see her at all. He didn't know whether he was relieved or not. But he knew he was tense. Only when he knew she was gone did he open his door and go out to greet Micah.

He held out his hand and grinned at the boy. "Glad to see you!"

"Glad to be back," Micah said. "Lots of work to do before summer."

"You've decided?"

Micah nodded. "Yeah. I read those AKC rules about a million times between here and Vermont."

Tanner stooped down to gush over Sophie for a moment. "You want to be an obedience dog?" he asked her.

She wagged her tail and threw herself at him.

"That's a yes," Micah said.

Still, Tanner thought, Micah seemed distracted, as if he wanted to ask something but wasn't comfortable enough. Tanner felt Micah watching him carefully. It was difficult to teach, and difficult to learn, under these circumstances. So, after about half an hour, he decided Micah needed something else.

"Tell you the truth," he said, "I'm bushed. Let's grab a can of soda and take a break."

He opened the old refrigerator and tossed Micah a soda and grabbed one for himself. He scooped

ice into a paper cup for Sophie. "Let's go out on
the porch," he said. He did not allow himself to
dwell on the irony that a few short weeks ago he
and Sally talked on his porch. That was the night
he wanted more than anything to kiss her.

With a little soda in his system, Micah began to
talk. He told Tanner about going back to Vermont.
"It wasn't home anymore. The house was the same
house, but it wasn't my home. My mom and dad
weren't there, and they weren't ever going to be
there again."

Tanner kept his eyes carefully on the sky, to give
Micah room to talk. And talk Micah did. He told
Tanner about going to the cemetery where his parents were buried. "I'm scared I will forget them. I
mean, they're the only parents I'll ever have, except Sally, and she's great, but she's not my mom."
He thought for a moment. "She's more like an
aunt. Or a big sister."

"Trust me," Tanner said. He wasn't comfortable
talking about feelings, but he liked Micah enough
to try, even if his words sounded hokey. "You won't
forget your parents. They gave you a wonderful
childhood and you've grown up to be a terrific
young man. Your folks gave you a strong founda-
tion that you'll always have inside you, and that's
why you'll do so well with your life." He realized
he sounded like a dumb Hallmark card.

"Sort of like your puppies?" Micah said. "They
grow up with puppy raisers who help them become
what they are. Then you train them to help people?"

Tanner nods. "Like our puppies."

Micah gave Sophie an ice cube. She broke the silence with her crunching. Micah gave her another one. He was chewing on a thought, as Sophie chewed on ice. Finally, he looked at Tanner. "I guess you had great parents, too. Because you're pretty great yourself."

Tanner looked away from Micah to stare up at the darkening sky. Great parents? Hardly. Still, as Micah had said, they were the only ones he'd ever have. Even if they parented by default, they were, indirectly, the reason he'd ended up where he was.

"Say," Micah interrupted his thoughts, "Are you going to a dog show on Saturday?"

"No."

"Can I ask you a favor?"

"Sure."

"I need to go up to Cleveland to see some people about sled hockey. Could you drive me?"

Tanner thought for a minute. "What about Sally?"

"Well, this is hockey. It's sort of a guy thing."

Tanner smiled to himself. "You sure she won't mind?"

"I'm sure."

"Then okay."

"Great! Can you pick me up about eight?"

"Sure."

Thursday afternoon, Sally sat on her front porch and watched Micah go through heeling patterns with Sophie. She no longer pulled at the leash, was no longer in danger of pulling Micah off balance. It was because of Tanner Dodge.

"Hey, Miss Foster!"

"Hey, Joshua Martini!" she called back.

"Hey, Joshua," Micah called the younger boy over. "Did you hear about the guy that had his whole left side cut off? He's all right now."

Joshua laughed so hard he nearly fell over.

That evening, Micah showed Sally the directions to the ice rink in Cleveland. "E-mail from Terry," he said.

Sally read through the directions. "Sounds like an easy place to get to."

"Good!" Micah let some excitement show on his face.

"Anything you need before you go up?" Sally asked.

"Nah. Terry said they'll loan me anything I need."

Friday evening, Tanner's phone rang. It was Micah. He wanted to make sure everything was set for tomorrow morning. Tanner said he had a tank full of gas and he'd be there at eight. Micah said that was cool. Tanner asked again if this was okay with Sally. Micah said sure. The boy sounded excited. Tanner assumed it was because of hockey.

At exactly eight the next morning, Tanner pulled up in Sally's driveway.

Sally looked out her front door and saw him.

She looked surprised. This does not bode well, he thought. With a sigh, he climbed out of his truck.

"Micah," he heard Sally call.

Then she opened the screen door for him. "Come in," she said. There was a frown on her face.

"Hi, Tanner," Micah said. He had guilt written all over his face.

"Micah," Sally said. "Please explain."

The boy didn't shrink away from it, Tanner thought.

"Well," Micah said, "you two weren't talking to each other, and I wanted to go up to Cleveland, so I thought I would ask both of you to take me."

This was awkward. Tanner didn't know what to say. Sally looked as uncomfortable as he felt.

"So will you?" Micah asked. "Will you both take me?"

Tanner stubbed his toe in the carpet. "I told you I'd take you if Sally didn't mind," he said. "You did not tell me the whole story."

Micah looked down at his feet. "Yeah. I'm sorry. I didn't know what else to do."

"You *lied* to Tanner?" Sally asked.

"It wasn't a lie, not exactly," the boy said. "Please, can't we all go together?"

Tanner watched conflicting emotions play on Sally's face. He knew how she felt.

"I don't know what to do," she said at last. "I don't like it that you were not completely honest," she told Micah.

"I know. And I'm sorry. But," he repeated, "I

wanted both of you there, and I didn't know how else to do it."

Sally sighed. She looked at Tanner. She raised her eyebrows.

"I guess I could drive you both," he said at last. "If it's okay with Sally."

As she locked the front door behind them, Sally wished she had on a better pair of jeans. She felt self-conscious.

"Did you bring the temporary handicapped parking tag?" Micah asked her. "We can hang it from the mirror of Tanner's truck. All the cars up there will probably have 'em."

Sally thought Micah wouldn't want—"I forgot them. Wait a minute." She stuck her key in the lock.

Finally they were on their way to Cleveland. Micah, sitting between them, held the directions tightly in his hand.

The closer they got to Cleveland, the more tense Micah became. Sally could feel the tension building in him, and she started to feel it, too. She glanced over at Tanner. While he didn't look tense, he didn't look as calm as he usually did.

Micah almost didn't breathe until they were at the ice center; Tanner parked the truck, and Sally hopped out. Micah was right—most of the vans in the parking lot sported handicapped license plates. Then, she noticed, that Micah's eyes were bright, his face was strained. He's afraid, Sally realized.

Inside the building, Micah took a deep breath,

breathing in the smell of the ice. Then a voice called out, "Micah!" and Terry Muldoon wheeled her chair over to them. "I'm so glad you came! Come on down to the locker room and meet everyone!" Then she remembered her manners. "Hello, Miss Foster," she said. "Can I take Micah?"

Sally nodded. "See you later," she told him.

Micah gave her a quick wave over his shoulder as he followed Terry down the hall.

Sally watched him go. "I don't know what I'm feeling," she said to Tanner. "I'm feeling so many things right now, I can't sort them out."

"Karen would say you need to take time to process it all."

Sally nodded. She looked around at lots of parents and kids with varying combinations of wheelchairs and braces and other devices, hauling bulging hockey bags. "Smells like an ice rink," she said. "In college Deb and I spent lots of time up in the bleachers watching Kevin practice. It smelled like this. Like hard rubber and cold ice." Then Kevin taught Deborah how to skate and Deb loved it. Sally never learned. Sally stayed home. She frowned at the memory. Somehow it seemed disloyal to Deb.

Tanner looked around, too. "Maybe we should go find the bleachers."

Sally nodded. "I guess so." She looked around again and pointed. "Through those double doors, I think."

They climbed up the steps to the middle row of seats. Classical music played over the sound system. Down on the ice a handful of young women were listening to instructions from an older man. "Figure skating lessons," Sally told Tanner.

She glanced at the clock high on the wall. They had almost an hour to wait before sled hockey. She shivered.

"Cold?" Tanner asked.

Sally shook her head. "Not really." Then she grinned. "I just lack adequate clothing."

"Wait here," Tanner said. "I'll be back."

He was back, a sweater draped over one arm, and holding two paper cups. He nodded to the sweater. "Take it. I keep an extra one in the truck." He handed her one of the cups. "Hot chocolate. There's a concession stand outside."

Sally slid her arms in his sweater. It warmed her. "Thank you."

"No problem." He settled back in the seat next to her.

Sally glanced at the clock again. She might as well enjoy the figure skating lesson.

It was difficult to sit next to Sally and not touch her. He knew the feel of her skin. His desire for it was strong. He had wanted her for so long it was almost painful. He had to think of something else. "I'm glad Micah decided to come today," he told Sally.

She nodded. "I am so glad about so many things, I can't begin to tell them all. But most of all, I guess, I'm not afraid of failing him anymore."

He smiled. "Good."

"You were right. The only way I could fail him

was not to try." Her smile was sweet. It cut right through him.

He realized he was failing her now. He failed her by not trying, by not trusting her with the truth. He had never lied to her but he had left many things out. It was a kind of deception, like Micah had not told him everything about coming to Cleveland. Sally had been disappointed in Micah. Tanner didn't want to bear her disappointment. He had to tell her. Even if it meant she never wanted to see him again, he had to trust her with the truth. If he loved her he had to tell her.

He cleared his throat. "I want," he said hesitantly, "to tell you why I left. After we . . ."

"Made love," Sally whispered.

Tanner nodded. "Yes. After we made love." He took a deep breath and began to talk. His parents were alcoholics. His father held down odd jobs when he could stay sober enough. Tanner grew up on the streets, mostly to keep from having to go home. He got into bits of trouble, lots of small stuff. "I was in and out of juvenile court so often I was practically on a first-name basis with all the judges." When he was fifteen, he became furious at his mother because she wouldn't give him lunch money so he got blinding drunk, stole his mother's car, and went for a joyride. Alcohol was nothing new to him. He'd been drinking as soon as he could hold a cup in one hand. His parents thought it was cute to see their son toddering around. He wasn't cute now, driving a car while he was way over the legal alcohol limit. He crashed.

"When you were talking on the phone and said

drunk drivers should be strung up and eviscerated, you were talking about me. The only difference between me and the woman who hit Micah and his parents is that I was lucky enough to crash into a tree instead of another car. My mom's car was totaled, but I walked away." He hadn't touched a drop of alcohol since.

This time, the judge sent him to a boys' school, a detention center. He had to stay there until he was eighteen. His parents never came to visit—they disowned him. He did his schoolwork there, at the center. A counselor made a difference in his life. She helped him learn to take responsibility for his own actions. When he was seventeen, the center decided to take part in a program run by a nun. Half a dozen boys would be chosen to raise puppies for a year. After that, the puppies would be trained as service dogs. Tanner was one of those chosen. For the first time in his life, Tanner found something he loved. He loved his puppy. Loved being with her, loved training her. The boys taught the dogs basic obedience, to come when they were called, to sit, stay, manners, that type of thing. By the end of that year, Tanner had been bitten by the dog bug. The counselor helped him apply to college at the University of Indiana for their program in animal psychology. When he was accepted, the counselor strongly suggested he see someone regularly at the mental health center. She made a few phone calls and set him up with Karen. They had become friends, bonded immediately by their love of dogs. When he graduated, Karen suggested he apply to Helper Dogs. She had even written a letter of recommendation for him. That's why he came here to Hartley. "Other than Karen, you're the only one who knows," he said.

So. He had told her. He could feel her gaze on him, but he couldn't make himself look at her, couldn't beg her to forgive what he'd been. So when he finished talking, he waited for her sentence. He was silent, staring at the hard, cold ice.

She hadn't taken her eyes off his face the whole time he was talking. She didn't look away from him now. She realized he had handed her the gift of his trust. She wanted to reach out to him, to touch him, to cross the chasm broken open between them. She reached into her mind and snagged one of the many thoughts whirling in her mind.

"Is training service dogs a subconscious way of apologizing?"

Surprise flashed across his face. He finally looked at her and the wall in his eyes was gone. She could see deep into his soul. Before he could answer, she said the words. "I love you."

His eyes opened wide. Sally rushed on. "You are what you are. The things that happened to you, and to me, when we were little, those are the things that made us who we are, the reason we are here and now." She reached out to lay her palm against his cheek. "All those rehab books say, in one way or another, it's not about the falling down, it's about the getting up again."

"Karen says what's important is not what happens to us, it's how we deal with it."

Sally nodded. "Jessie says Karen is fairly perceptive, for a psychologist."

Tanner leaned towards her and gave her a soft, gentle kiss. "I love you, too."

The door to the ice opened and suddenly, there was Micah, sitting on a sled, two short sticks in his hands. He looked up at the bleachers. Sally stood up and waved. Micah used a stick to wave back. "I can almost see his grin from up here," she said.

Another player zoomed out onto the ice and made a sharp turn with his sled. "That's a hockey stop!" Sally said to Tanner.

They leaned forward together to watch Micah learn how to maneuver a sled.

"Looks like he may play hockey again," Tanner said.

Tears sprang to Sally's eyes. "I hope so."

"I know so."

"You knew he'd come back."

"He knows you love him."

"I didn't know you'd come back."

"I didn't know you loved me. I was afraid to tell you I loved you."

"Right now," Sally whispered, "I want to be here, with you, watching Micah, more than anything else. But at the same time, I want to be with you somewhere private, where I can show you how much I love you."

Tanner put his mouth close to her ear. "Hold that thought," he whispered. "I'll take you up on it."

They settled back in their seats. Tanner put his arm around her and they watched Micah fly on the ice.

"And did you see that big guy from the Erie team? He's really into checking." Micah, sitting between them in the truck, had been chattering nonstop all the way from Cleveland. "Terry says I have to remember where my feet are. In stand-up hockey, when you check someone into the boards your feet don't get in the way. On a sled, you have to be careful not to hit the boards feet first."

"Your hockey player persona is showing," Sally said. She was mighty glad to see it.

"I guess so. Oh, and did you see me shoot the puck? I can really shoot with my right hand, but I have to learn to shoot with my left. In sled hockey you shoot with both hands." He made a few practice shots with his left hand. "You didn't lose the phone number of that sled company?"

"No. I have it in my purse. I won't lose it."

"Good. I have to call them first thing Monday. I wonder if they're open today. I know sleds are expensive." He turned earnest eyes at her. "I'll get a job bagging groceries at Abernathy's or something, to help pay for it."

"No." Sally put her foot down. "I will pay for your sled. I don't care how much it costs. You are *not* going to get an after-school job until you're at least sixteen. This is not negotiable."

Micah tossed her a grin. "You sound just like my mother."

"Good!" It was better than good, Sally thought. It was the best thing in the world. It was so good she wanted to burst with goodness. She stuck her arm around Micah and squeezed his shoulders in a hug. This time he hugged her back.

"I'm lucky," Micah said. "I got to choose my family. I picked you."

Tanner caught her eye. "I choose you, too," he said.

Sally wanted to tell them she chose them—but she knew the minute she tried to speak she'd fall apart.

"Sally's getting all gushy," Micah told Tanner. "She does that."

"I guess we'll have to get used to it, then," Tanner said.

"Yeah," Micah agreed. "I guess so."

"Say, Micah, did Sally ever tell you she was considering getting her own dog?"

Micah shot her a look of pure astonishment. "Really?"

"You never know," Sally said. "Someday someone may come up to me and say, Sally, here is the perfect dog, a dog who loves cats. And this dog is for you."

Micah snorted. "That'll be the day."

Then they were in Hartley, and Tanner turned onto Grape Street.

Micah sat up straight. "To Cleveland, to Cleveland," he chanted, "to play on the ice." He turned to Sally.

She understood. Micah was finally back. "Home again, home again, jiggity jice."

Tanner pulled into her driveway. "Let me drop you off. I have to go pick something up. If it's okay, I'll be back in a little while."

"Of course it's okay," Sally said. "I'm not going anywhere."

"I am," Micah said. "I'm gonna go over to the Martinis'. Is that okay Sally?"

Sally climbed out of Tanner's truck. Micah clambered out after her and set off down the street towards the Martinis'. "See ya later, alligator," she called after him.

"In a while, crocodile!"

Tanner reached out and wiped a tear from her cheek. "You're getting all gushy again."

She nodded. "I get this way a lot."

"I'll get used to it." He pressed a kiss on her forehead. "I'll be back."

"I know you will."

True to his word, an hour later Tanner pulled into her driveway. He climbed out of his truck. Then he made a motion and Wing jumped out, followed by a lovely reddish gold dog. The three of them came up the front walk to her door. She opened the door and let them in. "What's this?" she asked.

"Sally," Tanner said, "this is Maxie. You met her once before, at the mall. She is a perfect dog. She was raised with cats, and loves them. Part of my job is to find her a perfect home. If you want her, she will be yours."

"You think I'd be the perfect home for her?"

"Yes."

Sally looked into Maxie's face. Into her eyes. "You like cats?" she asked the dog. The dog wagged her tail.

Tess wandered by. Tess and Maxie touched noses. Maxie licked Tess's head. Tess rubbed against Maxie's legs.

"You can't argue with a cat," Sally said. "I guess I have two dogs."

Tanner took her in his arms. She pressed her cheek against his chest. She listened to his heartbeat. She reached up to kiss him. She threaded her fingers through his hair; she touched his face.

Tanner buried his face in her hair. "How do you feel about three dogs?"

Sally stilled. "Are you part of the deal?"

"Always."

"I feel great." And she proved it.

ABOUT THE AUTHOR

You can write to the author at:

P.O. Box 30401
Gahanna, Ohio 43230

A portion of the author's royalties supports Canine Companions for Independence, and also the 2002 U.S. Paralympic Sledge Hockey Team (and they brought home the gold!).